Mansions and Mills

a novel

Wanda Longshaw

Mansions and Mills. Copyright © 2019 Wanda Longshaw. Produced and printed by Stillwater River Publications. All rights reserved. Written and produced in the United States of America. This book may not be reproduced or sold in any form without the expressed, written permission of the author and publisher.

Visit our website at www.StillwaterPress.com for more information.

First Stillwater River Publications Edition

ISBN-13: 978-1-950-33904-4
ISBN-10: 1-950-33904-1

1 2 3 4 5 6 7 8 9

Written by Wanda Longshaw
Cover design by Kody Lavature

Published by Stillwater River Publications, Pawtucket, RI, USA.

The views and opinions expressed in this book are solely those of the author and do not necessarily reflect the views and opinions of the publisher.

Dedication

Dedicated to the women in my life. My mother Claire Lapointe Currier; her sisters Lydia, Helene and Elizabeth; my daughters Lydia Byrne Jefferson, Cheryl Byrne Dickson and the late Cynthia Byrne Kernan; and my granddaughter Sarah Jefferson Burke.

Acknowledgments

Sincere appreciation to my daughter, Lydia Jefferson. Without her wizardry at reassembling a dropped printer and taming onerous computers this book would never have been written.

Mansions and Mills

Rita,
Wishing you happy days and happy reading

Wanda E. Longshaw

Prologue

The eleven-year-old boy's day began as all days. How could he imagine that it would end in horror?

In midafternoon his mother read her newspaper, soon annoyed by the interruption from shuffling, nineteen-year-old Bridget. Yes, Bridget here in Boston, a city drenched in signs stating that no Irish need apply. Nevertheless, one was reduced to engaging a servant named Bridget or named Bridie or named Annie in order to obtain domestics. The advertisement had clearly stated—no Irish!

The city and the entire country were inundated with immigrants, coming from Portugal, Italy, Canada and all papists. The ones from Russia weren't pope lovers. They were cart-pushing Jews announcing their presence with noisy bells. She hated all.

Elizabeth wanted to engage a proper, British, Episcopalian girl but they flocked to the mills attracted by promised better wages. This city drowned in Irish girls seeking employment in private homes. Signs or no signs!

Bridget said, "Ah now, for sure, 'tis mighty weary I find meself and me feet are sore swollen. I would be thankful to go to me bed for a bit of rest. Supper is ready and I will be down to serve it and there is dough rising for a morning greeting of fresh, warm bread." She stood, long, reddened fingers by her side, head bent, aware that she would need to be as foolish as a leprechaun's doxy to be unaware of her employer's contempt.

"Very well, but be sure to serve supper at six."

"All the saint's blessings on ye, Ma'am."

Blessings, Elizabeth thought with scorn, watching the despised creature relying on the banister as she ascended the stairs. Never mind she told herself, for very soon this would end and never again would her eyes gaze on this wanton.

The room chilled, the fire needed fresh logs. She cursed herself for not remembering to have the worthless girl tend to it. Refueling completed, she resumed reading of Lizzie Borden, that Fall River lady with the hatchet. Her husband insisted no woman could commit such a crime, but though she never argued the point, she knew better. Long, vertical flames warmed and mesmerized, inveigling a nap, but Edward dashed in.

"Mother, it's snowing." he cried.

Drowsy, she replied, "I hadn't noticed."

"You would have noticed if you didn't keep the drapes closed. They don't do it at Eliot's house. Why do we? May I go sliding with him?"

"You may go play till supper but dress for the snow."

She hoped he would forget the first question, but he repeated it. What was she to tell this eleven-year-old boy? Considering his age, a simple answer might do. "Drapes are only drawn if there is a mother in the house. Sadly, Eliot no longer has one. Soon we will open them. Now, go play."

"Oh, but they are getting a new mother. They are happy because she is a good cook. They hate their father's cooking and they love her. She is their aunt. They can't wait till she comes from Baltimore."

Edward kept rambling as the roaring fire failed to prevent flakes of ice from tumbling through her veins. Within seconds, her hands trembled and her head throbbed. Eliot had only one aunt—Helen.

That homely, chinless woman returning to Boston! The only person knowing what none must ever know. Of course, there was that mumbling, old man who could no longer remember his name. No problem there, but only the delicacy of the matter had kept gossipy Helen from babbling. Under present circumstances, there would be no silencing her. To Elizabeth's dismay, Edward would not be stilled.

"When they have a new mother, will they close the drapes?" he asked, innocently.

"Go out, get the sled from the barn and go!" she snapped, out of character for she never raised her voice. Forbearance, stressed for months, cracked. Her shocked and bewildered son picked up dry clothing before rushing through the door.

So, Elizabeth cogitated, Helen would have a husband at last though it was not for love. She had been engaged once until even she admitted her intended was a dolt. To escape snickers, she had joined the Suffrage and Temperance Movements, traveling from rally to rally, shrieking through buckteeth for women's rights. Now, at forty, she would be substitute mother for a brood of six, no doubt to the immense relief of the groom to be. It did appear unseemly so soon after the passing of her sister, but the children would benefit in a well-managed household. That much could be said for her.

Elizabeth asked herself, however, why be distracted by idle thoughts of her neighbors, in view of the dilemma of Helen's return? She would rid herself of Bridget though her husband would object to the method. But when opposed to her plans, he was made to reconsider, one way or the other. Helen's return, however, posed a dangerous and different problem. Getting her out of the way was a quandary. After much thought, she devised a painful solution, the only solution affording protection from notoriety. If solving it her way caused her husband acute discomfort, so be it.

In spite of the situation, she smirked at thoughts of his reaction to news of the impending wedding. She pictured his brown eyes widening in horror as his swarthy complexion turned ghostly and that square chin quivered under his trimmed beard.

As Elizabeth planned within the house, the boys romped outside. Eliot called out, "Why isn't Bridget playing with us? She loves snow. Did your mother say she couldn't because she is Irish?"

Edward answered, "No, Mother said her feet hurt. I wish they'd get better. I miss the fun we had together."

He was fond of this servant barely eight years older. She played checkers and played with marbles and jacks. Until the last few months, she raced him downhill, always losing. Long skirts hampered her. They made cookies or molasses candy. After the candy cooled, Edward helped by twisting and weaving it to a golden color. Each time he'd say, "I'm not going to quit till I get it the color of your hair."

She'd reply, "Ye'll no do that. If me hair was lighter 'twould be white."

She told him stories of the old country and enthralled him with tales of fairies and leprechauns. She spoke of her mother making Irish lace in hopes of feeding famished, Irish tables and once she took him to the convent. He liked the nuns. They looked like penguins, but telling mother was a big mistake.

"Penguins," she hooted, "I suppose you are right but you are never to go there again. They are Catholics and Irish. Green is the proper color for them. You remember you are British to the core. Your mother is still a subject of the British queen and will remain so. I recall telling you that I once danced with the Prince of Wales. Did you forget?"

Recollection of that incident remained planted just as he recalled his father's mocking reply, "If you danced with him, it must have been ring-around-the-rosy. You were too young for his usual interests. Since then, all his high jinx don't involve little boys and girls. Remember that, Lizzie."

"Don't call me Lizzie. Someday he will be king."

Mansions and Mills

"I only call you Lizzie when you put on airs. His mother will prevent his reign if she must live to one hundred and ten." Mother flounced out of the room. She always did when Father teased her.

Edward didn't know anything about that prince fellow or why green was the proper color for Irish people or what was wrong with Catholics or why Bridget didn't play anymore or why Mother made her work from six o'clock till nine at night all seven days of the week. Other servants had time off. Why couldn't he see the penguins anymore? What was wrong with penguins? Mothers were so confusing.

Every night after dishwashing, Mother gave Bridget "rest work" like polishing silver or sewing on hooks and eyes or darning socks. Usually his. He did not know why he got so many holes in them. Mother would say, "Bridget, I'll let you know when it is nine o'clock. I imagine you will sleep well." Sometimes Mother sounded mean.

That evening at supper, when the sled was back in the barn, Elizabeth started to say, "Francis..." but Bridget stumbled in, cutting her off. Conversation, however, could wait. Let dear husband gorge himself, even to the point of wrenching indigestion.

Bridget said, "For desert, there is preserved peaches and cream from the top of the milk bottle."

"Mother, can I have some?"

She corrected him, "It's may I have some and of course, you may have some." She reached out to caress his russet hair.

"Elizabeth, my dear, remember what experts are saying about raising boys. Little handling is advised." He smiled while admonishing his wife.

Stone-faced, she retrieved a reluctant hand from the curly locks and sat back, studying her husband. He was a good provider with a tiring job, bending over fittings, straining eyes with needle and thread and mastering unpredictable machinery, which at times, had a mind of its own. Too, there was demanding clientele, as well she knew, for she had worked beside him for many years, some which she would prefer to forget. Sighing, she pushed memories aside.

And as she studied him, he studied her. When they married, a veil fell over her large, green eyes, but now they were opaque. The luster, once characteristic, returned only on beholding Edward.

So many years had passed since first they met but still her every pore held the same allure. At times, his need to know all the inner workings under that wealth of auburn hair was so great that he fancied placing a hand on each side of her head to squeeze out its mysteries. He did know of her lofty pride, but considering her ancestry, or claimed ancestry, he almost understood.

However, when it came to her son, there was no mystery. For her, insuring his future by fair means or foul prevailed. Francis' hopes were simpler. He did not want to raise a rogue. He had met many in his seafaring days and innocence had vanished with the speed of a Clipper ship.

But other than her feelings regarding Edward, what did he know of this woman he had so wanted? Did he possess one portion of her being? Had he ever? Did she think of Richard Spencer or not at all? Had all the volcanic emotion exhausted itself? If it had fizzled, his belief was that time could take full credit, not he, himself.

Appearing distressed, Bridget rushed upstairs, leaving unwashed dishes on the table. Strange, Edward thought. Stranger still that Mother hadn't noticed or didn't care.

With Bridget gone, Elizabeth cooed, "Francis, my dear, there are to be some nuptials. Eliot's father is to be married to Helen. She will be our permanent neighbor."

"Yes, Father. I forgot to tell..." Words stuck in Edward's throat as an ashen pallor covered his father's face and a large fist banged the table, rattling French china.

"No." he exploded.

In haste, Edward dabbed the napkin over his chin and left for the refuge of his room, forgetting to request excusal. As he stepped over the threshold, he heard his mother say, "I know what we must do though it will be most unpleasant."

Sleep did not come for Edward in spite of time spent outdoors. Perplexing months weighed him. He wanted things as they were. No snapping voice, no fist banging. He wanted games played with Bridget. He wanted to race down the street watching her hair escape from its bun. At long last, confounded eyes closed.

Hours later, dragged from dreams by strange noises coming from Bridget's room, he inched along the hallway. Looking over his shoulder, he noticed his father downstairs, illuminated by gas jets, pacing back and forth and finger-combing his black hair. The strange sounds swelled, echoing against walls as agonized, but muffled screams. Feeling his way in darkness, he paused before cracking the door open.

He stood transfixed at sight of a figure holding a pillow over Bridget's face. In scant light from an oil lamp, he saw blood-spattered scissors with long, sharp blades. Something else was there, something that looked ugly and there was blood, lots of blood on sheets and blankets. He shouted in alarm, "Father, come quick! Come help Bridget!"

Chapter One

Discounting early annoyances, their relationship started well, though the thought that they would marry was unimaginable. He had been deserted in a country that held no charms, a land that had recently abandoned slavery at the cost of brother slaying brother and one whose attempts at reconstruction were pathetic and perhaps futile. Blacks had signed on ships preferring unknown perils of the sea to known perils in the vanquished South, and tales coming from these men, coupled with his knowledge of treatment afforded to Native Americans made the cultures of so-called uncivilized Pacific Islanders appear to offer paradise. Given a choice, he would have preferred placement on an island rather than in the United States.

Elizabeth came to the land of opportunity where gold lined the streets, or so she thought, for a thorough education furnished by her Boston aunt's generous purse. She knew nothing of cheap, white labor in the North, cheap, yellow labor in the West or free, black labor in the South.

Her aunt's death, synchronized with a reversal in family logging fortune, caused her family to request that she remain in Boston seeking employment. She had been born to wealth on her grandfather's Canadian Land Grant and though accustomed to prosperity and social standing, she favored life in a cultured city to life in New Brunswick's woodlands. She considered herself the equal of any Boston Brahmin and planned marriage to one of that ilk, impatient of the hiatus while laboring as a dressmaker and milliner.

Elizabeth, at twenty-one, first learned of the existence of sixteen-year-old Francisco in her boardinghouse room while eavesdropping on Mr. and Mrs. Blackwood. By placing a curious ear against the crack of a slightly opened door, she heard every word.

Mr. Blackwood said, "The captain left him here last night, saying the boy was too sick for life at sea but was a sturdy lad and with rest, good food and a bit of nursing, he'd be fit as a fiddle in no time. Didn't trust filthy hospitals. Was told by dockhands to bring him here. Hated leaving the youngster but his ship sat heavy in the water and he had to weigh anchor at dawn. Left a good purse. Have it right here." he said, pulling a woolen bag from his pocket. "Fine cut of a man that captain is with the smell of the sea strong on him. Must think highly of the boy to bring him himself."

"Good 'twas the smell of the sea and not the forecastle. If the purse is good, probably didn't trust no bloody seaman."

"The purse is good enough for a mighty spell."

"Mighty spell," his wife cried alarmed, "hope it ain't a whaler's disease."

"No, said his men caught it moored in Recife and most left their bunks in ten days, unless they got a cough. Then it lasted three weeks. Hush all your foolish worrying. Wished that good man a hearty wind come morning."

The captain had laughed, saying, "If there was a day sails didn't belly out in Boston, I didn't see it."

Mrs. Blackwood said, "Pray tell me what the lad's name might be."

"Francisco, don't recall the other name but he ain't no limey."

As dawn streaked over the gangplank, a drained and sad Captain Addison climbed aboard. He despaired over the cabin boy who had become an able seaman and sail maker. He hoped the lad would never sign on a ship whose captain practiced flogging. He believed it resulted in a surly crew prone to desertion. In addition, he abhorred cruelty. Due to respect from seamen, he ran a tight ship. Confinement on bread and water had been sufficient for rare infractions. The captain plumbed the depths of gloom because he would never sail with Francisco again. After delivery of cargo in Brazil and after loading coffee, sugar and rubber and braving choppy waters around New Zealand to load teak, he would bid farewell to a beloved sea.

He had informed Mr. Hall, his first mate, "Going to make land in England, settle down with my wife, a cat and a pipe never to hear groaning timbers or singing sails again."

As the weary, old salt's foot hit the deck, Mr. Hall greeted him, "All standing, Sir. Yours has been a long day and a longer night. Perhaps some rest is in order. Is Francisco in good hands?"

"Yes, hoist sails with all speed." The skipper lingered on deck gazing at Boston as ships and docks vanished into the horizon, returning to his lonely cabin when the last church spire disappeared.

Two hours later, Elizabeth thought the captain right about wind as she pushed against gusts which winged him past Cape Cod while, at times, thrusting her light frame backwards. She grasped a jaunty hat which threatened to depart for the bay as she rushed, anxious to complete work on Mrs. Spencer's indigo hat, a match to a gown produced by Mr. Hood's sewing and her careful fittings. Pleasing the copious matron mattered for she would become Elizabeth's mother-in-law, though unaware of that fact. But, it was fact.

Richard Spencer had courted for two years and a proposal was nigh. Most men put less time into courting rituals but she attributed delay to shyness. She arrived at work breathless and late.

Mr. Hood said, "Elizabeth, are you forgetting that Mrs. Spencer will arrive at three for her apparel? Why so much niggling on the hat?"

"Having handsome headdress is important. If everything wasn't perfect, it would reflect on us." She lowered her eyes. "Do you know if her son plans to accompany her?"

"That, I don't know." he replied, scrutinizing her. Sly glances had passed between her and Richard. He deliberated on how unimportant her education and lineage were in Boston. Here, she was a seamstress, a talented milliner whose beauty, brains and upbringing carried no weight.

"Elizabeth, I hope you are not wasting dream time on him. His parents like all their lofty friends will select his wife for an advantageous marriage. Mrs. Spencer would find you unfit company for her son."

Mrs. Spencer's son, however, found her fit company and suitable for his needs, very much so, though only a few of his frat friends knew of the couple's association.

The seamstress hid a smile, remembering all the evenings spent at dinners or horse racing near the Mystic River. This evening she would wear the green gown manufactured on Sundays. Ben Davis would play host tonight.

Mrs. Spencer, never tardy, arrived two minutes before three, extolling pleasure. Exalted son was not with her. The tailor muttered relief.

"Mr. Hood, what did you say?"

"Nothing, just thinking out loud." Actually thoughts of Sam, former slave, dispenser of information had crossed his mind. Fortunate that the matron could not read minds!

"My," she exclaimed, "this hat would entice the Prince of Wales."

"Strange that you should mention the prince," Elizabeth said, "I once had the honor of dancing with him. He is so charming."

"Really, dear child, and when was that?" she queried, concealing scornful disbelief.

"Mrs. Spencer," interrupted Mr. Hood "I have received some material that would make a splendid ball gown. It is in the back room. I believe the shade would match your lovely eyes."

Giggling, she followed him. "What a thing to say, Mr. Hood." The intrusion had the desired effect. It spared Elizabeth the distain and mirth of this fraud.

Mrs. Spencer contained laughter, with effort, till she reached her carriage. She could hardly wait for tonight's party when she would mimic the seamstress for the amusement of guests and Richard. How he would laugh at the absurdity. He was out every evening, sizzling his father's temper. Paternity stormed, "High time for marriage and grandchildren." That could wait for their son's return from Paris. For now, listening to hoofs on cobblestone, she imagined a gown the color of her eyes. Was that old fellow flirting? She no longer had a girlish figure, but tightly corseted she made a stylish appearance. She relished merriment over that addled-brained girl. Dancing with the prince. Indeed!

Within minutes of his mother's departing carriage, Richard strolled into the tailor shop casting a cocky, sidelong grin at Elizabeth. Mr. Hood rolled his eyes, no longer doubting that dalliance was on the man's mind. Marriage, for certain, was not. Must he tell the girl again? He hoped telling her facts about the Spencers would prove unnecessary since knowledge would be distasteful.

After Richard's first visit with his mother, he had come often, always alone. He had buttons changed or a seam stitched but then overworked the tailor, having suits, jackets and coats made.

"Good day, Mr. Hood. My suits must be ready. I'll be leaving for Paris in two days and will have need of them. I'll send someone with a trunk tomorrow who will pack them up and put them on board. My parents expected I'd have them made in Paris, but why do that when you produce the same quality?"

This dandy takes me for a fool Mr. Hood thought. He will tell his parents they were made in Paris, quote Paris prices and pocket the difference. Despicable, as usual.

"Have a good trip, Sir. How long will you be away?"

Mansions and Mills

"Two months, but it will depend on how many interesting sites are offered."

The tailor eyed Elizabeth over his glasses. She appeared unconcerned over this man's departure. Perhaps she had digested his advice.

Elizabeth was not upset, certain the proposal would arrive at moonrise this evening. He would not leave without securing her with a promise. While away, he wouldn't trust all of his gushing friends. Would he? Of course not. He wouldn't do what two of his friends did to Lucy and Betsy, suddenly marrying socially prominent girls from New York.

Ponderings on any weddings, other than her own, faded as she rushed from work that evening. Her path took her past admiring dockworkers and seamen. Heeding Mrs. Blackwood's warnings to ignore turning heads, she ran faster. Anyway, only Richard held interest. With gray eyes and blonde hair, she thought of him as being made of silver and gold. Veins pulsed at the thought of him. As the tide in the bay flowed, so did her inner tide, surging with anticipation.

Mrs. Blackwood arranged her hair, winding its auburn abundance around her head in thick braids. Fumbling with hooks and eyes, she asked, "Tell me, why does his carriage driver come for ye and never his lordly self?"

"Saves time. He is always late unlike his mother who arrives on time without a displaced hair."

"If ye don't stop fidgeting, ye'll have everything displaced. So ye have met his mother. What does she think of this courtship?"

"She doesn't know. Only his friends do."

"Thought not, her sort wants a marriage to fatten the family fortune. 'Tis time for him to state intentions. Ye must be knowing that."

"He's not like his other friends. He's shy, but a proposal will come soon I'm sure."

"Sit still. This braid needs a hairpin."

13

"Why are you so good to me?"

"Ain't had a girl of me own. Lost two boys to cholera. The other two went west to make a fortune. Soon I'll have me own horse and carriage unless some filly takes all their coins. Ye do furrow me brow what with this high and mighty one. Take care. I can tell ye about..."

Elizabeth didn't hear her. Conversation ended with the sound of a clattering horse. She sprinted through the door and down the stairs, her racing heels pounding wood floors, uncaring about anything else, least of all of disturbing a sick seaman.

Within minutes, Mrs. Blackwood watched Elizabeth limp back into the room, clenching an envelope.

"He sends regrets. He cannot keep tonight's appointment. Family has surprised him with a farewell party and it is impossible to see me before departure. He promises to write daily." Unhooked, the pleated, bustled, green gown fell to the floor.

Had despair not decimated sleep, a kitten's plaintiff cry would have gone unheard. Looking into the alley, Elizabeth saw a gray bundle of fur which looked as miserable as she. Passing the seaman's door, she heard silence. Perhaps he died she thought. Nothing as worthless as a sick seaman, but dealing with a corpse might delay breakfast.

Cool air shrouded her as she picked up the kitten. On tiptoes, she found milk and a box which when filled with dirt served for litter. Placing the animal on top of the box, she balanced it with one hand and balanced the bowl in the other.

Rambling sounds came from the seaman now. She whispered to the kitten, "So, he's not dead." She heard Mrs. Blackwood coming to check him again and scooted to her room before discovery. Another boarder, a furry one at that, might not be appreciated.

The following morning, a sleepless, dejected Elizabeth dragged to work. Mr. Hood's foot fell off the sewing machine's treadle at first sight of her and he battled alarm all day as her moods rose and fell like a child on a seesaw.

Her thoughts ran. He must care. Why else would he spend every evening with her? But, why did he leave with such nonchalance? He promised to write. He must care.

Her ashen face looked up. "I didn't tell you. Mrs. Blackwood has a new boarder, a very sick one, freshly plucked from the brine. Surprising when she calls all seamen bilge rats."

"I expect she has seen her share. Didn't she run a boardinghouse in rough and tumble San Francisco? You would think she would chuck him out."

"Yes, but maybe it's because he's just a boy and sick enough to die."

"Does that upset you?"

"No, but it would cause a nuisance with the arrival of a mortician and maybe police thinking we murdered him."

Her employer concluded her moods had nothing to do with that young man and considering her good mood last night, it couldn't be about Richard's absence. Maybe it's that woman thing. He felt sorry for women. Either they had that or were giving birth or lactating. The poor creatures were always leaking something.

Deep in thought, he didn't hear Elizabeth when first she spoke. "What did you say?"

"I forgot to ask. Do you want a kitten? I found one and must find it a home before Mrs. Blackwood chucks me in the street."

"Mrs. Hood gets sick around cats but I know someone who needs one to keep out vermin. I will appreciate an excuse to stop by to see him tonight and ask, but I'm sure he will take it. Please bring it with you tomorrow."

Elizabeth was wrong regarding Mrs. Blackwood's attitude towards kittens for she arrived home and found the house owner playing with it. She said, "Such a sweet thing. 'Twill lighten me black thoughts."

"But, he is promised elsewhere. The man needs it to keep vermin away."

"Vermin! 'Tis me who needs protection. Vermin rings the doorbell when there is no vacant sign. But a promise is a promise. I'll have me another one and one not so scrawny."

The following morning Elizabeth offered to deliver the kitten. "No. No." said Mr. Hood, "I will do the delivery. It gives me an excuse to see a friend again."

That was not the truth. The truth being that he didn't want Elizabeth seeing Sam's scarred face.

Chapter Two

On the following workday, Elizabeth appeared to be waltzing. As she opened the door, her long skirts whirled around her high-buttoned leather shoes. Her eyes twinkled.

Mr. Hood said, "You must have enjoyed a glorious Fourth of July. What did you do?"

"Nothing exciting, read letters, some from home, but it wasn't quiet with that noisy fellow down the hall. He coughs day and night. Wish he would die and get it over with before he kills Mrs. Blackwood."

"Elizabeth, you don't mean that," the tailor said as he sharpened scissors, "but I understand your concern for her."

His employee remained jolly and unfazed by unreasonable clientele. He marveled at the difference from days ago. The answer to her joy, more akin to rapture, nestled in her skirt pocket. A messenger had delivered a note from Richard, written when he first entered his stateroom.

Both heads in the tailor shop bent over fabric, thread, feathers, lace, buttons and hooks and eyes while Mrs. Blackwood's head remained bent at her task—keeping the boy alive. She assured concerned boarders that he didn't have typhoid, diphtheria or cholera. She spooned water and broth into his mouth, waiting for each swallow. After food and a change of sheets, he fell into a deep sleep interrupted by coughs and mutterings in a language similar to the Spanish of California. She concluded he spoke Portuguese and he was reliving his life. Later, she would attempt deciphering.

She propped a weary head against a padded chair and began reliving her own, one that had dark-eyed, curly-headed boys gracing it. Boys resembling this one.

Though she had ample reasons to despise seamen, her adored father was a captain who carved her fate and her mother's sad one as well. While docked in Ireland, his eyes fell on a blonde lass selling produce. He called out to the elderly farmer, "Is she your daughter?"

"Aye."

"I will buy all your grand Irish potatoes if you give me her hand in marriage."

"Are ye daft?" But at sight of a rapt expression on the girl's face, he asked, "Child, are ye daft as well?"

"No, Father, 'tis me wish." One look into the tantalizing, laughter-crinkled eyes told her all she needed to know.

"For sure, 'twill be done by a priest." replied the astounded tiller of soil.

"By a priest or two or three if you wish, but she sails with me. She'll visit but be one less mouth to feed." Noticing her ragged clothing, he added, "Next you see her, she will be dressed like a queen."

And so she was, reserving silk dresses and fancy bonnets for display on land but still dressed like the captain's lady at sea. She strolled the streets of the world, arm linked inside her husband's elbow.

Both Ruth and her older brother were born at sea and they visited churches and museums while keeping a tight grasp on their beautiful mother's hands.

On calm evenings, Ruth perched on one knee and her brother on the other while their father explained the difference between a schooner, a bark, a sloop, a brig and a whaler omitting mention of slavers. If they learned of ships from him, they learned about saints from her along with heaven and hell and having devils in black hearts.

Ruth loved the smell of the sea and the first gray streaks of sunrise which soon colored the sky in brilliant hues. She loved sunsets with its bursting colors over undulating waves. She loved it all until the tragic meeting of the ship's bow and a still uncharted Pacific reef.

Remembrances took flight with sounds of Elizabeth's feet beating the hallway while tearing open an envelope. Mrs. Blackwood muttered, "Another precious letter. Would like to see him with me own eyes. Know scoundrels when I see them and that he is I'll wager." Her inert patient made no reply.

After supper and dishwashing, she returned to his side, settling in the chair, though knowing comfortable idleness would bring on usually avoided "black" thoughts. She wished her father had lived to sail a Clipper, rejoicing in its speed. Alas, only she, her mother and three sailors survived the killing reef. In a boat, they floated to the shores of a large, deep bay, surrounded by woods in lush, Mexican land and she would hate every minute she spent there.

They were found on the beach by Pedro, a fourteen-year-old, half-breed. A small dwelling sufficed as they awaited a rescuing ship. The first to drop anchor was a "spouter", hardly suitable for females. After warning Ruth and her mother to take cover, the second mate swam to the ship, screeching up, "My name is Lariviere. Ship crumbled on a reef like an eggshell. Where are you bound? Do you need hands?"

A voice boomed, "That we do. Can you provide five? Bound for the Arctic. It will be so cold you'll pray for hell."

"We can provide three. Can you supply warm clothing?"

"Yup, if you don't mind dead men's gear. The Horn picked off a few."

In hidden deliberation, the decision was for the men to go and inform an appropriate ship of the females' need for rescue. Unfortunately, all three perished, killed by a maddened, bull whale smashing their boat, killing two outright and drowning one entangled in ropes.

Though the captain's wife knew farming and the land was fertile, an unattended broken arm sustained in the shipwreck became useless. Ruth's extreme youth hindered assistance. Pedro, hated by the Indians, was a poor hunter. A Franciscan monk offered no aid for she had married a heathen Yankee.

"But we were married by a priest." she cried, brushing windblown hair from her face with her functioning left arm.

"That you say. Those at sea don't do Easter duties. Surrender the child to the mission." With enraged and taut vocal chords, he shouted, "Parted from you, her soul can be saved."

She'd surrender her daughter to no one, so she did what desperate women have done since the dawn of time. Gritting her teeth and closing her eyes, she resorted to prostitution. Her blonde coloring appealed to Mexicans and half-breeds. Word of her availability spread up and down the coast and ships diverted to San Francisco.

Years passed. One day, Pedro said, "Ruth, I will soon have to say you are esposa so sailors will not think you are what your mother is. You cannot hide forever."

"And what may she be?"

"You are old enough to know what I mean. Is all right. Un poco de dinero."

By the time she was sixteen, she was Pedro's esposa, though not legally, and at age seventeen she gave birth to the first of four sons. When she lost two to cholera, she turned to her mother for sympathy. Only a mother who had lost a child could understand that wound that never heals. Time could scab it, but a reminder pulled off the scab and started the bleeding anew.

Resourceful Pedro formulated what he called a respectable business. He initiated making and selling grog, that mixture of rum and water first introduced by Admiral Vernon and so appreciated by seafarers. Pedro delighted sailors with a bit of refreshment. Sometimes too much refreshment contributed to the discouragement of captains who sailed with drunken crews.

At times the skipper himself came ashore to round up his men. On occasion, some were not to be found at all and it was assumed that a miscreant had abandoned the animosity of the sea for a friendly land or a friendlier, smooth-skinned inhabitant. Often the captains came in, searching for missing men. One day a skipper, roaring with rage, saw two slumped over a table and in triumph kicked the chairs from under them shouting, "Where are the others? Upstairs, I suppose."

Ruth said, "No, only my mother is there and she is ill."

"Ill, that's not what I've heard of her. Occupied, is she?"

"She is ill and this wicked world is full of tales."

"I'll see for myself." he bellowed, taking the stairs two at a time. Bursting into the room, he saw a gray-haired, emaciated woman. Still not satisfied, he threw open the closet door, muttering, "All sorts of things have gone on in closets." It was bare of everything but meager clothing. Rushing past the withered figure, he shouted, "Too many men disappear from here. Have the squaws such irresistible charms?"

Pedro arrived. As he slid off a horse, the captain hissed, "Do you know where I might find my other men?"

"No hablo Ingles, amigo."

"You speak English. Your wife does and I'm no amigo. If you run into those sogers, warn them to avoid me." With that, he slammed the door.

His words about too many missing men caused a chill of suspicion in Ruth. Pedro behaved as lazy as a Spanish prince, but over the years the house enlarged and his dress improved, duplicating the attire of the wealthy. She kept the accounts and income from the grog shop didn't match expenditure.

Pedro encouraged seamen to gallop off with him for sightseeing and returned with just the horses saying the men had left for their ships. The day came when she discovered blood on his trousers. Ruth uncovered coins left by her deceased mother and headed for Boston. It was there, in an aromatic coffee shop that she met the man who would marry her, serve as an excellent father and never ask questions.

Abandoning reverie and her patient, Mrs. Blackwood went out to the porch. Elizabeth found her there, hugging a post with tears streaming down her face. When asked why, she said, "Thinking of me mother, bless her soul. She always knew what was in mine. 'Tis a terrible missing."

As she held the gnarled, arthritic fingers, Elizabeth whispered, "I'm so sorry. What took her?"

"Oh, 'twas the consumption and she was buried in the same dress she wore at her wedding to me sainted father. Right to the end, she was a fine, captain's lady."

She never mentioned that for many years the fine, captain's lady had suffered from syphilitic blindness.

Chapter Three

In a fevered state, Francisco relived his life beginning with his first memory—of lying in a sundrenched field beside his mother. He had positioned a hand on her large stomach, willing himself to remain in place, unmoving, least he awaken her for if he did, she could arise and go. He was too young to understand the significance of the enlarged stomach and there was no fancying the day when he would hate those distensions and his father's part.

Approaching twelve, he understood and when another baby was expected, he screamed, "The last thing we need is another baby. We have too many already!"

His furious father bellowed, "This is none of your affair. Tend to your chores. For your insolence, you will go without supper. It's God's will and who are you to question?" Believing it was his father's will and not God's will causing his mother's chronic fatigue, resentment towards the head of the household grew as Francisco attempted to assume more and more of her burdens, but he could not spare her the agony of a breeched birth and a midwife screeching, "We must save the child, not the mother."

The final straw was the widower's rapid marriage to the widowed, childless Dona who had served as godparent to the grief-stricken youngster. He was too young to appreciate his father's need for a female caretaker for all these children. Consumed by loss and rage, Francisco vowed to leave home.

"You'll be back when the hunger strikes." his stepmother predicted.

"Never!" but he wondered if courage would oblige.

He packed a satchel of food, hoping it would last, and with that and some clothing set off for the nearest port. First sight of the men swarming the docks would discourage hardier youths. A toothless sea wanderer approached, stating, "If ye be looking for a berth, best stay away from that yonder ship. For sure, there's a devil in her and the skipper is weighing anchor on Friday. He's a Finn, says he can tame her. Maybe, cuz those Finns have magical ways with the sea. Seen it meself. Calmed a tempest, scratching a mast saying some boogle thing, but no way would I board that black-hearted vessel. Not for double wages."

A British seaman, sitting on a barrel and whittling mermaids said, "Leave the lad alone. Don't go scaring him with hogwash."

"Hogwash! 'Tain't and ye be knowing it. Stop jawing and make ye mermaids."

"He makes mermaids cuz he's been too long at sea." said a Scotsman, lighting a pipe after dropping his gear on the dock. "I know cuz I was his shipmate. Three years, stay on land, urchin."

"Pay no mind to heathens. Seafaring is a good life, but don't go aloft on that ship. A killer she is and the ghosts she makes come out in the fog, moaning and screaming."

The Presbyterian Scotsman shouted to the whittler, "Did he call us heathens?"

"That he did. Him that goes around kissing rings on blokes wearing nightgowns and silly hats. Strikes me as a chap you would call a birkie." the Brit answered, enjoying himself.

"Well, 'tis better to kiss rings than to bow me arse to a daft, cold-blooded queen."

Mansions and Mills

"Wait a minute," a Teutonic ship carpenter said before heading towards a whaler, "at least she had brains enough to marry well."

"I'll be thanking ye to keep ye mouths shut and just leave the boy to me. I'll be telling him straight who to sail with and who to run from. If he stays here, the army gets him and may the saints preserve him from that."

Francisco, confused and frightened began not only to doubt the wisdom of his decision, but to wonder what was being served for supper at home. Noting the lad's anxiety, the Irishman began anew, "See that ship," pointing to one being caulked and having chains scraped, "she will be seaworthy by Monday, a good Catholic one with extra time given for the Sabbath. Ye best be taking me words. Never set out to sea on a Friday or on a ship that had a name change and stay clear of Finns. That yonder ship 'tis true all the tales. She should be set afire to put an end to her 'fore she puts the end to other ships. Rams them. Many men could tell stories of her witchery if they had lived, but some died with but one foot on her deck. Wait for the Catholic ship."

Considering his food supply, Francisco couldn't wait. He could depart for home but couldn't face the humiliating taunts.

The Englishman discontinued his whittling, and broke in, "Pay no attention to that loony papist. That distant British ship needs a cabin boy. You may have to lie about your age. Swear you are fourteen. Beautiful sight that vessel is with fresh varnish and brass polished with brick dust and brine. If you are certain the sea is for you, you'll have a capable, fair skipper to boot. Beware of agents. Some offer triple wages then you'll find yourself on a whaler. Might be gone for four years and have scars and missing limbs to prove it. I was once where you are, so I'm telling you straight. Wish someone had done so for me."

Francisco looked out at a calm sea, a blue sky garnished with billowing clouds, soaring seagulls searching for food and weighed his options. Home was out of the question as well as waiting for the Catholic ship. Terrified by a vessel possessed by the devil or ghosts, he had one choice. Through the chaos of a busy dock, he sought the berth on the British, merchant ship.

Captain Addison watched him walk up the gangplank. Turning to his first mate, he asked, "How old do you think he is?"

"I might stretch it to thirteen but they age soon after a taste of a gale or two. Rather pudgy, no doubt a well-fed, farm boy, but that fat will be muscle before long. Wonder why he wants to trade the plow for the mast."

"Mr. Hall, the young yearn for adventure then get more than imagined. The siren call of foreign lands, with no contemplation of the seas between, has turned many into permanent landlubbers, as you know. I sense spirit in the boy. His berth is to be in steerage and the crew is to keep their distance. That order is to be strictly enforced."

"Aye, Sir, and would a violation bring a keelhauling?" the smiling first mate inquired. Some levity existed between him and the skipper.

"This is not a warship, or haven't you noticed?"

"That I have, Sir, but I understand your orders and they shall be dispatched before the crew weighs anchor."

Francisco served meals, lit lamps and cleaned decks before noticing the crew's avoidance. One day, in the doldrums the captain called him to his quarters, asking, "How did you learn English?"

"Sir, it was from a former sailor who settled on a nearby farm. He visited and taught all of us. Well, all of us old enough. I'm the oldest so I learned the fastest."

"Oh, another man who decided the smell of soil was preferable to the smell of the sea. Did he tell you anything of sea life?"

"He said not to even mention it."

"Small wonder," he laughed then added, "I have some good books. Are you interested in reading them?"

"Yes, Sir. Will I have time to read all of them?"

"Hope not to be at sea that long, but choose some." Francisco shuffled through dozens, meticulously selecting.

Mansions and Mills

After knocking, the first mate entered, announcing, "Not a thimbleful of wind. I've held my palm to the wind a dozen times."

Captain Addison said, "I've been at sea so long that if it picks up, I'll smell it coming."

The first mate retreated and the captain studied Francisco as he piled books. Much solid wisdom curled under the old salt's white hair and having taken a liking to the chubby youngster, he decided to pass along his lifelong experiences. Well, at least most of them.

Checking out the lad's selections, he said, "Francisco, there is a bible on that shelf. Won't hurt to read it."

"Sir, the priests told us not to read the bible." He recoiled, terrified, as if confronted by a coral snake. "That is forbidden."

"Really, and did they say why?"

"Yes, Sir, they said only priests, bishops, cardinals and especially the pope could understand God's laws. They didn't want us confused about sins. There are an awful lot of sins that would send you straight to hell if God knew, but He was always watching us so I guess there was no fooling Him."

"I suppose not, but was there anything you could do that was not a sin?"

"I can't think of anything right now." Francisco replied, scratching his head, as if that action would supply an answer. It promptly did. "The priests were happy when we killed a pig or a goat so killing can't be a sin if you don't kill people and they said having babies was God's will. But, I stopped believing that. At first, when I thought it was God's will, I kept praying for them to stop but they kept coming, even two at a time."

Curbed grief began to flow from his eyes remembering his mother's repeated enlarging circumference. "I know it's a sin not to honor your mother and father, but I don't know if it's a sin to hate babies, but I will never have any because I hate them."

The captain murmured, "You will no doubt change your mind when you are older." He was flabbergasted at the lad's emotional outburst, being an undemonstrative Quaker, given to few words, although one who had taken a strong stand as an abolitionist. The end of slavery in Britain caused him jubilation, and he was saddened and amazed that the United States had lost so much blood, both black and white in bringing its demise. Cruel treatment of prisoners in Australian penal colonies had also moved him to speak in protest.

But now, he fell silent for he was not a parson and certainly not a priest. His training was competent command of a ship and a crew's sentiments were of no importance. After many breaths, he muttered, "There are books on navigation and sailing that could be useful if you do stay with seafaring, but don't be surprised if one voyage puts you permanently on land."

Days later, in his first oscillating sea, sickness struck Francisco, as it did to all "greenies" and did not abate for several days. The first mate advised ramming a piece of salt pork, attached to a string, down his throat in order to empty his stomach, but this he could not do. Thus, he never learned if it was, in truth, a remedy.

He found life in steerage cramped and dark with sounds of the stubborn vessel battering the equally stubborn sea near deafening.

Captain Addison hastened Francisco's customary dunk at first crossing of the equator since a brisk breeze promised a quick sail to Rio De Janeiro. Francisco was denied a shore visit though others sojourned.

"Staying on board will give you time for study." the captain told him. "What have you learned so far?"

Concealing disappointment, he answered, "I've learned one sail from the other, Sir."

"So, you know a jib from a spanker. Are you prepared to climb up the main skysail? You understand the rocking increases the higher you go?"

"Aye, Sir, but I would like to try."

"All in good time. For now, go on with your studies."

Mansions and Mills

The captain rejected Francisco's shore leave, fearing exposure to carnal knowledge before his discussion of the "sentiments of the senses" as he called it. It would be difficult, for as a childless man, he lacked experience.

Within a week, as the captain stood on the quarter deck, Mr. Hall approached, clearing his throat, but stumbling on, saying, "Sir, there is a problem causing distress with the crew."

Stunned, the shipmaster asked, "What could the problem be?"

"Francisco."

"Francisco. I fail to grasp that."

"You see, they are having great difficulty with the order to avoid him. He stands by their sides at the spoke, during watch and is drawn to Harry Gray, the sail maker."

"Indeed. I suppose he could seek worse company. Is he not the black man who escaped slavery by way of the sea? Appears upright. Is he not?"

"As good as may be found among seamen, Sir."

"Speaking of sail makers, the best sails will need hoisting for the Horn."

"That is to be done by next morning's light."

The skipper smiled, "Soon you will be able to command a ship. As to Francisco, expecting no fraternization is obviously irrational, but observe closely and he is to remain in steerage."

One day the boy stood by the sail maker's door, practicing making knots. Harry Gray looked up, "Have you mastered all of them?"

"Having trouble with the double carrick bend. Do I really need to know it?"

Harry's teeth gleamed white against his dark skin. "I can help you with any knot. Been at sea for years. Didn't learn navigation but what use does a colored have for it? That's white man know-how. Come in."

Francisco reveled in the company of a man who taught him to make sails and much-needed trousers and shirts since the clothing he had hung from a now muscled, lean frame. He also learned to tar boots, jackets and hats for shelter from wet weather.

"Take these to the cook. He'll dry them by the fire. Say I sent you. We go back to plantation days. His name is Amos."

Francisco took a special liking to this powerful man, strengthened by years of back-breaking work on a cotton plantation. Emancipation had freed him in 1863, but he fled from the South, fearing retribution from former slave owners. When moored in Southern ports, he stayed on board.

Sitting on a keg, Francisco listened to tales of the sea and the South. Addressing Harry, Amos said, "You ran before you met Sam, before he came to the Gray plantation so you never saw his face."

"How come your name is the same as your owner?" asked Francisco, lacking interest in anyone named Sam. At least for now.

"We were given no last names of our own so we took the names of our masters." Harry responded.

Turning toward Amos, the boy asked, "Isn't your name Gray? All hands call you Mason."

"That's right. Took the name of the first Union officer to say old Abe set me free and in all the confusion after the war, there was no one to say different. Packed a canvas bag and left fast." Mind dwelling on Sam, he continued, "Never knew Sam's first master's name. He was a man not given to mouthing, but the lash marks on his face might have made for sore jawing."

Harry said, "I never got the whole story about him. Tell me what you know."

"Not now. Breakfast comes early and the berth awaits my rest."

But there would be little rest for any that night for huge, steel-colored clouds manifested and before the ship reached the Falkland Islands, waves rose like monsters. The westerly wind seemed to have gone mad causing rocking and lurching. Three knocks on the hatchway with the call "All hands ahoy." brought seamen scrambling. Francisco awakened to the terror of the sea in its dance of unrestrained rage. Newly acquired nautical skills were tested but proved to be sufficient enough to avoid shipmate scorn, although at one point he found himself embracing a mast as men embraced their brides.

After three days of ocean fury, the exhausted crew saw sun breaking from an unremorseful sky. A dismayed captain, after checking longitude and latitude, realized the vessel was so off course that they could not round the Horn before late June or early July. The winter season in that area provided eighteen-hour nights and ice.

When they finally reached the tip of South America, it appeared that Satan owned its waters, churning the sea and lashing air. The ship plunged into frosty swells, covering her deck with ice. Freezing fingers fisted sails. Snow, hail and sleet fell without mercy and steering against such a heavy sea required years of experience. A Frenchman and a Swede washed overboard. Francisco almost followed, striking his head against a rail. The captain closed the gash by tying strands of hair over the wound.

Days later, they reached the calm Pacific, relit the galley fire, and saluted the crossing with cold, salt pork, a biscuit and tea laced with molasses.

While twelve-year-old Francisco experienced all this, seventeen-year-old Elizabeth enjoyed July in Boston, studying under sheltering trees, learning languages and how to entertain in genteel fashion. Her anticipated well-adorned home would be shared with an appropriate man of her choosing. Of course!

As she acquired skills befitting a lady, Francisco was on his way to becoming a man.

Chapter Four

Still dreaming, Francisco in his boardinghouse room saw himself at sea in the Pacific, running before the Southeast trade winds. They performed regular tasks, scrubbing the deck, tarring, oiling, polishing and unbending torn sails and setting up new ones. A caught turtle animated taste buds bored with salt pork and onions.

Captain Addison anchored at Valparaiso in order to replace the two lost men. One was a Scot who stated, "Good to be on a ship with no wummin. I canna mak do on a lady ship." Having just left one with skipper and wife, he swore never again. He was well-educated, sang baritone and excelled at seamanship.

After conducting brief, Sabbath services, the captain noticed Francisco pocketing rosary beads. A bible rested in his book-lined cabin and he offered its use but had no applicants. The crews main interests were grog shops and brothels when ashore, and onboard ribald tales abounded. Francisco differed, perchance it was accurate that the Church held its own. Just as well, he concluded.

From the poop deck, the skipper studied the water. Over so much time, he had seen it in all its mesmerizing shades, from turquoise, to royal blue, to green, to gray and menacing black. He had seen it smooth as glass and seen it roaring, swelling, its waves standing in trembling peaks or lashing ships, sandbars, reefs and cliffs, demanding surrender to its will. Also, he had seen it glittering in moonlight as it caressed his toes with tiny, white, bubbling ripples. He hated it and loved it. But, that could be said of a woman.

The sight of Francisco leaning against a mast terminated reveries. It being the Sabbath, the crew had hours of leisure. Soon the boy walked off with Harry who sacrificed time for the youngster. They made clothing for some shipmates who parted with coins in exchange. Francisco saved all his, hiding them in a locked chest, the key worn around his neck.

One balmy day, Francisco asked Amos and Harry, "Why am I not in the forecastle like the others?" The black men regarded one another, both considering a reply.

Harry answered, "You wouldn't like it there. They gamble and I suspect you hide your earnings up your arse. The smoke is so thick you can't see your fingers. They snore something fitful."

Amos added, "It leaks, all the caulking in the world can't fix it and those scoundrels grouse even on sunny days."

"You think steerage is cozy? I have to bolt or tie everything down not to get my head bashed in."

"Amos, tell us the whole Sam story." Harry said, changing the subject. He knew why the skipper objected to twelve-year-old Francisco mingling with the rascals.

"Aye, as I said he wasn't given to babbling but the story was that he tried to kill some white man that was being harsh to his boy. They brought him wrapped in chains from neck to ankles, bloodied from top to bottom. A maid for Mrs. Gray heard something about no sale papers. Why would the master take someone in that condition? Hard to believe Sam was the killing kind. Don't know which plantation he came from. Mr. Gray told us to call him Sam. Nothing else. Came right after Lincoln got elected and when freed, joined the Union Army. Wonder if he ever found his boy again."

Amos rotated on one foot as surly, black Rufus carried in canvas saying, "Here, compliments of the skipper. Now you can stop jawing and get to work." Laughter twisting from him, he said, "Heard what you said, Amos. Did you say harsh? I was there with Sam on that damned plantation." Bitter rage accompanied his exit.

A few days later, when Francisco cleared dishes, the captain asked how his reading progressed.

"I have read all the books." he said, steadying himself against a rocking sea.

"Then it is time to return them and take others. What have you learned now?"

"I learned how some waves come from one direction and others from another and they sort of fight." he replied while arranging chairs.

"Suppose that's one way of explaining rough seas." the captain replied, with humor. "But it's so much more. Keep studying. See those clouds forming out there? Soon, you will have another test of your seamanship. You have done well in the past. I expect you will again."

As Captain Addison predicted, by nightfall a gale struck. Waves rolled in huge surges, foaming white. The order came to "douse sails, look lively lads." The main royal tore before the crew could reach it. Francisco being quick but short was unable to grasp the sail while the stressed top gallant nearly knocked him into the sea. A Frenchman, tall and strong, reached him and together they caught tattered sails. Torn strips entangled spars, rigging and seamen. Later inspection of remaining canvas spoke of forthcoming hard labor for the sail maker and his willing assistant.

That same week, Elizabeth's aunt left "this vale of tears", ending the young woman's privileged education and instigating a consultation with family.

She asked, "How did you lose so much land?"

"We had a loan for improved logging equipment when in a flash flood, all our cut logs floated into the Bay of Fundy. The bank took most of the land. We have a small area left. Please find employment in Boston and though it is embarrassing to ask, would you send some of your income home?"

Visitors to her aunt's home had cooed over her dressmaking and millinery creations. Now her handiwork would provide employment. Confident, she displayed it to tailor after tailor, accepting Mr. Hood's offer.

He felt aptitude had walked in the door. She felt Beacon Hill would walk in the same door. On the day that she began labor with needles inserted in silks, velvet, wool, serge and cotton, Francisco continued labor with needles inserted in canvas, duck cloth and oilskins.

When Francisco turned thirteen, Captain Addison circled his imposing cabin several times before resolving to have the man to man talk, and then wavered.

How to tell him of Iliki? But since she had played such a huge part, how could he not? He didn't read his bible often but he thought he remembered the words. "Who can find a virtuous woman? For her price is far above rubies. The heart of her husband doth safely trust in her so that he shall have no need of spoil. She is like..." He couldn't remember it all, but he remembered, "Strength and honor are her clothing."

She was like rubies. She demolished his need for spoils. When she fell beneath his glance, swimming to the ship, her clothing was strength and honor though all she wore was the water glimmering on her slim, brown body. For what is a woman's clothing? If she stands disrobed, still she wears a thousand impenetrable veils. He ordered his men not to touch Iliki.

Like most islanders, she knew English, having learned from whalers. She inspected him, bewildered. "Why no? Girls do all the time. Men give beads and pots. My sister get whale tooth with pretty pictures."

"And what have they given you?"

"Nothing. This is first time."

"I would imagine since you look so young, but it will be your last time. Today, you will come to my cabin then you will take me to your father."

"Father big kahuna."

Later he told the big kahuna she was not to go to the ships for she would be his wife and he arranged to have the ceremony performed by a captain from a spouter. Her father insisted on gifts and he had an uneasy feeling that her father and other natives believed that she was purchased——that she was his slave, subject to all orders. He had but one firm one.

"No going out to the ships."

The kahuna answered, "I understand. No ships. No white men."

But, neither Iliki nor her father understood. They believed that she and her chastity were bought. No islander understood the significance of the wedding ceremony so foreign from theirs. He did not take her to England. His family would not accept her and he doubted she could adapt to another culture. It was of no importance. She reveled in the magical isle with its swimming and its hula.

The gold ring to her was the symbol of enslavement. To him, the marriage was cemented, but to her in her innocent understanding, or misunderstanding, it was no marriage. She could be traded like pineapples.

When angry natives surrounded him, demanding removal of the gold band, her father protested. Gifts from the captain for both him and Iliki caused him to seek other captains for purchase of three other daughters. No other takers came forth. A willing, female visitor on board was one thing, a Christian marriage to a pious woman at home was another.

Once on his return from a voyage to India, native women bombarded him. "Take ring off. Music of drums, singing, hula, no Iliki, no fun."

"She will wear that ring if I have to nail it on her!" he shouted in frustration. Why couldn't they understand? How to explain the significance of his grandmother's ring on Iliki's finger?

But as they turned to rage at her father, she stepped forward. Rubbing the symbol of servitude, she said, "Leave father in peace. Iliki wants ring."

He brought dresses from England. She slid one over her nakedness, declaring, "Dress pretty. Dress hot." An irritating rash developed around her neck and armpits. She fled to the water, cumbersome attire pulling with the outgoing tide. Calling back from sun-dazzled water, she announced, "Pretty dress no hurt now."

Birds fluttered and the sea pulsed. Suddenly, his surroundings seemed natural, islanders engaged in chores, children playing in sand, swimming, all unaware of clothing or lack thereof, all unaware of what his culture called sin. Looking at his garb and Iliki struggling with the soaked dress, he realized he was the odd one in this flower-drenched land.

"Iliki," he shouted, "take the dress off. I'll send all of them to my sister."

"Your sister be happy with pretty dresses. She wear to swim?"

"It's too cold. She wears much clothing to keep the cold away." And her husband to boot, he assumed. But, not so Iliki. They found isolated inlets and played like children, splashing one another, watching whitecaps and where the sea scratched sand they dug in toes. Where the surf struck rocks, throwing sun-kissed spray, they stood under, catching droplets. He taught her to build English cottages from sand. They made garlands of flowers and made two babies. One a precocious boy and one an impish girl.

One day Iliki asked, "Will you marry me?"

"I did, on the ship with Captain Frayne and the book from my cabin."

"Your book no good. Kapu wedding. Wedding good when Great Kane comes. Shine lights and wahine do hula with ginger flowers and maile branches. Priest of the Great Kane puts tapa on shoulders and you are wed."

He had a moment of irritation. Did she understand nothing at all of years spent together? But, looking into her guileless eyes, he liquefied. "All right, but tell me my part so that I can get it right this time."

The long, and to him foolish ceremony ended when the moon rose. When she slept, he tiptoed to his cabin. By lamplight, he found his father's ring. His velvet touch awakened her as he placed the ring in her palm. He extended his left, ring finger. For hours they remained entwined, having reached that point when silence spoke a thousand words.

He was homebound when he heard the call "Sail Ho!" from a whaler. A boat pulled up. A sailor shouted, "Best avoid Hawaii. There's measles there." Another white man's disease unknown to natives and a killer for them.

Not known to be a "driver", Captain Addison pushed to Hawaii as if demonically possessed. He arrived too late. Iliki had walked her burning body into cooling waves with a pitiful, ill child in each fevered hand and kept walking until blissful, chilling water covered their heads. Her son's tiny hand slid the wedding ring from Iliki's finger as he slipped from a lifeless grasp.

Years later, he married again. She was a British teacher, saved from spinsterhood and beyond childbearing. Never having another child guaranteed never losing another child and there would never be another Iliki.

No need to tell Francisco any of that. It was too personal, too painful. There was time to give it more thought. After all, the boy was still young.

The skipper surmised incorrectly. Harry and Amos had started the process, explaining the ravages of sexually transmitted diseases and the abstinence required to avoid such afflictions. They told him of Hawaii before the advent of missionaries and islands where the readiness to share a wife existed.

"You can't fault them," said big-hearted Harry, "it's sort of a religion."

"Why aren't they Catholics? It's the only way to salvation. Why does Captain Addison have a bible? Priests said that was wrong, but I like him." The youngster was torn and confused.

Mansions and Mills

"It's a good book," responded Amos, "that Scotsman has one. I've got one somewhere."

Francisco planned to get explanations from the captain, but he saw less of the mentor since three sailors had deserted and his role had become more sailing and less serving.

He reached for the needle in Harry's hand for aging eyes made threading difficult. Before leaving for watch, Francisco threaded dozens of needles for his shipmate.

The first flush of dawn skimmed over the horizon when watch changed and sleep enticed Francisco's aching torso. Without warning, the Spaniard who had come on board at Valparaiso tripped him. Face against the planking, he felt a finger snake-like slide up his thigh. The seaman whispered, "See you in your bunk soon, lad."

Before he could respond, two, large, chocolate-colored hands caught the sailor by the collar and the seat of his pants. The would-be lover soared over the rail like a gull. Spinning around, his protector said, "Now you know what harsh treatment to slave boys' means. Sam's son was my playmate, and you might say treatment was harsh. Those who don't see nothing stay healthy and you saw nothing tonight." A moment's fear crossed his eyes as turning, he saw a witness.

The big, blonde man spoke, "Ya dinna need to do it by yeself. Are ye of no mind for assistance? Ah, the pity of dose kind bothering the biddie lads. Couldna see a thing wi' no sunup."

On that night, these two large men formed a bond. Soon John taught reading and writing to a man eager to learn. Before long, Rufus could write letters, inquiring about Sam.

Francisco had obtained an unsolicited education regarding harsh treatment while Elizabeth had obtained a new customer named Spencer. She wondered if the lady had sons or nephews while Mr. Hood wondered how the Spencers had penetrated Boston society.

Chapter Five

The morning after the seaman disappeared, the stern voice of authority ordered all hands on deck, questioning the crew as to what they may have seen or heard. Francisco scanned the faces, searching for the ones of the night before. Both were blank and the dire threat from Rufus had been unnecessary for Francisco would never recount the experience. None had liked the man so after looking around, all shrugged, murmuring ignorance.

"Come lads, someone must know what happened. He is not on board and unlike Jesus, he cannot walk on water."

"Perhaps he slipped or perhaps he lost his grip on the rigging." suggested Mr. Hall. He was mindful of the man's unpopularity and suspected a helpful hand over the side. He knew none would speak up. He shifted nervous feet.

"What watch did he have?" stormed the captain.

"Lookout from midnight to four, Sir." The first mate rattled off the names of all on deck between those hours, including the names of the three who could have supplied the answer. Every man rotated his head, glancing at shipmates, but all looked as angelic as a boys' choir. John, unruffled and the picture of innocence, leaned on the very rail which bore no mark of the sunrise crime.

The log merely recorded man overboard.

While fretting the doldrums, the commander asked Francisco, "Would you care to learn chess? Mr. Hall plays in calm surf but without enthusiasm. It is obvious he has little love for it. He makes no effort to improve thus being an unchallenging opponent. I hope you take to it. It will offer relief from the isolation afforded a ship's captain."

Fascinated by the game, Francisco rewarded the white-haired man by supplying abundant competition.

Between games, the skipper instructed the boy on a head-wind against the Gulf Stream, and the benefit of the Humbolt Current for whalers who later caught trade winds in the Pacific. He explained how the Westerlies quickened the voyage from New York to England but lengthened the reverse trip. Francisco absorbed it all, learning of warm currents and cold ones, navigation and constellations. His intention was to spend life at sea.

After repeated postponements, the captain conquered qualms regarding Francisco's sexual education. Discussing the subject with Harry and Amos caused Francisco no discomfort, but a rosy blush skated over his face as the commander mentioned the topic.

"I already heard about that stuff." he stammered. "We don't have to talk about it if you don't want to."

"I'd like to hear what you were told."

"They told me about women that were happy doing things they shouldn't, but said it was all right because it was a religion. It mixed me up because back home everybody gets married."

"Lad, there are many religions and many different rules in different countries. You will learn this as you visit different lands. They no doubt told you about well-fed women. Did they tell you of hungry ones or those living under suppression? Hunger can make women devious in their need for survival. I believe men suppress women through fear of their gentleness but uncover that gentleness, if you can, and you will be humbled. Remember, Francisco, when you have one woman you have the world of them and always remember that every woman would behave like the Queen of England had she been born the Queen of England. It's just an accident of birth, sometimes a tragic one. Respect all of them."

As Francisco replaced the chess board to its niche, the captain tossed a questioning look in his direction. With starboard watch the boy must know something.

"Francisco, did you notice nothing amiss the night the seaman disappeared?"

Flooded with guilt, he answered, "No, Sir, nothing at all." He could never tell anyone what had happened. Bad enough John and Rufus knew.

When that evening's sunset brushed the sky, Francisco processed and digested words about women but two questions remained. Wasn't the Catholic Church the only way to salvation and did he really have to respect his stepmother?

At the next passage around the Horn when snow and hail blanketed the deck, he was thankful for John and Rufus. When Francisco sprang aloft, John followed and when the order came, "Lay out and furl the jib." Rufus was the first to leap, pushing Francisco aside and sparing him a difficult, dangerous task.

A week later, after passing the Falkland Islands, a thunderstorm came from the southwest. Moments of stillness, lifeless air, preceded saturation of hair and clothing. Wild, flashing lighting slashed, claw-like. Feet scrambled, some barefooted, some shod. Mr. Hall shouted, "Step up to it, boy. You are a seaman now. Isn't there another shot in the locker?" Though drenched, Francisco blazed with images of furrows at home.

When the ship dropped anchor in Terceira, he tramped to his place of birth. With no intention of visiting family and hidden by bushes, he stood overlooking the farm, gazing at father and siblings in the field. A woman, recognized as his stepmother, appeared in the doorway, holding and embracing a toddler——the child who terminated his mother's life. It seemed the Dona was a good substitute mother. Another woman deserving respect, he thought, grudgingly. Climbing a grassy hill, passing headstones, he placed spring flowers on his mother's grave, kissed the ground and never returned.

Later, in the galley, he asked about the seafaring career of the skipper. Harry, long at sea, stored years of scuttlebutt. He would reveal a bit.

"He is from Hull in England. Father did Arctic whaling. Sailed together in 1813 passing the Orkney Islands to get to Davis Straight."

Francisco pulled up a cask, sat on it, ate rice pudding reserved for the Sabbath but served against rules. The cook also favored him by drying his socks and mittens by the stove. Others donned them when still wet. He hung on every word. "Tell me more."

"They left port in April for the short whaling season. They wound up caked in ice. Ships crushed. Blasting didn't always help. Not in 1814. Lost all the whalers then, including his father. Francisco, how are the chess games going?"

"Great for him. Do you think he would tell me about all of his adventures?"

Harry wore a doubtful face, but John said, "Maybe aye and maybe na. Wouldna hurt to ask. Couldna meet a sailor that didna twitch to tell yarns. Na a skipper either."

Luck was with Francisco for the ship was becalmed. The captain growled, "Not a teaspoon of wind." Francisco rejoiced at the opportunity for tales of more oceanic exploits.

The skipper began, "Went Arctic whaling for one year. One season of that was one season too many. The following year, my father didn't return. Can't think of anything worse than a spouter unless it's a slaver. Could smell them for miles downwind. Can't explain the beasts that manned them but going back to whaling, they are the best seamen in the world, especially those New England captains. I wasn't man enough for that job."

"I'm sure you are man enough for any job." said the admiring youngster.

"Not for that one. Only went in the first place to avoid American frigates and Napoleon's warships. Visions of impressment bobbed in my head. That one year went for bowheads in Davis Straight then a greedy captain ordered us to Baffin Bay. Told the crew he'd break anyone who didn't work brightly. Meant it. He was a tyrant who wanted casks of whale oil and baleen for women's finery." As John predicted, he warmed to telling yarns, describing the clothing worn, the size of icebergs and the possibility of sinking from the weight of ice coating a ship. He said, "The worse, however, was the sight of suffering creatures, the blood and the smell."

"Had I been older and wiser, I would have embarked on cargo ships only, but I was enticed with promises of good wages on a ship transporting convicts to the penal colony. I exchanged the sight of whale agony for human agony. When I realized what I had signed up for, it was too late." He had rushed to the nearest tavern for his first drink. Whiskey, straight.

Francisco wanted more information but the wind picked up and he was relegated to innumerable duties.

One Sabbath, he went to the galley in search of more sea stories. He found one from a superstitious German who said, "Them that sink to Davey Jones Locker come back in the mist. They walk on water and skulk on ships. Had an officer killed falling down a passageway. He was haunting before we could say prayers. We had a parson on that trip and don't tell me that's not getting you worse luck than thirteen crewmen will get you. Once in the Caribbean, we went for a voodoo man. The hauntings were that bad."

Francisco, somewhat shaken, grasped the rosary beads in his pocket and ventured to say, "The priests told us there were no ghosts. There are saints watching over us and that's all."

"Who is this scamp not knowing a thing? You listen to them who know what they are talking about."

All looked up as they heard raindrops overhead. Francisco felt relief at the call "All hands ahoy." and at having the German precede him from the galley. Harry said not to believe old-wives

Mansions and Mills

tales but it took three weeks of nightly rosaries to dispel spirits lurking in corners.

When the opportunity presented itself for a chess game, Francisco asked, "Sir, do you believe in ghosts?"

"No, but many seamen do."

"Harry doesn't. Says it's nonsense and that means the priests are right. You said different people believe different things. If I think about that I get a headache. Do you know who is right?"

"All religions teach love of your fellowman, so all are right."

"But not everyone does and I don't care for everyone either." He thought of the tossed seaman.

"Strive to. At least, you must not willingly harm others. Life gives everyone problems enough. You need not add to them." The captain changed the subject to navigation, asking himself, "How does one preach from a tarnished pulpit?"

Several weeks later the cabin door squealed open. Francisco, with expectant face and a book in hand on winning chess marched in.

Noticing the book, Captain Addison exclaimed, "Came to win, I see."

"Aye, Sir, been studying hard."

The weary, weathered face smiled. He had been considering the sea and its casualties and how it could cause a man to lose his wits in grog shops or brothels. Some, on regaining their wits, sort quick passage home.

The lad was setting up chess pieces when the skipper asked, "Why do so many believe that seafaring is a jaunt upon the waters? Does no one tell them that it is hard, endless and dangerous work? Do they sign on to get passage to what they delude themselves will bring a better life? Did you leave to escape conscription?"

"No, Sir, but I did leave to get away from home."

"Did you think life would be better elsewhere? One thing is certain, the young and poor in every country are used for cheap labor or cannon fodder." Taking on a lighter tone, he continued, "Life at sea can be such a trial that instead of going themselves, they should send their in-laws first for a taste of it and wait for a report." He sighed, "Francisco, I believe I'm in need of a hiatus in Britain."

His mood rose as he won every game in spite of Francisco's best efforts. Undeterred, the youngster said, "Someday I'll win. Watch and see. Now, will you tell me of more adventures?"

"Not today. There is little time for it. You have need of your berth." His tone sharpened, "I believe you have watch at four bells and at all times, I want alertness."

Francisco's tone changed also, "Aye, Sir, and I'll check the scuttlecask."

They left Lisbon with a full crew challenged by the waters of the Atlantic flowing in circular, clockwise motion along with the sub currents, drifts and gyres. Bucking the Westerlies, especially strong that year, required repeated tacking.

Before reaching Nova Scotia, Captain Addison warned that a storm approached and ordered a bright watch. By morning, the vessel pitched and rolled. A huge wave hit and the ship could not lift for it. The bow went into the water, shuddered as waves covered her deck, but the gallant ship managed to defeat the sea's fury. The captain ordered, "Hold course as possible but keep her into the sea. I don't want these waves taken broadside." Within hours, the sky turned to brilliant blue.

They unloaded at high tide and reloaded at the next. The Labrador Current carried them with speed to Boston where Elizabeth had just met her dream man, tall, blonde and affluent. In port, Francisco always had anchor duty so his path did not cross Elizabeth's.

Running angry fingers through thick hair, Francisco approached Harry. His intention to refrain from expressing frustration proved useless. "Why am I still treated as an infant? Anchor duty, steerage with only you and Amos as companions. John and Rufus are always together studying." Harry opened his mouth to answer but Francisco continued, "I know what it is. I'm not to fall into seaman ways. I'm not to gamble or meet women who do things. What makes anyone think I would? I don't want ugly diseases and I want to keep my money."

"I've noticed that money part but I'm not one to talk. Still have the first farthing put in my hand. Let's find John. Maybe he can make you feel better."

"He's busy working on mending and replacing chafing gear. Can't figure what I did to the captain. He isn't playing chess anymore or telling me about his sailing days."

"Don't think he'll tell you about all of them." Harry declared, under his breath, and added, "He has a ship to care for. Ever think of that? You want to hear stories? I can tell you some to improve your education. The skipper loves his chess too much to forego it. Must have something on his mind."

When Harry mentioned education, Francisco's head flew up. He had an insatiable thirst for knowledge. "What are your stories about?"

"Ever hear of the underground railroad?"

"No," stretching to reach needles, he asked, "can I ride it? Isn't it dark underground?"

Harry answered, "Its dark but not one you ride. More crawling and hiding than riding." He shuddered in remembrance and dropped a needle. Knowing he could not see the faint glimmer on the floor, Francisco retrieved it.

"Don't know about Arctic whaling but New England whaling saved my life."

Forgetting the time, the youngster settled on a pile of canvas, eager to hear. He jumped as bells sounded. Cursed bells, he thought, always coming between his thirsty brain and its quenching.

Harry called to the rushing lad, "Not surprised you forgot the time. I always do because for me, days are all the same, except on the Sabbath." Alone with his thoughts, he ruminated about the captain. Wasn't like him to shun the boy and chess. Something must be bothering him. He was right.

The captain missed the games but most of all he missed the boy. A cordial, respectful distance existed between him and Mr. Hall. The crew understood their place and their duties and had shown no resentment towards the cabin boy, but Francisco approached fifteen. He was a full-fledged, capable seaman. How much longer could he be referred to as a cabin boy? How much longer could he be kept in steerage? How much longer could he be favored?

Mr. Hall informed him that Rufus had warned others to keep distant from Francisco. He had shielding from Harry, Amos and John but for how long? Harry's gnarled fingers warred against him. John and Amos could go separate ways and he was approaching seventy and would soon retire.

Admit it, he told himself. You want to adopt him, but how? Even his wife could object. Did he know her views regarding children or anything else? She liked cats. Would the boy want to exchange the sea for life with a staid, old couple?

He had gone to great lengths to avoid having another child in his life, marrying when aged, marrying a spinster. How had he allowed this attachment? He hadn't. It happened, just like Iliki happened. He had promised himself that he would never care for anyone again. Caring brings pain.

He paced his cabin, fingering papers and charts on his desk, moved to the bookcase, pulled out a book, gazed at the title and replaced it in its niche. Drawing himself up, he struggled to shut off all thought of Francisco. Hadn't he pushed him away recently? Hadn't he made a valiant attempt to drive Francisco from his days? He could forget him. Hadn't he forgotten Iliki? A piercing pain said otherwise. Regardless, the teenager was different. Someone to forget without effort.

He poured stout ale, selected a book, settled into a comfortable chair and forgot about it. At least, he thought he did.

Chapter Six

After Sunday religious services, Francisco settled on canvas once more, rearranging it, turning in circles, somewhat like a dog seeking comfort. No bells would sound this time. "Harry," he said, "now tell me about the underground railroad and whaling."

"I'll start at the beginning. A Quaker captain took me on board in Savannah after I ran from the plantation. Lots of them picked up darkies. Risked their lives."

Shifting position, Francisco asked, "What's a Quaker?"

"A religion. Your captain is one." He ignored a baffled expression rolling over the boy's face.

"He got me to New Bedford. Was supposed to go by way of a house on Pine Street in Fall River, but it was too dangerous. They hid me in a barrel of fish, took me to Rhode Island first then got me to Canada. Sailed on a schooner there. Canada was cold so made my way back to New Bedford and called it home. Have a wife there. Didn't know I was married. Did you? Yes, I have a wife there. She works as a washerwoman. Can't work as a lady's maid. Funny how Northerners wanted to free slaves but never want them in their homes. Why would you have a bloody war, let young men die for people you don't want around? Do these uppity people think a duchess will come in to serve tea?"

Francisco had no answer. He was finding the world beyond Terceira ever more perplexing. There it was simple. You tended animals, farmed, said prayers and had babies.

"Harry, I know where New Bedford is but where is Fall River?"

"Stop interrupting and let me finish. White men up North hid runaway slaves, hid them in their own houses, moved them under the noses of the law and got them to freedom in Canada. They called that the underground railway. See? After, I whaled out of New Bedford. It's a bloody, hard task but if you harpoon a calf, the mother stays around and you get her. You slip in oil and blood but the strange thing is the creatures die quiet. Not a sound while thrashing in torment. It was an awful silence."

"I bet that bothered the captain."

Harry sucked in an irritated breath, "You are interrupting again. Do you want to hear all this or do you want to jaw about the skipper?"

"I want to hear everything, but about those whales, have you thought a dog hears things we can't? Maybe we are too deaf to hear their screaming."

"Could be I suppose. Are you always trying to figure things?"

"Yes, but with all the ice and not hearing whales scream I understand why the captain only whaled once."

Once? He knew more of the old codger than anyone, but the best course was keeping lips caulked.

"Harry, tell about your worst trip. I think I'll ask all of you and keep a journal."

"Guess it was the one near New Zealand. Wind was blowing from the..."

"I suppose Captain Addison saw more bad trips than anyone. Once he..."

"That does it! You can't stop chinning so don't ask me again. Go see if you can bring back tea and molasses from the

Mansions and Mills

galley. While there ask Amos about his worst trip! When you see John, ask him about hen ships and crying bairns!"

Subdued, Francisco returned with tea and molasses and one biscuit for Harry.

As sunset's colored clouds darted across the sky, Francisco did not join the off-key singing of sea ditties and remained, almost unmoving, on the spar deck. He was still motionless as the sea swallowed the sun and Amos and John joined him. Amos asked, "What ails?"

"Nothing. Amos, tell me something, are you a Quaker?"

"No, a Baptist. Harry is one too, but like me, not the best specimen. Learned on the Gray Plantation."

"John, what are you?" the lad inquired.

Pondering the question, John replied, "Wouldna be decent to say I dinna haiff one." He boomed, "Presbyterian. Aye, laddie. Presbyterian." He repeated Amos' question. "What ails, youngster?"

"I'm not a youngster. I've been at sea for three years. What do I have for it? A hammock in steerage and I'm getting mixed up too."

Amos said, "Everybody gets mixed up. Makes no difference where your berth is. We all know you are a seaman to the bone. Soon we'll be in Cadiz. Shore leave will perk you up."

"Shore leave!" Francis hooted, "When do I get it? I'll be scrapping barnacles, tarring masts, holystoning the deck, painting, polishing, varnishing and dozens of other jobs. While smoking the ship, I might find dead kittens with the dead rats and cockroaches."

"No kittens. Chip's cat is a boy."

Aware of Francisco's dejection, Harry relented on sharing tales. "Gave it thought. I'm sure my worst storm was off Recife where the Malvinas and Brazilian Current meet. Devils with red tails were in those waves, fandango dancing. Could tell we were in for a nasty blow by the cat. A cat will let you know every time. When a storm is coming, they go below. Stay there just licking

51

their fur. Our commander wasn't worth much. After that, I signed on with Captain Addison."

Francisco groaned, "You said there were no ghosts. Now you are talking about dancing devils and magical cats."

"There are no ghosts. I know, never seen one. That's how I know. But devils, I've seen them riding waves with my own eyes and those cats know. Don't pay attention to those ghost talkers. Scare the knickers off the men. But not me, who has not one superstitious bone."

Francisco had never been told of dancing devils, but he was told of one he did not care to meet. He swore to say an extra rosary tonight.

A week later while making sails, Harry said, "Amos tells me he is thinking about his worst storm. He'll get around to telling you. Should be good. He has a lot of chin-music in him." He adjusted his glasses in a futile attempt to improve eyesight, "Don't know how much longer I'll be able to do this. With some cows, me and the wife will start a dairy farm in Westport, Massachusetts and sell milk to millworkers in Fall River and New Bedford. We can't do sums so will need some fellow who can."

"Harry, you can't do sums? You didn't get an education of any sort on a plantation, did you?"

"Sure not, no slave did. Didn't you notice me and Amos can't read or write? We both wish we could."

Francisco jumped up, "If you want I can teach both of you."

Sitting on sun-drenched decks, books in hands, both former slaves spent Sundays with Francisco who realized that Amos had a quick mind. Teaching numbed some of the teenager's inner turmoil.

The inspiration came to teach all the men chess. He approached John, "Can you play chess?"

"A wee bit but little enough to be verra poor at it."

"How can I get chess pieces made? Do you think the men will give up gambling if they learn to play?"

Mansions and Mills

"Donna know about gambling but buttons can make pawns. I canna mak queens and kings, but that maukit carpenter can mak some semblance if ye fasch him."

With a mixture of doubt and fear, Francisco replied, "He'll pull my ear till he sees blood."

"Na, the captain would haiff him in chains. He will not be scathful."

Francisco found a four-sided piece of wood and made a chess board by painting some squares black.

The crew impatiently anticipated the completion of the improvised chess game. The eventful Sabbath dawned warm and sunny. Appealing white wisps of clouds dotted a glorious, cerulean sky, but for Rufus, those cloud puffs reminded him of cotton fields. "A maggot eats that man." Harry muttered as the hulk walked past, disinterested in the game spread out on the deck. Sailors aloft, anxious to join the festivities, sang while shaking out canvas. Light wind cooperated as if its interest had been aroused as well. Patrolling the quarterdeck, the captain showed interest also.

"Mr. Hall," he bellowed, "what goes there?"

"A chess game, Sir."

"How did they acquire the pieces?"

"Carved out some semblance. Put a skirt on a queen, a crown on a stick for a king. Knights and bishops took ingenuity but they came up with it. They have strict rules I'm told, made up by Francisco."

"What are the rules?"

"No fighting and no blasphemy for they play mostly on the Sabbath. Disputes are settled by the rule book. Those who can't read trust the lad."

"I'd say well done. This will put an end to the gambling."

"Not quite, Sir."

"How not?"

"They wager on the winner."

53

Teaching reading, writing, arithmetic and chess lifted Francisco's mood somewhat, but the captain's remained sullen. His aloneness, his failing stamina and the arthritis from many salty soakings dragged him down. His emotional state fluctuated between depression and anger. His resentment of the chess game grew. He questioned his decision to keep the boy at arm's length. He fumed. What must he do to get the boy back without surrendering pride? He sat in a chair, fingered his pocket compass, looked out at the sea, at the glistening showers of spray thrown by cavorting dolphins and felt the heavy weight of emptiness. If loving brought pain, not loving brought nothingness. Why had he attempted to avoid what he knew, what he had learned years ago? Those children and Iliki. Why did he have to lose them all? Francisco filled some of the void.

The youngster must return to his life somehow. What did he mean somehow? He was captain. His was the law at sea. It made no difference about the crew. It didn't matter if they wanted to play chess. He, the commander, wanted to play chess!

Storming on deck he barked, "Mr. Hall, I want to see you." Orders were given. The crew would need to manage their games themselves. The boy would be back!

After one turbulent storm, the moment came for the happy teen to bounce into the captain's quarters. Francisco noted that the board was set up, an indication that his opponent hungered for the game.

"Lad, where is your manual? I believed you carried it as others carry love letters." He pulled up a chair and loosened his belt. "Did wetness ruin it?"

"No, Sir, John is directing with it. Many men are doing very well."

"Don't suppose you can devise a way to discourage gambling."

"I tried, but there is no way." he answered, lowering his head. He had a moment's fear of displeasure. He dreaded another dismissal although perplexed by the first banishment. What could he have done?

Mansions and Mills

The old gentleman chuckled and said, "Even you cannot make saints out of sinners or a silk purse from a sow's ear."

Francisco being Francisco, begged, "Sir, after our games, please tell me of all your voyages to foreign places."

"That might take a long time, far more time than we have. Some I don't remember and some I do not care to remember."

"I've been asking the men to tell me of the worst storms they have seen."

"How many have you heard?"

"Most, but some, like Rufus, tell me to go away and Amos keeps putting it off. I have been told that I'm a pest by a few. They say I ask too many questions."

Crushing laughter behind a large hand, Captain Addison said, "I'd say that is not possible."

One Sunday, when Francisco managed to pull Amos from the game he explained, "I have my notebook here. Tell me your storm story."

Impatient to return to chess, Amos retorted, "Now? Why should I let your nonsense come between me and a good wager?"

Astounded, Francisco said, "You told me you never gamble. Why are you doing it now?"

"I never gamble. I'm not gambling on the game! I have a wager with Harry that dumb German will lose. It's a wager on the loser, not on the game. It's different. No good Baptist would ever gamble."

Baffled, Francisco replied, "Amos, there is no difference. It's still gambling."

"How old are you? Are you fifteen yet? When you grow up you'll know the difference between gambling on a game and having a wager on a loser." He wheeled away, "Don't ever say I gamble!"

Soon, Amos was at his side, grinning from ear to ear, holding a small bag and jiggling it back and forth. "That didn't take long. Harry is one upset son of a gun. Prizes his money. Like you. Why are you bothering me so much about a storm? The worst was the Horn."

"Everybody can say that. I mean one beside the Horn."

"Why do you want to know all this? Are you writing a book? Tell you what, get a storm yarn from the skipper then I'll best it."

Chapter Seven

Captain Addison took on the ponderous task of writing to his wife about future plans. Esteemed wife, he began. He put the pen down and the paper aside. Esteemed, he thought. That was accurate. A more affectionate term, however, seemed desirable. But, what term? Why spend time fussing over this? He always began-—Dear Edith. He could not address her as dearest wife. She would scoff. Perhaps dear wife was preferable this time for he planned to mention his regard for Francisco and his concerns. His fingers clutched the pen once more. He ink-blotted the paper and picked up a fresh sheet. Perhaps she didn't like children. He didn't know.

This lack of communication required rectification. With most time at sea with brief visits home, sanity survived. But need existed for shared interest beyond the cat. She was a good, frugal Quaker but one who might become mulish if confronted with a young addition to the home. Did he know more of this woman than any other?

He suggested that when he retired they meet at Saint Paul's Cathedral where they had literally bumped into each other. From there, they could take in dining, the theater and other delights before settling down. He also suggested that she might be happier living in the outskirts of London. If she so desired, she could start searching for a house now. Whatever she wanted would suit him. Having buttered his bread on both sides, he eased into the topic of Francisco. Nevertheless, neither hand wringing nor an uncooperative pen produced a better salutation than—Dear Edith.

Before reaching Liverpool, Francisco pinioned the captain to long-delayed tales. After filling the skipper's favorite pipe to the brim, he placed himself on a stool, hanging on each syllable.

"You know I was born in Hull. You know of the Arctic whaling. When my father didn't return, I inherited his ring." He stroked the gold on his left, ring finger.

"I went to sea to escape conscription. England, burdened with two wars, needed to man warships. I wanted no part of war. I went to Portsmouth and went on a ship in desperate need of seamen. Had I been more sophisticated, I would have inquired of its cargo. The hold was already burdened with female convicts bound for New South Wales. Most of the poor creatures were guilty of minor offenses such as stealing a loaf of bread or a cloak. Hunger or cold was no excuse." A grimace crossed his features. "England had few prisons so they shipped them overseas."

He paused as he looked out the porthole, pondering the wisdom of saying more. But, he wanted Francisco worldly wise. He would be if he stayed at sea, but who knows?

He hadn't heard from Edith, but mail placed on ships for delivery sometimes saw watery graves instead.

They were interrupted by a subdued knock on the door. Amos, carrying tea and biscuits entered. Both arose, stretched and Francisco settled in a cozy chair for the welcomed drink.

Placing the cup in its saucer, the captain studied Francisco. The crew respected him probably because he held classes and devised inelegant chess sets. Whatever his charisma, he improved morale and crewmen's behavior. Every ship should have a Francisco. He untied his shoelaces and scrutinized the calm, cloudless day.

Francisco broke the quiet, "Sir, did you take many trips on convict ships?"

Mansions and Mills

"Hell no!" Suddenly angry with a world full of irrational cruelty, he exclaimed, "You are full of curiosity. You must know it all. Perchance a brain like yours is a curse. Adhering to ignorance may be the course of the wise. You ask so many questions. Do you know why?"

"No, Sir, but when I was a little boy, some gypsies came through. One came to the door to ask my mother for a cup of water. My father told her to go away, but my mother told him to go tend to the animals. She gave the gypsy water and sweet bread. The gypsy put a hand on my head and said, 'This one will thirst for knowledge. Much will be trapped within for there are those who will never wish to hear and much that he will never dare to say. Silence will be his cross.' The priest told my mother she had sinned by letting the gypsy in. My mother just laughed. I don't think my mother sinned, but what do you think the gypsy meant?"

"Can't help you there, my lad, but if your mother laughed, I suspect she didn't think kindness a sin either."

"The gypsy was right about me thirsting for knowledge, but if I don't ask questions and read, how do I learn?"

"You don't." With patience and resignation, the aged man added, "Fire away."

"About the convict ships, what were they like?"

"My voyage was bedlam. Some men kept the women rum soaked, and the rutting, which our own crew told you all about, was enough to populate England with convicts tenfold. What haunts me is the memory of an innocent, fourteen-year-old girl. When I say innocent, her brother stole a trunk of clothing. When he escaped, they accused her. This story is gruesome, but I suppose contributes to rounding out your education beyond the one received from your seafaring friends. She caught an officer's eye. Her screams brought me running. As I reached for his collar, two men under his command pulled me away. The next morning she was found hanging by the tattered rags left to her."

Francisco shuddered, eyes widening in horror. "But, she didn't want to do that thing. Did they hang her?"

"She hung herself no doubt to avoid repetition. The ship owners wanted a return of worthwhile cargo instead of a ship in ballast so they sent us whaling in a vessel hardly suited for it with inexpert men. Cursed whaling again! I'll tell you two things more then it's off to dreamland for you. First, when I was free of that ship and back in England, I waited in the dark for that officer. I smashed a fist in his face, breaking his nose and sending him crashing into the brine, arse first. Secondly, when I was told 'sling your hammock in the bloody hooker', I made damn sure that ship carried cargo only."

After Francisco departed, the captain brought a ledger down from an upper shelf, one speaking of wealth. Edith had agreed to all his plans but had not mentioned Francisco. He whistled in astonishment when he totaled his assets.

He held a fortune, one acquired only after Iliki's fateful walk into the Pacific. At first, in the depth of grief, he spent days gazing at a sea that enveloped her and their two creations. Natives left flowers, fish and baskets of fruit. He must have eaten but didn't recall. He was spoken to but recalled not a sound, except the sound of stillness. The sun blazed but he didn't feel heat, and when the wind blew, it was voiceless. He slept nights cuddling her garments, inhaling the floral odor of her until his hungered nostrils drained every iota of scent.

When the vault of his world smelled of the sea only, that sea that held her, rage engulfed him. A rage directed at greedy men. He saw greedy men as the cause of all misery. Greed brought underpaid and slave labor. Greed brought diseases to the innocent——measles, venereal diseases, smallpox, and death by malnutrition, filth and interminable wars. Wars made greedy men rich. Rules laid down by them for others, especially for women, inflicted underserved pain. That rage drove him into a need to best them at their own game. A game that must be played. For good measure, he would debauch their wives.

He had the charm, and the handsomeness to turn many a grandee into a cuckold. If an avaricious man neglected a comely wife, Captain Addison's graciousness consoled. With gold buttons, hat cradled within his elbow, a deep bow and grinning invitation he captivated. In addition, the thoughtful swain always left flowers on the pillow, or sachet or a billet-doux. A lady need not fear loss of reputation for he was most discreet, nor did she need fear for her daughters since the only woman he deflowered, he married——not once, but twice. He practiced serial monogamy. Only one woman to each port. He never bought one, he never wanted to, but his appreciation for the warmth and suppleness of female flesh bordered on reverence. No woman regretted bedding him. If he left a seared heart behind, he never knew, for like sailing men, he simply sailed off.

As all captains with luck and thorough knowledge of his ship and the sea, he profited. His was a good record of arrivals and departures. He did the main thing. He kept ships afloat. His financial unconcern before Iliki turned into a driving need for fiscal power. He wanted to best men. He succeeded.

He transported gold-seekers to California and two years later, transported disheartened gold-diggers home. Yet, he did more, consulting with shipwrights and merchants. He discussed dead rise, sharp-bottomed and flat-bottomed ships. Some old salts insisted that a ship should have a cod's head and a mackerel's tail. He weighed all.

When twelve shares were offered on a new ship at two thousand a share, he managed to buy one. With growing wealth, he bought more, but never too much on one ship.

Gauging wealth, his lips puckered. Edith mustn't know. It might quiver her Quaker heart.

Ledger replaced, sleepless, he strode the quarterdeck, then the length of the ship, exercising his cramped legs till four bells sounded. He noticed Francisco at the wheel, managing a choppy sea with dexterity. Fine lad with a fine mind who was born for the sea. The teen had the makings of a captain. He muttered, "Someday the youngster will make his own fortune."

Captain Addison addressed financial acumen a week later, "Never invest too much on one ship," he advised Francisco, "it might sink or be attacked. The Confederate ship *Shenandoah* by itself, took out thirty-four Yankee whalers."

Two hours later, while passing the galley, Francisco heard the German's voice, "Some bucket heads deserted in Brazil. There's a spider in Rio. One bite and you're dead. Same with coral, lance head snakes or pit vipers. Got to know where to jump ship. When I do, it will be in California. There's gold there. It's called wheat."

Harry said, "Some have jumped and encountered man-eaters. Heard of a few lost that way, boiled for dinner. They prefer men to women. Think women too fatty." Seeing Francisco, he said, "Good advice, don't desert where you might be dessert."

As they approached Liverpool, they saw seagulls soaring over vessels, seeking food. The ship docked there with ease for there were no sandbars between East River and King's Dock. The skipper took Francisco on shore leave with him. As they strolled, they fought a jungle of barrels, casks and boxes. Ships loaded and unloaded, merchants hawked their wares.

Captain Addison bought pastry. Checking his pocket compass he declared, "Traveling in the right direction." As long as the direction didn't take them to the brine or to a sawpit, Francisco didn't care. He was in the company of the skipper once more.

A woman caught the captain's arm. One look at the clinging hand told the story, but not to Francisco. As he contemplated the meaning, a short, balding man pushed her into the street, shouting, "Get away. Can't ye tell a gent when ye see one, slut?"

The white-haired skipper stooped, lifting her to her feet. Reaching into a pocket and handing over its contents, he said, "A little something for you, Miss." Turning to the man who almost reached his shoulder, he asked, "Irish I take it?"

"Ay, and proud of it, I am. Rafferty is the name." he barked.

"A noble name. Too noble to strike a woman."

"She ain't no woman. She's just a common..."

A firm grasp on his shoulder prevented a completed sentence. "Mr. Rafferty, allow me to correct you. She is a woman. God's improvement after He created man. Good day."

Francisco looked back at the astonished man as a strange premonition permeated that somehow this man would affect his life. He wondered if the gypsy stuff had pierced his brain. He shook his head to clear it.

Captain Addison found concealing his anger impossible. On the walk back to the ship, his pace quickened. He stormed, "Remember what I told you before about women. No woman is ever a slut."

"Sir," he said, "I understand what you mean. Now, I even respect my stepmother but something troubles me. You said all religions are good, but I was told there was but one way to salvation. You are a Quaker, John is a Presbyterian, Harry and Amos are Baptists. Sometimes I can't sleep. I want you all saved."

The shipmaster paused as he watched gulls diving onto docks, digesting their prizes before soaring to a cloudless sky. He flexed tired legs. Old bones complained. He didn't have a shot left in the locker. Not today, but the boy looked so devastated. Inspiration struck. In resigned tone, he said, "I have books on the world's religions. Stop by my cabin after watch. Thirsting for knowledge as you do, perhaps that reading should be included."

The sky branched with morning color when Francisco entered the commander's quarters. The skipper said, "The books are on that third shelf. Take all you want." Old fingers withdrew a book and turned it over several times, flicking pages, finally deciding. "Francisco," he said, "you might consider reading this one on the Spanish Inquisition."

The teen read them all. Fear, turmoil, and questions disappeared.

The following Sunday, Amos, chuckling, danced a jig that rivaled any done in Ireland. "We sail tomorrow without our German friend. He found a ship going to California. She weighed anchor yesterday. A bag of bones, she is. If she doesn't have a ghost, she'll make some."

Harry said, "Don't imagine he can grow wheat when he doesn't know the difference between a plow and a horse. I don't know about dairy farming but my wife does and..."

Amos, intent on his gyrations, didn't hear him. "Harry, I've got a secret."

"What's the secret?"

"If I told you, it wouldn't be a secret anymore. I'll tell you next time we dock."

In New York, Harry informed Francisco that sail making was now his full responsibility, "My eyes and fingers tell me it's time. Mate, I'm long in the tooth. You come to see me in Westport, you and John and Amos. Where is Amos? He has a secret to tell me. Not sure he'll tell you. Can't figure what it is."

Francisco, on the brink of his sixteenth birthday, helped the old seaman prepare for the role of landlubber, dragging and lifting the chest for placement on its last wharf.

Amos returned from obtaining provisions for the next voyage to Recife and released his secret. He was leaving the sea to teach colored children the three R's. "I owe it all to you, Francisco. You were a great teacher. I'll teach those little girls and boys chess too and I won't let them gamble, just as I and Harry never did. Did you notice I said I and not me?" The black man beamed with pride.

Francisco, dubious, asked, "Is it safe for you in the South?"

"Sure. They put troops in to protect colored people and settle things down. Don't worry. I'm going to be fine."

While moored in Savannah, John was heard shouting at Rufus "Damn ye, I canna fetch Sam. What do ye want fae him?" Without a goodbye, Rufus disappeared in the red earth of Georgia.

Taking on cargo in Recife, a few seamen succumbed to sickness. As some rallied, others fell. In spite of a cooperative Gulf Stream, progress to Boston slowed. Off of Cape Cod, Francisco and the captain indulged in a chess game. At sunset, as a medley of hues bejeweled the sky, the excited teen exclaimed, "I've finally done it! Checkmate." Then he collapsed.

Chapter Eight

*I*n Boston, Francisco awoke to a fine morning still fresh with dew and clinging to summer. Flowerpots perched on windowsills. A pounding sound, a thumping that seemed familiar rattled his ears. Thuds, like the crash of sea against bulkheads had pierced dreams. What was it? Straining auditory canals, he concluded the sounds came from noisy, hurried heels, even frenzied ones. Whose were they?

Slow-paced memory returned. Yes, he remembered the captain bringing him here, but where was his skipper now? How long ago? He thought of John and Amos, both strong enough to carry him from this place. Amos, the quick learner, the man who could tintype every letter would not have deserted him. Where is Amos? More memory surfaced. Amos was gone, teaching school. Francisco wanted to return to his ship, but where was it? He watched the shadow of a tree, its outlined leaves playing leapfrog on a flower-patterned wall.

A woman entered the room, hair gray-streaked, wearing a smile. "Well, laddie, appears the fever burned out. Ye'd be looking mighty well if ye weren't as gray as the ashes in me stove and no heavier than a sheet of lampblack. Need a bit of fattening, for sure. I'll see to that meself." She touched his forehead with the back of her hand. He recoiled from this strange woman.

"Cool as Saint Francis in his grave. Are ye named after him? Me favorite saint. Pray to him every day for patience. Lord knows, 'tis needed with that one across the hall trying me into me own grave. Her gentleman friend might have good intentions what with the letters every day, but methinks of him as a rascal. We'll see when he returns from his Paris trip. Him, the mighty with high-flying ways. The proof is in the pudding I tell Mr. Blackwood, but he ain't the noticing kind."

At present, he had small interest in saints or the female across the hall, probably the source of the slamming heels. He cut off this unknown woman's prattle with a question. "How can I get to my ship?"

"That ship is long gone, but there be a note for ye from the captain." She reached into the top dresser drawer, handing him a sealed envelope.

Two fingers held it as he asked, "How long have I been here?"

"Nigh on a month."

His attempts to open the letter failed. Astounded at his inability to unseal it, he sunk into the pillow, feeling as if he had been struck by guns on one of her majesty's warships.

"Might it be amiss to open it for ye?" she asked, face flooded with concern.

"Thank you, but I'll open it later when I can see straight."

She walked to the pine door, "Best ye have some tea and broth for now and plenty of bread and butter. The fetching will take but a minute. Broth is always to be had in this house."

"Do you put molasses in the tea?"

"Molasses?"

"That's the way we have it at sea."

"Molasses it will be but methinks 'tis a sin to spoil a good cup of tea."

Following a massive meal including pudding, the satiated sixteen-year-old fell into deep slumber only to be awakened by pounding heels. Sight unseen, he decided that the wearer was an unfeeling, overweight, dimwitted female deserving of insensitive treatment from a suitor. Daily letters were no substitute for daily attendance. Out of sight out of mind. Every sailor knew that. Furthermore, Harry and John had told him that a jaunt in Paris was memorable, but if that came from personal knowledge, neither confessed. They said the world knew. If "heels" did not know of delights in Paris, she was a fool.

One day he dared to ask, "Mrs. Blackwood, what sort is heels? That's what I call her because of the racket she makes coming and going. I suppose I'm in no position to complain."

She squared her shoulders and said, "Ye board is paid and ye may complain. Here are coins left by the captain." she said, handing him the small bag, "Mr. Blackwood took the price of lodging up to this week. Lodging is two dollars and seventy-five cents for men." He caught a backward look of disapproval as she swung through the door.

After his supper, she drew herself up to her full height of five feet three inches and held his eyes as she said, "Heels, as ye call her is a well-schooled, hardworking, sweet lass who made the mistake, in me opinion, of falling in love with a Brahmin. She dreams the colt will come back with the foolishness burned out. I say me beads at bedtime and do novenas for the besotted girl and I'll be thanking ye to speak kindly of her. The heels pound when she runs to meet the postman or when she runs to her room to read every word of blarney. For meself, 'tis blarney and methinks, the Brahmin will put blade to her heart." She brushed away a tear.

Contrite and barely whispering, he asked, "What's a Brahmin?"

"Them with highflying ways. They live on Beacon Hill, go to operas and the Parker House, not worrying about the lot of the poor. Me mind says there be no decent bone in that man, letters or no letters."

Now tears dropped onto the wood floor and Francisco flamed with regret. He vowed never to use the term "heels", except in secret. If she sounded like thunder, he would caulk his tongue to the roof of his mouth. It could be said he had experience in the grand art of caulking!

Mrs. Blackwood blew her nose and wiped salty moisture from her face. "She reads the blackguard's letters over and over. Reads parts to me!"

Francisco regretted mentioning "heels" but he wished the earsplitting woman could better contain her ardor. Without expertise, he had little sympathy for ardor.

Heels pulled him from a pleasant dream of his mother. He was with her again, just him, before the steady stream of births. No others tugging at her skirt, no others cradled in her arms. How he hated the next one, unseating him from her lap, and the next one, and again the next till she died so another could live. He pulled a blue blanket over his ears trying to dim drumming heels. He throbbed with heated irritation at the rhythmic racket. Murmuring into the pillow, he vowed to recuperate with speed. Howling winds, crashing waves and snapping sails were music compared to this imbecile.

The following morning Mrs. Blackwood walked in, breakfast in hand. "We can chatter today. Two boarders have gone fishing for a week and Elizabeth will be working late. Her special Mrs. Spencer wants a pile of gowns."

"Why is she special?"

"She is mother to letter man. Seems her son will be away longer than planned to see a bit more of Europe. That's what he wrote to Elizabeth. I told her 'like as not, 'tis party time, dearie' and she didn't like me words. Head all mashed up with the man. What do you think?"

"Don't think of it. I think of going to sea." He nodded off clinging to his rosary. She patted his hand in approval before tiptoeing towards the kitchen. Chatter would wait.

Next morning the tray, more burdened with food than ever, balanced on a diminutive table as he asked, "Did you ever live in California? I heard you tell a boarder that you had a son there."

Looking out the window, she declared, "For a bit. Need to shut this window. Appears to be blowing up for a big rain."

"How did you get to Boston?" He shifted in bed, rubbing a numb leg.

"By ship to the isthmus, rode a bloody mule across, then took another ship to Boston with water going one way and wind the other till me head was where me feet should be. Ye know, 'tis starting to rain. If not for it, I'd be weeding me garden." She wanted to avoid the topic.

"What did you think of sunny California?"

"Ye do ask questions." She was grateful for the sound of bells and rattling tongs and whirled towards it. "Oh, 'tis the ice-man. Icebox is near empty. Going to have me a big piece." She hurried down the front stairs, chasing the iceman through pouring rain.

Rain stopped with dawn's arrival and Mrs. Blackwood appeared carrying, as usual, enough breakfast for two men. With head averted and in atypical silence, she busied herself dusting furniture. With some nudging on his part, tears gathered at each eye, "Elizabeth had me read the letter last night. She said it was proof he would ask for her hand but 'tain't the way I see it. He ran around Europe. Now he goes back to Paris. Why?"

"Even as Paris heals from the Franco-Prussian War, it is a jolly place for aristocrats. Does he fall into that category?"

"For sure, he thinks so, but the letter sounds like he wants her to see Europe. He ain't saying with him. She says 'tis a different meaning. Methinks not."

"In January of last year, starving Parisians ate all the rats. One happy thought, without rats he can't bring back bubonic plague."

"Methinks he's the plague. I pray that he comes back and marries her. Francisco, pray for that."

He reached for his rosary, saying, "I promise you. I will pray for THAT!"

Elizabeth harbored antipathy towards Francisco also. She had complained to Mr. Hood. "All Mrs. Blackwood says is 'go quiet' because she thinks the bilge rat will recover strength with sleep. How can I be quiet when I must rush back and forth? There are too few hours in a day. Mrs. Spencer is killing both of us. I can't imagine what kind of social season she is planning."

Boston had a hot summer season and a perspiring Mrs. Spencer came in one August day, asking, "How should we ornament my new gown?"

Elizabeth answered, "It could be adorned with roseate feathers."

"I've never seen any."

"The plumage is beautiful. Allow me to show you." Elizabeth scooted into the store room and scooted back with brilliant feathers.

"Exquisite. Mr. Hood, won't that color flatter my complexion?" How could she forget what the sweet man had said about her eyes?

"Without question." he assured her while escorting her out.

Elizabeth weighed the reason for Mrs. Spencer's excessive clothing requirements, "All this apparel must be necessary to lift her spirits. Her husband offers little company."

"Her spirits seem fine. Goodness, the way she spends the old boy's money. But, how come you know so much of her affairs?"

Crimson color raced over her face. She couldn't tell him of Richard's chatty letters.

Mr. Hood repeated the question, "How do you know?"

Averting a direct glance, she answered, "Gossip, talk. Things get around."

"I suppose you hens cluck during measurements. Should have thought of that. Women." Relief sucked the breath from her.

Two nights later, Elizabeth arrived with predictable click and clack. This time, the door slammed behind her. Charming, Francisco thought. Now she has added that to her repertoire. He would have tolerated her apparent unconcern for others had it been possible for him to fathom the gyrating emotions surging through her. Emotions beyond his imagination. How could he understand that every word from Richard was lyrical, that every stanza fed a flame of hope so consuming that another's annoyance at short-lived noise seemed infantile? The unintentional door slamming gave voice to panting eagerness to touch the paper, to run her fingers over the inked words, reinforcing a crucial belief that upon his return all would hear surprising news. But, at times, the delay, the uncertainty, the wrenching thought that Mrs. Blackwood might be right so overwhelmed that usual concern for others flew away. Pull the petals from the flowers. He loves me, he loves me not. Francisco's dream of life at sea was not a dream but a certainty. At sixteen, his life was a bundle of promises. At twenty-one, her life was a bundle of letters.

Francisco could not see them but he heard them as the duo sat on the front stairs. A soft, cultured voice said, "Read that part again. Doesn't it mean we will honeymoon in Europe?"

"For meself, no." Mrs. Blackwood always picked up a suggestion that Elizabeth should go alone. That she should go away. She was wrong on that score. Richard's plans included Elizabeth with hopes of success.

"Look what he says here. Remarkable! He suffered no seasickness."

"Ain't remarkable, 'tis a calm sea for all that time that's remarkable. Pray tell how anyone going to Paris added Cork, Dublin, London and the International Exhibit. Now, he goes back to Paris after visiting Norway where daylight lasts to eleven o'clock. You'd think he would bring himself back to Boston for a good night's sleep. Norway! All heathens following that Luther man."

"We followed one with too many wives and not always widowed, unless you think lopping off heads is the road to widowhood. He will return ready to settle down. He'll get it out of his system, as they say."

"Methinks there's much in the system. 'Tis me love for you that makes me say this man has a black heart." She begged, "Find yeself a decent one."

Once more, Francisco asked himself, "What is wrong with this girl? Is she too stupid or too ugly to find another man? Why not listen to advice from someone with years of boardinghouse experience?" His bewilderment stemmed from a captain's failure to tell him that love blinded and consumed as it was blinding and consuming Elizabeth.

Though Mrs. Blackwood told him that Elizabeth was lovesick, she had no understanding of it. Pedro was just there like a pimple. Leaving a righteous man would produce no more tears than leaving an outlaw. Mr. Blackwood was a gentle, humorous helpmate. He felt love; she felt sustaining companionship. Love for her was romance in lovely hues—the billet doux, candlelight and handholding in the park, devoid of heat. Her sons, parents and humanity she loved, but the highs and lows of sexual passion unoccupied her life. To her, the gentleness displayed by her parents was love and no suspicion existed of the wild passion concealed behind cabin doors. Mr. Blackwood had what she called "a man's moments" without disproportional expectations. Since his behavior was her definition of lovesick, she had no idea of the forces raging within Elizabeth.

Though Elizabeth was in many ways naïve, she was knowledgeable in the ways of procreation. Having been born adjacent to farmland, she had seen animal births, and likewise, conceptions. At the age of nine, she witnessed that lascivious Colpitts girl and a boy or two in barns, limbs entwined. She was a disgusted child at nine. She was not nine now. She had juices flowing and hormones jiggling beyond imagination. Her fingertips tingled at the thought of touching Richard, hands clasped in his hair, her luxuriant, auburn locks tumbling over her shoulders, over his shoulders as she arched closer under fevered hands.

All this fervor remained concealed in starched dignity, in white gloves, a ladylike hat perched at the correct angle and a calm, cool exterior only ruffled by a postal delivery. Neither Mrs. Blackwood nor Francisco, both with limited or no experience, understood Elizabeth's lovesickness. She swung like a pendulum between joyous dreams and unacknowledged fear, worsened by petals whispering, "He loves me, he loves me not."

One hot day, Mrs. Blackwood found her patient hobbling around his room, "I do declare ye'll be sitting at breakfast before the week is out."

Wiping wetness from his brow, he asked, "Is it always this hot in Boston?"

"Indeed not, sometimes 'tis hotter. Best get a shave to show the dimple."

"What dimple?"

"The one in ye chin." Noticing the unopened envelope, she said, "Not read ye letter, yet?"

"I can't read goodbye." he answered, dropping his eyes.

"Well, this one bespeaks of hello, so read t'other first." Her right hand brandished a letter.

He bolted, "From the captain?"

"One and the same. That put a jig in ye."

The first expressed regret at leaving him, explaining no other choice. The second informed him that after his retirement, John and Mr. Hall would stay with the ship and John could be contacted for the permanent addresses of Amos, Harry and himself. We must stay in touch he wrote. Please contact me if you encounter any difficulties. I hear that Harry will reside just outside of Fall River. Story is that it is a reeking, mill city.

He didn't mention Rufus. The man must have fled with every intention of remaining hidden. That suited Francisco. The thought of Rufus caused a shiver no longer attributed to fever. He could shake off all thought of Rufus. That man could never come back into his life. Could he?

Radiating sadness, he told Mrs. Blackwood, "The captain is retiring. Won't sail with him again."

Mansions and Mills

"Have ye given thought to leaving that killing place? Stay on shore, Francisco. In a few years, get married. Have little ones."

"Little ones! Children? Hate the sight and sound of those runny-nosed, wet-bottomed things. There will be none for me."

"Ye'll take what the Lord sends ye." she cried in indignation. "No little ones! An indecent thing to say."

"Mrs. Blackwood, I want to see the world, every stream, every ocean. I want to wiggle my toes in every rivulet. I want to see mountains and volcanoes. I want my own ship to survey it all, the earth's beauty and its vileness. I want to see icecaps and sunsets over a screeching sea and the glimmer of moonlight on a silent one. I want to see every island and the colors of every bird. I am not a nester and would never nest in this nation." She blinked in wordless astonishment, rattling china on a tray as she tripped over the threshold.

Francisco craved the sea. Captain Addison battled despondency over leaving it but his aged frame had no other choice. He would not return to England, however, without stopping in Hawaii. For the last time, he would walk in the sand, swim the surf and smell the flowers Iliki wore.

How anguished she must have been, stepping over bodies, unable to ease the children's torment or her own. Better to end agony than suffer the burning, closing stages. If he had been there, with his knowledge, he could have saved them. The eternal if. He took flowers to the ship so he could have the scent of her for a little while–just a small while.

Francisco heard voices as he headed for breakfast, his gait almost brisk as before. It was the same argument, "See, he said he'd make all arrangements. He knows about schedules all over Europe."

"The man should, that's for sure." Scanning the letter, she continued, "Still tells me he will make arrangements for ye only." Wanting to change the subject, she asked, "Did ye get all the gowns done for his mother?"

"Yes, and she said he'd be home for the holidays."

"The holidays! He left before the Fourth of July!"

"He met with unforeseen delays. He'll explain."

"That he will, for sure. Lass, open ye eyes!"

Francisco held back, waiting for termination of the conversation, fearful of being caught at his eavesdropping. There was no mistaking the fact. The girl had ballast in her brain, or worse, hay. He pictured hay protruding from her ears like a scarecrow and swallowed laughter. Dimwit "heels" couldn't calculate the obvious. She had to be plain and dull as yesterday's dishwater. He'd wager against any gambling, tobacco chewing seaman, on any worm-eaten vessel that the dandy had found a perfumed, playful Frenchy. He retreated backwards down the hallway, coughed, and returned with crashing footsteps.

Francisco saw the auburn head rise from her breakfast of bacon and eggs, dabbing at crimson-colored lips, napkin in long, graceful fingers. Slowly, heavy lids rose, revealing large, emerald eyes and with that one glance, he knew wrenching yearning would not be for the sea.

Chapter Nine

Slack-jawed, Francisco watched Elizabeth arise, hug Mrs. Blackwood and ignoring him, leave. The gray-haired woman said, "Will need to close the shutters against the sun. The likes of this hot summer!" Looking out the window, she cried, "See the weeds in me garden. No time for wasting."

"She is as valuable as whale dung." he pronounced, raising a hand to forestall a blow. "To him, I mean to him. Does she not know how desirable, how beautiful she is?"

"Appears not. She has no fanciful notions of herself."

"If he cared at all, he would not turn his back for a moment. Others must be in pursuit."

Leaving the room, she said, "She pays no mind to other men. Must do me chores and take me thoughts from that girl." His thoughts lingered.

Elizabeth's thoughts were on him also. She told Mr. Hood, "I have seen the rattle boy who rose from the sea. Not bad looking in a dark sort of way. I wager one of the Conroy girls will be visiting."

Assumption proved correct for when she returned home she found not one but all five Conroy girls surrounding him as he sat on the shadowed steps.

Francisco nodded, "Good evening, it is cooler out here."

"I know, Mrs. Blackwood and I frequently sit here."

"Oh, then I'm imposing, am I not?"

"No, you are entitled to comfort," she answered, and fixing her gaze on the girls, continued, "as a lodger, you have a right to be here, enjoying shade." All five girls retreated to the sunny side.

It became habit for him and the two women to sit on the front steps till the mosquitoes drove them inside. When Mr. and Mrs. Blackwood went out for the evening, Elizabeth and Francisco attempted to fashion conversation. At first, awkwardness prevailed for they had little in common. One evening he began, "Once, I was almost swept overboard by a Gray Back."

"Is that a whale?"

"No, it's a wave ten to thirty feet high." She seemed unimpressed.

She began, "I was born in New Brunswick on a cold night and..." Faltering, she murmured, "I suppose that's of no interest."

"No, I'm interested. I was born in Terceira on a warm night. The coast of Canada is often foggy. Makes for dangerous sea travel." He fumbled for an interesting topic while feeling foolish.

"I never gave much thought to fog."

"You would if you were a sea captain."

Lamely, she replied, "I suppose." Boredom yawned. She twisted curls, adjusted her skirt and studied the lamplighter's labors. As flickering light illuminated her beauty, the lamplighter noticed. Lucky fellow, he thought, unaware of the fellow's squirming, tongue-tied discomfort.

The envious man's wife heard of the loveliness, "She's an unstoned beauty."

"And what is that?"

"You never heard of them? Way back, every woman who didn't have smallpox marks was thought to be a witch. They stoned her to death. Those who survived without pits and weren't stoned were the unstoned beauties. Understand?"

"I'm not sure. Are you putting me on?" She smelled his breath, "Well, it's not that. I believe you are dimwitted."

Dimwitted was how Francisco felt he appeared to his well-schooled companion. One evening, Mrs. Blackwood filled the gap by reading a letter from her cattle rustling son. Hot there, he wrote. Hard on women. Place is full of bachelors. He asked them to send a wife or two.

Needing little excuse, Elizabeth pulled out Richard's letters, providing conversational fodder. Not Francisco's version of entertainment, but he surely wasn't entertaining her. It kept her by his side, sometimes with heads touching and it fostered a friendship. He pretended interest as she effervesced over Richard's description of carioles in Norway, which were somewhat like a sulky, requiring a change of horses about every ten miles. "He says he believes the horses are grateful because he is not overweight. He is so amusing!"

Overhearing as she came to join them, Mrs. Blackwood said, "Amusing, that he is. Amusing!"

Elizabeth brushed damp hair from her neck, ignoring the last remark. "See how he describes the Memorial for Prince Albert. Such a fine man. You would think he had been born British. The Queen chose well." Her companions exchanged patient gazes, but Irish Mrs. Blackwood wiped vexed perspiration from her forehead.

Finally, Elizabeth sought his counsel, hoping his opinion would differ from her female advisor, but he voiced amazement at Richard's insistence on secrecy. "You would think he'd be showing you off. You only go to parties and dinners at his friends' houses? Who chaperones?"

"There are many women at these affairs. They are chaperones. His carriage driver never leaves us alone. All is proper and I'm certain on his return a proposal will be forthcoming." But, an impatient tug on her collar revealed unexpressed annoyance.

"How long has this courtship been going on?" he asked, agitation moving him closer on the stair.

"He's shy." She leaned away, inserting a hand on the space between them. Noticing the obstruction, he moved back. Pausing and inhaling deeply, she answered, "In truth, it has been two years."

"Two years! Some courtships don't last two months. When he returns insist on being seen publicly and if he..."

"A lady does not insist in that fashion."

"And a gentleman does not behave in that fashion!"

A whirl of annoyed petticoats ran upstairs, leaving him to wish upon a star that Richard's ship would sink and that someday he would fill Richard's shoes.

Elizabeth avoided him. Mrs. Blackwood and he sat alone. He told her of his advice and berated himself for supplying any. "Ye spoke the truth. Methinks if she has a drop of sense, she'll heed wise words."

"Did you ever think there would be a marriage?"

"Doubted from the first." She sighed then began again, "Ye be but sixteen, but can ye say what sort of game the man plays?"

"I have heard of many games from men who couldn't caulk tongues. Did she ever describe the women at these affairs? How many mothers or matrons?"

"Didn't ask. They must be decent or she'd have no truck with them. She says he's shy. Is any man that shy?"

"No, educated she is but as naïve as a duckling."

She wiped a slaughtered mosquito off her hand. "Don't know why this fellow died. 'Twas but a wee blow on the head. If I don't mistake, are ye thinking of fancy women who carry on as harlots? Good Lord, there be no way she'd be a fancy woman. She makes all her finery and no man pays for it. Are ye suggesting that?"

"No way, but ask her someday about the guests. Why wasn't she here for your fine meal tonight?"

"She's at a church affair."

He looked toward the firmament. "She may be coming home in an Irish hurricane."

"What might that be?"

"Steady drizzle in calm wind."

Later, as she sat in a rocking chair, she asked, "Can me son be thinking of two wives? Are there Mormons in Texas with too many?"

"I think they are all in Utah. Are you afraid he'll become one?"

"Indeed. Other religions are false."

"I won't deceive you. I no longer believe it is the only true religion though I say my rosary. Elizabeth is an Episcopalian. Do you think she is damned?"

"Give it no thought." she answered as she fidgeted and twisted her apron strings. "A headache 'twould give me to dwell on it. But, the pope says so and he is infallible."

Leaning his olive complexion closer, he said, "If it will rid you of a headache, let me tell you, that not God or Jesus said the pope is infallible. The Ecumenical Council established that dogma less than three years ago and I don't think your son wants a bunch of wives. More than one wife could make a man loopy, and as for Elizabeth, her soul is fine, though there might be some who wish to tarnish it a little."

Rising with slow, painful movement, she stood before him, "Never told this to a soul, but Mr. Blackwood is a Congregationalist. Thought marrying one indecent. Told a lie to the priest that married us."

Slapping his thigh, Francis doubled over laughing. "How did you manage that? Found a priest with a muddled brain, did you? Where I come from, church records are precise."

"Mr. Blackwood had a brother living on the frontier. 'Twould have been sinful not to go find his only brother stating our intentions and have him at the wedding. He knew a priest who went to save Indian souls but had no love of wolves or losing his scalp. Said he was packing, dead set on leaving. The redskins could save their own souls for all of him. 'Twas his very own words. 'Twould be nice to have a wedding there we said. So no questions asked, me and the husband had a grand wedding before putting the priest on a fast coach to New York. Ye would think if he preached the wonders of heaven to them Indians, he'd be anxious to get there himself 'stead of high-tailing away from wolves and tomahawks."

"By now, he's probably a bishop."

She opened the front door, grasping the brass handle with one hand and a painful hip with the other. Looking at dampening streets, she said, "Seems ye are right, here is ye Irish hurricane. Ye know, me bones knew hours ago."

After supper, Mrs. Blackwood scrutinized him. Handsome, with wavy dark hair, a square, dimpled jaw and brown eyes fixed on the back hall. He voiced concern, "The days are still long, but should she not return before dark? Not to mention the weather."

"Fear not, someone will see her home, 'tis the wee boys in danger what with a fiend torturing them. Here, read about it." She handed him a copy of The Boston Post and a copy of that new paper, The Boston Globe. "Told Elizabeth not to spend the four cents for it. Bad news from one paper was bad news enough but she didn't listen. When does she?"

The boarders passed sections of the papers from hand to hand. He read both editions twice in a useless attempt to distract himself from worry about Elizabeth.

After all others had retired, he crept to the mustard-colored hall, sat on the floor, planning swift escape to his room at first sound of welcomed footsteps. Footsteps once detested. He was unaware of her approach till she tripped over his sleeping form. A small cry of surprise preceded her asking, "What are you doing here?"

His sleepy voice blurted, "I was worried. It's dark and wet out there."

"How nice of you after my nastiness. It was an awful thing to do after I sort your opinion. Grandfather said never to ask for opinions unless you are prepared for an answer. It's late. We must go quiet as Mrs. Blackwood says."

"You didn't miss much with supper. Mr. Blackwood said the beef should be shoe polished instead of eaten. Goodnight." Giggling, she removed her shoes and slipped to her room.

The following day, Mrs. Blackwood and Francisco, alone in the kitchen, discussed his future. She asked, "Will ye be seeking a berth soon, lad."

"You know, Boston is a great place for education. I'd love some."

"What need have ye for schooling? Ye read and write and do sums. The rich don't take to paying taxes for Catholic schools. Public school might make ye faith more feeble."

"Going back to sea could do more harm to my faith. Did you notice that letter for me?" Not waiting for an answer, he continued, "It's from John." Her perplexed expression made him explain, "John was onboard with me. Others went different ways, but he gave me the address of all. I can stay in touch and still get an education here."

"But, what is this talking about education? What happened to the lad wanting to see the world? Indeed, stay on land but what would bring about this change of..." Before she finished the sentence, his ravished expression provided her answer. "By all the saints, say t'aint so. She is daft for another man and twenty-one. Ye be but sixteen. A child to her!"

Laying hands over his face, he placed elbows on the table. A low sound escaped, half sigh and half sob. Distraught, falling into the chair beside him, she stroked his head.

Two minutes later, Elizabeth whirled around the kitchen with paper flapping in one hand and arms over her head like a ballerina. "He will not stay away till the holidays. He is searching immediate passage and has a present for me. Tonight I will begin making a new gown." She grimaced, "Didn't get to show off the green one yet, but now I'm thinking of pink, lovely pink, trimmed with leftover roseate feathers."

Francisco could not bear the sight of her jubilation, but raising his eyes in the opposite direction caught her twirling, shadowed form upon the wall.

Waving the letter before Mrs. Blackwood's eyes, she exclaimed, "See right here where he says he's returning in haste and can't wait till I meet him at the dock?" She imagined the gift was an engagement ring.

Richard's rush home had nothing to do with Elizabeth. It was instigated by an irate father's irritation at an extended and expensive vacation. "Vacation," his father snorted, "from what? Not one banking duty falls on his shoulders. He isn't as useful as a spittoon." He roared at his wife, "Your son is getting no more except the price of a one-way ticket!"

Reluctant to meet his father, Richard planned a midnight docking, asking Elizabeth to meet him. Wouldn't onlookers be impressed by her beauty especially when she climbed into his carriage? After she dropped him off, a hackney could take her home. His travel-weary body would plunge into a lonely bed. At least, it would be lonely that night.

The inconvenient arrival time for a working girl was Elizabeth's problem, not his. He had his own problems. One was postponed arrival of his Paris love due to his father fastening the mint. His other was paternal wrath. He would postpone the confrontation as long as possible, knowing what he would hear.

Why couldn't he be left alone? Why force an unwanted marriage on him? There was no avoiding it much longer although he had sidestepped for years. It was crucial that Dad never discover his youthful, frilly paramour. Guaranteed disinheritance would follow. His father would even prefer Elizabeth.

He had hoped fatherly rages, coupled with excess weight, would carry him off. Now, to postpone the unavoidable explosive quarrel, he'd claim extreme travel fatigue, then swear to another indisposition. If the old lecher fell down a flight of stairs, with assistance, would Mother help cover the crime? Bank employees knew of their odious relationship. Did he dare?

Mansions and Mills

As his ship approached Boston, Richard pulled himself from thoughts and filled a travel-battered suitcase. Balancing on deck, he belatedly remembered Elizabeth's gift and cursed. Grumbling, he returned to his cabin. Frantic fingers searched and found the box under a blanket.

On that docking evening, Francisco insisted on accompanying Elizabeth to the wharf. The day had returned to summer, refusing to surrender to autumn's demanding call, but by evening the season had won the contest. Cool air surrounded their trekking. He despaired over her fatigue and the dwindling coins in that small bag——a barrier to a rented buggy. He needed employment soon. Otherwise, he would be dangling from a spar, torn from the sight of her.

She couldn't afford a buggy either. Her dimes went to siblings and dictates of fashion. She theorized with her lineage, image mattered.

Ambling beside her, Francisco felt the weight of poverty and lack of formal education. If he went to sea, he knew he could become affluent, but there was no wrenching himself from Elizabeth. Fractured at the thought that she cared for Richard as he cared for her, he watched in agony as Richard disembarked and handed her a box.

Once Elizabeth burrowed into the carriage, Francisco wandered home cursing Richard's inconsideration at such an inappropriate arrival. Why didn't he consider that morning brought another working day for an overworked seamstress? Why be so cavalier with her reputation? Why not take her home first?

Francisco's aching feet dragged through dark streets, barely lit by flickering gaslights while listening to night's small sounds—a raccoon foraging around trash cans, a meowing cat, a barking dog in the distance, the rustling sound of wind tormenting leaves and twigs snapping under his forlorn footsteps. What do raccoons eat he wondered. Perhaps it wasn't a raccoon, maybe some other small, nocturnal animal. What difference did it make when she was with Richard? Why was that man born handsome, blonde and gray eyed? Why do the gaslights seem to be dancing? What is there to dance about?

The next day a well-rested Richard pivoted on a polished shoe into the clutter surrounding exhausted Elizabeth. "Look, Mr. Hood, I brought this tweed from Scotland." He winked. "Managed not to pay duty on it. Won't it make a fine suit?"

While the man adjusted his glasses for close inspection, Richard slipped a note into a basket of ribbons at her feet. The dropped note speeded Elizabeth's pace homeward. She was deaf to fellow boarder's greetings and blind to their smiles, but the missive was merely another dinner invitation. Tomorrow at seven it said. You will meet a gentleman from New York, a wealthy, Dutch one and have the pleasure of seeing Betsy and Lucy again. It baffled that these two jilted women would be there. Who would escort them now?

She vowed this was the last private party. He would present her to his family. Concealment of their association would end. In spite of behaving in a brash manner, she would tell him it was time for an engagement.

The following evening the sight of him as he handed her down from the carriage melted resolve. Sometimes she thought his name was tattooed onto each of her vital organs. She would enjoy this evening, forgetting anything Francisco had said about Richard and forget his criticism as she prepared to leave in the green gown, "That neckline is too low. You look like Empress Eugenie. Why dress like her when she is cowering in exile?"

"She knew fashion and who are you to comment on my attire?" she flashed, while resisting an impulse to remark on his faded clothing.

Sparks of rage shot through the air like bolts of lightning till Mrs. Blackwood led him away, understanding that jealousy motivated his outburst.

Dwelling on Francisco's condemnation faded in Ben Davis' mansion. Crystal sparkled, flowers abounded and music overflowed in every candlelit room. Ben said, "Allow me to introduce you to Mr. Klass, he's one of those New York Dutchman and Bill, this is Miss Elizabeth Gilbert." Betsy clung to his arm. Could this be a new courtship so soon after her last suitor's wedding?

During dinner, Betsy commented on the elegance of the green gown. Leaning towards Richard, a rude and jealous voice questioned the price. Blushing, he answered, "I can't say."

Outraged, Elizabeth sputtered, "How would he know? I make all my clothing."

Astounded, Betsy cried, in a tone rattling off walls, "You make all your own clothing? All of it?" Conversation stopped midsentence, silver utensils clashed onto bone china and every head turned to a ruby-faced Richard.

Amused, Bill Klass asked, "Is the bank doing poorly?" Elizabeth ignored her escort's crimson face, but gauged all others. Some registered surprise, some shock, and Ben's, like Bill's, amusement. John White, unable to stifle it, roared with laughter.

The red face composed itself to say, "The bank is fine. This is a different situation."

"How different?" The Dutchman enjoyed the moment. At first meeting, he disliked Richard, judging him a worthless dandy.

"Elizabeth is very honorable, as are my intentions." he responded as embarrassed fingers locked under the table.

"Then why take her here? Take her to the Parker House."

Louise, Ben's companion spoke, shifting her gaze towards him. "I've never been there. Would you take me?"

The rich man, rich enough to thumb his nose at the world, answered in the affirmative. "Sure thing, honey. We can make it a foursome. You two girls decide when. Any night except an opera night will be fine."

Elizabeth replied, "Next Saturday would be fine with me." That would give her time to complete application of the roseate spoonbill feathers along the hem of the pink skirt.

Icy voiced, Richard asked, "Mr. Klass, why not join us?"

"I would if my wife could accompany me, but at present, she visits her brother in Washington. Please excuse my early departure but I have an early meeting tomorrow and need rested wits.

Thank you for the entertaining evening, Mr. Davis. I expect to hear from you upon your arrival in New York." Shaking off Betsy's clinging hand, he said, "As for you, Miss, thank you for your delightful company. Goodnight."

There was no pretense in this man. He was what he was, a canny trader, and an astute judge of character. His acumen assessed the relationship between Elizabeth and Richard. If it takes a rogue to know a rogue, I must be one he told himself.

Elizabeth riveted on the withdrawing back. Wife, she thought. Had these bachelors planned a match for this married man? Of course they had. He probably hadn't fancied Betsy. Had Richard exposed her to what she now knew was unsavory conduct simply to be in the company of treasured friends? No matter. He had said the word honorable. She would forgive him but the association with this lot would end. Two hours later, Richard drove Elizabeth home in silence pleading a headache. The only sounds came from the horses' hoofs clattering on cobblestones and the beats of her joyful heart. He had said it. Honorable intentions.

Ben had misgivings about the Parker House dinner with Richard. He had held suspicious but now he knew. He had been told by business associates that the man was as useful as a baptismal font at a funeral.

He need not have worried. On the evening of the scheduled dinner, Louise's cousin went into premature labor and regrets came in the hands of a waiter. Elizabeth rejoiced. She had Richard to herself. Dates could be set. Wedding plans made. "Good Lord," Richard declared, clenching the note, "this is unnecessary, but I'm hungry and we might as well have dinner." At her surprised expression, he forced a smile and said, "Allow me to order for you." He ignored admiring, male glances fixed on Elizabeth.

Reflected on silver and crystal, candlelight crawled through his hair turning it into golden wedges. She slowly tilted her water glass to capture the mirrored color. A hurricane of desire pelted her flesh at visions of their wedding night. Imagination of the fusion sent hot, steel needles coursing through her veins. It was him and no one else—not ever. She sat back scrutinizing every feature. Uncomfortable, he asked, "What are you looking at?"

"You." He fidgeted, feeling pique at Bill for getting him into this situation. Suppose someone saw him with a seamstress?

Over his shoulder, she caught sight of his mother, holding an ostrich fan, wearing black velvet. Engrossed in conversation, Mrs. Spencer did not see her, but the corpulent man with her had noticed them.

"Look, there is your mother. We can..."

He blanched, whiter than snow, grabbed her elbow, pulled her from her seat and half dragged and half pushed her towards the kitchen. She gasped, "What are you doing?" She heard tearing fabric, saw feathers scatter, having been caught beneath his frantic feet. Shocked waiters and cooks stood frozen. Soon she was out the back door in a downpour. "Richard, my cloak."

"Stay here. I'll get it. Where is my damn driver? I'll fire that bastard! I forgot. It's their anniversary. My father must be with her. Did they see us?"

"If that is your father, I'm sure he did. Richard, it's pouring." She watched what was left of the pink dress gather stains.

"I can't go back in there for your cloak. Wait, I'll find my driver." He found him sharing beer with other hackneys.

For some time, the only sounds were of hoofs slipping on wet cobblestones and of dripping water from her skirt.

"How will I explain the likes of you? I know what my father will say. Everything he will say."

"In the light of this treatment, how can you say your intentions were honorable? Why did you say it?"

"Because I had to. Otherwise, they would think me a failure. Too strapped to keep a woman."

"You made them think I was kept! Why didn't you tell me you never intended marriage?"

"Never thought you would think someone from my station would marry a seamstress. I would need to be insane. Better to be called a cad than a lunatic. I know what I will tell my friends. I'll say that though beautiful, you are too ignorant."

"Ignorant. Do you know Latin, French and Greek?"

"Enough French to get by. Yes, you did have schooling but it didn't prevent you from being stupid. If I cared about you, would I have trotted off to Europe? Wouldn't I have behaved differently? Did you really think I would marry a hat maker? Did you? You have nothing to complain about. You had great dinner dances. You had good food, the best wines. I owe you nothing, not even explanations. Don't worry. Someone will marry you. You go by the docks daily and the fellows always said you were a tasty morsel."

Struggling out of the carriage in a soaked, torn, pink dress, she blessed the rain. Drops on her face made the tears indiscernible and salvaged a scrap of pride. Better he believe she sought money and status than suspect how much she cared. On reaching her room, she held her forehead against the window and every raindrop rolling down the outside matched every tear rolling down the inside. Rain fell through the night and through the next day as did the tears till the final one was driven back to its glandular source, where it congealed. She could never and would never cry again.

Chapter Ten

On Saturday, November 9, 1872, dawn broke the silence of the Boston night, filling the streets with activity and raising five troubled heads from fitful sleep. Francisco and Mrs. Blackwood worried over Elizabeth. The dazzling eyes had dimmed and were embraced by dark circles. Animation disappeared, replaced by formal rigidity. Wrapped in a thin mantle of pride, which held no warmth, she would spend all of her earthly days with a stiffened gait and erect head.

Distressed Richard, out of excuses to avoid his father, promised to meet him that evening at eight.

The fifth distressed spirit was the head of the fire department. The city dotted with wooden roofs, poor water pressure, old pipes, too few hydrants, irregular couplings and flu-infected, fire horses courted disaster. He concluded should fire break out, means to combat it would be close to impossible. He checked the horses' worsening condition in despair. At seven twenty that night, fears became reality.

Flames sprouted in a warehouse basement on Summer Street where goods caught fire, spreading flames across the business district's streets. Blazing, red tongues licked dormers in tenement houses and gobbled French Mansard roofs. Panicked citizens rushed to banks, withdrawing uninsured funds. Looters and Richard rejoiced.

Before the elder's tirade began, the inferno's clatter began. "Quick," Richard's father boomed, "we must get to the bank."

"Right behind you. Let me get my coat." But the son made a rapid retreat across the Charles River. If all of Boston burned, along with his father, he would collect from all the over insured family holdings. Like Nero, he relished the red glow. The more red, the greener for him. Of course, it hinged on his father's demise, and with all the explosions coming from across the river, he gloated on the prospect.

Exploding gas lines sent flying debris around Francisco as he attempted to save the Old South Meeting House by dousing it with wet blankets. Efforts appeared hopeless before a pumper engine arrived from Portsmouth, New Hampshire capable of pumping water to the top of the belfry.

Broken glass, slashing his legs, felled him. A policeman called out, "This boy needs a doctor."

"The best doctors are sea captains. Where can I find one?" he replied, holding a wet shirt over the gashes. Thrown over a shoulder, he arrived in a shed manned by doctors and nurses.

The following night, after hours of recuperative sleep, Francisco awoke to Mrs. Blackwood saying, "So, ye find yeself back in bed. Must fancy the life."

Ignoring the remark, he asked, "Is it out? Is the tailoring shop all right?"

"Mr. Blackwood has gone for word. 'Tis still smouldering. Thank the Lord that it stayed away from here, but the smell. Methinks 'twill last for years." Casting a fretful glance outside, she continued, "What would it be keeping me husband so long? Dangerous 'tis out there. Black as tar 'twill be soon what with blown gaslights and shorter days."

"I'm sure the man is clever enough to take care." With words barely out of his mouth, the back door creaked open.

"Door needs a glob of grease." the carpenter stated.

Mansions and Mills

Swinging bandaged legs out of bed, Francisco asked, "How bad is it. What of the tailor shop?"

"The shop was spared the flames, but it appears the material is covered with soot. Mr. Hood must have insurance. The business district is gone. Sixty-five acres, they say. Two newspapers are gone, both The Herald and The Globe. Some people killed, we'll learn how many in a few days. The politicians should have paid attention to the fire chief. Think his name is John Damrell. Heard about him two months ago when having a taste of brew." Smiling at his wife, he added, "Not that I sip often."

"Ye best be wary of pubs full of ward bosses. Never was there an honest one."

Holding her chin between thumb and forefinger, he said, "Come on, you lovely wench. If I say I'm voting their way, we'll get a free turkey. Better than your leathery beef."

The fire bankrupted many insurance companies and rendered many homeless, but it was a boon for Francisco, supplying employment. Needed muscles cleared charred debris, dumping it into the harbor. He spent a year building a better city.

The inferno was also a boon for the Spencers, enriching them through insurance payments for over insured and overstocked warehouses, but unlike others, they made no contributions for Boston's renewal.

The only fly in that elderly man's ointment was a lazy, worthless, playboy son, but he was determined to have an unspoiled grandson. He blamed Richard's flaws on his wife's leniency, clueless to his poor example. He considered himself a man's man, one who gave no quarter.

Although Richard's elaborate home had been spared the flames, as had all Beacon Hill dwellings, he despaired. His father had raced into pandemonium, pulled horseless, fire apparatus, had been hailed a hero, and worse, survived.

Nights later, at his father's home, a different fire blazed. Richard sat in an overstuffed, wine-colored chair, running a finger inside a stiff collar, tapping panicked feet on a Persian rug, awaiting Father's arrival.

His mother picked at cuticles and bit her nails while seated on an armless chair which accommodated yards of material, complete with flounced skirt, many petticoats and a merciless, ever-present, boned corset. Such a device had concealed her one and only pregnancy. Mr. Spencer had always contained himself so well, even in youth, sparing her baser demands perhaps out of respect for her person. Now, age was a factor, if not alcoholic excess.

Richard inspected the portrait of the vain, lecherous old goat, which he knew his father to be, hanging somewhat askew. "Better straighten it before he blows a gasket over that too."

Apprehension heightened as his mother gazed toward the window. "Mother," he said, "I would like you to stay."

"Very well, if you don't raise his ire to fever pitch. I don't."

"You don't because you do as he says. I resent interference." In spite of her misguided belief that hers was a perfect marriage, he could tell her a thing or two. He smiled, contemplating their lack of information regarding his activities.

The front door slammed and his father strode to the liquor cabinet before acknowledging his son. After two, large gulps of the amber fluid, he bellowed, "It's high time for you to marry and settle down. There will be no more of your carousing!" He glanced at his wife. She did not suspect her son of cavorting with low women. Her husband had shielded her from knowledge of rampant, male practices.

In a sneering tone, Richard replied. "I don't wish to marry at this time. There is no young lady who I find suitable."

"Suitable! What of the Bates girl? She is attractive and of good family."

"Excuse me, dear, but the ladies have whispered that she has a suitor and it looks promising but the Lee's niece is visiting. We might make discreet inquiry and..."

Richard interrupted, "I remember her from the Newton wedding. A stupid female. Do you want me bored to death?"

Banging his fist on a table, his father roared, "Damn you! I don't care if you are bored. I want a grandson and you will provide it or wish you had."

Mrs. Spencer, after twisting and untwisting tassels on a pillow, excused herself. As her footsteps hit the upstairs landing, her husband hissed, "I will no longer pay your expenses. You squander my money on red-haired sluts and refuse me a grandson. A child that may have some intelligence. I spent a fortune on your education and you failed every subject. I bought your diploma."

"I failed because of inferior professors."

"You failed because you don't have the brains of a herring. You excel at one thing. Chasing petticoats."

"Are you the one to chastise me? As I recall yours didn't own petticoats."

"Mention that outside this room and there goes your social standing. You would be on a street corner without me. Wipe that smirk off your face, for if I see it again, you will be penniless. How about that Carlton girl?"

"That fat cow!"

"Somewhat heavy, but she has a pretty face. Come on son, you know that in the dark, under the sheets they are all the same."

Thinking of his French love, adorned with red lace, Richard disagreed. They were very different.

His father's voice, no longer mocking, slashed his daydream. "Choose fat, stupid, hook-nosed or cross-eyed but choose. Choose now!"

Neither wits nor looks influenced Richard's decision. There was something else to consider. Inheritance. Marjorie Carlton was an only child. He remembered a mention of Daddy Carlton having a heart problem and Daddy was the richest man in Boston. If English Queens could close their eyes and think of England, so could he. "Father, I've decided. Marjorie Carlton."

"Somehow, I thought you would."

Marjorie waxed more enthusiasm than her parents but the girl begged approval. Female hearts swooned over handsome and charming Richard Spencer. She planned to be a dutiful wife, leaning on her husband and consulting him on all decisions.

Proclamation of the engagement came at a festive dinner at the Carlton mansion, with invitations sent to the cream of society. Richard scrutinized the crystal, the silverware, gold doorframes, marble walls and silently congratulated himself on his choice. Nothing had prepared him for this display of wealth. If he could bear Marjorie somewhat and produce a son somehow, the day would come when all this and the Spencer money would be his. He counted his chickens, all unhatched.

Ben sidled up to Bill. "I like this marble. Think I'll have some installed. I'm wondering, what happened to this bloke's honorable intention as far as Elizabeth was concerned?"

"He never had any."

"Don't know why not. She is beautiful and intelligent. Her morals don't matter."

"Ben, there's nothing wrong with her morals."

"Then what was she doing with him?"

"Sorry to say, being a fool. A shame. I can read women and she's an admirable one. The cad took advantage of her affection for his own purposes."

"Can't figure that out, but I think I'll go to this wedding with a strumpet on each arm."

Bill laughed, "Only you would have the nerve to do that, but it sounds fitting to me."

Looking at Marjorie, Ben said, "She is pretty enough in a dull sort of way, but what does he see in her?"

"An heiress."

Fall withdrew, making room for winter with shortened daylight peeking through naked trees, devoid of lush covering. All noted that the carriage no longer came to the door. Mrs. Blackwood said, "Girl, ye believed what ye wanted to believe and we all do at times." A scorched Elizabeth went back and forth to work in a scorched city.

Mansions and Mills

Francisco participated in reconstructing ravaged Boston but was powerless at reconstructing ravaged Elizabeth.

On Tuesday, December thirty-first, 1872, many fellow boarders and the Blackwoods went out to celebrate the coming year. Francisco, exhausted, retired early. When all was quiet in the house, Elizabeth took the tattered, pink gown and incinerated it in the kitchen stove, tearing it further as she dropped piece by piece into the flames.

January 1873 brought the death of the ex-emperor of France. Mrs. Blackwood said, "God rest his soul." Later, she read of the death of John Stuart Mills, "Will that take some music out of the women's movements?" she asked, but blessed his soul also. Her concern over every soul in every continent solaced the German boarder for she'd bless his if he dropped dead over her indigestible beef.

In addition, January's newspapers announced the engagement of Marjorie Carlton and Richard Spencer. A prolonged honeymoon in Europe would follow the March wedding. Mrs. Blackwood attempted to conceal the news from Elizabeth, knowing the attempt futile. She always scanned the newspapers spread out on the round, kitchen table. Not seeing them in the customary place, she asked, "Where are the newspapers?" An unwilling hand produced copies from the sideboard. Standing, leaning over the table, turning each page, Elizabeth read the announcement without comment. The only indication of emotional response was that first, sudden grasp at her skirt. She tottered to her room, appearing with jacket and shawl in hand. "I will return in time for supper."

Mrs. Blackwood stepped forward, "Elizabeth, is there anything..."

Raising her hand, discouraging conversation, she passed through the mustard-colored hall and out the back door.

The next day, in Salem, a seaman purchased boots. Noticing a newspaper discarded in a wastepaper basket, he asked the proprietor, "If you are finished with that, may I have it? It would be something to read on a long whaling trip."

The salesman asked, "You can read?"

"Sure can. I'll catch some news."

"I know what. I'll wrap the boots in it."

The mariner looked at the wall clock, picked up the package, tucked it under an arm and hustled toward the dock as two customers walked in. "See that man? He can read. Imagine a negro reading."

The following morning, a jovial Richard walked into the tailoring shop. He swung a shy girl forward. "I have a surprise for you. This is Miss Marjorie Carlton, my fiancée. She would like to have Miss Gilbert make her wedding gown." Icy crystals covered her bonnet and frigid air followed them.

At sight of him, a magnitude of sensations washed over Elizabeth—anger, humiliation, crushing pain, yet still that warm, trickling desire, all mingling with self-hatred at her inability to control turbulent emotions. Lace fell from trembling fingers, tumbling helter-skelter on the floor. "Allow me," he said with a mocking smile as he retrieved it, "none other than you can be trusted to make my bride's gown."

Mr. Hood developed a vicious headache as he complied with Richard's mandates. Richard said, "I'd like three striped shirts and show me fabrics for a wedding gown." Marjorie threw a longing glance at a bolt that he tossed aside.

The tailor sat at a sewing machine, one foot on the pedal, and holding a cold, wet rag to his forehead said, "I thought he'd never leave. Now we know why Mrs. Spencer ordered so many items. This marriage must have been in the wind for months. Is it possible to design a gown to make the bride look slimmer?"

"I have a design in mind." Elizabeth's tone was light, hooded eyes hid feelings as she rummaged through a box of buttons.

"She appears to have a sweet disposition. She could have served as a dutiful daughter. So many do. Perhaps they have no other choice. The war carried off so many young men, but better a spinster than a wife to him. Tell me, what woman, unless insane would want him?"

Mansions and Mills

Tumbling thoughts accompanied her walk home. Elizabeth muttered, "I must be insane." Could this have been in the wind for a long time? Why didn't he ever speak of it? Yes, she thought, I am insane.

Two weeks later, Marjorie came in for a final fitting. "I just have to sew this seam and you may take the gown with you." Elizabeth said.

"Let me try it on first." the seventeen-year-old said. She twirled around the room as a man of uncertain age walked into the hubbub. Pushing his chewing tobacco to the roof of his mouth, he walked out.

Before closing time, Mr. Hood said, "It's a marvel. She looks so much slimmer."

In a saddened whisper, Elizabeth said. "Every bride deserves to look beautiful on her wedding day. She appears to be a nice girl."

"Very young, but I wager with that husband, she will age fast. Poor thing."

Stacked books greeted Richard in the green-carpeted library. His sire nestled in an overstuffed chair, glass filled with a favored liquid. Wordlessly, he raised an index finger, indicating where Richard was to sit. The chair was stiff, armless and uncomfortable. The son broke the silence, "How big a bundle did you get from the insurance?"

"We are not here to discuss my finances. Just yours."

"Which, as you know are none. Since you have promoted this marriage, how am I to support this wife in customary fashion? It will require a substantial allowance."

"Just instruct her to use some restrain and send all bills to me. Remind her that she married a Spencer and not another Carlton."

"My embarrassment would be too profound. Submitting bills like school children! I won't do it! I'll cancel the wedding to that cow."

"Have I not made myself clear? Not another dime if you do not marry. She need not know our arrangement. She gives you the bills and you send them to me. You will be provided with pocket change and you might still be able to keep your red-haired harlot. She is very beautiful. You should share her with someone who could keep her in better elegance." A lewd glint passed over his eyes.

"As I recall, red hair was not your style."

"Watch it, boy."

"You call me boy!" His temper flared.

"Just habit. Forget it." For the first time, he feared his son as well he should. One quick blow with the poker. The senior attempted to placate, saying, "Son, some men know how to make money. I figured the gimmicks."

Richard flared, "You certainly did. Didn't you? Wouldn't pay for a slave. Why should you when you manufactured your own? Did you keep count of your mulatto bastards? Probably made a handsome profit selling mulattos to other planters. Especially females. Did you keep records on the daughters you sold?"

"Lower your voice, your mother will hear. She's a decent Christian from prominent family. That's what got us accepted in Boston. But I convinced them I was an abolitionist. Sold those darkies and the plantation at a profit. Yankees never knew because I got here before the war and helped transport slaves to Canada."

"How did you know when to pull out?"

"Easy. Abe got elected. Knew there would be war, knew the North would win. Took only a lick of sense to know that. They had the industries, we didn't. The Yankees would hit our Virginia plantation long before they could ruin Georgia. They would turn our negroes free. If they didn't slaughter us with their black hands, I'd be as broke as those fool rebels. I knew slavery was doomed. Sold everything fast to a deluded confederate, confident of his calvary. Another fool! I got out while the getting was still good."

"Must admit, you always win." His eyes, still fixed on the poker, remained icy. "Returning to my situation, I want a better deal."

"I have a deal for you. If a grandson survives till age two, you shall have a substantial allowance. One that you will manage."

Making his way home through darkened streets, Richard hoped siring a son would take few trials. How would he manage it? Nausea overwhelmed him. Marjorie revolted.

At that very moment, Marjorie received that obligatory, mother, prenuptial talk. A red-faced Mrs. Carlton stuttered, "Dear, things will occur on your wedding night that may seem strange, undignified, but it is part of married life. Endure it in silence. It won't last long."

"Mother, what sort of things?" Marjorie whispered, eyes flaring apprehension.

Face a deeper shade of red, Mrs. Carlton answered, "Don't concern yourself. Your husband will guide you." She calmed the innerved girl, giving tender pats to trembling hands.

As Richard rode home, under cold stars, he pondered on his father's lack of consternation when confronted with his visits to enslaved women. What a triumph knowing of his father's peccadilloes while his own remained secret. He'd continue outsmarting them all. Nothing to worry about. He'd have all those chickens.

Turning into his driveway, he noticed a flickering bedroom light. The cursed session with his father faded. That light meant a boat from France had arrived. All the pent-up craving rose. He raced up the circular staircase, designed by Charles Bulfinch. In throbbing anticipation, he tore off his jacket, waistcoat and shirt. "So, you decided to surprise me. How marvelous seeing you and wearing the red lace. I've missed you so much! Oh, my darling, little Henri."

Chapter Eleven

Francisco opened the door to the hallway, looked in the kitchen and saw three shadows on the wall, one unmoving and two in dynamic motions. Mrs. Blackwood cranked the handle of a meat grinder while Mr. Bruncken shook spices in ground beef as it fell into a blue bowl. On occasion he paused, tasting raw meat then dropping more unnamed spices into the mixture, attempting to make gourmet fare out of inexpensive cuts of beef. It was his landlady's concession to economy, kept secret from her husband who often complained, "How come your roast beef is more suitable to the soles of my shoes than my stomach?"

The third shadow cast on a beige wall came from a seated Elizabeth, bent over notes from home. Francisco had hoped for a calvary type entrance, though minus a horse, but he limped in, groaning. Dropping to the nearest chair, he attempted to remove boots which seemed to have succumbed to sorcery by shrinking two sizes.

Mrs. Blackwood released the wood handle and by pulling with all her might, succeeded in removing constricting boots over protests coming from a German intent on completing the task at hand.

"Hush," she said, "look at the poor lad's swollen feet." She filled a tub with water, added powder, rolled up his trouser legs and submerged his feet. "For sure, 'twill do a world of good if ye soak for twenty minutes. There is fresh Sapolio soap by your door for washing."

Claus Bruncken's narrowed eyes focused on the grime-covered youth who, in his opinion, received pampering. Defiant Francisco returned the German's gaze. This one, he thought, is not like the ones I met at sea. They were not like this diminutive man who resents me. He recalled reading that the Teutonic race descended from the Franks or the Goths. Maybe one race produced powerful offspring and the other produced little, sausage-loving weasels. He was convinced this man needed work more vigorous than running errands for a law firm and interests beyond his obvious yearning for Elizabeth.

Francisco's scrutiny switched to Elizabeth rising from the chair, clutching letters and gliding, with rustling skirts, to the window. She crossed her arms, holding an elbow in each hand, silent in her observation of passing humans. Her dress was plain and a drab brown. Her matching hat dangled from a coat rack. Once she wore colorful clothing—bright plaids, vivid hues, and feathered hats worn at rakish angles. Now she was stylish but not feathery.

Weary of the silence within Elizabeth, Mrs. Blackwood said, "What would it be? Bad news from home?" She resumed the meat grinding, throwing concerned glances in the young woman's direction.

"No, actually things are picking up." Moving to the center of the room, she said, "Francisco there are several letters for you hiding under the newspapers."

"They will have to wait. I can't keep my eyes open."

Mrs. Blackwood washed her hands and towel in hand walked towards him. "Best have supper, tired or not." He wiped his feet revealing a dark, unwashed ring above his ankles. "My," she exclaimed, "ye be two-toned. Methinks the soap will come to good use."

Attempting, without success, to engage Elizabeth, she said, "Look at the news. They caught the fiend torturing little ones because one boy remembered he had a white eye. Think he can see out of it? His name is Jesse Pomeroy. 'Twill knock devils out of him going to the Lyman School for Boys in Westborough."

Francisco said, "Don't know about that. Cruel stays cruel, but you have to wonder what made him that way." An image of Rufus crossed his mind and he shivered.

Disgusted with interruptions, Claus attempted to leave his flavoring task only to be told, "I'll not be letting ye off. Ye started this. 'Tis to be done and don't be telling me husband why. Cuts of beef and all. Methinks, if a husband goes to bed with a full stomach, best he never knows what he eats."

Francisco managed supper and ablutions after Mrs. Blackwood brought heated water. He fell in bed only to have a nightmare probably induced by the fiend, Jesse Pomeroy. In his dream, Rufus stood, surrounded by tortured children, and seeing Francisco strode towards him saying, "You know too much." As he walked forward, his hands grew to a tremendous size, dwarfing his body. Francisco crumbled between his palms. Massive fingers opened, revealing wet sand. Francisco awoke trembling both from the dream and a room that had grown cold. Barefooted, he removed an extra blanket from a drawer.

The next day was Sunday, affording time to linger, to sip hot tea and read letters. One from the captain questioned if he would be interested in permanent residence in England. Leave the States with speed he advised. The States are full of Indian massacres and rioting Irishmen. This Francisco found amusing. Obviously, the British man could now forget his country's history of riots, wars, rebellions and subjugation of others. Francisco could not tell him about Elizabeth. In patchy knowledge of the cerebral captain, he was convinced that scorn would result from confessing fixation on a woman. Francisco had more to learn.

He tore open the letter from Amos, one free of advice or questions. The former cotton picker, now teacher, searched for his parents and from an old darky, heard of a former slave, renamed

Baker. He said, "He found de wife still on de old plantation. Deh jumped the broom, den made it lawful 'bout de time de Yewwnited States said dat was all right for de culluds."

As Amos related the long, convoluted tale, Francisco placed the letter on the large table with its pedestal leg and clawed foot. He surveyed the room with its large stove, dull walls, and slate sink, one hand resting on a chair's arm, the other hand clutching the envelope, wringing it between his fingers, immersed in worry. Amos didn't mention that he might find himself tarred and feathered or lynched. The trusting man trusted the Federal Government and wasn't fretting. Francisco fretted about conditions south of the Mason-Dixon Line.

He reread the letter while no longer seated. He stood or circled the room in agitation. Mrs. Blackwood stopped dishwashing and stacking dishes to ask, "Lad, is there troubling news?"

"No, Amos found his parents and extends an invitation." He considered it. A visit might take the bullet called Elizabeth out of his brain. The beckoning sea might do that also. Staying made him as witless over her as she was witless over Richard. He knew it and hated it and he hated her heartbroken moping.

Sighing, he opened the letter from Harry. It was buoyant. His wife's savings from being a laundress in New Bedford along with his own provided the purchase of several cows. White men made the milk deliveries. He didn't explain why. Omission spoke for itself.

Before settling down, they had gone for a brief spree in New York by way of the Fall River Line. They saw New York sites, and for their return, boarded a ship from a pier on Murray Street. They had an excellent meal for fifty cents and disembarked at the foot of Central Street in Fall River. Harry relished the novelty of relaxing at sea. When was Francisco planning to return to it?

Brushing uncombed hair from his eyes, he realized the time and asked, "Where is Elizabeth?"

"Not at a Catholic mass, saving her soul."

"Are you still dwelling on that? Thought that was straightened out. Where is Elizabeth?"

"Me boy wrote he is driving cattle through Kansas. Might there be Mormons there?"

"Not that I know of. Stop worrying, remember what I said. With too many wives driving him crazy, his soul will be saved. Now, where is Elizabeth?"

"Don't be funning about people's souls."

"Where's Elizabeth?"

"They went off to a Protestant sermon."

"Whose they? Not the dumb German."

His agitation increased as she answered, "He is the right age for her. Best she get her mind off the scoundrel and Claus is a good man. Just slow in the head."

"Right age! I'll soon be seventeen and have crowded ten years of life in four years at sea. Add ten to my first twelve and that makes me twenty-two. I'm a good man. Can't she see that?"

She rested an elbow on the table, fist under her chin, considering his words. His new-found income provided two pairs of trousers, a lined jacket and he had made three shirts by borrowing Elizabeth's sewing machine. A former sailor gifted him a Russian's fur hat, once bartered for rum. Seamen's universal currency!

"Fine that ye remember sums. Twelve and ten make twenty-two, for sure. A man ye say. Like as not, 'tis so and Elizabeth seems fourteen with her mooning and wearing old lady hats. Did ye notice the brown one?" Her mind wandered to her usual anxiety over Elizabeth.

She was brought back to the present problem by Francisco's pressing question. "When will she be back?"

As if on cue, an icy blast of air blew her in, swirling the brown shawl around her head and challenging the gloved hands to keep the cavorting covering in place. The same explosive wind blew the letters off the table. Frost, shellacking her rosy cheeks, sent her running to the stove. She pulled off her gloves, blew on chilled fingers, held them to the heat and filled Francisco's hungry eyes with every movement.

Mrs. Blackwood noticed twisting emotions on his face and wondered how Elizabeth failed to notice, but she always said the girl was blind, "Tell me, what have ye done with Mr. Bruncken?"

"Bored him I fear, what with the sermon and my talk of family. We couldn't discuss Socrates, Virgil or the Celtic tribes. Conversation was at cross-purposes when it existed at all. He had a mission of sorts on the corner of Washington and Bedford Streets so we parted company."

Francisco didn't ask about those foreign blokes. No sense reminding her of his lack of education. Library books would tell him. He had several stacked in his room. He cherished the ones on history, convinced mankind should learn from other's mistakes. That dumb German, extolling Germany's recent victory over France, declared that his country should plan more. Dumb German.

Mrs. Blackwood scrutinized Francisco again. He was kind, wise beyond his years and always seeking knowledge in spite of returning at night with facial features hung with fatigue.

Once, she had attempted to match him to the eighteen-year-old Conroy girl but he had asked, "Is she the carrot head with freckles going from her forehead to forever?"

Blushing, she had replied, "Hard to say where her freckles let off. 'Tis wicked for ye to think of it." She arose to brew tea. Grasping a hip and flinching, she declared, "Me son had best decide when these old bones can move to warm Texas. Needs more funds he says."

All contemplated Mr. Bruncken's long stay in the cold. Brown's Apothecary stood on the corner of Washington and Bedford. Elizabeth said, "Maybe he went for lozenges."

Noticing the overflowing pan of water under the icebox, Mrs. Blackwood jumped up and with help from a steadying chair, pulled it from its den. "Ah, wouldn't you think with this cold, ice would never melt?"

Leaping up, Francisco took hold of the container, headed down the porch stairs and tossed the water over the railing, spilling some on the steps. It would freeze, jeopardizing Claus' ascent. He had a brief moment envisioning the hopeful suitor sheathed in splints, but on reflection, requested ashes from the coal stove in order to spread them over the stairs.

While outside at his task, Elizabeth remarked, "What a thoughtful boy."

"Man, Elizabeth, man. Can't ye tell the difference? As I have said so many times, ye are blind and I fear ye will keep paying for it."

March brought streaming sun through kitchen windows, stippling over newspapers announcing the merging of the Carlton and Spencer families. The almanac stated spring had arrived, but the elements ignored calendar dictates. The weather was as cool as the façade encircling Elizabeth. Reacting to the wedding announcement in like fashion to the engagement announcement, she picked up a shawl and strolled out the door. She would never mention the event and never suspect how often she was mentioned at the event.

It began with Ben Davis complimenting the bride's gown. She thanked him stating it was the creation of talented Miss Gilbert.

He gulped, took a sip of champagne and then choked. Alert Bill Klass pounded his back while a distressed bride clutched her own throat. Bill led him away to a nearby bench and sat with him until he returned to his normal physical state if not his emotional one.

"Bill, did you hear what she said?"

"No," he stared at the befuddled face, "you look like a man in shock."

"I am but will recover. Can you imagine the audacity of that man having his bride's gown made by Elizabeth?" Ben sputtered in indignation, "The unmitigated gall."

Mansions and Mills

"That would be more than gall. It would be callowness." He pulled a watch from his pocket, checked the time, calculated protocol as to how soon he and Isabel could leave Richard's company. A waiter walked by with a tray of champagne. Ben plucked a glass of bubbly liquid, handing it to Bill.

"Good stuff! Carlton spared no expense." Ben downed his glass and chased the tray for another. "The impudence of introducing your bride to your para..." He checked himself. "I know what you think, Bill, but convince me."

"Since you insist. You went to college with him. Tell me of his behavior. Was he a good student?"

"No. Flunked. Hung around with younger students. No competition I guess."

"With his scholastic record, how can he be a business asset? Probably can't earn a dime. You said he hung around with younger boys. Didn't you notice weird behavior? Ben, you are a man of the world. Come on, Ben, think!"

Ben decided he needed another glass of golden elixir. "To be honest, some of the fellows were beginning to wonder, but then he showed up with a beautiful, richly dressed woman. He claimed financial success and after dark refreshments."

"There were no after dark refreshments, at least not with her or any woman. He used a trusting, enamored woman as a front."

Ben felt ill. Maybe too much glass lifting, but he didn't think so. "So, what does he do with a wife?"

"Continue the charade for fortune. Fear romance will rub off soon for this bride. Seventeen! Poor child. Hear his father clamors for a grandchild. Might take a miracle for Richard to accomplish that."

Russet gown flaring, Bill's wife waltzed by with a former Calvary officer. "This is the third dance. That's two too many."

Ben laughed, "Don't worry about him. As a medical assistant, I was stationed in Washington. He was married to a devoted wife, devoted enough to cross battle lines to visit her hospitalized husband. Would have been praiseworthy if he had a wound but he was more gifted at pushing troops forward than leading them forward. His days would have ended at the end of a rope had he served with Sherman, but the Army put him to pushing papers in Washington, a place full of politicians and prostitutes, alike in principals. His unsheathed saber became more visible to camp followers than it had been on the battlefield. When his wife discovered the nature of his illness, she ran off with a colonel. He had no talent for papers and couldn't seat a horse either because riding would hurt in the middle you might say. Upon discharge, resplendent with vanity if not valor, he ran for Congress. Failing two elections, he found the Lord. As a minister, his souvenir sword gets frequent use beheading bats in the belfry. I can't kill bats so that roué has one up on me."

Gulping down more champagne, Ben swayed towards the door. He caught Bill by the shoulder, "You know, I've decided on proposing to Louise but I'm going to wait till tomorrow when I'm sober just to be sure."

Bill watched his wife dancing with a gentleman wearing a handlebar moustache. He decided to cut in, "Dearest," he said, "it's time for you to say your pretty goodbyes. You have had enough fun for one evening."

Richard managed a forced smile as his father waddled towards him. "Great show, son. Carlton opened a bank vault for this. All I want is a promise to be a good husband."

"Of course, I promise." He thought of an old English proverb. Promises are like piecrust, made to be broken.

Marjorie went to her bridal bed clad in a "modesty" nightgown with buttons running from neck to hem, a gift from her mother and wasted money for the bride went through a tortured night. Mother said it was an initiation into marriage, so did chains symbolize the marital bond?

Richard vowed not to repeat it for two months. Maybe she was more fecund than her mother. Had Marjorie not complied with every demand, the deed could not have been accomplished. His luck held. She conceived that night.

Mansions and Mills

On the honeymoon, he padded bills sent home to the cash register, stating that due to her happy condition, she deserved spoiling. Added greenbacks allowed him to afford Henri.

The morning after the wedding, a sober Ben proposed to his consort, and to his consternation, was turned down. He sat in amazement on the lavish settee that had cost a fortune asking, "Why not? I want to make an honest woman of you."

"Why? What would your friends think?"

"There is no reason for me to care what anyone thinks."

"You'll be excluded from their clubs."

"No problem. I will buy all the clubs and exclude them."

"Why do you want to marry me?"

"Because I'm accustomed to having you around and I don't want anyone else to have you. All these other fellows think you are as smashing as Elizabeth. You are sincere and funny. You make me laugh and that's important. Louise, I want you for keeps."

"Fiddlesticks. When I'm old and fat, you'll be chasing a young, skinny and equally funny girl."

"Fiddlesticks yourself. When you are old and fat, I'll be older and probably fatter. You should have seen last night's guests. A room full of fat, old codgers. Too many cigars and too much whiskey lubrication but all the women were still slim except Mrs. Spencer and that poor bride."

"There, you have said it. A proper Bostonian wife. The teas. The charities. The bowing and fawning. Gossiping and speculating on who can outspend who. That's not what I want. That's what Elizabeth wants. That's what she wanted Richard for."

"She wanted Richard for himself and that's the highest compliment a rich man gets."

"Try it. Propose to her. Watch her jump."

He drew her close, crushing the velvet dress. "Let's talk about us."

She pulled away, holding him at arm's length. "Have you ever wanted to live in a log cabin or build one, or watch crops grow, or take a wild ride down rapids?"

"Heavens, no."

"Well, I do. I can't suffocate in all this starch. I'm going to the frontier. I've been thinking of it more and more. Can you imagine me in homespun? I'm more suited to a hoedown than a waltz. I would become miserable here and I would make you miserable. That's the last thing I want to do. I will always remember you and pray for you. Your proposal was an honor. Thank you." She brushed her tear-streaked face across his chest.

Elizabeth reread descriptions of the wedding beneath an oil lamp. The only sound came from angry, howling wind. Soon trees would wear tiny, yellow-green buds. Spring again. Sunlight claiming more hours, shining upon her, ignoring the darkness of her days. New life bursting through softened earth. There would be the song of returning birds, chirping for a mate. Last year a nightingale had screeched for a companion. Every organ within her, bearing Richard's etched name, screeched. She wondered if those organs were bleeding. She sat in unmoving silence under a circle of lamplight, thinking that Marjorie was the luckiest girl in the world.

Chapter Twelve

Sun sparkled, but Mr. Bruncken hugged the buildings in useless attempts to obtain protection from shifting gusts of wind. He took a circuitous route, not because he had developed paranoia, unless wanting to avoid meeting his cousin could be classified as paranoia, and not because he wanted exercise.

In fact, he was hungry. He longed for supper and yearned for bed. He dallied from embarrassment and the horrifying thought that neither food nor rest would be furnished that evening. Restaurants were plentiful but lodgings were not. The fire destroyed tenements and the influx of immigrants didn't help. No, he decided, Mrs. Blackwood wouldn't throw him into the cold streets even if Elizabeth had told them of the incident, but he wasn't certain of Mr. Blackwood. The man of the house was known to chuck miscreants to the curb. Mr. Bruncken feared it might be his turn for a heave-ho, considering he was a man given a heave-ho by his mother. His refusal to serve in the noble cause of defeating the French had been, for her, the last straw.

Head bent against blustery weather, eyes cast on cobblestones, alert to horse droppings, he drew his jacket closer with his left hand and inserted the right in a pocket, feeling the source of his problem. His hand flew out as if bitten by a rattlesnake. One quarter of a week's salary invested and for what? If landed in the gutter, it was his cousin's fault. Why had he listened to someone who had been dropped on his head as a baby? He slackened his pace to a crawl as shadows lengthened.

Nevertheless, reluctant or not, he arrived at the backstairs. Drawing in a deep breath, attempting to draw courage, he placed one hesitant step on the first step then on the second one and froze. A kaleidoscope of voices and laughter wafted towards him. "Heavens," he told himself, "she told everyone."

Mr. Blackwood spotted him and called, "Here you are! We have held supper and are all famished." The German didn't understand that word. Famished? It must be all right. Everyone, except Francisco, seemed pleased to see him. The host patted him on the back and stated, "Invited half the neighborhood over for a taste of your sausages. Don't ever leave unless you give us the recipe."

A thought buzzed in the chef's head, "Can't share the recipe. Promised my mother that the family recipe would never pass to a soul. Looks like I must stay." He smiled at wincing Francisco.

The more praised the fare, the more the two rivals for Elizabeth eyed each other, one with glee, the other with burning animosity. Telling himself that Elizabeth would never succumb to this uneducated foreigner brought little comfort to Francisco for he too was an uneducated foreigner.

Discussion of education arose when a teacher announced that he was seeking different employment because Boston's boys were unruly. Some had pounded nails into the bottom of his chair, towards the rear, pointing upwards. Protruding, imperceptible points produced puncture wounds. He had administered cane to the youngsters' backsides but heard them laughing at recess. They had felt nothing, having cushioned their undisciplined posteriors with towels. In addition, whenever he left the room, the boys closed the door over a belt, wedging it shut. Nothing short of removing the hinges had freed the door. As insurance against the practice, he had insisted on relinquished belts before any entered the classroom. Then they stuffed their pockets with pieces of discarded rugs and achieved the same results by jamming those under the door. His patience shattered, however, when they brought in frogs and larvae. The creatures that didn't croak crawled. He slipped on mealy bugs, sustaining a back injury. "What is galling is my replacement by a young, inexperienced girl has produced model students."

"It's probably because she is pretty and pretty girls can change things." volunteered Claus.

Mrs. Blackwood swallowed convulsing laughter by asking, "Elizabeth, have ye found out if the kitten is a she?" Her eyes rested on each male face before continuing, "Methinks it could be just one more tomcat."

During the following week, Mrs. Blackwood often broke out with fits of laughter. The tale had to be shared or she would explode but never shared with her husband. His would be a difficult choice—his principals or his beloved sausages.

At last, she told Francisco, saying, "This German tries me soul what with me husband fired up about his sausages. I be bursting to tell someone but remember if ye put one hand on Mr. Sausage, we may both be seeking lodgings if we are not dropped in an outhouse first. For sure, 'twas a mistake grinding me bloody arm off. Me beef was fine, was it not?"

"Superb," he lied, "but I promise I'll not touch him."

Through laughter she related Elizabeth's anecdote. Weeks ago, his cousin had told Claus Bruncken about this marvelous elixir. "Two teaspoons a day and you will put women into swoons requiring smelling salts." Claus didn't believe him. Who listens to a dunce who was dropped on his head at two months? New thoughts formed after the Sunday spent with Elizabeth. He didn't impress her with his wits so he gave consideration to the advice from dented head. On his route to the apothecary, they met. Cousin told Claus, "They don't have it. I have bottles of the good stuff. Got it from a man on a wagon. I'll sell you some. It will turn her into a wildcat, clawing you." A guaranty of a clawing Elizabeth sold at any price.

After cultivating courage, his vacillating hand knocked on the door of the creature brewed by Greek gods. Modesty held a wrapper to her chin. She asked, "Is something wrong? Are you ill? Mrs. Blackwood has remedies. Wait, I'll get her."

"No! Don't get her. I have something to show you. Don't wake any of them. Let's whisper."

Perplexed by this strange presentation at this hour, she asked, "Is that medicine?" She examined the green bottle in a faint light from a full moon. It was said that some people behaved in a weird manner at a full moon. Chances were he was being affected but he was such a nice man that this behavior could be tolerated for a moment.

"It's sort of like medicine. Makes a person healthy and strong. Soon, I'll be able to show you how strong I am."

"If you want to be strong, lifting weights helps. I am going to tell Mrs. Blackwood to get some of this. She looks so tired sometimes. Where did you buy it?"

He stood speechless and openmouthed. Picking up his sagging lower lip, he managed to croak, "Please keep it a secret. It might not work."

"If it can help her, I must tell her. Goodnight." She closed her door, convinced that this bizarre behavior was caused by the full moon.

In early rays of sun, Elizabeth saw another dropped lip. When speech returned, Mrs. Blackwood said. "Dearie, the only thing they give women is big, pink pills."

To make her point, she opened a cupboard door, "See. Pink pills. They fix everything except sweating all night and aching bones."

After telling Francisco, Mrs. Blackwood glanced at clenched, male fists, veins apparent in young hands. Several minutes later, they relaxed, as she said, "Francisco, there be no harm done. She didn't hear the stallion neigh."

He circled the table, running fingers through his hair until booming laughter erupted, "You are so right. Such a stupid approach, but he is dumb. Isn't that naivety in her amazing?"

"No. She's been sheltered till she went to work and what does she see 'cept the trappings of the fuddy-duddy rich?"

"This thing between men and women is spoken of at sea but never on land. Do women ever speak of it?"

"Not till they be old enough to fan themselves. Have ye not noticed matrons with ostrich-plume fans? They talk of little pink pills. Most doctors give big ones."

He could not follow her. This talk of pills and fans! "Why do girls flirt if they don't know what it's for?"

"Compliments. Bet Mr. Hood knows that. Fat, thin, old, tall or short, they are all beautiful, graceful and charming he'll say. Good for business."

He had the modus operandi. If Elizabeth fluttered her lashes, say something nice, except she was not a flutterer.

Mrs. Blackwood interrupted his ruminations, "Are all ye questions answered?"

"No. Who tells the young girls about baby making?"

"Their mothers. The night before they get married. Except the poor ones. Crowded in tenements, working in mills. They learn too soon, too fast what with ruffians grabbing at them."

"Captain Addison told me not to act that way. He told me to respect all women."

The skipper had so influenced him that Francisco wondered if the story of Adam and Eve could be correct. Perchance deviltry had been instigated by Adam who lied and told the Lord, "The woman is to blame." and she had no witness to refute what the muscled one said.

A wisp of dark hair fell over one eye. Mrs. Blackwood brushed it back with gnarled, arthritic fingers. "Ye are in need of a haircut." Hair fell in the same place when he nodded agreement. Once more, she brushed it back.

Having solved the riddle of women, Francisco sat back to sip tea and molasses. But he and Mrs. Blackwood missed two vital things about Elizabeth. First, she was incapable of separating love from lust. She didn't understand that others could and she didn't understand men. She was unaware of nature bestowing on men a need to bond through the flesh and to bond with a trusted friend. How could she know men never confided in other men? She didn't know that men shook hands, slapped backs but were in constant competition with each other in business, sports and the pursuit of women. How to fathom that a man might need a place to cry?

Secondly, when she would have followed Richard through jungles and arid land, his rejection did more than shatter her. It made her feel unlovable. How could she have appeal? She had never been personally vain, never seen her features as meeting beauty's criteria. Strong family pride resided within, but a mirror whispered that there was too much red in her hair, a silly dimple centered at the tip of her nose, eyes that should be blue were green and hips should have been somewhat narrower.

As Francisco drank his tea, Mr. Blackwood tramped through the kitchen from his basement project, oil dispenser in hand, "Have to fix those creaking door hinges. Elizabeth insists we have a ghost."

Task completed, he said, "Any tea left?" He picked up the pot, shaking it. "This will do. Any chance for an early supper?"

The lady of the house shook her head, "No. 'Twill be delayed. Mr. Felix is going to visit his sick father."

Francisco groaned, "I wish I had a horse."

"Pray tell why when ye have no carriage?"

"I'd eat it."

"Not without giving half to me." intoned the carpenter, "A delay? I'm starved. I know what you are thinking, woman. I've no right complaining when I forgot to take out my garbage this morning. Beats all hell, it's always your money and it's always my garbage."

Francisco looked out at a ferocious rainstorm. Elizabeth's umbrella sat in the stand. He paced to the window, then back to the chair, then back to the window. "Sit," said Mrs. Blackwood, "ye be cluttering up me kitchen."

"Did she take her boots this morning?"

Mansions and Mills

"Methinks not, but will check." She returned clutching brown boots. "Mighty good match to that bloody hat! Promise you will borrow it and bury it with me."

"One question. How will I return it?"

"Funning with me, are ye? Sit I said. No, ye won't sit. Ye want to fetch the lass. Get on with it!" She tossed the boots into his lap and handed him the umbrella.

On his way down the walk, he met the saturated, sausage man. His feet squished in sopping shoes. Francisco laughed, remembering the tonic tale and wondering where it was.

The green bottle had been tossed into the bay to be retrieved someday by someone making jewelry out of beach glass. He often cursed a cousin who though dropped on his head was a clever swindler. Besides, the contents gave him indigestion.

Francisco found Elizabeth with pins in her mouth and a tape measure around her neck. Mr. Hood looked up. "Good afternoon, though it is a foul one. What may I do for you?"

"Nothing, Sir. I brought rain gear for Elizabeth. You must be Mr. Hood. A pleasure to meet you."

"You must be Francisco. The pleasure is mine." He scrutinized the youngster, liking what he saw. Turning, he said, "Run along Elizabeth. You can finish that tomorrow."

Changing into boots and reaching for her coat, she retorted, "Isn't he a thoughtful bo—man?" Francisco swelled. She had called him a man. Was she beginning to discount the age difference? Was there a chance? Could she be forgetting Richard?

Before exiting, her questions tumbled, "Didn't you work today? What's for supper?"

"Weather made work impossible. Left early. Supper is lamb stew when we get it. It's delayed."

"That's better than bangers or rashers. I love lamb."

Perplexed, Mr. Hood asked, "What are bangers and rashers?"

Francisco answered, "Sausages and bacon made the Irish way, but you haven't lived till you have tasted Mr. Bruncken's sausages."

Elizabeth's laughter and the storm rushing in the door drowned out Mr. Hood's question, "Who is he?"

In pouring rain, her drenched skirt clung to Elizabeth's legs. Francisco avoided his eyes. Admiration of a lady's "limbs" was considered offensive. He hoped she hadn't seen his approving glance.

Wet clothes dried by the stove and all boarders ate and retired to their rooms with the exception of Francisco who lingered with Mrs. Blackwood. He sat listening to ashes falling away from a former, fiery state and a mood assailed him.

Mrs. Blackwood, tidying up, asked. "What ails ye?"

"Saudades."

"Is that something ye ate?"

"No. It's a Portuguese word that is hard to translate in English but it means being sad, but more, like having a deep longing for someplace or someone."

"Are ye missing home? Ye never speak of it."

"I never miss home, but I miss my mother. It's been years so I can't say I'm grieving."

"If ye be missing, ye be grieving and ye'll call for her with ye last breath. Ye can put any meaning to your Portuguese word, but for sure, missing her is in the middle of it."

His head dropped against this woman as he wept for a woman on a field in the village of Sao Pedro. The only motherly warmth, comfort or guidance for this seventeen-year-old youth came from this woman as it did for Elizabeth.

Once when Elizabeth appeared to be lost in saudades, Mrs. Blackwood said, "Lass, the way to forget a man is with another man. Open those eyes. A good man may be closer than ye think."

"Not for me, but did you forget a man that way?"

"Well, dearie," she answered, scratching a spot behind her ear, "guess I never found one worth forgetting or remembering but 'tis for sure, ye golden one ain't worth a thought. He's deserving of brushing off like a squashed bug."

"How do you know? You never met him."

"I know his kind and they all fall in the same cesspool."

One rainy night the house was quiet by ten o'clock, but a bit later Elizabeth heard squeaking hinges. Must be a ghost again she thought, aware that those ancient hinges had been oiled.

In the middle of the night the rain stopped. Drops of water rode on branches. At times, halted by a bud, silvery beads stood still, standing for a moment like sentries before falling as if struck by a pellet. She watched a few drops clinging in a crook refusing to plummet. These were caught in the faint, misty beam from a gaslight and looked like diamonds. Diamonds for Marjorie's hair. That sweet teen could have all the jewels on the planet if she could have had that one golden one. Before dawn she awoke to renewed rain stabbing the roofs, the windows, and the cobblestones of her narrow world.

Chapter Thirteen

Many days later, Elizabeth rose with the sun, its beams migrating through juvenile honeysuckle blossoms. Last week crocuses, harbingers of warmer days, made a saffron and purple appearance by the door.

She prepared for a busy day, dressing in haste and twisting her hair into a bun. In spite of uncooperative, squealing hinges, she left soundless. Gone were the days of pounding, rushing heels.

By ten o'clock Mrs. Spencer bounced in with a companion. "This is Mrs. Carlton, a dear friend. She and I require summer garb for concerts, operas and all other social events. She insists we accompany her and Mr. Carlton." She spoke to the proprietor only, ignoring that silly, mendacious girl.

Mrs. Carlton said, "You must be the talented girl who fashioned the wedding gown. Dear child, you are a dressmaker, not a seamstress. There is a difference. In the past, I had dressmakers come to my home but Mrs. Spencer adopted the pastime of coming to this establishment and wishes me to do so."

They left after several selections. Mr. Hood mopped his forehead, moaning, "They are planning to bring half of Boston here including husbands. Don't misunderstand, I'm not complaining about more business, but I can't work us both to death in cramped space. Expansion and more hands are needed."

Riding home in the carriage, Mrs. Carlton said, "I don't believe you noticed the teaseled material. Imagine that all those bolts are manufactured by overworked millworkers. Sad, is it not?"

"Since they teem into the country filthy and illiterate, they should appreciate any employment. Mills can't be that bad."

"I'm told they are, and devastating for children." The younger matron, weary of forced, congenial, family relationships, counted each block before her feet could alight from the carriage.

That evening Elizabeth dragged in for supper. Francisco sat, allowing Mrs. Blackwood to grease his palms with some reeking concoction. His voice whined complaint, "It smells awful. I've had plenty of blisters. I was at sea for four years! Those ropes don't tickle." His grousing continued. "Now they want me to plaster walls. I told them they will have the lumpiest walls in the world. Ouch!" A resisting hand pulled away.

"Hush. Be still so you won't delay supper any longer." She threw an apologetic glance at hungry boarders. Nursing chore completed, she washed her hands, set out plates and served corn beef and cabbage. Apple tarts sat on the sideboard.

"Elizabeth, ye look like ye be working fingers off, just like this one." she said, inclining her head towards Francisco.

"What about me?" boomed her husband as sawdust clung to his hair.

Waving a dismissive hand, she answered, "For sure, 'tis work keeping ye young. Elizabeth, what's the news on the kitten?"

"He's growing healthy and he is a tomcat. A pretty black and white one visits Anvil. That's his name. Mr. Hood says be patient, but why wait? The world is full of kittens."

"I'll bide no other than the kitten of the gray one."

Soon bashful buds sprouted open into vivid, summer flowers. They rushed through fences, multi-hued, certain of their welcome. Tree manes, emerging a pale yellow-green, changed to lush green. With heat and lengthening days, front stair practices returned, complete with admiring glances from five girls across the street. At Francisco's displeased groan, creamed laughter erupted from Elizabeth. She suggested, "Come on. Give one of them a tumble."

In aromatic awakening, summer brought him a bonus. He had permission to tag along, like a happy puppy on Elizabeth's Sunday walks. She displayed interest in his nautical yarns, in trade winds, in cold and warm currents, asking how the Gulf Stream remained warm when the cold North Equatorial ran into it. Jabbing fingers into a map she asked about the Agulhas, the Benguela, the North Atlantic Drift and the Humboldt. She asked numerous questions and he wished he knew all the answers.

They walked through the Commons, they viewed the new Brewer Fountain. Still questions continued, "Why did captains keep weapons and handcuffs?" He wondered, was this feigned interest or was she becoming interested in him? Hope soared on wings.

He said, "Let's talk about you."

"You know I was born in New Brunswick, in Petitcodiac. In French, that means little elbow. My grandfather received a land grant for heroic service to the Crown. They logged, sold to shipbuilders and did well till 1867 when New England set up trade barriers and sank our economy. The big blow came when they mortgaged the land and all their cut logs, ready for market, washed downriver in a flash flood. Let's talk of you."

Wild delirium rocked his senses. Tumbling words spoke of his birth on Terceira, "That means third because it is the third island discovered in the Azores by Prince Henry the Navigator. My father said I was born so ugly that I should have been drowned."

"You are not ugly. You are quite handsome. That Conroy flock thinks so."

"Let's not talk of them. Tell me more about you."

He tilted his head towards her, clinging to each word as she spoke of siblings. Though both were primogenitures, it soon became apparent that their views regarding family additions differed. She tingled with excitement at each birth. She had wished for a dozen siblings. His head snapped away. Rather than state his opinion on infant accumulation, he asked, "Do you know what's for supper?"

"A Spanish dish. It's made with chicken, rice, red peppers and spices. It's called arros con pollo. Oh, I meant to ask, have you heard creaking at night? Do you think the house is haunted?"

He hesitated, then murmured, "It's not haunted."

They watched as sunset covered the day with florid colors and the waters of the bay drank each tinge of blue and gold and inhaled deep rose indicating another hot day. Lengthening shadows proclaimed a need to reverse course. She caught his elbow, turned him around and gasped at a tall figure rushing forward. Sunlight revealed gold hair. The startling charisma of the thirty-two-year-old male sickened Francisco.

Elizabeth's clenched fingers clutched his sleeve, pulling him through sweltering streets as her gait became a frenzied trot.

Francisco's hopes deflated but Richard intended to inflate his. After leaving tearful Marjorie with tearful mother, a rapid pace brought him to his father's home. He had tired of his wife's complaints before interference from a mother-in-law. How dare she contact his father?

Holding needlepoint in her hand, his mother met him at the door, "Considering Marjorie's condition it is just as well that the honeymoon was cancelled. Mrs. Carlton is so concerned."

"Dear Momma Carlton should have kept concerns to herself."

She brushed yarn from her taffeta skirt, "She was concerned enough to call on your father. All the traveling and sightseeing must have taxed the girl. Hurry. He's waiting."

Sightseeing, traveling, he mused, gliding across a gleaming floor. She wasn't taxed, she rested while he and Henri traveled to art galleries, restaurants and vineyards.

An angry door banged behind him as he strode towards the maroon, velvet, smoking jacket wrapped around an expanding frame. The patriarch sat in a sturdy chair, a glass of muscatel in one hand and a well-chewed cigar in the other.

"For a man who savors money you are not cultivating favor with Marjorie's parents. Let's hear your story, boy."

"Stop calling me boy."

"Just habit."

"You never exercise that habit elsewhere."

"At least, you have noticed that."

Richard suppressed temper. He needed additional funds in order to get Henri a ticket back to Boston.

"You want my story. Fine. I have a spoiled wife. My mother-in-law meddles. I understand she called on you. With my wife's extravagant demands, I find myself in the embarrassing situation of requesting more funds."

"Fat chance! Do those extravagant demands include a measure of your time?"

He hesitated before asking, "What did Mrs. Carlton say?"

"Nothing. She allowed me to read Marjorie's letters. I'm no fool. Tell me about your carousing."

Richard blanched. Did Marjorie know of Henri? What was in those letters? Balm came with his father's next words. "Took along your red-haired harlot at my expense didn't you? Get rid of her or get a cheaper one."

The younger man masked relief. If Daddy surmised a playmate, Elizabeth had proved useful again as a cover.

"Let me tell you something. You married for money. Many do, but pretense is the rule. A man can love his wife or not love her, but if he doesn't, it is not for exhibition. He can find her vain and boring, but he cannot humiliate her in public by traipsing around with a slut, especially on a honeymoon, especially when she is with child and especially when she is a Carlton. What happens if Carlton finds out about your curvaceous harlot while his daughter lacks attention, even common courtesy? Often I have said you have the brains of a herring. I stand corrected. You have none at all."

"Spoken by the perfect husband. What about your visits to the slave quarters? Why does your wife know nothing of your assets either? What are they?"

"Your mother knew nothing about the affairs of the plantation. Southern gentlemen didn't disclose all activities and a word from a slave—you know what that would have got them. Of course, her family inheritance contributed to its purchase but it sold at a huge profit." He laughed remembering the ill-starred purchaser. "As for my assets, dwell on yours at present. Our deal isn't cut in stone. I want that grandson and a semblance of a happy family. See to it. By the way, that new suit. Did I pay for it?"

With a mock bow, Richard answered, "Of course, dear father."

"Shut the door on your way out."

His mother watched him pass under the archway leading to the front hall, shoulders slumped, not stopping for farewell. Things must have been unpleasant, but they always were. She threw handcraft into a basket.

Drapes were drawn aside as the father watched the son march down the street. He wanted to know about the father's assets. More than the fool could manage. Richard's mind could never comprehend the device of charging capital expenditures to current operating expenses so that net worth would always be larger than shown on books.

At home in a silk smoking jacket, the son contemplated the situation. He would appear to play the game. He had married that cow for money and he would get it all. That brat had better not be female. He swirled brandy in a glass before letting it roll around his tongue. He poured a refill then another. Increasing heat penetrated thick, stone walls. He rolled the jacket into a ball before casting it aside. In this heat, his father wore velvet. More blubber than blood, he sneered.

He needed to think. All the brandy wasn't helping. How could he survive without Henri? Though, in truth, the boy stimulated less. Disconcerting fuzz germinated on his chin. Replacement was possible. What of those underpaid mill boys? Boys could be bought for a silver dollar. Why hadn't he thought of that before?

With his luck, his child would be a boy, sparing him revolting retrials. Hadn't he been lucky enough to fool them all? Nobody, not even his frat friends suspected anything. Yes, luck would hold.

Elizabeth had served her purpose and if Marjorie dropped a boy, he'd be forever free from the nauseating lumps, bumps and crevices of a woman.

Chapter Fourteen

On that blistering night, while Richard counted unhatched chickens, the boarders discussed the merits of arros con pollo. Dimmed gaslights failed to lessen heat. Face gleaming with perspiration, Mr. Bruncken declared, "It's too spicy."

"Belike I slipped a bit with the spices." Mrs. Blackwood confessed as she danced around the room swatting flies and mosquitos.

Francisco, a wealth of sea knowledge, chimed, "It's better than gurry stew."

Elizabeth asked. "What's in that?"

"The refuse of a whale."

Rising queasiness did not deter Claus Bruncken, "Why do they eat that?"

"When they are desperate for food they eat anything. Whalers waste little. They make scrimshaw from whale teeth and sweetheart valentines from shells."

A curious Mr. Blackwood asked, "What does gurry stew taste like?"

"I don't know. I never tasted it."

"Then how do you know it isn't worse than chicken a la Spanish?" asked a now sickening carpenter.

Claus squeaked, "Anything must be better."

Elizabeth chirped, "I liked it."

Mr. Blackwood scanned her in disbelief, "Well, if you are not sick to your stomach, you are sick in your head. Ruth, sit down, your sweat is dripping."

"Captain Addison once said, 'Men perspire, horses sweat and ladies glow and he..."

Mrs. Blackwood interjected, "For sure, 'tis made into fertilizer."

Her husband asked, "What, people sweat or horse sweat?"

"Neither. That whale stuff."

The vision of it on growing cabbage sent the ailing German running for the backyard, pail in hand.

Francisco laughed, enjoying the German's discomfort.

Francisco continued, "Did you know that besides lighting, whale oil goes in soap, medicine, paint and softens leather? Whalebone makes umbrellas, fans, hoops and springs and if a whaler losses a leg, he gets a whalebone cane. Mr. Blackwood, did you use whale oil on the hinges?"

"If so, didn't work well. I'm feeling seasick besides being sick of sea talk, I'm going to bed."

Stumbling, white-faced into the room, Mr. Bruncken followed his example.

"Pay no mind to me husband. 'Twas the heat that got to them, 'twas not me supper."

Silk petticoats rustled as Elizabeth headed for the window, asking, "Do you hear thunder?"

A lightning bolt, resembling an inverted tree, spread contorted branches across the sky. Cooling rain joined earthshaking blast. The scent of moisture on parched earth rose like perfume. Hypnotized, they watched unleashed fury. Thunder, rolling like cannon fire, prevented sleep. Through darkness, sometimes eliminated by zigzagging light, water pounded roofs and pavements with hammer blows.

Disheartened by thoughts of that blonde, incomparable man, Francisco sat up in bed at sounds of creaking hinges. Can't be the ghost in this weather. He muttered to himself, "Those hinges need replacement, oil won't do. Perhaps the wind pushed the door open." Arising to fasten a latch, he stopped mid-step at the vision of Elizabeth standing on the sheltered porch, her loosened hair blowing around an upturned face. Wrapped in white, illuminated by lightning, she looked like the pictures of the Madonna garnishing walls in that Azorean farmhouse. Unwilling to intrude on thoughts, perhaps engendered by the sight of Richard, his muffled feet moved backwards.

Tardiness prevailed the following morning. Many overslept, many arrived at work with bloodshot eyes. Francisco struggled with plastering, too sleep deprived to care. He slapped a blob on a wall, gave it a useless swish or two while a good-natured Italian followed behind. Three, swift movements produced perfection as he said, "You gotta do it lika dat."

"I'll never do it lika dat. I've got to find different work or go back to sea."

That same morning, Elizabeth found Mr. Hood with a gray-haired woman surrounded by bolts of every material ever produced. She ordered for every season promising to return with family members.

He rubbed aching, bony wrists and fleshless hands. "This is a deluge! Said she wanted to join the fun started by Mrs. Spencer. She is sending her husband for a new suit and a Mrs. Baxter is coming this afternoon with Mrs. Carlton and her daughter."

All three fluttered in at one o'clock. The new customer approached Elizabeth, saying, "I found this piece of silk on the floor. Such a lovely dubonnet color. Do you have more?"

Elizabeth answered, "I'm certain there is a bolt in the backroom." She held a piece of thread to the swatch. "A perfect match."

Marjorie came close, whispering, "Miss Gilbert, do you think you could make expandable garments in the event that I gain weight?"

Elizabeth reflected, was it? Could it be so soon? Yes, it could be. A stabbing feeling rocked her. Rubbing a fist over her forehead, she answered the soon to be eighteen-year-old girl. "Extra wide pleats can be let out as needed."

Demands of all three satisfied, Mr. Hood held the door and escorted them to their carriage. Returning and gazing at his sleep-deprived employee, he said, "The country may be in an economic slump this year, but there is no slump here. Haven't their husbands suffered financially in this crash? Imagine that woman saying dubonnet. It is called wine as far as I'm concerned. There is no longer a question about it. We must expand and hire more help." He rubbed his lower back, "Do you know of anyone who can even sew a seam?"

"Francisco makes shirts. Do you want me to ask him?"

A weary nod was the answer. His had been a sleepless night also. "Lord," he said, "wasn't it a racket last night?"

Elizabeth dragged home. The smell of baked beans greeted her nostrils but no one was in sight except the landlady. Pulling long pins from a straw hat with one hand while patting hair in place with the other, she asked, "Where is everybody and how did you bake beans on such a hot day?"

"Took to their beds, two still complaining of stomach pain and the beans baked themselves while I took meself to a good nap. As for Francisco, he was too tired for anything but bread and jelly."

"Did he say if he liked plastering?" With a large chunk of bread in hand, she dug into a plate of beans. "I have another job for him if he doesn't."

"Said not a word. If ye had any sense, ye'd dine on the back porch and catch some breeze."

The hot kitchen caused chaffing as sleeves smothered her armpits but the prospect of battling hovering flies kept her damply in place, "I'm not going to share beans with them. Look at the buzzing fellows." She pointed towards the window saying, "I need to talk to Francisco about that job."

Mansions and Mills

"For sure, 'twont be tonight. The bo—the man's face hung on his knees and just where might that job be?"

"We are inundated with work and he can sew."

Mrs. Blackwood paused but overcome with concern, asked, "Could it be that ye still see the Spencers?"

"Her, but never him." Blaming the stifling kitchen for her reddening features, she rushed to her room. She lifted the cover on the dry sink, poured water into the stoneware bowl and washed away the burdens of the day, except one. A baby. Richard's baby.

The following evening the recovered boarders gathered. Elizabeth wondered why supper wasn't leftovers. Where did all the beans go? Elizabeth whispered, "Francisco, who ate all the beans?" Looking at the ceiling, he shrugged.

After others scattered, she nudged him to the front stairs. Coolness had dissipated yesterday's heat and cool air enveloped them, a coolness discouraging mosquitos and encouraging them to stay long after the rounds of the lamplighter. They discussed his future as a tailor. "I can do that. I made trousers for my shipmates. I'll take it."

The moonless night concealed them from nearsighted eyes. Elizabeth spun around as a figure skirting bushes appeared through darkness, "That's Mrs. Blackwood. Where is she going at this hour?"

He clasped a gentle hand over her lips. "Shush, she will hear you." Leaning close, he whispered, "Watch and you'll learn something. She does this when there is leftover food. It's her secret."

Carrying a bag, Mrs. Blackwood approached a frail woman. Scant light revealed poverty of dress. Elizabeth's straining ears heard the murmur, "Here, ye don't have to work tonight."

Removing the silencing hand, Francisco said, "That's your ghost and that explains the missing beans. They probably got passed around last night."

When Mrs. Blackwood withdrew, Elizabeth said, "Passed around where? Who is that awful looking woman?"

"She is one of them. Don't ever ask Mrs. Blackwood about this."

"Why not?"

"Because of what this woman is."

"What is she?"

He coughed, "A lady of the night."

"What's that?"

"Gosh. Where is your mother when you need her? But being in logging maybe she doesn't know either. I have an idea. Does she read the bible?"

"Yes, but what does the bible have to do with this?"

"Did she tell you about Delilah? She's in the bible."

"Francisco, tell me what it's about."

"Well, Delilah met this fellow named..." She sliced through his words by grasping his collar and shaking him.

"Tell me about these nocturnal trips or I'll break your neck."

"All right if you stop shaking me. How to begin? I know. There was no question about you because you were employed and lived in the low-rent district, but when you went to fancy dinners did you suspect that those men were paying all the expenses for their companions?"

"Not at first. Only at the end did I realize they were fancy women, but what does that have to do with this?"

"I'm getting there, although you really should ask someone else. How about Mr. Hood?"

She made another move for his collar. "Stop. I'll tell you. Be patient and I'll get there. Now these fancy ladies, with luck may wind up rich but usually not. They aren't trained to be teachers or milliners or anything. The mills hire only young women."

"Get to the point!"

"I'm getting there. Calm down. Sometimes women are widowed with young children, but they are illiterate immigrants and..."

Mansions and Mills

She had him by the collar again, shaking his head back and forth. He managed to gasp, "All right. These ladies of the night sell their bodies to men, lots of men."

"What?"

"They walk the streets at night. That's why they call them that. They are poor. They need the money. Mrs. Blackwood wants to give these women some nights off the job."

"That's disgusting!"

"No, Elizabeth, that's sad."

She stood on a stair, rubbing hands over her eyes as if to dispel unpleasant images. She dropped a look of hatred at him before closing the heavy, front portal.

He muttered to uncaring stars, "She wanted the truth now she acts like all evil is my fault. I didn't create this world, not the men who shovel misappropriated gold in vaults or women who grovel in streets. Didn't she say don't ask if you don't want the answer?"

Shifting his weight, he studied a diamond studded firmament, each star brilliant against the dark, moonless sky. He thought of men using constellations to navigate. He thought of the Southern Cross which he would never see again, not if he remained in this hemisphere. He thought of how Elizabeth would process new knowledge and be well-disposed towards him again, male creature that he was. He stretched, yawned and made his way to bed. She'd behave as usual tomorrow.

But she didn't. Her distaste included Mrs. Blackwood. Her gaze bubbled with revulsion. After days of this treatment, Mrs. Blackwood corralled him. "What ails Elizabeth?" The tone menaced.

Raising his hand as barrier to more womanly fury, he hedged, "Maybe too much work."

Slapping his hand away and clutching his collar, she shook him, "Don't ye shillyshally with me. With all that porch jawing, ye know."

Thoughts raced. What is it with the women in this God-forsaken country? Are they all dedicated to shaking a man to death and destroying all of his collars? Since I'd like to wear a decent shirt on my new job and start without a loopy brain, I'd better tell her. He begged, "Just stop shaking me." All this female violence taxed a man.

After hearing him out, she said, "The lass rides too high on the horse. I'll see to this." Marvelous, he thought. The matter rested in good hands.

On Sunday, preparing for her walk, Mrs. Blackwood corralled Elizabeth as Francisco had been. A cataclysmic, motherly blast followed, "Lass, 'tis fine to have pride of person and family, but pride that looks down on the poor is too much pride. Had ye married his majesty, ye would be fried in glory and detestable. Best dwell on humility and a bit of charity. Pride does come before the fall. Take care that ye pride is not ye undoing. Sometimes I fear, 'twill be."

A subdue Elizabeth along with Mr. Hood celebrated Francisco's first day of tailoring by raising glasses of orange juice. A raised roof as well as extension backwards supplied more room in the shop.

The cream of society rushed in for shirts with detachable collars and cuffs, in fashionable stripes. By late summer, winter tweeds and plaids arrived. Ladies planned fall and winter wardrobes. Roguish Prince Edward set male fashions and Mrs. Blackwood rustled papers reading about that villain, Boss Tweed.

Vivid colors of summer turned to vivid colors of autumn. Sunday walks under gold and red leaves clinging to life became for Elizabeth a study of birds winging south. She asked, "What kind of bird is that?" Francisco wished he had all the answers but was blind to birds. All he could see was a lithe figure framed under an arch of brilliant hues. Working with her, sometimes accidentally touching her worsened his misery.

As they reached the bottom of the year, she remained remote, isolated in a private world. If unhappy memories intruded, she concealed them under questions of currents and birds.

Mansions and Mills

To occupy thoughts and increase knowledge, Francisco enrolled in classes. Somewhat piqued, Elizabeth enrolled in a painting class. One whiff of the paint and Mrs. Blackwood cried, "Ye'll not bring that smell into this house. Take a history class, like Francisco's about Napoleon. Napoleon will smell just fine." Elizabeth cancelled enrollment.

At Christmas everyone exchanged greetings. Letters arrived from New Brunswick, from Captain Addison, Harry and Amos. The only sour note came from John. On becoming Captain Hall, the man became a "driver" on a money mad frenzy. Crews believed he would land them all on the rocks.

One rainy day in late December, a drenched stranger left an envelope for Mr. Bruncken. His landlady weighed it on the tip of arthritic fingers. More than a letter, she thought. Later he eyed it with suspicion. He asked, "Who left it?"

"A wee man, bald as a baby's backside."

"Sounds like my cousin. Probably wants to rob me again for something that just gave me a sick stomach."

Impishly, she asked, "Now, what might that be?"

Crimson faced, he lapsed into prolonged silence continuing to eye the missive with suspicion.

"Holy Saints, just open it. 'Twont bite." She threw it in front of him as he sat, elbows on table, biting a fingernail. Trembling, he opened it. Photographs fell beside a note. She saw likenesses of a solid woman. "This one misses no meals." she said. "Ah, I forget meself. Could she be a relative?"

"She is a relative on his side. He is bringing her from Germany to marry me. My mother likes the idea. This can't be good." He looked over his shoulder as waterlogged Elizabeth and Francisco walked in.

"Best get ready for a wedding." Mrs. Blackwood said, holding up a picture. "See the bride. Now ain't she a healthy one?"

Thus 1873 ended with Claus awaiting a bride chosen by a dented-headed cousin. She would tower over him and help make him the wealthiest sausage vendor in Boston. Francisco rejoiced at the forthcoming evaporation of a man obsessed with ogling Elizabeth, not suspecting that soon he would be tormented by a far more formidable rival.

Chapter Fifteen

The year one thousand, eight hundred and seventy-four proved to be significant for the inhabitants of Boston who saw restorations, widened streets and an improved business district. Enchanted citizens observed gold leaf being applied on the dome of the State House, among them the group from the boardinghouse with the exception of Mr. Bruncken engrossed in wedding plans. The tall, solid, good-natured woman had a contagious laugh a zest for work and bed romping.

The significant year brought forth Richard's son. The grandmothers rushed in the tailoring shop gushing over the beauty of the infant. Slicing through the room with customary drama, Mrs. Spencer, waving a piece of sienna colored paper, announced, "He is the very image of his father and grandfather." Casting a smug glance at Mrs. Carlton, she consoled, "I'm sure he will have his mother's grace." Holding the paper aloft in proximity to Mr. Hood's aquiline nose, she demanded, "You must find material this very color. I want to wear it to the christening."

Mrs. Carlton wore the predictable fixed smile, Mr. Hood the accustomed expression of patient endurance and Francisco a look of concern directed at Elizabeth.

The aged tailor rubbed his harried head, "Mrs. Spencer, finding a match to that scrap of paper is impossible."

Pushing it in Elizabeth's hands, she ordered, "Girl, you find the match. Come, Margaret, let's visit the baby."

Mrs. Carlton begged off, sympathizing with Elizabeth and the daughter who drew this mother-in-law out of the deck—the Queen of Spades, adjacent to other cards of the same suit.

That year was also significant in the birth of another child, a girl born in Liverpool to a boisterous, squabbling, whiskey-saturated, Irish dockworker named Rafferty who felt her unworthy of the name chosen by her mother. "She don't deserve an Irish Saint's name," he roared, "she'll not be named Brigid. Name the unwanted thing Bridget, after a bloody Swedish Saint." Many tides would ebb and swell before she crossed Elizabeth's path.

That year brought a possible daughter-in-law into Mrs. Blackwood's life. Letters from Texas spilled. He wrote, this might be the year when I get a wife. She is beautiful, funny, talented and industrious. In no time, she had become a valuable cowhand. She mended fences, trained horses, handled a gun and had shot a vulture hovering over a sick calf which she nursed back to health. He informed them that vultures tasted like venison. Cattle rustlers feared her aim. They didn't want to tangle with her, at least not that kind of tangling, if you know what I mean. She snorted before continuing. She said, "Francisco, it takes eighteen years for a mother to make a man of her son and eighteen minutes for another woman to make a fool of him."

At his sad nod of agreement, she patted his hand soothingly, saying, "Ah now."

Snapping up his head, he asked, "What else does he say?"

She handed him a second sheet. He read it, quoting, "We have a cowpoke with the deep chest of someone born in high altitudes and he's bowlegged. Probably put on a horse too young. He's smitten with her but I think I have a better chance." The letter continued saying it was time for her to move to Texas since she'd have the companionship of a god fearing, decent, clean-living woman just like her.

Mansions and Mills

God fearing the girl might be, but thinking of Pedro, she could not claim decent, clean living herself. Fortunate that he was too young to remember and fortunate that children have no interest in a parent's young life. They seemed to assume that before their birth, parents lived in a sanitized limbo where neither the seven deadly sins nor the Ten Commandments had collided with heated blood.

"Francisco, what else does he say?"

"Start packing so you can be there before snow flies." He hesitated before tumbling the postscript, "He says she has learned to do a fandango that sets his spurs jingling."

She giggled as rosy color flooded her cheeks, "That lad, you might have omitted."

At being informed of the missive's contents, Elizabeth jammed angry fists into pockets, "You can't move and leave us."

"Me bones feel no better and methinks the old back will break."

The young woman argued, "You are not that old."

"Talk to me bones. Tell them."

"You nurse us, you scold us. You are like a mother. What will we do?"

"You, lassie, will grow up. High time methinks."

"But you'll sell the house. Where will we go?"

"The Lord will provide. Ask me priest."

"Hang your precious priest! Your churches are popping up all over the country. Irish, Portuguese, French, Polish, Italian all reeking with the smell of priests."

Caressing a painful right hip, Mrs. Blackwood rose asking, "And what might that smell be?"

Elizabeth spat, "That stuff they wave around at stupid masses."

The pain-wracked woman paused at an inviting door before saying, "Ye have gone too far."

At her departure, Francisco said, "Elizabeth, to her the faith is sacred. She prays every night for us and for street women."

Elizabeth sat holding her head, "I can't bear the thought of being without her, but why did I behave like that?"

"I'll explain it to her tomorrow."

When Francisco began speaking, Mrs. Blackwood interrupted. Her understanding and forgiving nature said, "Loss of control ain't her way and the blocked emotions in the lass troubles me soul. 'Tis more than a move to Texas, but tell her she owes me an apology."

Days later, peace restored, the gray-haired woman considered her own sensations which rose to the surface and dissipated. If sad, she cried. If funny, she laughed. If angry, walls quaked. She wished Elizabeth always did likewise.

The cupboard door opened with a thud. Worried, she reached for the bottle of magical, pink pills. After all, those pills fixed everything!

One steamy day in midsummer, Mrs. Blackwood inquired, "Francisco, why not let the lass know of ye feelings? She might give it thought." She took a towel from his hands to apply her brand of scrubbing to his dripping hair.

"She doesn't want or need the burden of my feelings when she must bear her own." Agony always cruised in Elizabeth's eyes on beholding the Spencer infant.

Mrs. Blackwood asked, "Are ye sure 'twould be a burden?"

"I'm sure. I must say nothing." He recalled the gypsy foretelling that silence would be his cross. "Whoa, you are taking the skin off my scalp. Give me that towel."

Summer sauntered forward in fragments of soft air, harrowing storms, sizzling heat and refreshing rivulets of rain. Leaves frolicked, bouncing against each other as did playing children in streets. Weary mothers dragged protesting cherubs from parks. Overheated, overworked horses pulled heavy loads. Dockworkers welcomed bay breezes as did men in shipyards. Nails flew into crates, obeying commands of hammers. Men delivered milk, others clanged bells as they sold chunks of ice or called for rags which would be made into rugs.

Mansions and Mills

Mrs. Blackwood chased the ragman, shouting, "Wait, there's not a soul to be found with more rags." In frantic packing for the move, she discovered well-worn knickers and blankets, forgotten shirts, faded aprons and undarned socks. Crammed closets saw daylight. Some clothing no longer fit expanded waists. Cart full, the happy man headed home early.

Papers for the house sale were to be signed on Tuesday, September 29th but on the 25th, news arrived that hordes of grasshoppers had inundated the southwest, devouring everything, curtains, bedclothes, ropes, even wagon boards.

Mrs. Blackwood wailed, "Best unpack. 'Tis the Lord's will. 'Twas time for a cleaning out of junk anyway." Rubbing aching fingers, she said. "Belike, next year."

California did not beckon where her other son went from unfound gold to a worthless silver mine. When penniless, he accepted work in a salt mine. She shuddered at memories of the state. Pedro might no longer be there. He might have met a knife quicker than his own. Nevertheless, she'd stick with Texas.

With difficulty, Elizabeth concealed joy over ravenous grasshoppers. She had neither fumed nor panicked over leaving her own mother but she had never been close to her parents. She had bonded with siblings. Mrs. Blackwood filled the role of substitute mother.

Several days later, newspaper in hand, an indignant Mrs. Blackwood cried out, "Now the bloody Brits have annexed the Fiji Islands. The Irish can tell ye there's no limit to those villains. Don't repeat me words to Elizabeth."

Francisco barely heard her. He was deep in study of Napoleon. "Do you know he said that if you wish to be a success, promise everything, deliver nothing?"

"Sounds like a man, not a genius."

"And he also said that four hostile newspapers are to be feared more than one thousand bayonets and that history is the version of events that people have decided to agree upon."

"Can't agree with French or English history and methinks that Napoleon should have feared bayonets up his arse more than news."

Mr. Blackwood removed the book from the student's hands and said, "Says here that he said, 'Religion is what keeps the poor from murdering the rich.' Not sure of that. Seems to me that nothing keeps the poor from murdering the rich except high walls."

Leaning over her husband's shoulder, she said, "He said that England is a nation of shopkeepers. Ah, 'tis a bit of good sense. Don't tell Elizabeth. Hush, here she comes. Best rid yeself of that book. Quick, under me apron." She worked on a smile, "Greetings, have ye been to a lecture?" A picture of innocence, she added, "We have been chatting about British shopkeepers."

"How nice. No lecture. I've been talking to a watercolor teacher. Her classes are on Thursdays. I can begin on the twenty-ninth of October or the fifth of November. It has been months since Mr. Bruncken left. Now that you won't be going to Texas, have you thought of a replacement? How about a young woman with my interest?"

"No, 'twont be a woman. Men are less fussy."

Francisco almost whimpered, "Another man. How about an unfussy spinster?"

The new boarder was a man aged twenty-six said to be from Bristol, Rhode Island. He was two inches taller than Francisco and slim. It would have pleased Francisco to know that he was almost engaged to a woman of his sister's choice but displeased to know that the man was not engaged to a woman of his choice. His name was Joseph Bishop and the clothing on his torso suggested wealth. He shared breakfast and supper with them and left after his last bite. With rusty hinges replaced, none heard his late arrivals. Mr. Bruncken was stupid. This polished, attractive man was not.

Elizabeth attended her first class. If Francisco could take classes five nights a week, she could take a class once a week and refrain from being a nuisance about it. The previous evening

Francisco had shared lessons on Bourbon kings. Everyone fidgeted and yawned except Mrs. Blackwood who escaped in blackening the stove. Elizabeth vowed to never burden anyone with her classes. One mighty bore was enough.

In her first class, a classmate interrupted, supplying unsolicited advice. "Those flowers look washed out. Try brighter red on this one." She placed a finger one inch from the poppy. Picking up a tube of yellow from her own supply, she continued, "This will wake up that tulip."

Elizabeth glanced over her shoulder at a slapdash of color, asking, "What do you call that?"

"It's a method started by students in France. I've read all about it."

France again! A small table sat at the stranger's elbow, covered with brushes and an array of colors. Elizabeth asked, "How long have you been painting?"

"This is my first week, but as you can see, I come prepared."

Nonplussed, Elizabeth whispered, "Mrs. Prescott said start with two shades of the primary colors and this brown." She held up a sienna shade.

"She's not the best in town you know. No other teacher had room for me. Can you imagine twenty classes filled to the brim? How many did you apply for?"

"Just this one." Elizabeth couldn't imagine twenty filled classes not with present circumstances. Last year the economy sank and unemployment had soared to twenty-five percent. Not that it was felt at the tailoring shop but Mr. Hood said the rich always had money stored in vaults.

Distraction came once more with the grating voice. "You'll never show in Paris, but that's not important. The important thing is the rights of women."

"What rights?" Elizabeth studied her art. This weird woman was right. Brighter shades improved both flowers.

"The rights they don't have. Where are you living, girl?"

"In a boardinghouse."

"A boardinghouse! Even mill girls live with family except those Lowell girls, but that system did keep most out of trouble. You know what I mean, don't you?"

Exasperated, Elizabeth snapped, "I have no idea what you mean. Mill girls, Lowell girls, rights women don't have. I'd really like to work on my painting!" She turned her back to this annoying woman who refused dismissal.

Grasping Elizabeth's shoulders and turning her, she spat, "Haven't you heard of exploited mill workers, hungry children, orphanages and inhuman treatment in mental hospitals? Don't you think women should vote to end all this suffering? Haven't you heard of the Women's Rights Movement or the Temperance Movement? Do you like the sight of starving babies?"

"All the babies I've seen were overfed."

"After class, follow me for your first lesson."

To her later regret, Elizabeth did just that, taking unfamiliar turns. Her classmate pulled her through a door. The smell of cigars and liquor seared her nostrils. Four men sat at a table and two at a bar. One, in a plaid shirt, had two feet planted on a brass rail. His companion's feet hung deathlike over it while his head rested on the bar.

Approaching them, the rasping voice barked, "Shame on you. You have been created to emulate angels."

Bleary eyes looked up, "Iss that sho, lady? Then I'm shurr in trouble." Before his head fell back to its former position, he held out a glass of beer to her, "Have shum."

Elizabeth attempted to pull her incensed companion away but her hands were shaken off. "Shame. Your children are crying and waiting for you." His head lifted off the bar to look her over.

"Are you shurr. Do I have shum? Tell me their names." Looking at Elizabeth, he slurred, "Diss one is pretty. You want shum beer, pretty lady?"

The unmelodious vocal chords derided, "You are disgusting. I will pray for your children."

Mansions and Mills

At last the plaid shirted man spoke, "He ain't got children. He ain't even married. Jack, give me another beer." Placing a dime on the bar, he said, "On second thought, give me two. It will take two to make the noisy one look good."

Elizabeth stammered, "Come with me or stay here alone. I'm going."

The bartender reached the door before they did. Handing out what had first appeared to be brown sticks, he laughed, "Pass these out at your next meeting. Give the do-good ladies a cigar."

On the sidewalk, an embarrassed and confused Elizabeth looked around at unfamiliar surroundings. Twilight had bowed to darkness hours ago. How to find her way back? That voice said, "Untwist your knickers. You're the wrong type to ever help. I'll lead you back to where you belong."

Elizabeth held a tight scarf against the cold as they trudged back to Mrs. Prescott's now darkened house. She felt the same anger at the knowledge of rummies as she had at the disclosure of streetwalkers. Worse, this time she had not hammered for enlightenment. What possessed her to go anywhere with this unhinged character? She fumed over a restraining arm. Lowering her head to whisper, the woman said, "You know, there is something funny about this teacher. She seems to have a lot of money and did you notice that boy painting in the corner? The stories I've heard about his family you wouldn't believe."

"If I wouldn't believe them, don't bother to tell me. Mrs. Prescott must be a rich widow. Where did you leave all your brushes and paints?"

Pulling a burlap bag from underneath a bush, the bucktoothed woman replied, "Here. Since there are no classes till after the holidays, I won't see you till the seventh of January. You have time to think of voting rights at least. Bye."

One week later, the occupants of the boardinghouse planned Christmas. Glaring at Francisco, Mrs. Blackwood exclaimed, "For sure, 'tis a bloody disgrace the manner in which ye miss mass every Sunday. Ye'll not do it on Christmas!"

After religious observance, all gathered for a sausage dinner, compliments of Mr. Bruncken. Mr. Felix had moved in with his father and Mr. Bishop spent his holiday in Bristol. The household was down to four.

On the eve of the New Year, they celebrated at an Irish club filled with singing and dancing. Children, struggling to keep eyes open, attempted to teach Elizabeth the jig. She practiced on the way home, dancing in the streets. A passing couple stared and the matron exclaimed, "These Irish! Even the women sip too much sauce."

Elizabeth planned to arrive late for the January class, hoping that others would be situated around the galling artist. A scrawny man left the studio as she settled herself and paraphernalia close to the boy of alleged family scandals. Watered brush in hand, she heard an arched voice, "Excuse me, little man, but kindly set yourself up elsewhere. I wish to speak to this young lady."

For several minutes blessed silence prevailed as the irksome female wrapped a green apron around her thin, flat frame and arranged brushes and multiple paints. She shifted everything back and forth several times before asking, "What do you think of him?"

Brows furrowed, engrossed in her artistic efforts, Elizabeth pretended not to hear.

Again, "What do you think of him?"

Elizabeth, yielding to sure knowledge that this woman would not tolerate being ignored, straightened, placed a brush loaded with the desired shade on the table, inhaled and took four steps toward her classmate's painting. Perplexed, she looked at a garish splash of zigzagging color, lacking a "him". She asked, "Where is him?"

"Not the painting. Him. The man who left when you came in."

"I didn't notice."

"Nobody does. Everyone says I shouldn't marry him because he is stupid."

Mansions and Mills

Returning to work on her peacock, Elizabeth stated, "If you want to marry him, do so. Why care what others say? Women's rights, remember?"

"But I don't want to marry him. He has no interest in social problems. I really want to be a midwife. That would help women."

"Single women are never midwives."

"Women can do what they please. Women's rights, remember?"

Looking towards heaven for succor, Elizabeth told herself, "This woman's stated concern for the mentally ill is logical. She is a candidate for a padded cell."

"Talking to you has been helpful. Thank you. I'm going off to the lecture circuit. I'll care for orphans and become a midwife."

"But your him might be gone."

"No. Nobody wants him. If I come back, he'll be here." Handing Elizabeth the burlap bag, she said, "You can have this. I won't paint anymore." The sounds of her footsteps diminished on each stair.

Elizabeth was standing, openmouthed when the teacher approached. "Mrs. Prescott," she stammered, "is that woman sane?"

Amused, Mrs. Prescott answered, "Believe it or not, she is. She is far before her time. That can be quite uncomfortable and confusing if not downright lonely. If she doesn't collapse under the weight of conformity, she might bring change and women need change. She does have a distasteful love of gossip, but everyone is entitled to one vice. Do you agree?"

"I suppose, but I don't want one."

"Rest assured if you don't have one, you will."

"I just realized something. I don't know her name."

"She's a Manchester. Her given name is Helen."

Chapter Sixteen

*E*lizabeth enjoyed classes without rasping interruptions and with the belief that she and Helen would never cross paths. Snowdrifts, winds and numbing cold failed to dishearten her from faithful attendance even though she often arrived with reddened nose and stiffened fingers.

A huge, glowing, coal stove stood in the room's center. Massaging and warming her hands by its heat, she brightened at Mrs. Prescott's words, "You have made so much progress in such an unforgiving medium. Surprising that you didn't choose oil."

"The odor was not welcomed in my living quarters." She smiled recalling the forewarning, "This art best not stink!" Inspecting her latest endeavor, she murmured, "Praise or no praise, my art does stink."

Before long the Blackwoods insisted on evaluation. They placed paintings on the table, circling it and commentating. The man of the house frowned in concentration, thumbs pulling suspenders, "Ruth," he said, "I'm a natural critic. The peacock is best."

"No, 'tis the apples and peaches. Fit colors for the parlor." She handed him nails and a hammer.

"I'll not hang it. I'll hang the peacock. Besides, it's a better frame, almost as good as any I've made."

"Ye'll hang the other or 'twont be me dusting it."

Lifting a defiant chin, he stormed to the cellar, assaulting ears with loud hammering sounds. Huffing and puffing, she commanded, "Francisco, ye'll hang it!"

Handed a fresh box of nails and a smaller hammer, he protested, "I like the seascape, besides he'll be angry enough to give my room to a spinster."

"Glory be, 'tis me doing the cooking and cleaning. Ye'll hang the bloody thing or 'twill be me showing ye the curbstone." He held up the excuse of a bandaged finger, drawing no sympathy. With exaggerated sigh, he headed for the parlor while Elizabeth stuck a sassy tongue in his direction. Napoleon would not grace the walls.

One hour later, Mr. Blackwood stomped upstairs, walked into the parlor, and after careful inspection stated. "Looks good there. Just like I said."

"Ye said ye wanted the peacock!"

"Never said any such thing." He scanned the room, daring anyone to disagree. None did.

"Since ye have come to ye senses, let's read the letter from Texas." The gaslight's rays fell on the bold script. They gathered around, both men pulling a chair closer.

Elizabeth looked on, masking disgust. She wished Texas would fall off the map. She asked. "This time did he remember to tell you her name?"

"That he did. Oops." The paper had slipped from her hand. Her attempt at retrieval produced a painful groan.

Francisco bent, handing it back.

The gray-haired woman smiled, "So pretty. 'Tis Louise."

Francisco asked, "Doesn't she have a last name?"

"To be sure. 'Tis Morgan."

Elizabeth felt her face fall. It couldn't be the same Louise. Both were common names. The Louise that she knew was at this moment carousing with Ben Davis at his expense. Besides, that strumpet reveled in being a kept harlot. Only a stupid or moral woman would leave a champagne world and Louise was neither. Forget it she told herself. The Louise Morgan you know is here in Boston.

On Tuesday, February 2, 1875, a slimmer Marjorie appeared at the tailoring shop. Weight loss, in combination with a strained look, gave the impression of illness. Mr. Hood entertained another suspicion. The bounder, he concluded, couldn't be a considerate husband.

The young mother noticed Francisco's bandaged finger. She asked, "What happened?"

"Pierced by a sewing machine needle. My clumsy fault."

"That must be so painful." Distress shadowed her eyes.

Francisco wondered how such a sweet girl could marry a man said by Mr. Hood to be putrid. Must be his looks. Why do women fall for good looks? But then, why do men? Elizabeth's sent hot, wild arrows spinning through his arteries. Who was he to question?

Musings scattered when Mrs. Spencer's voice carved through the shop. "Come, come, girls. I'm finished here. Marjorie, you can return another day to have seams taken in."

Mother and daughter exchanged sympathetic glances as they hurried behind, but Mrs. Carlton bit her lower lip. Did she need to keep up this charade for her daughter? Marjorie appeared miserable and Richard appeared bored. He ignored his son and his late-night walks were questionable although he explained that he needed exercise but could find no other time. Strange when bank employees were rumored to say that he did as much work as a mop without a handle.

On the Monday of Holy Week, spring attempted to push winter aside and that stubborn season pushed back. Two cold boarders returned from work to the pungent aroma of fish. Mr. Blackwood dove into a plate of baked potatoes and cod. Elizabeth exclaimed, "Not cod again. We had it last Friday. I hate cod."

The avid diner announced, "I love it and my good wife always wishes to please me. Note the painting in the parlor."

Elizabeth reminded them again, "It's Monday."

"Indeed, the Monday of Holy Week. Ye'll eat fish all week. 'Tis well to remember that Jesus had a bad week. Lad, ye'll go to mass on Easter."

He ran a finger around a damp collar. "My, it is hot in here." A disapproving look silenced him but not Elizabeth.

"Isn't there a piece of meat left from last night?" Then, remembering the street women, she said, "I suppose not."

Francisco whispered, "Just do it her way." She filled a growling, midsection vacuum with potatoes, green beans and two pieces of custard pie.

Spring soon won the seasonal battle, vanquishing cold, blustering skies. The northern hemisphere took on pastel hues, waiting for the rich colors of summer. Winter wools were anesthetized in mothballs and lightweight clothing viewed the sun again. Rugs hung on clotheslines awaiting floggings from carpet beaters. Soot disappeared from walls. Washed windows opened to breezes and Bill Klass walked into the tailoring shop.

Elizabeth, covered with tailoring chalk, a pin cushion attached to her wrist and hair disheveled did not see the troop of women being handed down from the carriage by a lone man, but Mr. Hood did. At his groan, always indicating the approach of Mrs. Spencer, she looked up, met by the sight of four women and a male——a male she preferred not to see.

She greeted three women by name. The fourth, a striking brunette, was a stranger. She had an aristocratic air about her in contrast to the huge woman making the introduction, "Mr. Hood, I bring you an acquaintance in need of your competence. This is Mrs. Klass and her charming husband. She is desperate for a gown for an unexpected event demanding her attendance. Only you can produce it on such short notice."

"Only Miss Gilbert can produce it on short notice."

"Whatever." She waved a contemptuous hand, but her jaw tumbled to her knees when Bill, blind to Elizabeth's dishevelment, held out a hand, saying. "Seeing you again is such a pleasure. I hope you are enjoying good health." His voice was deep and as warm as the hand clasping hers. Speechless, she nodded.

Bill sat, as comfortable as possible, in a small, wooden chair, leaning back and preparing for a long wait. He pulled a gold watch from his vest, snapped the case open and mentally noted the time. Having completed business, there was nothing left to do but indulge the ladies. He had informed Ben this morning that he would need thinking time before investing in cotton mills. In spite of grim statistics in 1873, having hit rich, coal veins, both had prospered. Certain that railroads would someday crisscross the country from sea to sea and northern to southern border, Bill had suggested more investment in steel. But cotton mills? He'd give it more thought.

He studied his surroundings. How to spend the time? He shifted to one of his favorite pastimes, studying the room's occupants. Mr. Hood was assessed as honest. He knew Marjorie and mother as examples of fair womanhood and knew Mrs. Spencer's rich attire and jewels adorned a two-cent character.

His appraisal fell on Francisco. Foreign born, no doubt. Too muscled for a tailor with skin somewhat weathered. Might have spent time at sea. Appeared to be about Elizabeth's age, but seamen grow old very fast. Then he caught the sadness in the limpid eyes each time those brown orbs rested on Elizabeth. His unfailing insight told him that Francisco knew about Richard and he twisted in the wind with unrequited, unspoken love.

Richard! If this fellow knew the truth about Richard, would he stop twisting and assert himself? It was not his place to interfere but he decided, as had Captain Addison, that this was a worthy fledgling. Addressing Mr. Hood, he said, "I've decided I want an overcoat. I'm sure this young fellow could make an old geezer like me look like the cat's meow."

The tailor laughed, "You are not an old geezer, but I am."

"After thirty-five, we are all old geezers."

Mansions and Mills

Bill chuckled at the bedlam as women chattered of this material or that color and what flattered and what didn't. Now he knew what idle ladies did when not drinking tea or attending charities. Their men supported it all by plotting deals. That brought thoughts back to cotton mills. With limited knowledge of mills, he would need to learn.

Bill made frequent business trips to Boston that summer receiving torrential wordage from Ben regarding booming mills and while there, made frequent visits to the nineteen-year-old, perfectionist tailor. The shoulders had to be a perfect fit and the sleeves had to break just so. Francisco had Bill bend his elbow several times to ascertain the proper sleeve length.

Bill reached for the door handle. An impertinent hand swung the door open, pushing him against the wall. Unconcerned of an individual pinned behind the heavy portal, Mrs. Spencer said, "Mr. Hood the hat in the window. I must have it if the buckram is of good quality."

"By now, you must know that only the best quality is used particularly in hats. The oblique slant would collapse without accurate stiffening. Miss Gilbert takes great pride in her millinery."

"In that case, have her try it on. I want to see how it sits on the head."

"There are mirrors here. What matters, Madam, is how it sits on your head."

"I said the girl is to try it. Are you plagued with deafness?"

Bill stepped free. Facing an incredulous matron, he said, "The girl's name is Miss Gilbert. She is neither your employee nor your model. If you have need for a model, I suggest that you employ one."

Stunned at the sight of him, she stammered, "What a sur...surprise! What brings you here?"

"The same thing that brings you here. Fashion." She scrutinized Elizabeth with suspicion and he knew what she was thinking. How stupid, he thought. What man of his means would have a working paramour? Mistresses were expected to rest by day and be zestful by night. Only a foolish man would expect anything but apathy in an exhausted woman.

"Did Mrs. Klass accompany you?" she asked, eyeing a seamstress too intent on her work to notice.

"Of course, she almost always does even if it entails bringing along pets and tutors." He checked the moving hands on his watch and replacing it in a waistcoat pocket, said, "How time flies. I bid you all a good evening." Rushing feet took him out the door.

"The impudence of the man!" she squealed. "I'll inform Mrs. Carlton that an invitation will be declined if there is a simultaneous one sent to him. Have you ever encountered such rudeness? I'll have him blacklisted. Mr. Hood, I've decided against buying the hat. Perhaps later, there will be a better choice than this one."

The tailors shook their heads back and forth, eyes raised to the ceiling. Francisco asked, "How do you stand her?"

Both palms cradling his forehead, he answered, "I don't know and I don't know why, but it was worse when putrid son came also. We could do well without her business."

"But she would take her friends with her."

"Francisco, I find it difficult to imagine that her obnoxious influence is that great."

Had he known, the gray-haired man would have enjoyed his summation for when Mrs. Spencer threw down the gauntlet, she and husband were crossed off invitational lists in favor of the Klass family. In Boston's pecking order, the Spencer hen ranked last.

Francisco advanced to handling the bookkeeping and Elizabeth advanced to selecting materials. Her eye picked up the smallest imperfection. With that double weight removed from his shoulders, Mr. Hood's frame gained weight and he looked healthier, less tired. With his business in capable hands, he could plan to follow doctor advice and accompany Mrs. Hood in a search for a more suitable climate.

Mrs. Blackwood unpacked once more because the ravenous grasshoppers had returned this year, as devoted as last year. She buried a weeping face in her hands. Consoling Elizabeth concealed elation, saying, "Now, now, you always say the Lord knows best. That could be true. You might not like his wife. What kind of unwomanly woman stops stampedes? Did he send a picture?"

"How can ye think someone can take a picture dancing around bloody bugs and cows?"

"He calls them steers."

Slapping her away with an apron wet with tears, Mrs. Blackwood cried, "Be gone with ye foolishness. Cows, steers, bulls or cattle, the Lord best strike down grasshoppers with a mighty hand or explain Himself. A bit of explaining is due."

Another attempt to console brought another swipe with the soggy apron. Elizabeth retreated, saying, "Things will be better tomorrow."

But the following morning offered overcast skies. Clouds grew darker as the day progressed, making summer flowers appear dull and forlorn in their hopeless straining for sunlight. Weather increased the boardinghouse keeper's gloom and Mr. Hood's despair over travel constraints. Trains were slow and stagecoaches more so. Connections were chancy. His wife would need to try different areas for accurate assessments of climate. It appeared the process could take months. Mr. Hood wailed, "Without her months will seem like years."

That dark day seemed bright to Ben Davis. Bill had decided to invest with him in cotton manufacturing, adding, "I had more interest in wool. Any chance for a wool mill in Lowell or Fall River?"

"Can't see it now, but I can keep my ear to the ground."

Bill grinned, "I'm off to pick up a new overcoat. Will get to see Miss Gilbert again. She's still beautiful though she is fatigued." He walked around a desk, fingering Ben's lapels. "Getting shabby, old pal? Get some new trappings. Can't get better workmanship. Hand me that pencil and I'll leave the address." Ben crunched the scrap of paper into a ball. He popped it into a pocket.

Bill left with his overcoat just as slate-colored clouds released sprinkles. Seeing the gentle warning, Francisco said, "We should start for home before it starts pouring." He had swelled with pride over Bill's praise. As they rushed through heavier drops, he said, "Can you imagine I did it all by myself? Everything! No help from Mr. Hood. Mr. Klass reminds me of Captain Addison. Don't you think he's fantastic?"

"I've never known what to think. I never gave him much thought." What was she to think of him after she learned of the true relationships in that group? He left alone that night, but did he always? Small matter to her.

"Why not give him much thought? Aren't you curious about people?"

"Not really. When people are of no consequence to me, they are of no consequence."

"Don't you think you should be curious about people?"

"Why? I said when I don't care, I don't care!"

She hopped over a forming puddle and added, "Would you have me be a busybody, like Helen?"

"Whose Helen?"

"Thank your lucky stars if you never even see her."

"Elizabeth, don't you like anybody? We all inhabit the same imperfect world."

"The imperfections of the world are outside my door and can never touch me if I don't open it and I never will."

"I hope all your doors are well fortified."

"I am very well fortified. At times you are exasperating! I imagine you can't tell me what's for supper."

"No, but let me ask you a question. I'm curious. Has Mrs. Spencer always been so rude?"

"She got worse after the merger with the Carltons. Their lineage goes back to 1655 with judges, ministers and governors.

As for me, why should her coarseness bother me? It doesn't, because it's hers and not mine. She is easy to ignore."

He was puzzled about Bill. How long had he known Elizabeth? Maybe he was in that party group. Saying that his wife often goes with him doesn't exclude the possibility of a kept mistress or discreet, extended lunch breaks. If charity covers a multitude of sins, a man's employment sometimes covered more. Seafaring and warfare did. Did Elizabeth know? In keeping shoddiness outside her door, would she say?

If he posed many questions, her emerald eyes would take on an Arctic frost. He would venture one more. "You don't like Mr. Klass. Do you? Why not?"

"Ecce homo."

"What?"

"That's Latin. It means behold the man. Francisco, you behold the man and leave me alone!"

"You know I don't know Latin. Why are you putting on airs?" His lack of broad education stabbed again.

The gentle rain began plummeting. She ran both to escape the rain and his questions. Rushing feet splashed mud onto her skirts. "Darn it, I washed this outfit Sunday and pressed it early this morning."

Checking out the splattered skirt, he said, "Mud you might brush off but be careful not to step in horse leavings." The remark made her hitch the skirt and petticoats higher, affording him a tantalizing view.

That evening when all was quiet, an uncomfortable Mrs. Blackwood tiptoed to the kitchen in order to swallow the forgotten pink pill. Under a gaslight, turned low, she almost stumbled over a slumped figure.

"Glory, nearly didn't see ye. Eyes no better than me bones. What ails ye, lad?"

He mumbled, "Not anything your powders, salves and pills can fix. Not even the pink ones."

"Methinks them pills fix nothing," she said, taking one with gulps of water, "but must be wary of not taking them least things get worse." She leaned over him to turn up the gas flame, gasping when bright light hit his dejected face. "Have ye need of a doctor?"

"No doctor can fix this. Sometimes I'm happy just being with her, sometimes I'm miserable. No matter how much I study, read and go to classes, I'll never learn Latin or Greek. Compared to her, I'm a simpleton. I can see myself in her eyes."

"Blarney 'tis, up to me eyeballs."

Stunned, he demanded, "Tell me what blarney."

"Begging ye pardon, lad, but 'tis blarney and get done with it. Ye have something that this lass, God help her, will never have. I love her like me own but I know her like me own. Her Latin and Greek is naught to what ye know just by breathing. Her learning 'tis in her lovely head, but what ye know is deep in ye vitals and 'tis a better knowing."

In reverential tone, he said, "Much that I learned came from the captain and other seamen for good or ill."

"Ah, and ye drank it and thirst for more. Ye cup will never fill, but her cup was filled with the correct way to serve tea. Life ain't peaches and cream but she has no wish to know. Methinks harsh awakenings await."

"Yes, she hides from reality and how will she cope if reality is served raw?"

What they couldn't imagine was neither the rawness of Richard's goodbye nor the coping mechanism set in place. If pride was to be her undoing, as Mrs. Blackwood feared, pride of family, not self, was her only salvation. She would keep all others at arm's length and close her eyes to the world's shoddiness, certain it could not be forced upon her unless she allowed it. She would wrap herself in that prideful cloak, patching it when worn thin, and stitching opened seams, convinced, if nothing else, it would protect her from infiltration.

Footsteps on the porch stairs halted late night ponderings on Elizabeth. Mrs. Blackwood held an index finger over her mouth, "Hush, here comes Mr. Morgan. Methinks there is deviltry in that man." Voice rising, she said, "Good evening, are ye arriving a bit earlier than usual?"

"Not early enough to answer questions." He circled the table and headed for his room.

"Friendly chap, and to think I worried about his appeal." Shuffling off to bed, Francisco could not resist a parting whisper, "Told you to get a spinster."

Mrs. Blackwood insisted that lonely Mr. Hood join them at Christmas. Mr. Bruncken delivered his usual sausages and his usual warning, "If my cousin tries to sell you anything, don't buy it."

Mrs. Blackwood received letters from both sons and a grainy wedding picture from Texas. Elizabeth cast an eye over it, leaning on an outstretched arm. The Louise she knew smiled at her while standing behind the seated groom. Elizabeth wondered why the bride was never seated, displaying fashionable skirts. Not that fashion existed in Texas. Haute couture didn't blend with dust, steers and suckling calves. Louise had fashion here. Did Ben send her packing? Convinced that Louise, like Helen, would remain in the dustbin of history, Elizabeth concerned herself with thoughts of the shock to Mrs. Blackwood when confronted by the strumpet.

Mr. Hood announced, "Mrs. Blackwood, I have a present for you but you must wait a few weeks. You will have your kitten. I presume you want a male. What will you name him?"

In dry fashion, Mr. Blackwood answered, "Napoleon. We heard so much of him, we must have our own."

"No. 'Twas enough to drive us all daft. Methinks Bourbon might be an improvement."

Mr. Hood asked, "Isn't that a drink?"

"Indeed not. 'Twas a line of kings. Let's name him after an Irish patriot. One martyred by the bloody Bri..." She threw a hesitant look at Elizabeth.

Mr. Blackwood boomed, "How about naming him after a good Yankee like Washington."

Francisco piped, "Correct me if I'm wrong, but I don't think a Virginian is called a Yankee. How about Adams?"

"Never, 'twill have an Irish name."

Inspiration struck Elizabeth, "I know and it is Irish." The room fell silent. "Shamrock."

"Indeed, 'tis a fine name. Me kitten's name is Shamrock."

Elizabeth reddened as all applauded. "See," she exclaimed, "it's like you said, God has his reasons. Imagine if you had gone to Texas without him."

With calloused palms pressed together and fingers pointing skyward to form a steeple, a carpenter implored, "Lord, let it savor grasshoppers."

Shamrock, however, would not see Texas soon for the grasshopper plague would continue for two more years, and the kitten would not see any in that holiday group before it had seen Rufus.

Chapter Seventeen

Ben Davis strolled up his sidewalk and his front stairs, thin ice cracking under each footstep. He peeled off one glove in order to pull a key from his pocket. Servants were not expected to delay early bedtimes in order to open doors. They arose at dawn to daily chores while his social activities ran late.

The visiting belle he escorted under duress had been as boring as her father was penniless, having lost his fortune in General Sherman's march through Georgia, but political ties kept him afloat, perhaps nefariously. Regardless, playing with politicians was necessary. Tariffs were a consideration. Even so, he hated their company, but more, hated the company of daughters hungering for matrimony.

Their annoying hunger merely kindled his. He missed Louise. As he placed a ponderous, gold watch and chain on a bedside table, he quizzed himself. What made her so fetching? Where was she now? Long shadows flicked on a wall from an oil lamp. The rest of the room was as dark as his mood.

A crumbled paper fell from his pocket as he reached for a hanger. Opening it under the light, he recognized Bill's handwriting. His eyes read the address before it landed in a wastepaper basket.

Louise once filled this room with pealing laughter, playing coquette, enticing, then rejecting, then reconsidering. Memory lingered of her sitting up with speed and grace, saying, "I'm hungry. Are you?"

"Very, but not for food."

"I'll tiptoe so the servants won't hear and make ham sandwiches." He groaned.

Donning a silk wrapper, running barefoot, she raced through the door and within minutes returned with a tray of sandwiches, milk, pickles and lemon cake.

She giggled, "What will your valet think about all the crumbs on the sheet?"

"He will think we did some snacking."

"You'll see. Everything is better on a full stomach."

He grinned at remembering that accurate statement. She was joy in an often joyless world.

His childhood had joy until 1853, in the city of New Orleans, when an epidemic of yellow fever put a period to his father's life. Ben, born Confederate, became a Yankee when his mother moved him to Boston, a city no longer cursed with that plague which had migrated south, years before the Union Army did. He recalled the yellow flags, called yellow jacks, on quarantined ships anchored offshore and recalled how his mother dispatched him out of the city with a servant. She nursed his father alone through fever, yellowing eyes and kidney and liver failure.

Officials denied requests to see his beloved father before the body, with many others, cluttered the streets. His uncle served as trustee for substantial holdings. He did so with honesty and shrewdness while instructing Ben in financial sagacity.

His mother remarried two years later only to die from puerperal fever soon after stillbirth, taking gaiety into the grave. Singing, piano playing and games gone by the time he was fifteen. Laughter lost from his life until he met Louise.

Louise was right. She wasn't made for starched living, as she called it. Her advice was to marry Elizabeth because she would fit in his world. She had said, "A happy wife makes for a happy husband." Marry Elizabeth? A man could be proud of her. All the frat boys, believing that things were racy, thought Richard a lucky man. Marrying Elizabeth now, what would they think? Whoa, since when did he give a damn what anyone thought? The only man whose opinion he valued would applaud, and considering his fellows in sin, not one would ever dare to say a word. Hijinks discussed with relatives? Not likely. Elizabeth? One certainty, he would never victimize her by deception. Not him. All cards on the table, Ben, old boy. All fifty-two of them.

    The decision vacillated as the grandfather clock struck the hour. Two o'clock! Even so, he sat unmoving, weighing pros and cons, listening to ticking time. It ticked for him. Just before retiring, he rescued the discarded, furrowed paper from banishment. Placing it in a pajama pocket, he slept on it.

    Morning peeking through his window did not awaken him but his butler's activities did. Charles stoked dying embers and inserted fresh logs. In a chilly room, Ben stretched, yawned and felt sluggish. He welcomed the blue robe handed to him. Gazing out the window, he noted stairs and walks still dressed in glistening ice.

    "Charles," he said, "I have two questions for you. Do you think this day will be any warmer and do you think my wardrobe needs improvement?"

    "No Sir, and yes, Sir."

    "No to what and yes to what?"

    "This day will be colder and your wardrobe is in need of serious overhauling. Some things are frazzled, others are out of fashion."

    "What's frazzled?"

    "For one thing, your shirt collars. Poor women turn frazzled shirt collars over and I was about to ask Mrs. Murphy if she would mind doing that to spruce you up, at least a little."

    "Interesting. How do they turn the collars?"

    "First they remove them, turn them over, frayed side inside instead of outside and stitch them back on. That way the frayed side doesn't show because it is now inside." He hoped his explanation made it clear. The wealthy have no notion of poverty's need for inventiveness. He added, "Cuffs are also turned over in like fashion."

"I believe I can afford new shirts. How are my suits?"

"Some trouser seats are so worn I fear pink flesh will show through very soon. I dared not say after only a few months of employment, but I would have needed to or be unworthy of my post. I wonder why your last valet hadn't mentioned it."

"In all likelihood because he never liked me, or rather, never approved of me. Tell you what. I give you permission to discard any unsuitable clothing and make a list of what I require."

"Yes, Sir. I will do so and layout a suit for today."

In his marble lavatory Ben shaved, using a long handled razor blade. He preferred a clean-shaved look. He wore his chestnut colored hair somewhat shorter than fashionable. If attire mismatched his station, impeccable hygiene atoned. He never used tobacco and in spite of indulgence at the Spencer wedding, liquor was almost a stranger. He had one weakness. Not women. Just Louise.

When he returned to his room, the closet door gaped like a hatchling's hungry mouth. He noted that his wardrobe now consisted of one business suit, one overcoat, one lounging jacket, two hats, four pairs of shoes, one pair of warm boots and his formal attire. A gunmetal-colored suit rested on the bed. Great! That meant he had two business suits.

He checked the drawers. These contained three shirts, five pairs of socks, all his pajamas and two pairs of gloves. He would somehow manage at present. Tonight he had to appear at the Carlton's bash to welcome the country's Centennial Year. Consoling that his evening clothes passed inspection with Charles when the country celebrated one hundred years since the Declaration of Independence.

The country greeted the year with cheering and flag waving, a fitting salutation not only to independence but to the nation's survival of a devastating civil war. One that had ended less than a dozen years ago.

Charles dumped piles of clothing on the kitchen table, saying, "His last valet was a disgrace. Why didn't he tend to his duties? No wonder he was discharged."

Surprise blanketed Mrs. Murphy's face, "He was not discharged. He quit because he didn't approve of some shenanigans. A holier than thou type. I liked Miss Louise even though you might say she wasn't the right sort. She always remembered my birthday and my grandchildren at Christmas. They say no man is a hero to his valet, but I hope you can find it in your heart to see his qualities. I do, and I miss his sinful Miss Louise."

"I consider my position with Mr. Davis an honor." Past employers indulged in worse than womanizing!

Darkness covered Boston when Ben donned the mandatory apparel for a Carlton dinner and ball. When the mansion's doors opened to him, he noticed Bill chatting and his wife wearing a mauve gown and amethyst jewelry. All were seated before he detected the absence of the senior Spencers. While waltzing with Marjorie he asked if her parents were ill. She replied, "Haven't you heard? Everyone else knows, much to my embarrassment. After all, they are Richard's parents. I might as well tell you before someone else does in vicious manner." Her eyes circled the dancers before explaining, "My mother-in-law told my mother she would not attend any event if Mr. Klass did. He offended her in some silly way and my mother respected her wishes. The invitation to Mr. Klass had already been mailed so my mother had no choice except to discard the one to my in-laws. What else could Mother do? How does one retract an invitation previously sent? I don't understand why Richard isn't upset."

Ben understood. Richard was Richard striving to remain in favor with the Carltons. None but a fool such as his mother would push Mrs. Carlton too far. In Boston, a snub from the savoir-faire and super-rich Mrs. Carlton was a death knell.

While dancing with Bill's wife for the second time, she started coughing. He walked her to a balcony noisy with bells and noisemakers. At last she caught her breath, saying, "Too much dancing, I suppose. I have danced every one of them."

"Are you sure you are all right? Would you care to leave? I could find Bill through this horde." He looked over his shoulder but didn't see him. "I'll go look for him."

She caught his arm saying, "No. I'm fine. How many people do you think are jammed in here? This mob swallows all the air." She laughed and laughter brought on another coughing spell.

"You must be coming down with something. I'll get Bill."

"No, and don't say anything to him. He goes into fits if I sneeze. It's the dancing and the throng. Let's go inside. I want to ask Marjorie about the little boy."

Ben stood by her side, afraid to leave. He did not believe she was fine. Something was wrong. Where was Bill? Fervent eyes swept the crowded room as Marjorie said, "Mrs. Klass, is this not a delightful evening? I will be overcome with loneliness when all this gaiety ends."

Engulfed in anxiety, Ben hadn't noticed Richard's approach but heard him say, "My dear, there is no need for loneliness. Talk to yourself. On second thought, don't. You might discover how boring you are."

Following a gasp, a mauve-gowned Isabel fell to the floor. Ben deduced it was illness and not the remark causing Isabel's swoon. After administered smelling salts, strong arms elbowed through massed humans and placed her in a carriage.

On the way to the hotel, she assured Bill, "It was all the dancing, the heat and being packed like sardines. It was everything and nothing. It's a new year. Let's have none of your silly worrying."

In the streets and in the boardinghouse, festivities continued beyond dawn, until none except the sentinels from the police and fire stations remained upright.

Ben tacked a do not disturb note on his bedroom door and slept late on Saturday, January 1, 1876. Many citizens emerged from scant sleep to renewed merriments. Former rebels had more to celebrate than others. The government had granted amnesty to confederates with the misguided hope that one mighty stroke with a goose quill would improve southern tempers.

On awakening, Ben reconsidered the matter of Elizabeth. This year he would turn thirty-five with no wife and no issue. Bill, one year older, had three children. How old was Elizabeth? Possibly a year or two younger than Louise. High time for her to consider marriage. Richard had married almost three years ago and had tooted at last night's dinner that his son would turn two within days. Maybe Elizabeth had washed the imbecile from her mind like a spider down a rainspout. Maybe.

Tomorrow she'd be at work. He'd ask Charles to have the list of his needs prepared. It was just a matter of bringing it to the tailor shop. Where was that address? He remembered putting it in the jacket pocket of his pajamas but where were those pajamas? He rang for Charles.

The apologetic butler rushed in. "Sir, you left a note not to be disturbed. Otherwise, the room would not be so cold."

"Never mind about that. Four blankets are keeping me warm. Where are the pajamas I wore the night before last?"

"Out to the laundress." He bent, inspecting the fireplace, but there was not a spark. "Mr. Davis, please stay there till this room is warm."

"The cold room is my fault because of the note. It's a holiday. The laundress can't be washing today. I want those pajamas."

"I'm sorry. Holiday or not, she picks up the laundry every Saturday. I don't think one day or the other matters to her." He could understand a fuss over an icy room but not a fuss over pajamas. With difficulty, he managed the task of creating a fire.

Ben wiggled far down under the blankets, pulling them over his head when an outstretched toe felt something scratchy. Sheets were changed on Friday mornings. The note. Was it? It was. "Charles, I would appreciate the list specifying my clothing needs, at your earliest convenience of course."

"The list should be completed by noon tomorrow."

"That should be fine." At least it would be if he accumulated sufficient courage.

On Monday afternoon, complete with Charles' long list, Ben set out on his mission, radiating false confidence. The first to spot the broad-shouldered man was Francisco and from his seated position, this stranger appeared tall. Perhaps at least six feet. Mr. Hood and Elizabeth were in the storeroom evaluating fabrics. The unfamiliar man removed gloved hands from deep pockets, stating, "It's mighty cold out there. Are you the proprietor?"

"No, the proprietor is Mr. Hood and here he is now."

The elderly owner greeted him with a smile, but Elizabeth's face registered astonishment and displeasure. A reminder of those days she thought. Is there not another tailor in this expanding city?

Forcing cordiality, she exclaimed, "Mr. Davis, so delightful to see you again. Hope you are well."

Two tailors exchanged amazed glances. They asked themselves, how many dandies does she know? Francisco had the answer to how but not the answer to how many, while Mr. Hood remained clueless and puzzled.

Ben unfolded the list, saying, "It's rather long but my valet insists on all of this and my cook wants me to look like a hero. I must comply."

After three heads bent to the inventory, Elizabeth purred, "I agree with his color choices for someone of your complexion. Mr. Hood and Mr. Castro will make you appear a hero." All missed the mockery in her voice as she raised her eyes from printed instructions.

She looked at the clock, exclaiming, "Goodness, I have only one hour to complete Mrs. Fisher's hat." She pretended that application of white feathers prevented her from seeing his departure.

Mansions and Mills

Disappointment clung to Ben like the cold mist that permeated Boston as the day uttered a drab farewell. He hated these short, colorless days as colorless as Elizabeth's interest in him. Neither Francisco's measurements nor fabric selections had warranted her notice. Absorbed in work, she ignored him.

She was so beautiful, but her once silky glide had changed to a majestic stride with head held higher, carriage stiffer. He recalled her as friendly, now she was formal. This courtship thing did not appear promising. Nevertheless, the situation might change if given enough time and he hoped dressing to his valet's satisfaction would supply abundant opportunity. He fancied goldenrod in bloom before completion of his wardrobe. After all, patience could be a winning ticket.

Another consideration was a good word from Bill. She must have a high opinion of him. Why wouldn't she? He knotted a brown scarf around his neck, shoved gloved hands back into deep pockets and told himself this frigid walk was healthful.

Francisco tramped home in a foul mood with Elizabeth attempting to keep up with him. He had noticed admiring glances cast in her direction. How many rich men from her past would traipse in? If he asked her opinion of this one would he receive the same answer?

She called out, "Please slow down. What's wrong with you?"

"I hate that hat! Just because you think brown flatters that rich peacock doesn't mean it flatters you."

"You are rushing me because of my hat? Are you unhinged?"

"No. I need a vacation. I think I'll visit Amos and get away from this cold."

"You can't go now. Mr. Davis has ordered tons of things. Who will do his fittings? Me? Besides, it's dangerous down there. That reconstruction problem! Will you slow down?" He kept up a steady march.

"All right. Have it your way. Don't slow down. This is the last time I'll ever walk with you."

The words stopped him in his tracks. He waited and then matched her easy stride.

If he thought of escaping the constant bayonet of Elizabeth, that hope migrated when Mr. Hood climbed an old ladder which broke, plunging him to the ground.

A doctor, summoned from across the street, palpated the injured right ankle, declaring, "I don't feel a broken bone. I believe you have a severe sprain. However, I'm going to splint it. Considering your age, I would prefer using caution. Crutches will make it possible for you to work, but for one week it's bed rest in order to recover from shock."

Snowflakes pockmarked the sky when Francisco went in search of a hired hack. He felt certain that he could carry Mr. Hood on his shoulders as he hoisted him up the stairs outside his home. White flecks began whirling around in a dizzying spatter before he located a vehicle, but swarming snow did not blot out his vision of Ben hurrying towards the shop.

Damn the man, he thought. Others of his station sent servants to pick up items. All, but this one and Bill Klass. It was possible that Bill's visits to Boston were too brief to haul a servant along, but this bloke had servants to spare. Where was his exalted butler or valet, or whatever he called Charles? What prompted this man's trek through snow for two completed shirts? As if the reason wasn't obvious!

Ben assisted in lifting Mr. Hood into the hired hack and offered to supply his carriage for Mr. Hood's use. The tailor said. "Thank you, but that won't be necessary. After a week of rest I will have my own carriage at my disposal."

As the hack carrying Mr. Hood and Francisco left curbside, he looked through the window as a smiling Elizabeth handed Ben a wrapped package.

Nervousness prompted constant chatter from Mr. Hood, "When I return to work, I won't be able to peddle the sewing machine. Much of it will need to be done by Elizabeth. It will strengthen muscles in her le...limbs. We must remember that ladies have limbs, not legs." He chuckled before continuing, "I will give you Sam's address. He'll put shoes on my old nag and fix her harness, but I must warn you that he has a facial disfigurement. I want you prepared so you will not register shock. He is the friend with the kittens. Please pick it up for Mrs. Blackwood. Don't let Elizabeth go there. Better to spare her unpleasant facts. Don't you agree?"

The young man nodded in agreement, though he was thinking of how everyone spared her unpleasant facts, no doubt sensing that she didn't want to know.

He raced back through thrusts of wind and snow only to find a shop in darkness. Of course, worsening weather had hastened her departure. Did she leave with Ben? Would he have left her to fend alone through gathering drifts, dragging sodden skirts? No, Ben wouldn't.

Within seconds of arrival in the back hall, he received the perforating answer in hearing Mrs. Blackwood gurgling to herself, "Such a fine gent, that he is." Surprised and flustered at being heard, she tittered, "Look outside at all five Conroy girls romping in the snow. They wait for the sight of ye and three are not the least bit dotted." She crumbled, and said, "Ah, to be able to change it for ye, lad."

Ignoring this flood of words, he ate and retired to his room to study, shutting his mind to a gathering storm.

Two days later, Francisco trudged through slush to Sam's blacksmith shop, leading the horse with one hand and carrying the harness in the other. The sun's slanting rays were warm for February. Snow melted and dying icicles dropped off roofs making small, tinkling sounds as they fell. He braced himself against the first gaze at disfigurement, not knowing why, since he had seen so many maimed men, shredded by wrathful seas, sliced by merciless ropes and mangled by vengeful whales.

In spite of the clatter of worn horseshoes, he heard the clink of rosary beads on stone. They had dropped through a hole in his pocket. He thanked whatever angel had caused him to hear the faint sound. Picking them up and placing them around his neck, he vowed to take greater care. Caressing the beads always filled a need for solace or courage. At this moment, unease plagued. What was causing a foreboding? He fondled the beads again.

Sounds of argument assailed him as he reached the wide entrance. A voice said, "Come on, Sam. You have the strength. It's like pulling a nail from a horseshoe. Straight and you'll do it quick."

Taking no notice of Francisco, the leather-sheathed man growled, "Go to Dr. Adams."

"Please, Sam. His muscles are all in his head. He wiggles and twists for ten minutes. You did it for Mr. Hood and Joseph. They told me."

"Only because they are friends."

"Please I'll pay you twice as much as Dr. Adams."

"Don't want your money."

The man dropped to his knees, "See, this one, please."

The blacksmith stood before the kneeling man, tool in hand. In less time than it took to howl, the right, upper cuspid was out. Muffled through a handkerchief, sincere gratitude buffeted the walls.

"What can I do for you? Just don't tell me you have an aching tooth." the colored man grunted while turning to face Francisco.

Crisscrossed scars covered his forehead, cheeks, both hands and the visible part of his arms. It was obvious that eye protection came from balled fist. Francisco could not imagine what clothing concealed. How did anyone survive this? How often did this happen? Amos spoke of it. Was Sam the same Sam? Dare he ask?

"Don't bother saying. I know this horse and I heard of the accident. How does he fare?"

"Well enough considering the fall."

"Give me a minute to finish this." A high-pitched sound rose from the anvil as metal obeyed hammered commands. Sparks flew

Mansions and Mills

while Francisco inspected his surroundings. He saw ancient hoops, rusting wheels and broken iron railings resting against walls. Bellows spat air, encouraging flames. Doused, hot iron protested with an angry hiss. He watched, fascinated.

At last, Sam spoke. "I take it the old girl needs shoeing. Leave her, but can't say she'll be ready before four. Where is her saddle?"

"In her stable, but here is her harness. Can it be fixed?"

"Afraid not. She'll need a new one, but how do you ride her without a saddle?"

"I lead her. Never rode a horse, not even before I went to sea."

"A seaman? Many from the plantations went to sea."

Bells rang in Francisco's head, too many. "A shipmate was named Amos. Did you know him?"

"The Amos I knew would be about twenty-eight now. Was on the Gray plantation. Does that fit?"

"It fits. He was our cook."

"A cook? Imagine that!"

"Is Gray your name too?"

Sam chuckled, "The army gave me the name Turner. The sergeant told me to turn just as a private asked for my name. Cannons had deafened the man. When the sergeant told me to turn around, the private thought he was being supplied the answer. He must have thought my name was Turner because that's the name he put on the paper. The colored people thought Nat Turner was a hero so the name pleased me. Do you know what ship Amos is on now?"

"He's in the South. Gave up the sea to teach."

"Teach? Where did he learn enough to teach?"

"Aboard ship."

"That must have been some ship. Did you come across anyone else I know?"

Francisco gulped before saying, "I don't know his last name, but do you know someone named Rufus?"

175

Sam's face darkened before brightening, "Rufus. Yes, him and my boy played together. He might know where my son is. Where is Rufus now?"

"Nobody knows. He was searching for you. He was so determined that he might succeed."

Fighting tears, Sam said, "I hope so. They were good boys. I'd like to see Rufus."

Hiking to the tailor shop, he asked himself, "What could ruin my day more than the sight of Rufus? The sight of Ben?" He reasoned that seeing Rufus was improbable but opportunity would arrive to pose the question again. Ben or Rufus?

Chapter Eighteen

Three warm days decamped like wandering vagrants and frosty patterns garnished windows again, pedestrians shrank necks into collars while hugging coats against shivering torsos. Winter reasserted domination of its season while Francisco rejoiced at greeting the ever-proper Charles instead of Ben. The valet picked up two woolen suits and a fleece-lined overcoat. The young tailor relished a theory that absent Ben had found a more accommodating female. Conveying cheerfulness, he assisted the encumbered manservant through a wind-blasted door.

His jubilation would have evaporated like boiling water had he known that Ben hadn't forgotten Elizabeth. He was in New York assisting Bill with a troublesome business matter. As a rule Bill coped with ease, but now he was overwrought over his wife's health. "A cough shouldn't last this long. She gives me one explanation after another and refuses to see a doctor. I haven't seen her cough up blood but I fear consumption. Here is all the paperwork. I'm sure you can sort it out." His distraught conversation shifted back and forth from business to Isabel. "I can't think straight. I'm bringing a doctor to the house. Once here, she will submit to an examination."

Ben returned two weeks later, having handled the business matter by advising a quick sale of stocks, "Just get out of this. It smells bad."

While Ben was absent, three kittens arrived, all males. Everyone knew Mrs. Blackwood would want the gray one so like his father. Sam sent reports to Mr. Hood, informing him when feline eyes opened, saying that a royal heir drew less fanfare. Anybody seeking services from a blacksmith or a dentist appraised each one.

On the day Francisco planned to pick up Shamrock, Sam had an early morning visitor, an angry, bitter one. At first the man of color was not recognized.

He asked, "Do you remember me?"

Sam squinted at the huge man standing with his back to the morning sun, casting a long shadow across the floor.

Without waiting for a reply, he threw a newspaper at Sam's feet, saying, "Why didn't you kill them? You have lived in the same city. Killing them would have been simple."

"Killed who?" Sam took two steps backwards. The hammer was beneath his hand. Muscle for muscle he was a match for any man.

Indicating the newspaper, the man stated, "Don't tell me you didn't read this." He dismissed the menacing hammer with a smirk. It was poor weaponry when compared to his.

Sam snorted, "Read? They don't pass out diplomas on plantations. You read? You must have been a free darkie." He relaxed, abandoning the hammer, concluding that he was not facing a lunatic.

"Wasn't free. Worked tobacco same as you did, Sam."

"What are you here for? Can't be to teach me to read this newspaper and what is this talk of killing people?"

"I'm here for two reasons. First, where is Josh? If anyone knows, it must be you. I hope he made it out."

Sam stepped closer. Scrutinizing facial features, he exclaimed, "You are Rufus! You saw Josh last. Don't you know where he is?"

Mansions and Mills

"No. Maybe he did make it out, but if he did, why hasn't he found you? I want to see him. That hellhole didn't keep us from having some fun." He smiled, remembering tree climbing and games concocted with stones in the very young years. Later, they worked fields side by side, whispering of escape by reaching the river. Dogs would lose the scent.

Sam placed a barrel next to him, saying, "Sit down and tell me everything."

"When they took you away, Josh nearly went crazy. All his family sold and you gone too. Said he couldn't take it anymore, that he would kill the master and be whipped to death. We ran for the river. The dogs got me but I heard a splash. The plantation heir told overseers he'd deal with me. That meant chains in a shed. Never saw the light of day but saw plenty of him." He swallowed hard, "Sure you know what that means."

Sam grimaced, "Go on, Rufus."

"Before the war they sold the place. The new master unchained me and was good as it gets. Everybody ran when the first Yankee bullet sang. They were so busy saving their white asses that they didn't know which way any of us went. I went to sea. Don't know why I left my first ship but I landed in Salem. Thought I'd settle down. She was a mulatto. Never saw a lighter one. Should hate her for being so white, but I don't." Mist filled his dark eyes. He ran a distraught hand over them.

In a hushed tone, Sam said, "No law saying you can't stop if you want to."

"Might as well finish. She wouldn't marry me. Said she wasn't bringing any colored babies into this world. She could pass for white and she married white."

"Rufus, there's no beating a white man."

"Maybe there is. That's my second reason to be here." He pulled something from under his cloak, saying, "Ever seen anything like this? Traded rum for it. Ship out with rum and you can get anything. This is called a yataghan. Came from a Turk."

Sam looked at the weapon with its curved, double-edged blades without a cross guard and about two feet in length. Gnashing teeth and blazing eyes accompanied Rufus' next words, "Only met two whites I didn't hate, one a stubborn Scot and the other a cabin boy. World would be before off with a few less, don't you think?" He ran a finger over a sharp blade.

Sam drew back, alarms ringing, "How did you find me?"

"Your ad in this paper alongside of this happy Spencer announcement." Stomping savagely upon the news, he continued, "Found both in one newspaper and didn't even pay for it. How lucky can a man get?" Bending and rereading the announcement, he added, "Or how unlucky can a man get?"

"Did you say Spencer?"

"Aye, right here in Boston and someone with that name is going to be unlucky."

Surveying the blade, Sam said, "Rufus, you aren't thinking of doing anything foolish, are you?"

"What's foolish about disposing of garbage?"

"Don't do it! Think of the consequences!"

"They aren't going anywhere, so I'll tell you what. I'll take another berth and think real hard about it. The consequences if caught, but you'll never tell. While I'm thinking, you do some. Think of what they did to all of us and to Josh. Spit the truth, you want them speared!"

As Francisco approached the blacksmith's wide doors, he heard Sam shout, "Don't do it!"

The colored man noticed him, stopped and said, "Well, another from my past. Won't ask what you are doing in bean and cod land, but I will say, if you heard too much, remember what I told you years ago about staying healthy."

An overwrought blacksmith watched Rufus trot down the street. Overwhelmed with memories, he began shivering. The younger man led him to the barrel vacated by Rufus and sat him down. "I'm sorry," Francisco said, "he must have upset you. I knew he was no longer that nice, little boy but an angry man. If I had dreamed he would show up, I would have told you. I thought he might have been lost at sea."

Sam blabbered, "I didn't know they lived in Boston. I can't read. I didn't know." Sobs racked him now.

"Who are they?"

Sam pointed at the papers scattered on the floor. Francisco stooped to gather and smooth them, and then gasped, "Do you mean the Spencers?"

"Yes. I didn't know they sold the plantation. I went to the Grays. They grew cotton, not tobacco. They were kinder. Not like them." He pointed at the newspapers. "After the war, I went back to look for my son but people were dead or scattered." He gazed at the papers held in Francisco's incredulous hands and repeated, "I didn't know they lived in Boston."

"Sam, quiet down. Have a drink of water. Do I have it clear? Did the Spencers own a plantation and were you and Rufus owned by them?"

"Yes, me, my son and Rufus. They sold my wife. The new owner made her take another man. She had lots of babies. Those slaves they don't pay for and those babies barely walk before they work the fields. Oh God, I didn't know they were in Boston."

Francisco mulled over the seaman cast overboard and what Rufus had said of harsh treatment. "Was it true what happened to little boys there? Did that old man, you know, with little boys?"

"The father went for grown, slave women, but the son never went near a woman, not ever, not any woman. The son was the one and how those little fellows suffered."

"But he's marr..." Dawn surfaced. Logically, in Richard's elevated position, he had to cover, but the means to inseminate escaped imagination.

Francisco reached for the glass of water, took a sip, then said, "This will never do. Lock the door and stay here till I come back." He returned with two bottles of whiskey. He poured stiff drinks. When quickly swallowed, he poured more.

Hours later, Francisco slurred, "I'll take Shamrock and call it a day. You should too."

An emotionally mangled Sam agreed, "Thank you for the whiskey and all."

Francisco, with kitten tucked under jacket, stumbled home. Once there, unanimous kitten bewitchment masked the sway in his gait and the quick exit to his room. He ruminated that had it not been for Anvil's rescue, his reunion with Rufus and disclosure of Spencer savagery would not have occurred. Strange how inconsequential acts produce huge results. It all resulted from Elizabeth's response to cries from a distressed kitten!

So what to do with his newfound knowledge? Nothing. He wanted to protect Elizabeth from not only the world's evils but knowledge of the world's evils. Besides, how could he explain pedophilia to one who didn't need to know? He didn't want to speak of slavery which was never practiced in Canada and abandoned by England before she was born. She knew of problems in the South but deduced it was all due to emancipation. She believed that as valued property, slaves received bountiful treatment. What he had discovered would remain a secret. Just as the gypsy said.

Sam awoke the next morning, feeling secure that Francisco had heard nothing gushing from Rufus. He had not seen that lethal weapon nor had he heard the word hate. Sam had trusted Mr. Hood enough to tell him of the brutality but had never revealed Richard's habits. As for Francisco, he already knew of abused slave boys. Who had told him? It must have been Rufus.

He had a roaring headache. Over worn floors, he placed one agitated foot before the other. He poured water into the washbowl from a pitcher, oblivious to a thin layer of ice resting on its surface. Wash, dress, unlock the door and live around the dictates of the clock. Only today, he couldn't. Josh, Josh. That name, never said, was said. Memories, always pushed aside, permeated. The unremitting wound hemorrhaged.

He picked up a kitten, held it to his cheek. It was soft like white woman's hair. Not that he had ever felt white woman's hair, but Jonah said it felt silky soft. Sam didn't ask how he knew. That was lynching knowledge.

One whiskey bottle sat half full. It beckoned. Its light amber fluid fell down his throat in narrow drops. He turned the clock around, its frontage to the wall. Its moving fingers would not command today. Settled in comfort, he raised the bottle to his lips.

By the next afternoon, Rufus had committed to a ship bound for England and sailing at dawn. That last evening in Boston, he sat on a dock watching the sea swallow the sun. Think of the consequences. They would manage to hang him not once but twice for murdering one of the cream-colored, Beacon Hill Bostonians. The consequences. How much had Francisco heard? He hadn't played Judas at sea but that was a different situation. He was a frightened kid and the deed was done for him. Now, as a grown man safe on land, what? Would he have to do him in first, then the creamy one? He didn't want to shed Azorean blood but the other—how he hated that man, recalling the darkness, the solitude, the ever-present dread of painful visitations and those heavy, steadfast chains, slicing a child's growing frame.

What kind of white man did Jesse marry and what would happen if husband discovered the lie? He studied his white nails and palms in dimming light. He muttered, "Turn them over, fool. See the chocolate color. Washing dozens of times won't make them white. Not white enough for Jesse and scrubbing skin raw won't make you feel clean. Not after Richard."

At first, Rufus thought the moisture on his cheeks came from sea spray. He raised both hands to his face. Saline fluid ran through his fingers and the racking sound of sobs scattered gulls across the pink-tinged sunset.

Days later, Francisco raised his eyes to the mullioned paned windows of the shop seeing Ben not walking, not in a carriage but astride a sable-colored stallion, whose black mane swirled and lifted in the wind. He reined the horse, dismounted without effort and tied it to a hitching post before striding in with his usual confidence.

"Good morning. May I suggest you branch out to making drapes?" He wore a broad smile. "My present problem is windows in need of new draperies. I have measurements here."

Mr. Hood, crutches beside him, looked flabbergasted. Drapes? Francisco paused to study the shine on his left shoe before looking out to appraise the horse. Damn this man again. He sits a horse like a medieval knight while I'm afraid to feed an old nag an apple, plus he finds more reasons to come in here than a bride seeking a trousseau. Now it's drapes. What could ruin my day more than the sight of him or of Rufus? I know. Six of one and half dozen of the other.

Mr. Hood collected himself, "I hear readymade clothes and paper patterns are the wave of the future. Perhaps our future encompasses making drapes. I suppose you want then lined. Have you decided on colors and material?"

"I just brought measurements. Charles will select colors and fabrics when he recovers from a runny nose."

Wearing a puzzled expression, Mr. Hood asked, "Then why not hold the measurements till he recovers and supply all information at one time?"

Francisco fumed. Yes, why not wait? The tall gallant had an answer, "My horse needed exercise."

Francisco shot him a knowing glance while Mr. Hood quizzed, "Would not a gallop in the woods be more beneficial?"

Stepping out of a fitting room, Elizabeth spared him a reply, "Good day, Miss Gilbert." he said.

A familiar voice penetrated the dividing curtain, "These contraptions! Why don't men design sensible fashions for women? Years ago, my aunt caught her foot on the lowest hoop in those foolish hooped skirts and fell to her death."

With the barest nod in Ben's direction, Elizabeth stepped behind the partition, saying, "Let me help you."

The men exchanged sheepish glances. No doubt she referred to the bustle, a foolish contrivance.

Unabashed, Mrs. Carlton emerged, "I recognized your voice, Mr. Davis. A pleasure to see you."

"The pleasure is mine," he responded, bowing, while his right hand touched her extended, manicured fingers. "Your daughter has not accompanied you?"

"My daughter, like your Charles, suffers from a runny nose."

"A pity. I trust all others are well."

He detected a tensing of features before a halting reply, "My grandson does well, growing taller every day and Mr. Carlton is fine." He thought the omission noteworthy. "And what do you hear of Mr. and Mrs. Klass?"

It was his turn to tense and offer a partial response, "A voyage to Italy is planned." He did not elaborate.

"How nice. They will enjoy that beautiful country. Here is my driver, always punctual." Bidding farewell with minor tugging at an askew bustle, she disappeared into a carriage.

Ben looked around, hat still tucked under his elbow, by all appearances dismissed. Mr. Hood bent over scissors; Elizabeth slipped thread into a needle. An expression sharp as a needle passed between the young men. Ben had no choice but to flee.

Jamming his hat on his head, stroking the horse's gullet, he untethered it and mounted with ease. Propelling the animal, he trotted down the street, feeling like the fool that he was. Both tailors knew his intentions by now. In addition, Mrs. Carlton had heard his idiotic excuse of exercising the horse. Everyone was aware except Elizabeth!

He decided to exhaust equestrian exuberance in a gallop through fields. The whirling dust from racing hoofs equaled whirling thoughts from a racing mind. How could he court under these circumstances? How does one court anyway? Impossible when attending the war wounded. All the camp followers and brothels in Washington held no appeal. Besides those don't require courting. In 1866, Louise attached herself. Ten years ago!

Had he proposed before she discovered the pretentious life, would she have married him? Probably. But what of those proper, gossiping Bostonians speculating on her roots? Well, they would have accepted her or he would have jammed her down their throats. They would have swallowed her, digested her and absorbed her. When money talks, society walks. None, except Carlton had more, but with current investments that was subject to change. Railroads needed lumber for ties and for homes in expanding prairies. He and Bill had a good hold on that.

He raced the horse back to its stable still weighed with no genteel woman at the head of his table, no tiny voices scratching the silence. He functioned as an attendant for the hopeful or hopeless spinsters. Too old for belles in coming-out parties, he watched them flutter eyelashes and fans at targeted college boys. Pretending interest, some would say, "Mr. Davis, do tell me what you did in the war."

The nation had many war widows on both sides of the Mason-Dixon Line but he wanted his own children, not a ready-made family. Elizabeth would be an ideal wife. He recalled her at those parties, always correct, animated, dressed to perfection and emitting velvety laughter from a velvety throat.

Charles' runny nose became life-threatening pleurisy stalling courtship till bulbs opened earth.

Regardless, other things had progressed. Mr. Hood had doffed crutches. Francisco had resumed classes. Mrs. Hood had written of the tribulations of travel, "Once off the train, you take rattling, dusty stagecoaches to the backwoods but it was worth it for I feel marvelous here." On her return, sickness had returned. She approached her husband about a permanent move, "Is there anyone who will buy the business? How about Francisco? Can he afford it?"

"He hordes every dime, unlike Elizabeth who sends trinkets and just about everything else to New Brunswick. I have warned her about rainy days to no avail. Yes, I believe Francisco can afford it but does he want it? I wonder if he misses the sea."

When broached with the offer, Francisco replied, "I need time to consider. It would take most of my savings and wed me to Boston."

"Would that be so distasteful?"

Mansions and Mills

"Under certain circumstances, it would be unbearable."

In spite of his employees doing all the sewing machine peddling, Mr. Hood's ankle still ached. He placed it on a cushioned stool, asking, "What would make it unbearable?"

Francisco's face reddened as his eyes darted from one wall to the other. His feet ringed the room, his hands jammed pockets and his fingers gripped the rosary beads. Finally he melted onto a wooden chair, "I think you can guess."

"It's Elizabeth, isn't it?"

"She doesn't see me from the lint on the floor. Why would she ever when a rich cavalier is available. He can give her the world she once had. What can I offer? Do you realize the extent of her education?"

"Francisco, her education and ancestry are obvious but his kind will not marry a seamstress and she will never accept a backstreet life. She is not blind to your character. Give it time."

"I have given it four years and all I have is respectful friendship!"

Puffing on his pipe, the employer said, "Friendships have grown into marvelous marriages. Mine did. Sad the lack of children, but without the expenses of a family we have savings enough to retire and offer you a readymade business at a reasonable price. I would demand more from a stranger."

Francisco studied the bolts of summer material, some printed to commemorate the centennial year, one with flags, and one with the Liberty Bell. He stared at scrolled images of the Constitution. Faces of the Founders Fathers and Paul Revere on a horse stared back. He asked, "How would you handle things if I went South for a few weeks to weigh your offer?"

Mr. Hood knocked ashes out of his pipe and reached for his hat, replying, "I would employ someone to replace you. If your decision is to purchase the business, the new employee will replace me. If you decide against it, I will sell lock, stock and barrel to another. My wife is to leave within a month to prepare arrangements in a suitable climate. Traveling at this time of the year is preferable to travel in cold, railroad cars. When do you plan to leave?"

Francisco unwrapped his feet from the chair's rungs and looked outside to a surge of heat supplied by a July sun. Wiping his brow, he said, "I've written to Amos. Of course, the mails both ways are slow so I can't say just yet. I would like to stop off at the Centennial Exposition. This marvelous invention is on display. It's called a telephone."

"Yes. Elihu Vedder's illustrations are there as well as sculptors by John Rogers and William Storey. Look, I don't want to pressure you. You need a vacation after hauling me in and out of a carriage. As long as Mrs. Hood leaves this climate we can work out everything else. Once there, it will take her months to buy furnishing and whatever. You have time to make up your mind."

"Making up my mind, if I have one, is the problem. You might say my brain is just filled with fiber."

Patting the young man on a shoulder, Mr. Hood said, "Having Elizabeth leave early today gave us a chance to talk. Don't tell her of my plans yet. She gets rattled over people leaving. Is Mrs. Blackwood close to her move?"

"She's postponed again because of grasshoppers." They left together. Francisco locked the door, slipping the key into a pocket.

Not hungry and reluctant to walk home alone, he headed for Elizabeth's classroom hearing her teacher explaining, "Make it darker under the pier and keep the boat white. Bear in mind your focal point."

He waited till the teacher clapped her hands, saying, "Class over. See you next Thursday." Francisco persuaded Elizabeth to take a circuitous route, taking them to the waterfront, in spite of protestations. "Just fifteen minutes additional time. Look how bright the stars are on a moonless night" He looked overhead at constellations, missing the sight of the Southern Cross. Oh, to see that again and breathe salted air winging over plummeting waves. He stared at debris riding between dock and ships thinking that his mind was like flotsam, flowing back and forth between what he wanted and what was obtainable. The tempting sea would always be there, but if he waited too long deciding would towering waves overpower flaccid muscles? A life of nothing but needle and thread without the sea and without Elizabeth would be intolerable. It was intolerable now.

Her voice shattered his thoughts, "What ship is this?"

"Too dark to pick out the name but it is a British merchant. Might be the one carrying our Scottish wool."

It was carrying their wool. It also carried Rufus back to Boston after considering consequences. He considered them onboard and while wandering streets in Liverpool where a crying toddler clung to her father's leg and an angry mother shouted, "Ye'll burn for this, Paddy Rafferty." He considered consequences in pubs as he rotated glasses of stout ale between his palms, asking himself, "Is it worth hanging for?"

Chapter Nineteen

On a hot morning in June, mist fled from daybreak's first hot rays which promised to grow hotter. After a fitful night of deliberation, Francisco arose from dampened sheets. Plato's words danced in his head, "When desire disagrees with the judgment of reason, there is a disease of the soul." Yes, he had a soul disease and a nagging, inner voice saying, "Go see Amos."

He dragged a troubled mind to a breakfast served in a kitchen sweltering from boiled eggs and fried bacon. Mrs. Blackwood thumped both toaster doors open, revealing two golden slices timed to perfection. Francisco always burned them and Elizabeth unfailingly produced black, inedible ones and a smoke-filled room. Mrs. Blackwood had banned its use to all boarders, screeching, "Keep ye paws off it. One of ye chowder heads could set me house on fire."

Elizabeth made her appearance looking as crisp as the green beans gifted from the Conroy girls. She teased, "Francisco, did the freckled one or the broad one make the delivery? That third one is passable. Why not give her a tumble? Why not ask her to the fair? Come to think of it, I will when I trip over her on the curb, swooning over you. Isn't she named Beatrice?"

Mansions and Mills

He grumbled, "Eat your breakfast before you wilt. I'll wait on the backstairs." Clinging to shadow-draped walls, they ambled along in increasing heat.

He oiled a thirsty sewing machine. Pausing to wipe a dripping forehead with a damp sleeve, he scowled at the appearance of Ben and a frail Charles. As they removed their straw hats, the patrician boomed, "At last, after many delays, we are ready to proceed with the drapes. I expect you have retained the measurements."

An incredulous expression flooded Mr. Hood's face, "I thought you changed your mind." Scratching a balding, perspiring head he asked, "Now, where could I have put them?"

Dispirited Francisco drawled, "They are in the drawer under the gooseneck lamp."

Reaching for the papers, Ben said, "I think we need a woman's input. Miss Gilbert, these first measurements are for the library which contains blue upholstery and a multicolored, Persian rug. What do you suggest?"

They deliberated on each room, comparing swatches of material. She laughed in merriment as the two men bickered, conscious all decisions rested on her and Charles.

Her laughter, subdued for four years, gushed. Francisco had not heard the like since Richard's letters. Had she retained them? Didn't most women wrap them in red ribbons and encase them in lavender scented cachets? Some burned them. Had she?

The tailors exchanged glances. Mr. Hood's arched eyebrows worried. Did another grandfatherly talk summon? Didn't take long for that Spencer rake to marry a goldmine. Did it?

At closing time Mr. Hood remarked, "He's old enough to have decided on his heiress. Maybe that's what the drapes are about. All this will cost him a pretty penny. Lined and tasseled! He must understand there can be no rush. This is our first effort at making drapes. Elizabeth, are you planning a vacation this summer?"

Francisco's head shot up at her response, "Not now. Certainly, not now."

Ben left in festive mood having encountered an energized Elizabeth. He fretted over the impossible situation. How could he see her alone? He devised a plan. A private detective! She must do something other than work.

In early July the detective reported on her occasional attendance at church, fairs, lectures, museums and art openings. "Two weeks ago she went to a fair with an older couple, a girl and a dark haired, young man. The fair was great fun." His huge grin collapsed before a huge frown. "Getting back to business, she does not have a suitor but she is faithful to a Thursday night watercolor class. She walks back and forth. Here is the address." He handed Ben a hefty bill. "Is this enough or do you want more surveillance? There will be an additional charge, of course."

"Of course. This suffices." Pocketing a paid bill, Ben considered his options. Joining a painting class held no appeal. Inspiration surfaced. He would wait for a rainy Thursday and just happen to be riding by in a roofed buggy.

Luck was with him the following Thursday when the heavens delivered torrents of water. Wearing raingear, he harnessed a reluctant gelding, rearing in objection to the weather. Ben pressed on. No taciturn horse would deter him from his mission! Lamentably, due to deplorable weather, the class had been cancelled. Pulling up to a darkened building, he cursed, "Damn," he said, "Mr. Expensive Detective did not check on a rainy Thursday. Rain or shine I will be back next week."

On a balmy evening, Francisco witnessed Elizabeth exit from a splendid conveyance, smiling and nodding at a departing tipping hat. Bypassing her as she climbed rickety stairs, he made no comment when she quipped, "If these stairs aren't fixed, there will be no buyers. No buyers, no move to Texas. Isn't that nice?" Rankled by his silent snub, she asked, "What ails you, nitwit?" A brisk swish of an aqua skirt and silk petticoats registered annoyance.

Mansions and Mills

Aimless, Francisco walked narrow, twisting streets. He ambled through parks, inspecting statues with unseeing eyes. He passed mansions affordable to Ben and his sort. His sort didn't marry seamstresses. Did they ever? She was bred to hold court in manors and would settle for no less from Ben but how long could that man resist? He didn't want to observe a courtship.

Still, how could he leave Mr. Hood burdened with that drapery order? Would another reliable employee be forthcoming as hoped? She had called him a nitwit. Once he thought her a nitwit. Identical diseases of soul—unreasonable desire. At least, she hadn't called him an ignoramus. Being called a nitwit wasn't so bad.

Stride slowed. He studied his surroundings realizing he had wandered far. How much ground had he covered? Where was he? A woman stood in a window, one that ran from floor to ceiling. She paced back and forth, on occasion stopping to gaze out as if looking for someone. As she turned toward the lamplight, he caught her profile. It was Marjorie! Lord, in wandering, he had reached her residence.

Francisco had an eerie sense of a presence. He glanced over his shoulder. Did a shadow move? Was there a faint, rustling sound from dark bushes close to the front door? He thrust the thought aside. Imagination gone wild from restless nights and trying days. Heavy with fatigue, he retraced his steps.

On the following evening, frolicking winds sent clouds skimming over stars. Opaque night covered the mill town of Lawrence. It covered the activities of Richard Spencer but did not conceal him from anyone intent on finding him.

According to his estimation, it had been a good evening. The boy was worth two silver dollars. The doffer didn't earn that in a week. Perhaps it would buy him shoes to shield him from wooden splinters. Richard had heard mill workers wrapped rags around their feet as protection. Well, it wasn't his problem. His pockets clinked, thanks to the surviving heir, so safeguarded by generous grandparents.

He heard a sound in the alley. He stopped to listen. Silence. He looked behind. No one was there, but then a hulking figure stepped out of a doorway, blocking his path while holding a pistol in his left hand.

"Don't shoot! Money is in my pockets."

"I promise I won't shoot you if you just listen."

"That's a promise?"

"Yes, a solemn one. I really don't want to shoot you."

With forced calm, Richard said, "I'm listening."

"Once you kept me chained. It's too dark to see my face so I will tell you my name. It's Rufus."

Richard felt his knees buckle, but croaked, "I was a teenager. I'd never do anything like that now. I've changed."

"No, you haven't. I missed you last night but got there early enough tonight and have been following you. You sure haven't changed. Conversation over. I'm keeping my word not to shoot."

With a sigh of relief, Richard moved to step to the left when Rufus' right hand came up from under the cloak, thrusting the yataghan at a horizontal angle, severing the abdominal aorta and piercing the right lung. Relishing satisfaction, Rufus felt warm blood flowing over his fingers. Wide-eyed, Richard heard those last words, "Kept my promise not to shoot."

Placing a foot on the prone body, Rufus retrieved the weapon, looked around, saw no one and said to accusing stars, "He wasn't worth a bullet but worth consequences."

Two mornings later, Mrs. Blackwood cracked open the morning newspaper, uttered a cry and fell back into a chair. Francisco found her, gasping for air. "What's wrong?" She grasped his leg as he reached for a water glass.

"There be no help in water. 'Tis the news." She handed him the paper and saw his eyes turn into huge orbs. "Get yeself to work. Have breakfast in an eatery. 'Tis me who will be doing the telling. Get off with ye, I say." She pushed him towards the hall and into an obedient gallop.

Mansions and Mills

Ten minutes later, she sat still slumped in a chair. Elizabeth's morning smile fell from her face. She, as Francisco before her, asked, "What's wrong?"

"Sit here, lass, by me side." Holding the paper under her apron, she said, "The news, 'tis bad."

Elizabeth pulled a chair to face her and placed both hands in hers. They drew so close that knees touched through layers of fabric. "Is it the obituaries?"

"Worse. Ye might call it a sort of accident." She withdrew the paper but held it folded. "First page. Don't know how ye will take it, but something evil…" A firm grip held the bulletin as Elizabeth reached for it. "No, 'tis best I tell ye meself. 'Tis Richard, 'tis Richard Spencer."

Elizabeth snatched the paper, unfolded it, read it and wide-eyed walked to the window and looked down at disappointed Conroy girls. They had missed Francisco's early dash to the corner.

Life goes on she thought. The milkman's horse clopped down the street making a stop at every familiar delivery, knowing each one as well as the man clanking bottles. She heard him climb the stairs as he dropped off a day's supply and as he picked up empty bottles. She wondered why he delivered milk like every other day. Didn't he know today was different? Didn't he read the papers? Does he care? Do those twittering Conroy girls care? How come the world keeps revolving? Soon the green world would turn to orange and gold then brown. White snow would cover ugliness, but how could it cover the ugliness of Richard's murder? Does anyone or anything in the universe care? Remembering a tattered, burned, pink gown, she asked herself, "Should I care?"

Mrs. Blackwood's arms wrapped around her, offering comfort. Elizabeth patted the gnarled fingers, whispering, "Thank you." Lifting her head and straightening her shoulders, she asked, "What's for breakfast?"

That morning, Francisco didn't stop for breakfast. He took the shortest route to the blacksmith shop, running all the way.

Sam hauled him in by the lapels, scanned the street, slammed the double doors and threw the huge bolt.

Breathless, Francisco sputtered, "He did it. Didn't he?"

"You shouldn't have come. He just left. He knows where you work but I persuaded him you heard nothing that day and there was no way you'd connect him with them even though he saw you outside their house. He didn't take the Spencer name any more than I did, but if he sees you here, he'll suspect you put it together." He paused, meditating, "Any chance you can leave town for a while?"

"Thinking of it but not because of him. He's probably high tailing fast. He'll be safe in Haiti. The States recognized its sovereignty fourteen years ago."

Ignoring the information, Sam said, "Rufus won't be tied to the Spencers. Me, yes. I told Mr. Hood what happened except that boy stuff, but he never told me they lived in Boston. Might have been scared I'd do this. Gosh, maybe he thinks so now. Maybe he thinks I found where they lived and did it." Agitated, he continued, "If he told the police, they could show up at any minute. You better go if you want to stay out of this." Turmoil walked across his face. He asked, "Are you going to finger Rufus?"

"Not a chance." He speculated on what might have been his fate had Rufus not intervened on that ship, but most of all, there was Elizabeth. There was always Elizabeth. An apprehended Rufus might tell all. If knowledgeable reporters used customary discretion to spare the ladies, the motive would still surface as slave revenge. How debasing the acknowledgement, even to herself, that she had wanted a slave owning beast. She had to be spared the embarrassment of facing those like Ben and Bill who knew of her association with Richard.

Sam dragged him from cogitations, "Do you owe Rufus silence?"

"I'm late for work. We can talk about everything later." He knew he never would.

Mansions and Mills

He started for the door but a restraining hand clamped on his wrist. "Go out the back. How would you explain your presence here?"

"Easy, I'll say I have an aching molar and won't spend money on a dentist." Francisco paused, "Sam, tell me he won't go after the father."

"I doubt it. The boys had a special hatred for the son. I'm sure you understand."

Mr. Hood never suspected Sam, believing that illiteracy and hermetic lifestyle prevented tidings of the Spencer family. He felt Richard's obnoxiousness had grated someone to the point of murder. Ben and Bill concluded overtures had been made to the wrong man.

Authorities questioned family members. The elder Mrs. Spencer, horizontal with grief, withdrew behind closed doors, attended by a physician. The brief interview of the widow interested. She sat, not in widow's weeds, but in a rose-colored dress, dabbing at dry eyes with a lace handkerchief while swearing her husband had been in Lawrence on business. The men from the prescient remained unimpressed. Had they seen the nights when she paced in fury over Richard's neglect of his son, they would have delved deeper. Mr. Spencer would never mention a revenge motive or plantation ownership and insisted to experienced officers that Richard must have been murdered in Boston by a thieving ruffian and his body moved to a Lawrence alley. "The scoundrel wanted to cover his tracks." he explained.

"Sir, why would a thief not take the cash immediately and run off? What would explain so much blood in that alley?"

"Since you are expert criminologist, you tell me."

Later, one detective said to the other, "If the old man wasn't so fat, I'd think he did it himself. Not helpful or tearful. He's hiding something and isn't the masquerade interesting? Believe this one will go unsolved."

Marjorie had her first and only quarrel with her mother, announcing that she would not wear black, not even to the funeral.

The dispute lasted through the hanging of black crepe on the door, through the mortician carrying the remains into the parlor, through the setting up of chairs for all to show proper respect and through the first flower deliveries. Argument flew by bewildered men coming and going in fevered preparations.

Mrs. Carlton pleaded to no avail. "Mother," Marjorie said, "I will wear brown but no veiling and I will never wear black."

"Dear, only for one year so people won't talk. You mustn't embarrass us and think of your child. After a year you can start receiving attention from men and might marry again."

"Mother, bear with me while I tell you what I will do. Brown only till I leave the city. Have you noticed that marriage has made me as slim as a girl? Have you noticed that I have a small, pointed chin and high cheekbones once concealed by layers of fat? When I leave I will be the most sought after woman in Europe. The only Carlton and Spencer heir will help make it so and men may dance attendance till they drop, but I will never marry again. Marriage is distasteful, to say the least. I don't know how you stand the chains of marriage."

"I don't feel chained in my marriage." She wondered why her daughter wore a confused expression, but ladies never asked personal questions.

After the headlines, Francisco skimmed every blank expression carried on Elizabeth's features. He queried Mrs. Blackwood and met vexation. "Pish!" she exploded, "Don't ye know that lass at all? Crumbled to dust, she'd not abide the likes of anybody thinking so. She'd tighten the corset till it squeezed the life from her, for sure. She may not be puffed up with the beauty part but her pride can leapfrog a mountain. Can ye not learn the difference?"

"Maybe she doesn't care anymore." But it sounded like a question. Remembering Elizabeth's soft "Thank you." she didn't reply.

Ben continued picking her up every Thursday, never lingering until a day under disrobing trees. Chilled breaths from the sea buffeted their former brilliant gold and red clothing. He offered a plaid blanket. She encased her shoulders with one corner and wrapped the other corner around his. They drew closer in conversation as dropped reins dangled under the horse's bit.

In flooding agony, Francisco watched the windswept conversation. He withdrew from the window engaging his thoughts in the vital matter of a correct flow of molasses into his tea. Elizabeth sauntered in followed by swooping, crispy remains of blossoms. She had the customary question, "What's for supper?" She added, "Don't cook for me tomorrow. I'm going to the Parker House for dinner." Molasses curled in Francisco's steaming cup.

The following night as two ladies fussed over hair, shoes and costume, Francisco sat in a darkened kitchen listening to the hissing and crackling of logs sitting on reddening coals. Even with the heat, he felt as if icicles perforated every bone. Remarks wafted from Elizabeth's room, "A wee bit of rouge so ye won't look ghostly."

"Would you have me look like your streetwalking friend?"

"The shame, speaking of the poor creature. She comes by the paleness honestly."

"Sorry, I retract the comment. Think I'll wear the green gown. I've enhanced it with ruffles around the neckline."

Scrutinizing the alteration, the housekeeper exclaimed, "More modest, for sure, but I prefer the pink one." Searching the closet, she asked, "Where could it be?"

Turning to disguise a flinch, Elizabeth replied, "I no longer fancy pink and did away with it."

"Ah, the pity. Such fine, rosy feathers. Methinks the color becoming to auburn hair such as ye be blessed with."

"This color is horrid!"

From his slumped position by the cast-iron stove, Francisco paid little heed to the rise and fall of feminine voices. Neither the sounding doorbell nor Ben's voice roused him from thoughts. When the couple receded from the house, myopic Mrs. Blackwood ambled into the kitchen, almost bumping the back of his chair. "Glory," she cried, "Methought ye to be a bundle of laundry."

"Might as well be."

Placing an understanding hand on his shoulder, her words dropped, "Ye knew this was bound to be. 'Tis more than time. She's twenty-five. Hear tell the dotted Conroy girl has found a well-intentioned dotted boy. One less for the picking, not that ye cared for her spots but the one named Bea..."

"I'm leaving. My things are boxed and Mr. Hood will pick them up and store them in his attic for now. Here is a month's rent. It might take that long to get another boarder. Maybe you should try a spinster."

After several dumbstruck seconds, she stammered, "Want no more of the stay out all night sort. Will ye not be back?"

"Not here. After a stop in Philadelphia, I'm going to see Amos, but I'll write. Have to come back for my things. If you are not in Texas, I'll see you then."

"Bloody grasshoppers again this year. Me bones will be done in before I get meself there." She sat on his lap like a child, crying, "Ye'll be sorely missed."

He left within an hour. He headed for the train; Marjorie headed for a ship. She would attend the Grand Opera House of Paris, its completion delayed by the Franco-Prussian War. She would see the painting of General Prim painted by Alexander Henri Regnault, who at twenty-five lost his life in that same war.

Later that evening, neither boardinghouse proprietors heard Elizabeth's subdued return for Mr. Blackwood was upstairs trying to soothe his sobbing wife. He said, "I don't know what you are bawling about. If it wasn't for grasshoppers, you would leave him."

"Different things for the lad would make it better."

"What things?"

"Different things. Ye can't see what's under ye nose. Men are blind without a fig of understanding women either, that's for sure."

He agreed. There was no understanding women—that's for sure!

Chapter Twenty

Nature's insistent rhythm commanded the birds southward and Francisco followed with one detour to Philadelphia to view the newly invented telephone. A marvel, a potential timesaver! No other wonders impressed as much.

Complying with orders from home, he visited the Liberty Bell and stood in the hall that had housed the Founding Fathers.

Commands obeyed, he stood, brown suitcase in hand, waiting for a train. He heard its deafening sound before seeing it round a curve, smoke broadening skyward before mingling with sunset's colors.

Men jostled for seats, elbowing each other, while allowing ladies to pass for best choices. One man in his thirties sat on a trunk, confident of aid. On closer view, Francisco saw his right sleeve folded upon itself, secured by safety pins. Another war casualty. A teenage boy noticed the veteran's dilemma and started toward him just as Francisco dropped his suitcase to assist. Combined effort placed the heavy trunk under a long bench. Francisco wondered if in want this veteran would sell the hard-won medal now pinned on a tattered Confederate jacket and still worn with pride. The stranger sat alongside immigrants who crowded side by side in third-class accommodations, holding meager belongings and exuding uncertainty. They disembarked in Pittsburg for employment in steel mills.

Settled in second-class accommodations, Francisco studied surroundings. Stoves placed at each end provided scant heat. He anticipated the warmth of southern states, but when struck by extreme heat in Georgia, the cars became stifling when porters closed windows to avoid flying dust.

The train jostled, jerked at stops and at times lingered to pick up migrant workers. A boy called a butch sold nuts, dried fruit, soap, tea, coffee, books, papers, candy stuck to wrappers and cheap cigars. Mrs. Hood had not exaggerated the horrors, but Amos was worth it and anything was worth avoiding the shrapnel of Ben.

A ten cent magazine informed of recently freed slaves in Portugal and Cape Verde. If Elizabeth knew she'd scoff since Britain abolished the trade in 1808 and the Crown even purchased freedom for many. Why was he thinking of her? Wasn't half of this trip to forget her? Think of his reunion with Amos and a chess game.

He looked out at a colonnade of trees, many different from any in New England. The red earth of Georgia fascinated. He saw rivulets running in gullies so red it looked like blood. He reflected that Georgia had seen its share. With all his delving into history, he never saw a war justifying its massive destruction. Thoughts continued to wander. This trip was too long. With sleep unachievable, he fished his pocket for two cents and bought a local newspaper.

At the next stop, a beefy man settled next to him, replacing a small, silent woman whose false hairpieces fell on the platform, knocked off by exuberant greeters. The new occupant's girth took up part of Francisco's seat, his leaning weight a heavy cargo of heat and discomfort, augmented by prying questions. Discouraged by vague answers, he fell asleep with his snoring head on Francisco's shoulder.

Gilded hands on his watch dragged. After monotonous ticking, its shackled minutes proclaimed arrival. Amos' father appeared, a study in black and white, for his head wore crimped, snow-colored hair over a crinkled, tar-colored face. He drove a weatherworn buggy pulled by two mules.

Smiling from ear to ear, he said, "Youse lookin' trabelin daid, shonuff. Rid from Bawston jus' to see mah Amos."

"We have been friends for years. I was just twelve and always hungry. He gave me extra food. Counts on a ship."

"I's knos. He dun tol me 'bout all the furriner folk an' de Inlish massa. We's comin' to Morgan Creek. Doan know whut dis mule gwine to do. Magnolia doan take tuh water."

It soon manifested. She stopped in her tracks and after scrutinizing her, the other mule followed suit. He tossed a helpless glance over his shoulder. It was obvious which mule ruled the roost or rather the buggy.

Francisco's eyes, longing for sleep, fixed on the driver. "Can't you get her to move?"

"Dat mule gointer g'wan wen she be afixin' for supper. Ah oughter git a hause. If I's pushin' her, she gets real cussy."

Francisco hated the thought of her getting real cussy so they waited till hunger overcame her hydrophobia.

When Francisco jumped off the buggy, Amos sped from his log house, vaulting a fence and wrapping his arms around the younger man. Entwined, they bounced up and down, fell and rolled over the ground. Amos said, "My mother came to fix supper." Pointing at the mules, he added, "Feed them fast and hurry over. Sorry I couldn't pick you up but this is the day for tutoring the old folks. Must educate them enough to vote."

"Heard voting is a problem for you."

"Weird the way the plantation owners don't mind as much as poor whites. We all vote Republican, Lincoln was one. They are all Democrats so they don't want us at the polling places. At least, the Freedman's Bureau is some help."

Seeing his mother at the door, he changed the subject, asking, "How was your trip?" The answer hung unanswered. The expression fixed on the woman's face glued Francisco to the top stair.

"No bureau good 'nuff to save yo black ass." She wiped her hands on a towel before reaching out for both of Francisco's. "G'wan in. 'Speck youse mighty tired." She was a thin woman, wearing signs of toil and worry. She stepped aside pointing to a chair, cushioned in red and yellow. He had dozed through Magnolia's bullheadedness or rather, muleheadedness and once seated, dozed again.

Awakening an hour later, Amos waved apologies aside, saying, "We enjoyed your sleep. The meal could wait. Eat up and I'll show you to your bed."

The following morning they walked to the shack his parents called home. Farming equipment, tools, many worn, some rusting filled a shed. They hitched reluctant Magnolia for sightseeing. He asked about the usual speed of a mule. "Two and one-half miles an hour except for Magnolia who, if in a bad mood, slowed to two miles an hour and if she got cussy stopped till she was darn good and ready."

During one of her stops, Francisco heard of the swift, slave ship built to outsail pursuing British ships. Taking advantage of trade winds, it made a quick run, bringing Amos' parents to Cuba before they were smuggled into New Orleans for sale. With tar smeared on them to conceal wounds they brought a good price.

As darkness dropped upon them, Amos lit a lamp and its glow fell on his mother's blue-dotted dress. Light tumbled across a faded rug, coming to rest on his mother's fingers. She spoke of perpetual worry, "Take Amos outa heah. Dey mad Amos teaching. De whites heah doan like learnin' for cullards. Hayes got 'lected. Dey fizin' tuh take troops Naught. W'en de Yewnited States take de troops, Amos gointer git buhnt or lynched, dat de truth."

"Ma, that's not going to happen. I can't leave. Our people need schooling."

"De white's gwine to get yo kilt!" she wailed, stomping around the room in agitation.

"Amos," Francisco said, "I can get you work up North."

"Where in a mill? Hear tell those workers work harder than slaves, although they move back and forth without fear of the lash or worse. Besides they hire white immigrants. I want to teach. My chance of doing that in the North will be limited."

His mother went out to the well, pumping water into a cup. Tears mingled with each cool sip. "Ah knos. Ah jus' knos."

Francisco trudged to the schoolhouse to sit on a long bench supported by forged stakes and witnessed student tenacity, free from tomfoolery.

He stayed till the next year arrived, planning to leave on Wednesday, January 3, 1877. They sang hymns on Christmas and danced in the New Year, galloping barefooted to notes from Amos' harmonica. His mother wore her best dress though its once brilliant yellow color had faded.

Their last evening's setting sun found the two friends seated on a rail fence. Francisco brushed dust from his trousers as he approached the sensitive subject. "Amos, make your mother happy. Come with me."

"It would make Pa happy too. He never says anything except to sooth Ma, but I can see his fear. He rocks, smokes his corn pipe and pats her arm, but why should they bother over a small classroom? I avoid white women, those curious or wild enough to try a colored man. I've heard they lynch even if the white woman is a prostitute. It's not going to happen. In fact, did you notice that high-yellow girl in class? She's nineteen, a bit young, but when no one is looking, she gives me inviting looks. With luck, I'll die from amorous excess. As for you, any interesting filly around?"

He spilled out his hopeless situation, his certainty that Ben would propose and she would accept, "Why not, when it offers a rich life? I have nothing to offer and she would be perfect in that role."

Amos' fist came up to administer a gentle blow on the chin. "The world is full of women. You're twenty. You'll find another as fetching." In the gloaming, he didn't see Francisco's head shake back and forth. Sounding cheerful, Amos asked, "Do you have news about Rufus? Do you know if he found Sam?"

Caught off guard, crushed again with the guilt of accessory after the fact, his tongue paralyzed. Amos' dark, perplexed eyebrows shot skyward, "What's wrong? Was he shipwrecked?" Impatient for an answer, Amos jumped down from the railing, catching Francisco's arm and shaking him.

Hedging and thinking, Francisco replied, "Didn't know you were that chummy."

"Right, but he earned his peevishness. He had the same bloodthirsty master as Sam."

Having mulled all possible answers, an unsettled voice began, "We both found Sam but didn't find his son. Don't know where Rufus is now but don't believe he will return to the States." He hadn't lied and the sin of omission was not a mortal one. He didn't warn that Rufus was as dangerous as an oversized sail on a small ship. No need. Rufus would not show up here.

Francisco underestimated Rufus' ingenuity. He stowed away on a coffee ship going to South America. Crouching and listening, he heard the moans of a feverish, disoriented seaman and caught conversations of shipmates lamenting Adelard's hopeless condition. In a gale, with all able hands on deck, he stole into the forecastle and found papers belonging to Adelard Gramont. A telltale splash followed a brief eulogy. Rufus had a new name! Perusing papers, he realized the man was twenty years older. If he lived till age eighty, his death certificate would report him to be one hundred. He shrugged. Not his problem.

Francisco suspected none of this as he sat, lingering on that fence with Amos, despairing over their imminent separation.

The following morning, as dawn broke, Amos took him to the station. For reasons known only to her, Magnolia's performance improved and they arrived early. At farewell, Francisco's handshake held until the schoolteacher laughingly said, "Could I have my hand back?"

Letting go, Francisco said, "Thank you, Magnolia. You could have made me late." The mule threw him a churlish glance, flinging an impatient one at Amos. "You'd better go, Amos, before she gets cussy. I'll fill time reading." A whirlwind of emotions engulfed them. Sorrow tinged Amos' features and worry shadowed Francisco's.

Mansions and Mills

At the ticket window, Francisco placed the brown suitcase on a cracked, cement floor and sat a small one on top. It carried souvenirs for all with the exception of Elizabeth. He wouldn't be seeing her and what would a little trinket matter when she would be decked with jewels?

Pulling cash from a pocket, he asked the uniformed man behind a window, "What time is the next train to New Orleans?"

"One leaves in an hour and twenty minutes. Do you want a round trip?"

"No thanks! One way is more train travel than I want." Extending a handful of money, he said, "Help yourself to the fare."

The fleshy, red-faced man took several coins, counted them, returned some and handed him a ticket, scowling throughout the process.

Francisco collapsed on a bench next to a middle-aged woman who whispered, "He don't like you. You talk nasty about his trains and you all don't sound like us. You going to stay in New Orleans?" Leaning closer, she said, "Hear tell it's full of bawdy houses. My son and me are going to Montgomery."

"And I wish you a good trip. If you will excuse me, I must read important papers." He pulled out old letters and tried to seem engaged, ignoring the pimpled son seated next to her. He asked himself, "Are all travelers like this? The only bearable one wore artificial hair."

To his relief, in hustled activity, mother and son left for a connecting train, but the woman's vacant seat filled with a bible-carrying teenager who dumped suitcases and bags of fruit, some of which landed on Francisco. Clad in black suit and white shirt complete with cravat, he offered his fellow traveler a wormy apple. Opening the Holy Book, the boy asked, "Do you all read the Scriptures every day?" On being told that Catholics did not, he jumped up in horror. "Catholics kill Baptists." He scrambled to the most distant corner, scattering and tripping over paraphernalia.

From behind his cage, the ticket dispenser showered Francisco with hostile expressions. He had spotted this one as a

Northerner, but a Catholic was more than a self-respecting rebel could stand. Heathens, idol worshippers filled their cities. Federal troops were full of all kinds but they were going. He assured himself, "Once they disappear, we'll show them who's really in charge."

Francisco ran a finger around his collar, pushing perspiration from one side of his neck to the other. It trickled down his shirt. He hoped his train would arrive before schedule. Avoiding belligerent glances, he returned to his letters. He understood mortification in the vanquished and anxiety in the dispossessed, compounded by competition with the Negroes for the same jobs and the same acres of land. Rage flourished but there was an all-consuming fear.

When asked, he would report encountering a healthy Amos, great parents, fine chess games and a cantankerous mule. Nothing else.

He hoped to board the first ship bound for Boston. In New Orleans, he stepped around cotton bales destined for northern mills and found passage on a vessel bound for New York. Good enough, but it would not weigh anchor for two days. Having found suitable hotel accommodations, he soaked in hot water for an hour easing train-weary muscles.

Sun, peppered with clouds, beckoned him outdoors. Through a warehouse's unwashed windows, he saw zealous men carting bundles for loading. He hesitated at a blacksmith's shop summoned by sharp blows on an anvil, fascinated again by flying sparks. A curved Creole, escorted by her father or elderly husband, smiled an invitation from under a broad-brimmed hat.

This city was a vastness of sun, shade, color and activity. The French and Spanish architecture with its patios, courtyards, gardens, balconies and wrought iron railings so differed from New England with its stone fences now cloaked in snow. High noon arrived, tourism and exotic Creole aromas drifting from Bourbon Street awakened a ravenous appetite. He devoured gumbo soup, crab bisque and a desert of small cakes topped with French chocolate, all washed down with wine or coffee. He lingered as afternoon sun filtered through large windows, its rays creeping along tables, illuminating one then moving its light to another as minutes followed minutes.

At nightfall, following that first hush of evening, the Negroes' baritone chorale rose from the levees, a haunting, sad sound. Drawn by refrains, he wandered towards wharfs of ceaseless activity, bananas unloaded from one vessel and French wine from another. Ships of all sizes, some mooring, some weighing anchor and some in repair. New Orleans never slumbered.

He drifted to the red-light district where drunks stumbled out doors and into streets. Some fell and stayed there till morning. He hoped they didn't have families. That thought brought back Elizabeth's love of babies. Well, Ben could afford them. Lots of them.

On his second day of sightseeing, he stopped in his tracks, drawn to a store window displaying a color-splashed pillow. The owner asked, "You lookin' for voodoo woman? She come back soon. She make pretty girl wild for you."

He laughed, "Voodoo won't help. Pretty girl finds me resistible. I'm interested in that pillow."

"Oh, very soft. Made with dry moss. You sure you no wait for voodoo?" Francisco bought the pillow. He didn't know why.

Stepping on deck, he felt familiar bewitchment. Cooperating winds and the Gulf Stream sped him to New York. From there, he sailed the luxurious Fall River Line to that city. At the foot of Central Street, he boarded a train.

Soon he was in Boston and soon he rounded a corner to a house concealed by junipers and pine trees. Warm light spread through Mr. Hood's kitchen windows, revealing a man leafing papers. Embracing welcome followed Francisco's low tap on the door. "Why didn't you tell anyone you were returning? What route did you take?"

"I returned by sea. Trains are ghastly and the ocean always sings a siren's song."

"Not for me. I think a shot of rum will warm you. You look frozen. Come here by the fire." Reaching for a glass and a bottle of rum, poured with generosity, he said, "I hope the song was resistible. A permanent move for us is necessary and the offer still stands."

Letting the liquid roll around his tongue, savoring its taste, Francisco replied, "Good stuff. You have been most kind in giving me so much thinking time, but I have tasted the sea again and it calls. Sorry for all the inconvenience I've caused you."

"No inconvenience. I have a buyer come April but not at your price. Hand me your coat and I'll heap more logs on the fire." He hung the coat on a round peg. "Be certain of this decision. You will close the door on an opportunity which may never present itself again." He bent towards the heat. "Life as a tailor, though dull, offers longevity and death in a warm bed. The ocean offers, perchance, a cold, watery grave. I took one trip to Europe and swore never again."

"And I swore never a train again. I took the water route to avoid trains and test my sea legs. It's possible to survive a long life at sea. Captain Addison did. John seems happy managing the watery demons. The one in awful danger is Amos." He had promised himself to conceal conditions in the South and now he had blabbed it. He moved closer to sinuous flames, watching blazing, popping wood shoot sparks like fireworks. Smoldering coals, lying beneath, parted into ashes.

Mr. Hood tapped a fist on Francisco's knee, "Now he's the one who should go to sea. Have you suggested it?"

"No use. He insists on teaching his people. Besides, he is enraptured with a girl and plans to die not stretching hemp, but as he puts it, amorous excess."

His host guffawed, "Wouldn't we all wish to?" A knock on the door interrupted. "Forgot, Homer is here with muffins fresh from his wife's oven. You will meet your fellow tailor, if you so decide."

Homer Anderson shuffled in, balancing a platter of muffins while clutching his scarf. He was oval from his nose in an elongated face to shoulders sloping almost to mid chest. The only horizontal thing about him was his wide grin. After introductions, he said, "Heard all about you. Working with you will be a pleasure. Spring is just around the corner and we'll be busy. I'll run along. You have catching up to do." As he opened the door, he tightened his coat against the kiss of cold. "Did I say spring is around the corner?"

Mr. Hood said, "Real nice fellow. Oh, Mrs. Blackwood left a pile of letters here weeks ago." He pulled a package from a cabinet drawer. Letters tumbled onto a table from John, Harry and the skipper.

Mr. Hood bent towards stacks of shuffled papers and said, "Francisco, here among my mail is a letter for you sent to this address. Strange. It must have arrived today."

Francisco stared at the large print, read the return address and dangled it between quivering knees. His shaking hands made opening it difficult. He leaned closer to the oil lamp. A trembling voice informed Mr. Hood, "It was sent by one of his students saying Amos' school was set on fire and a warning was nailed to his house stating worse would come if he taught again. Amos refuses to quit teaching but his parents want him to teach up North. They want me to convince him and want to know if I can provide immediate housing."

Francisco had believed that all he would need was a ship's berth. How could he provide housing? Even Mrs. Blackwood couldn't board Amos. Other boarders would object.

A grieved expression rested on Mr. Hood as he continued, "How can I find housing for him when I don't have a place to live? But I must somehow. Otherwise, they will lynch him or set him on fire. Another method is tying them to a galloping horse. This they call a civilized country!" He paced, ran his fingers through his hair and said, with irritation, "What are you grinning about?"

Mr. Hood threw more logs on the fire, sat, put his feet on a stool and said, "Sit down, be comfortable. We will chat. Look around. Care for the furniture? Guess you didn't consider that this house has to be sold. If I know you, you have enough saved for a down payment on a package deal. Other than clothing and sentimental stuff, we will take nothing with us. If the neighbors don't like a colored person in here, tell them you spent your childhood in the South and you are accustomed to a manservant. As an orphan, I got a break. Now you accept one. You want to save Amos. There is a school in Connecticut where he can teach. Francisco, don't be a fool. You'll never get another deal like this one."

"I have no choice but to take it if I want to spare Amos a lynching."

Settled in a guest room that night, the sea lover dreamt of oceans and gulls. He rejoiced at seeing billowing sails through Captain Addison's porthole. Then blood-soaked Amos appeared. He woke shuddering. He reached for his mother's rosary beads.

The following morning he and Mr. Hood went to the bank, sealing him to Boston where Elizabeth's head rested on another man's shoulder. He didn't inquire about her. He didn't need excruciating details of how Ben got her.

Chapter Twenty-One

Ben didn't get her. Francisco left too early to witness her return from the Parker House. There, Elizabeth's entrance, as usual, turned male heads, much to her escort's satisfaction. Yes, she would do, he thought. The emerald green gown twirled around slender ankles and a sequined comb, holding hair piled high, trapped silvery, candlelit beams. Light, caught in decanters, escaped in rainbow colors journeying over silverware and crystal. Still, everything paled compared to her luminosity.

Satisfied with the modest addition around the neckline, she sat back, relaxed. The gown, before alteration, invited proposal. Once, she had dressed for such a thing but not now. Ben said he wanted conversation without clatter from horses' hoofs, but she wanted one night of enjoying such surroundings assured of not being dragged out a kitchen door. Memory contorted facial features.

He asked, "What's wrong?"

"Nothing. Nothing at all." The waiter extended a menu.

Wistful and lacking forethought, she remarked, "Remarkable isn't it that this lighting can make blonde hair look like gold?"

Jaw tightening, Ben answered, "All that glitters is not gold. I'm sure you know that." So, he pondered, it's still Richard and she doesn't suspect there wasn't an ounce of gold in him. Speak not unkindly of the dead, but how powerful his wish to unveil the truth. Impossible, of course. Concealing annoyance, he ordered, then said, "I suppose you are wondering what I wanted to speak about."

"Yes, but what can't be said in your considerate carriage rides?"

"Some conversations require ambience. First have some wine in preparation."

Taking a small sip, she looked over the rim of the glass and spotted Mrs. Prescott accompanied by a much older gentleman. The teacher's questioning eyebrows shot up but she brushed by without acknowledgment.

Distracted by the snub, Elizabeth said, "I'm sorry, Ben, did you say something?"

"I said will you marry me?"

Her head jerked back as if struck. "You can't be serious. Have I said anything to mislead you? Have I not said to you as to all others, that I will never marry?"

He waited till the waiter served them before continuing in a low, controlled voice, "Let's be honest. You would have married Richard so you have no aversion to marriage."

"That was different. I lo..."

He grabbed her wrist. "Don't finish that sentence, Elizabeth. You might not use the past tense."

"What difference does it make? Past or present. It's the only reason for marriage."

"Don't be silly. There are many reasons for marriage. There's position, money, children, titles, escaping stepparents, a lonesome old age or mollifying a father with a shotgun."

She looked around in desperation. What was it about this place? Was it cursed? Why was it impossible to enjoy good company, a lovely atmosphere and an excellent meal?

"You want honesty, Ben, so tell me. Just which reason do you have for wanting marriage to me?"

"Children, a hostess, grandchildren. Those reasons enough?" He scanned the room for the waiter. He ordered a whiskey on the rocks. Why wouldn't this woman jump at this chance for a fortune? "If you want love, I can't offer it and never will."

Sarcasm blanketed her face, "Oh, because you can't love, you choose a seamstress who will drool in appreciation of a mansion. Will no woman of your station accept that deal?"

"Dozens would and I can love but she wouldn't have me." Eyes clouding, he looked towards the ceiling. "Either she didn't care at all or she preferred life on the prairie."

She stammered, "You can't mean Louise! Do you? You proposed to her? Why would she pass you up for her present situation?"

"For present situation! What situation? She always liked you. She must have contacted you. Where is she?" He threw the napkin on the table. "Tell me that she is well."

He had said honest. He had been honest. It was her turn to be honest. She couldn't tell him where Louise was, but she could tell him how she was. "If we are talking of Louise Morgan from our past, she is well. Ben, she is married."

He stiffened and then relaxed as relief flooded. "At least, she's safe. I've worried so. So many things can happen to a lone woman. You should marry, but I take it you are turning me down also. I still think you would make a great mother and all that stuff. If you change your mind, let me know. On that, let's check out the dessert."

"I'm sorry. I know you are the best man any woman ever refused. Imagine a man in your position proposing to two women lacking money or titles. Rather unusual." She lowered her lids. "I'll have the apple pie."

They made a deal. Mutually enjoyable companionship would continue unless he found another. Darkness enveloped Ben as he directed the horse home. The animal's mane and tail twisted in a wind as turbulent as his emotions. Bruised by Elizabeth's rejection and slashed by Louise's marriage, he wrestled gyrating feelings. He tightened his grasp on the reins and urged greater speed on a mare also anxious for shelter. Solace at knowing Louise was safe battled the agony of knowing her soft warmth belonged to another man. Of course, luscious Elizabeth could have lifted spirit.

The lock opened in silence. He turned the bronze knob only to see a sleeping Charles propped in a chair. Why did he insist on waiting up when he always fell asleep? Not in the mood for chatter, Ben glided to his room. He removed polished shoes and studied the chamber with new, gold and wine drapes. He surveyed cherry furniture and teak flooring leading to a marbled dressing room and wondered why. What good was it? How many months before he would be thirty-six? What was wrong with him? How could two penniless women refuse him? In a house vacant of sound, he saw winged time flying swiftly.

The following Thursday, Mrs. Prescott, pleading a headache, excused the class early. At the last sound of departing feet, the teacher detained Elizabeth with a firm grip on her elbow. "Well done," she chortled, "I didn't think you had it in you. Ben Davis, no less! Is he the one picking you up?"

"If you know him, why didn't you stop by our table?"

"My dear, I don't know him. I know of him. Everybody does. I couldn't introduce you to my escort. It would have been embarrassing. How did you meet him? Better still, how did you land him?"

"We do his tailoring." She reached for her shawl hoping to signal an end to the conversation, but Mrs. Prescott grasped her elbow again, holding fast in spite of her captive's attempt to wrench free. "Why are you interested?"

"Everyone is interested in Ben Davis. Every widow, every politician's ambitious daughter. They thrust dance cards at him and wait around like potted plants clamoring for fertilization."

"I don't know why you didn't introduce your escort. Pardon frankness, but your behavior was uncivil then as it is now."

"Too discomforting. Mr. Davis would have recognized my patron's name. He is married. Yours is not, at least not yet."

She surveyed Elizabeth from head to toe before continuing, "With your looks, you can keep him even after he marries."

"Me with a married patron! Never."

"Well, foolish girl, if you are going to end it, you'd better get as much out of him as you can now." She raised jeweled fingers to brush back a strand of chestnut hair.

Outraged, Elizabeth hissed, "How can you suggest such a thing?"

"Don't be a fool! How else does a woman make it if she doesn't latch on to some man? Do they invite women into colleges? How many women doctors, lawyers or professors do you know? How do you think I made it?"

Elizabeth took a deep breath, closed the door with a firm click, pulled up a chair and said, "Do tell me how you made it."

"I started out by marrying a rich, old man, childless, of course. The inheritance was substantial."

"You married a man you didn't love?"

"Love?" With a deafening bang, she placed a four legged stool two feet from Elizabeth. "Love gets you nowhere."

"I would never marry except for love."

"Then be careful not to fall for Ben Davis because all you'll get is a broken heart. His kind has only one intention for our kind, sweetie, and before he's eighty, it will not be honorable."

Infuriated, Elizabeth blurted, "His intentions are honorable!"

The teacher snorted, "Idiot, what would give you that idea?"

"He proposed. Is that honorable enough? Women who have—who have, you know what I mean, with men they don't love are no better than streetwalkers."

Sadness crossed Mrs. Prescott's face, "I was put in an orphanage at four with nuns neither famed for kindness nor educational skills. I'm sorry you disapprove of my methods, but I was not inclined to mill drudgery nor the degradation of a brothel. At least, I have had my choice of men."

"I've never heard that word." Curiosity won over indignation. She asked, "What's a brothel?"

The older woman exhibited disbelief, "God, how sheltered can a girl be? The activity is the same as a streetwalker, but thankfully, behind protective walls. That brick building on the corner is a brothel. Haven't you noticed all the male traffic? You know, you thought Helen insane but she is clever enough to be aware of the desperation of poverty. She speaks at rallies and she assists at deliveries of illegitimate babies as well as legitimate ones. She is there for the women of botched abortions. No, I won't explain that one! Helen may have a weakness for gossip but she atones. If you want to remain in your pristine, ivory tower, with or without love, I suggest you grab Mr. Davis."

Elizabeth remained frozen to her seat, absorbing revelations she didn't want to believe. Helen, an unmarried woman delivering babies! She'd shut this conversation from her mind. How did she let it happen? Why didn't she force her way out? She picked up paints, paper and brushes, saying, "I won't be back."

In a voice no longer harsh but slipping to a soft tone, the older woman said, "I know, but heed my advice. Use your God-given beauty. Marry him soon. Elizabeth, be safe."

Revulsion attended every step home. How dare that woman suggest a loveless marriage? How dare she suggest using her body as a commodity? There would be no loveless union for her. There was never an excuse. All these women must have one family member somewhere. As for herself, she had guaranteed sanctuary in New Brunswick. A canopy of stars rode overhead. Before long, the luster of stars would be obliterated by smoke in a blistering city in another country.

1876 passed as Ben and Elizabeth attended lectures and openings of art exhibits. Weeks slid into the January of Francisco's return. One evening, cold, wet slush clung to Elizabeth' skirt. She stood on yesterday's newspapers watching them darken from melting snow while she tugged at her boots. Mrs. Blackwood spoke of meeting Francisco on Devonshire Street. "Ye'll be working for Francisco. He bought the tailoring business. Fancy that."

"Why didn't he tell me himself? He wrote to the rest of you. I thought we were friends. Now I'm expected to slave for him."

"I pray ye'll take me other tidings with better heart. As of today, this house is on the market." Buoyancy accompanied her task of washing and stacking pots and pans.

Mr. Blackwood said, "She is anxious to escape this cold but I'm staying to paint and patch."

Elizabeth battled a mixture of angst at news of Francisco's purchase, his failure to announce his departure months ago, his subsequent lack of communication and rage at Mrs. Blackwood. Why can't the woman take different pain pills? None of them cared a fig for her. She still had Ben as a friend till he found a wife, then what? The older woman's twittering over Texas had always irritated her. Everything about this woman irritated Elizabeth now. She deserved a slutty daughter-in-law and the misery of life with Louise. In stocking feet, she stepped off the soggy newspapers, calling over her shoulder, "Whatever is for supper, I don't want it."

Mr. Blackwood exclaimed, "Ain't that a new one? She ate everything except the wallpaper, even that shoe leather you used to cook. Oh, I forgot, not cod."

Within days, hustle, bustle and a boxed Shamrock accompanied a boardinghouse keeper's flight. She left with high anticipation of meeting the new Mrs. Blackwood. Elizabeth continued to steam. This Irish woman will wear out her rosary beads after meeting Louise. How could Mrs. Blackwood have gone unmindful of her welfare when she had said Elizabeth was like a daughter? The British were right about the Irish. They were never to be trusted. Couldn't even grow potatoes. Louise will poke fun at the mangled English and dump future diaper changes on an arthritic back. She might be eaten by grasshoppers for that matter. Good.

She drew herself up straighter, squaring her shoulders, remembering she was a Gilbert. She wouldn't buckle. She hadn't buckled after the night of the torn, pink dress. Somehow she hadn't. Somehow.

On arrival in Texas, Mrs. Blackwood extended an invitation. She wrote, "Come with Mr. Blackwood when he finishes patching and painting." Her ink flowed as she rhapsodized over Louise, the only problem being suspected barrenness but she had a failsafe Irish potion for it.

Elizabeth's aversion to Louise made the option of life in Texas impossible. The panic she once felt over Mrs. Blackwood's move turned to deepening anger which grew with each acclamation of Louise.

Mr. Hood set Francisco to packing boxes. Moaning and rubbing his back, he said, "I thought you were leaving all this stuff."

"Yes, all the furniture but not books or mementoes."

"You have a lot of mementoes!" Although Francisco had removed his jacket hours ago, his blue shirt clung to gathering armpit moisture. Another box of books appeared as if by magic. "Where did these come from?"

"The attic. There are a few more. Be of good cheer. For the next week, I'm doubling your wages. When done here, take time to rest. It will be April before the ladies start clamoring. Montgomery Ward's catalogue gains in popularity but you'll retain the regulars. There's no competing with fitted apparel. You won't see Mrs. Spencer. She never leaves her room."

"Marjorie?"

"No, the mother. Marjorie spends most of her time in Europe. Wears bright colors for a widow. I'd say she deserves them. Did I tell you the Blackwood house is for sale? Would you have preferred that one?"

"No way, but if they are off to Texas, I will miss them. Do you have the new address?"

"I'll see that you get it."

Francisco stumbled down narrow stairs, carrying boxes of books, anticipating an evening of drinking hot toddies by the fireplace. At nightfall, both savored the liquid and the twisting flames while toasting good fortune. Nodding ears did not hear Francisco say, "Guess the first thing is to replace Elizabeth."

Mansions and Mills

With trepidation, the new owner of the tailoring business walked towards the oak door. Spring's balmy breezes claimed its early days as he stepped backwards into the cobbled street to gaze at his acquisition. Not what he wanted but he could sell it once he succeeded in getting Amos here. A hesitant step took him across the threshold. For the second time in his life he reeled at the sight of the luxuriant, auburn hair and the arch of neck. Emerald eyes penetrated like a spike. Why was she here? Why was she not luxuriating in a soft bed? Ben wasn't the type for an extended engagement. Why wasn't she married?

Her level glance dropped to a garnet-threaded bobbin. Suppressing sarcasm, she said, "I was told you ventured into reconstructing the South and now you are my employer. How nice." She managed a deceptive smile.

He struggled through labored breathing to say, "I thought you were m..."

"What?"

An answer came in a flash, "I thought you were moving. Aren't they selling the house?"

"Yes, but I'm staying unless a new owner doesn't want a boardinghouse."

He wanted to ask about Ben, but wavered. The whirr of Homer's sewing machine sobered him, "Tell me where to start." He removed his coat as she slipped a lining into a jacket.

"This needs stitching. It's for Ben. Feel the quality of the wool." Well, the man was still around but what happened? He reasoned, stick around and you'll find out.

Before the day ended, animosity softened somewhat. She told him of her enjoyable friendship with Ben. "He's like having a brother here." He listened with pinched lips. "Mr. Hood is happy you bought him out and I'm happy you did. How was the South?"

"Unsettled." He didn't mention Amos and declined an invitation to join her and Ben for a lecture on Greek art. Though he planned to read a book, he told her, "I must get things settled in the house."

Ben and Elizabeth enjoyed a quiet evening while Francisco laundered thoughts as he watched vertical flames rise from a robust fire. Did she say Ben was like a brother? A brother?

In Texas, Mrs. Blackwood's world exploded. It started with feminine chitchat, and in its course, stories of the boardinghouse. The name Elizabeth jumped from the mouth of the gray-haired matron. "That sweet la..." Severed words fell like guillotined heads at a solid grasp of both gnarled hands. "What ails you, Louise?"

"Red hair? Green eyes?"

"For sure, do ye know the lass?"

"She was so nice, so bright. We thought she was kept by Richard Spencer, but unlike his friends he was too cheap. His type marries darn rich."

Mrs. Blackwood's eyes strayed to a closet jammed with expensive clothing, "Ye were not born to riches? Ye knew both of them?"

Louise asked, "Does she know I'm here? Does she know I married your son?" A slow nodding of an aging head caused a hairpin to fall on the table. Louise picked it up and handed it back for replacement. "And she said nothing?"

"Not one word." She rubbed her eyes in disbelief and took a second look into the closet. "Where do ye hide the jewels? Methinks ye had a blackguard not so cheap."

Small, pink flowers darted between the folds of Louise's skirt as she circled the room. "Why would she let me marry your son and say nothing?"

"Ah, 'tis naught. Lass, I know you be with child."

A keen eared, large form filled the doorway, thunderclouds covering his features. Whiplash in hand, he reached for Louise, tearing a sleeve as she pulled free. Staring at the hanging piece of material, he roared, "I married a slut? If she is with child, I'll rip it out of her."

Mrs. Blackwood tore into her son, "Ye'll do no such thing. Holier than thou, are ye?" Wrath overpowering reason, she raged, "Ye be naught but a bastard yeself! This babe ain't no bastard."

Doubtful, he peered at her, "You would never have a bastard. Not you."

"Had four. Ye sire was a half-breed, a thief and a murderer and me only wedding ring 'tis here." She held up a finger. "Ye be of poor stock. Best stock here eats fodder and moos."

"You said my grandfather was a great captain and my grandmother was sainted."

"For sure. The Gospel truth. Ye'd best be good to their great-grandchild. Pray for a girl meself." She ran knobby fingers over a distraught forehead. "Never had a girl of me own and lost Elizabeth."

In early May, Mr. Blackwood left for Texas, placing the unsold house with an agent. Mr. Bishop disappeared. One female tenant remained with Elizabeth. She arose one morning hailed by policemen asking the whereabouts of the missing Rhode Island man. Expressing doubt at her story, they searched every cranny in the house including shaking out her bloomers and corsets. In ruby-faced embarrassment, she inquired, "What are you looking for?"

"Jewels." The brawny man looked her over from end to end, "You live here alone with him?"

"No. A teacher boards here also."

"Is that so?" Once again he scrutinized her. "Little lady, if you hear from your second story man, let us know."

Second story man! Horror washed over her as when she had learned of streetwalkers, prostitutes, rummies, marrying old men for money and murder in back alleys. If her family knew, what would those country bumpkins say of life in the cultured city? She took comfort in believing there could be no other earth-shaking revelations. She thought she had learned it all.

Chapter Twenty-Two

May worked its sorcery with flowers emerging from ground softened by April rain. Breezes drove nomadic clouds but Francisco saw them as curling smoke from a growing inferno. Everything was wrong.

Letters from Texas changed to frantic telegrams. The agent reported that the house could not sell without a lowered price. Neighborhood quality deteriorated as an influx of immigrants produced crowded tenements and crime. In their search for Mr. Bishop, police knocked on unwilling doors. Known neighbors vacated. Mr. Blackwood implored Francisco to find a suitable boarder for protection of two females and while he was at it, could he keep an eye on the agent? Was the man honest? Sighing, Francisco took on additional burdens.

Otherwise, the carpenter reported all was well except Louise's slight, health problem. When informed, Elizabeth said, "It must mean a family addition."

Francisco answered, "Maybe she is truly sick."

"She's as healthy as a racehorse."

His clicking scissors fell silent, "What makes you sure?"

She pretended engrossment in stacking spools of ribbon, dodging, "I can't reach the top shelf. Would you kindly pass the stool?"

Handing it, he said, "I asked you a question."

In exasperation, she answered, "Can't you see I'm too busy for chit-chat? I have this to finish and I must start on Mrs. Thorpe's riding outfit today." She hated reminders of Louise and bygone days. "I hear from Mrs. Blackwood, you know. Try thinking! Now, leave me alone. I'm busy." She blazed. If Louise refused Ben's offer, she must have married for love and now the joy of a baby. All fulfilled for a trollop. Fury slapped material on a cutting table.

Francisco found a boarder. Scant protection! He was a deaf, retired professor who spent his days feeding pigeons or in libraries. But he was nonthreatening and additional rent.

Francisco set aside the evening of Tuesday, June fifth 1877 to go over April's income. He checked it against earnings of previous years. Revenues were down, much lower than the recession year 1873. If reports that the economy, after four years, was improving, what's wrong? Even paper patterns could not explain it. Not with the level of their clientele.

Faithful Mrs. Carlton ordered in grand fashion as usual, asking Elizabeth, "Do you think the new First Lady's simple attire will kill off the miserable bustle? But no one will get me in her Columbus dress. Imagine never serving liquor in the White House?" She railed like a miffed Democrat, "Plus her husband is withdrawing troops from the South! I predict one term only for this pair."

Two nights later, Francisco checked customer's names. Many who replenished wardrobes every spring had failed to appear this year. He listed names of unseen customers. Cox, Barlow, Hawes, Cliff, Otis, Bates, Field, Baker——the list went on and on. Millinery sales did well. He needed Elizabeth as well for female measurements. He dreaded giving Homer notice but it might come to that.

Setting records aside, he picked up paper, a stamp and an envelope. Amos could teach colored people in New England. Connecticut had approved black education eleven years ago. He understood Amos' stubbornness. The Southerner's opposition to black literacy drove him, but Francisco wanted him to stay alive. Thoughts tumbled upon thoughts. If the tailoring business failed, he could toss it and make a profit on the sale of the house. The house deal was equal to theft. In less than two weeks he would turn twenty-one. Still young enough to start over at sea, but what of Elizabeth? She could find employment elsewhere, return to her family or coax a proposal from Ben. Why hadn't it happened? As for himself, he had abandoned hope. She treated him as employer and no longer as friend. He faced one fact. He couldn't make any decisions before Amos was safe, but the roar of the ocean coming through back windows still beckoned. He dipped the pen in ink, frenzied words covered pages.

The following morning Elizabeth complained of cooking measures at the house. None existed. Neither woman cooked. The professor contented himself with fruit for breakfast, cheese and crackers with the pigeons and all other meals at his nephew's house. With her bountiful appetite, meals out strained resources. Yet, she had sent cameos to her mother and sisters and cravats to father and brothers.

Homer asked, "What do farmers or loggers or whatever they are do with cravats?"

"Wear them to church. Grandfather set rules long ago. You know, he fought with great gallantry at Waterloo and received a large land grant from the king."

"Is that so?" asked the unimpressed Swede. Steam rose from a damp cloth as he pressed a seam open, "Day's getting hot."

On the following Sunday, the church fair took place. Ben visited for a short time. A packed suitcase sat in his carriage waiting for a trip to New York. "My goodness," Elizabeth said, "Bill can't seem to do without you."

"We need to check out some Jacquard looms. Thinking of adding some in a mill. This might take some time. With all the investments he has in this general area, he should consider moving this way." An index finger brushed her chin. "Think you can survive without me without suffering?"

"Though difficult, I will try."

It was a beautiful day, having dawned as pink and cream as baby flesh. The river, helped along by mild breezes, crawled by as they sat under an elm sipping lemonade. For that moment, all was right with her world. She had a long summer of concerts, fairs and picnics before her but the thought struck. Who would accompany her? Feelings of abandonment crushed again. Would she ever forgive Mrs. Blackwood? Ben gone again! He shook hands of well-wishers in farewell, but when he seized Elizabeth's hand her lingering fingers detained him. Amazement crackled in his pupils as he pulled away.

A glazed-eyed and dispirited Elizabeth wandered to a solitary bench. What should she do in a friendless summer? Join another painting class? Take a trip home? Yes, that is what she would do but requesting vacation time or anything from Francisco galled.

Monday morning wore the same pastel shades as the day before. Her silhouette, elongated by morning shadows, raced in front of anxious feet.

Francisco heralded a vacation, "I shall hold a nonexistent flock from the door. Have you noticed a downturn?" Butterflies swarmed in his stomach as he asked, "Do you have sufficient funds?"

"Just about, but I'm looking forward to millinery income on my return. Summer has always been our slow season. Things will pick up." She flashed an optimistic smile.

Certain of her welcome, Elizabeth mailed a letter home that evening, requesting a reply by telegram. Did they have a telegraph office in the vicinity? She recalled isolated homesteads and dense forest, but things might have modernized. A thirteen-year-old boy's hand delivered the reply. She tore it open in the kitchen, for years the site of all tidings, but no one was there to cushion the blow. No Mrs. Blackwood.

Her brother Michael was twenty-two. Ann's husband was twenty-five. Both men lost in the fire in Saint John on the twentieth, sparked in a hay-filled storehouse following a warm, rainless month. They were last seen at the docks where flames swallowed eleven schooners. Philip, the only other male child, excelled at school and planned attendance at the Royal Military College. They would require hired help. Years of Elizabeth's gifts had been appreciated and since they represented American abundance they asked if she might provide financial assistance as in the past.

Staggered by tragedy, she stood, message in hand, contemplating how through generosity, she had promoted the fallacy of gold-strewed streets. Gold for the picking!

After meager food purchases and rent payment, she sent all that was left. She couldn't afford the extravagance of mourning. Tight-lipped, communicating nothing and dejected, she returned to a needle and thread existence.

Ben never wrote when away, but did on this trip explaining that he would be detained because railroad workers objected to a ten percent wage cut. The Baltimore and Ohio railroad laborers agitated for a strike. He feared things would become nasty and he was right. Railroad travel came to a standstill as strikers set fire to railcars. Rioters and Federal troops clashed. It was a tumultuous time but the strikers lost.

On the seventh day of August, a jubilant Francisco said, "The house is sold! One less problem. The buyer will be running a boardinghouse so you won't have to move, Elizabeth. He got a cash advance from a relative who wants him to get a good start in this country."

The corners of her mouth curved down before she opened it to speak, "They sold to an immigrant! Is he British? Mr. Blackwood is."

"I don't know, but I'm an immigrant. For that matter, so are you. They needed to unload it. I just hope they got their price."

Mansions and Mills

She sniffed, "We are immigrants of a different quality. You have acquired culture, at least."

"Started by a self-educated sea captain. Elizabeth, get off this culture thing. Mrs. Blackwood lacked education but you thought her marvelous. Didn't you?"

"She was different, at least till now." Like summer flowers, bitterness continued to bloom.

"What do you mean till now?" The tinkling bell on the door prevented an answer. A customer. The first today but it was still early.

Six days later, the new boardinghouse owner took possession and announced a rent increase without benefit of food once lavishly included. The teacher snorted, "For that much I can acquire better accommodations. Elizabeth, I suggest that you and the professor do the same. Let him bring in his unwashed relatives." Brandishing the classified section of the paper, she howled, "Look where you could live for just one dollar and fifty cents more. I intend to look into this tomorrow."

Elizabeth couldn't afford any rent increase. She adopted the professor's eating habits without benefit of a nephew. She grew tired of fruit, cheese and crackers. Ben wasn't around for frequent meals in posh restaurants. The strike was over. What delayed him?

Work slackened even more. Unsold hats, shielded from sun, remained in the window. The loss of her extra fifteen percent on each sale pinched. One evening, seated in a brown, sagging chair she worked on her budget, attempting to turn pennies into dimes. Crumbs from tonight's dinner of crackers and cheese sat in a tray as she scratched figures on sheets of paper. What was she to do?

On the same evening that Elizabeth added, subtracted, erased, recalculated and fell into a restless bed, Ben returned. Around midnight, he shed a damp, wrinkled shirt and jacket, kicked off shoes and blessed alleviation. It had been awful. The strike, the extent of damage and the economic losses. But he would recover financially. He shuffled through stacks of mail. One envelope jumped at him, an invitation for an affair being held this evening by Mrs. Marcus Hollingsworth Cheever. He cursed, knowing he had to attend, even with short notice.

He was still cursing that night as Charles rearranged his tie, "What boring belle will they pair me off with this evening?"

Charles said, "Sir, you seem to be in a foul mood."

He groused as he swept through the door, "Charles, I will plaster a smile on my face somehow. Why this in August heat?"

The evening was a disaster for guests and humiliating for the hostess. That morning her temperamental, French chef quit, booking passage to France where he would receive proper respect from discerning tongues. He had contempt for Americans who added salt and pepper to his faultless culinary creations and on that day, disapproved of Mrs. Cheever's new stove. He screamed, "Le fourneau. Pouvez-vous le changer?"

She explained the stove had arrived this morning. She rhapsodized over features, but no, she couldn't change it. He viewed her with distain and screamed at the butler, "Commandez un taxi pour moi." Ignored by the butler, he stormed out with his employer at his heels imploring, "Please, guests are coming." He waved her aside like a fly. There was no alternative except engaging the only available caterer.

He was available because he was dreadful. Courteous guests took one bite of every course. Vacant abdomens filled on fruit. The hostess' face flushed as ostrich feathers flew from her overworked fan.

When possible, Ben excused himself. His stomach commanded him home. Unwilling to disturb bedded servants, his famished feet marched up a graveled driveway leading to kitchen leftovers. From the stable came the stallion's neigh for attention. He whispered, "Hush, you are full. I am empty."

Ben's hunger savored a chunk of ham when he saw it. A soft, white, twisted bundle rested on the floor. Rushing to the bottom of the staircase, he bellowed everyone awake. They rubbed sleepy eyes as he dangled an object, shouting, "Which one of you

Mansions and Mills

can explain this? Speak up? What goes on behind my back? Charles, can you tell me?" A befuddled valet shook his head. Ben turned to Mrs. Murphy, "You know. Of course, it would be you." He grabbed her wrist.

Pulling away in tears, she answered, "I wanted to tell you but I promised."

"This is a promise you will break!"

Shuddering at unaccustomed vehemence, she answered every bombarded question. Within minutes, a well-fed horse galloped the streets carrying a very hungry man.

On that same night Francisco paced through rooms asking, "How can I boost income?" He hated terminating Homer but had no other choice. The day's heat held and a shadowed, porch bench beguiled a sleepless, troubled man. Cool breezes shifting from east to northeast played on his cheek. He thought the city had turned off all sound but he heard a clashing on cobblestones. The clamor hurried towards him and turning, rushed under a streetlamp, revealing the rider's profile. Had he not recognized the face, he knew the finest stallion in Boston. Where was Ben going at this hour? He hadn't made an appearance in weeks. Dare he question Elizabeth tomorrow?

The following day, looking over his shoulder, he ventured to ask, "Haven't seen Ben. Is he another lost customer?"

"No, he's away because of the railroad strike. I'm sure I'll know when he returns."

He hesitated before saying, "You must know the strike is over. How long does it take to hear when he returns?"

"Usually within two days. Never longer."

Ten days passed without a sign of Ben. Elizabeth became increasingly nasty and Francisco felt forced to complain, "What is troubling you? We were friends once though it doesn't appear we are now."

Through lowered lashes, she replied, "You showed you were no friend of mine. While away you never wrote. I have no friends. Not Mrs. Blackwood who is in love with her daughter-in-law and my only friend can't get his head out of business."

He preferred strangulation to letting her know he had seen Ben several days ago. He reached out a hand but she slapped it away. "Elizabeth, I know you are upset about Mrs. Blackwood and no doubt about Mr. Hood's departure as well, but I am your friend. I didn't write because I thought you and Ben were a twosome and he wouldn't appreciate correspondence from another male."

She bent, plucking pins from the floor before asking, "Why would a man object to letters from someone so young?"

From her position, she didn't see the painful grimace. So, he thought, she still thinks of me as young. Too young. "Look," he said, "I have a present from New Orleans, I didn't think with your attitude, I'd ever be able to give it to you." He climbed to the loft, pulling a bag from behind bolts of cloth. "See some of the shades match your eyes." Now he realized the pillow's irresistible draw.

She said, "This is the prettiest gift I've received since I was little. When my grandfather was alive, everything I had was pretty. It was my father who lost most of the land."

The last gift from a man came from Richard, shoved in her hand when he got off the ship. She had expected a ring, but from the shape of the box she knew it contained expensive, hand embroidered handkerchiefs. She never opened it.

That evening the new lord of the house approached. "You," he said, "you rent up." She bargained with him. If her rent stayed the same she would clean the kitchen and parlor on Sundays. He stuck a cigar in his mouth, contemplating the offer. "Hokay, I lika you." He flashed his tobacco stained teeth in a huge grin. Within days he added making breakfast for him if not for the other residents. She practiced with the toaster, counting seconds and finally producing ideal toast.

The disgusted teacher proclaimed, "I have found the perfect place at slightly higher rent but it is worth it." She slapped the classified pages into Elizabeth's hands, "Find another place, marry an idiot or enter a convent. Next he'll expect you to clean his smelly spittoon!"

Mansions and Mills

When the door slammed behind her, the smiling owner told Elizabeth, "Be astuto, cara linda, and pay nada."

No longer a naïve creature, she knew what he meant and shook her head with vigor. As she left the kitchen, he opened a cupboard that had once held big, pink pills and now held homemade wine.

In her room, the last rays of sunset yielded to moonbeams as she went over next month's budget. She wished pride did not stand between her and a loan request from Ben. She had seen him this afternoon ride by with an occupant in the carriage. Probably Bill. She'd hear from him within a couple of days. Pencil still in hand, she dozed on the desk. She heard a key in the lock. A sleep-fogged brain saw a swaying figure in the doorway. He had a key!

Her body was pulled from the chair, his drooling, fruity breath plastered her cheek. As she attempted to wrench free, his hand tore the gingham bodice from neckline to waist. He said, "No scream, man deaf, no hear, you rent nada." Shafts of light glimmered on hatpins within reach. She struck him in soft, midriff flesh. Yelping, he released her long enough for a mad dash. As she stumbled down the porch stairs, the hall echoed his voice, "Estupido, rent nada."

Holding tattered blouse to her neck, she looked to the naked Conroy windows once dressed in Irish lace. The O'Brian house wore a for sale sign. She rushed around the corner that once rang with the sound of Richard's carriage. The policeman on the beat ignored her obvious distress, muttering, "Well, well, the little Bishop lady. If we hadn't caught him, I'd pinch her for streetwalking. Probably tried swindling a customer and got her due. Fine with me." He marched in the opposite direction.

Where could she go? Knowing he had returned, she started for Ben's house. Yes, she would marry him. Mrs. Prescott was right. Women needed husbands for protection, for survival. She liked him. She wouldn't be marrying some old man for money. He wanted children as she did. They would be a respected couple with well-mannered offspring, but did she dare knock on his door in this condition? The humiliation of being met by Charles! Then she remembered it was Ben's opera night. She'd go there. Wait by his carriage.

An hour later Elizabeth searched a prosperous, exiting throng. Ben shouldered his way through emerging groups with one hand on a woman's back, shielding her from jostling humanity. A diamond bracelet flashed on her arm as he guided a dark-haired, dark-eyed beauty to his carriage. With wild, disheveled ringlets and a torn dress, Elizabeth didn't want to be seen by this elegant image. She resembled Louise but it couldn't be. Louise was in Texas. Lamplight fell on the woman's face as she turned to smile at Ben and Elizabeth saw the small mole situated one inch from her left eye. Good Lord, it was Louise!

She crawled behind the carriage and backed into an alley. Without warning, the skies opened, inundating a fleeing assembly and a bedraggled Elizabeth. As the foyer emptied, lights switched off. For the second time in her life, she huddled alone wearing a torn, soaked dress.

In total darkness, she staggered to the street, tripping and falling into a puddle. She howled, "God, it wasn't supposed to be like this. Did you not notice? I danced with the Prince of Wales!"

Chapter Twenty-Three

The following morning Ben awoke first. Louise's hair streamed across the pillow like black lightning. He raised a strand to his lips considering how fortunate that her glove fell on the kitchen floor. Had it not been for the inedible dinner, he wouldn't have scrounged for food. He pondered mighty Fate and how it targeted with small arrows.

Her lashes fluttered open. Her head shimmied up his arm to his shoulder, "I will need to adjust to the time change."

"You will. I want you to see Elizabeth Gilbert for new clothes."

"I can't. She must never know I'm here. She communicates with my mother-in-law. Can you imagine the rumpus if Mrs. Blackwood finds me?"

His index finger stroked her cheek before an extricated arm reached for a robe. "Elizabeth won't tell."

"Of course she will. They are as tight as canned sardines."

"No, she won't." At a discreet knock at the door, he handed her a pink, silk robe before saying, "Count to twenty, Charles, then tend to your fire."

Grabbing the robe, she skipped to the dressing room then peeped around the corner at this butler, remembering the frowns of the former one.

Ben said, "The lady behind the door will soon be Mrs. Davis."

"Very good, Sir. Mrs. Murphy informs that she is a charmer." Soon vibrant flames wove through the logs. "Mrs. Murphy wants to know when she should prepare breakfast."

"As long as she keeps coffee available, we'll be content with fruit and cold cereal. Tomorrow, we'll arise at an early hour and she can bring out her ham, eggs and toast." Charles closed the door behind him.

Ben pulled her towards the fire, feeling the lash scar at her waist, "If it wouldn't reveal your whereabouts, I'd go to Texas and kill the bastard. How did you get away alive?"

"His mother hit him with a broom handle and his father hustled me into a wagon. Next day he brought my clothing, cash and put me on a stagecoach. You weren't supposed to know any of this. I just wanted to give Mrs. Murphy Indian moccasins. She broke a promise."

"If she hadn't, I would have broken her neck. You would have sailed off to Philadelphia and out of my life. Would your mother have taken you in?"

"Under these circumstances, I think she would, sitting my stepfather back on his haunches."

"Under these circumstances, I want you comfortable. We'll see Elizabeth on Tuesday."

"Under these circumstances she will surely tell my mother-in-law."

"No, she won't."

She stamped a slippered foot, "She will!"

"She won't."

"What makes you so sure?"

"First, because I will ask her not to. Second, that failing business needs me. Well, not me. It needs Bill and that I can deliver."

"Failing? What's wrong?"

"Boston snobs. When it was owned by a Yankee, they rushed for the talent, but now it belongs to a Catholic immigrant. Problem is I don't know when Bill will be ready for business. His wife rallied after rest in Italy but I haven't heard from him in a few weeks. I hope she is doing all right."

That same morning, because of the sun's inability to pierce dense clouds, Francisco toppled out of bed in darkness thick enough to contradict his clock's compelling message that morning had arrived. Leaves glistened dark green from the night of rain. In a couple of months, as days shortened, those same leaves would be brilliant before turning to depressing brown.

In that ebony dawn, was it thoughts of Amos' stubbornness or sinking revenues that so dispirited? Or was it the sting of discharging Homer? He combed sleep-matted hair and dressed for another day.

Elizabeth sometimes arrived early so finding the tailoring shop unlocked did not surprise, but tripping over her clothing did. She slept in the backroom, yards of material serving as a make-do mattress and wearing a purple gown fashioned for Mrs. Wingate.

"Elizabeth, what the devil happened?"

Through tangled, clinging, wet hair, dark-ringed eyes opened. Explanations began and halted and flowed again. He spewed rage, "Hold it, I'll lock the door. No need for customers now." He secured the "closed" sign.

"After that happened, I didn't know where to go. I thought Ben's back and he might have a solution but she's with him. How did he find her? Why did they let her go when they think she is marvelous?"

This reminded him of Sam's babbling, "Who is she and who is they?"

"Louise and the Blackwoods. I can't go back home either. I can't milk cows or shear sheep. I could feed chickens but never wring necks. I can't plow fields. I can't stand the sight of worms and Philip won't stay."

He ignored a banging on the door, "Can't people read?" He asked, "Who is Philip and why would you work fields?"

"Philip is my brother. My father can't do it alone and the others were killed."

He filled a well-worn peculator with coffee and water. Placing it over a gas flame, he asked, "Who was killed and how?"

"My other brother and brother-in-law in that fire in Saint John. Emily is married and living in Nova Scotia, Ann is frail and the other girls are too young. I can't afford more rent and send money home for farmhands too."

"Elizabeth, please start at the beginning. I understand what happened to your family but this Louise and Blackwood bit is confusing."

She started by telling him how she met Louise and Ben together and ended with saying that they were together again. "I never told Mrs. Blackwood any of this thinking that before she ever met her, Louise would revert to former habits and disappear. Appears she has. She must have tired of the heat, the dust and the cattle. Figures." She told him everything, omitting one thing. She didn't mention Ben's proposal.

Francisco paced the room, agitated fingers sweeping his hair. "We have to get your belongings out of that house. How much is involved?"

"Not much but first you must promise. No altercation with that household lout. I don't want to chance contact with the policeman on the beat. Those empty spool boxes will hold all my clothes and a few books."

By noon her possessions were stacked in a wagon. Fearing Francisco, the boardinghouse keeper hid in the cellar. She checked her handbag. All was intact. She sneered, "Seems the scoundrel has some honor in him." Picking up her mail, she asked, "By the way, where are we putting this stuff?"

"Where else except my house? You can stay there and I'll sleep in the shop."

"That's not fair. I'll sleep in the shop."

"Don't argue. Read your mail."

Mansions and Mills

The wagon rattled over fog-drenched cobblestones as she read one from home thanking her and remarking how fortunate she was to be earning such good wages. Another letter requested her assistance at a bazaar. She gasped at the third. Tearing it open, she exclaimed, "This is from Mrs. Blackwood. She is in Philadelphia, hoping Louise will show up at her mother's. According to her, Louise had a valid reason to leave and she wants continued association." Elizabeth read on, "Goodness, no. Louise couldn't be in the family way. She must be mistaken. Wouldn't you say that's the wrong time to leave a husband?"

She pocketed the missive while conjecture flooded her mind. Louise was back to stay. Did Ben still want to marry the hussy? This business of Texas husband disposal could become nasty. She couldn't be expecting. She theorized that even brazen Louise wouldn't dare to contact Ben in that condition. A sane man would throw her out.

Mist ended and drying breezes destroyed remaining dew. Elizabeth sat on Francisco's porch, envying the uncomplicated lives of ants crawling over ballast stones.

From beneath pine trees, Francisco's voice shattered her thoughts, "You look exhausted. Scoot off to my bed while I scoot off to the shop. Spare me an argument about this and take a couple of days off."

On the following Tuesday, Ben introduced Louise as Mrs. Davis. Elizabeth's brain swirled. Was he a bigamist? Had that Blackwood wedding not taken place or was Louise denying it?

One thing was certain, Louise was with child and it could not be Ben's. She calculated this birth would ring in the coming year.

Stepping from the fitting room, Elizabeth met Ben's steely glare, "No one knows the circumstances regarding my wife and forthcoming child more than you do. I request that those circumstances do not pass these walls, not to anyone for any reason. Mrs. Davis' welfare and the child's depend on it."

Elizabeth recommended hip length jackets for Louise with triple rows of buttonholes and tied skirts. "All can be changed later. You have chosen material well worth subsequent alterations."

As they left, Ben tipped his curved-brim hat and used a brass-handled cane to hold the door for a flustered lady. She carried a huge bag saying, "You must help me. I purchased expensive material and this pattern but find I can't assemble it." She smiled, "As you can see I managed the skirt."

Elizabeth unwrapped cloth riveted with pins, "The skirt will need to be undone." She held up a piece of paper, "This is the apron front. You placed it where the bustle belongs."

"I need it for a wedding. What would you charge to make it?"

"Between undoing and redoing the skirt plus the gored bodice, I will need to charge ten dollars."

"That's outrages. That's my husband's weekly wages. You can do it for less."

"Sorry, but I must charge ten. If you choose to do your own sewing, I suggest simpler patterns."

Gathering trappings, the stranger stormed, "I'll go elsewhere. You are charlatans."

As she struggled with paraphernalia, Francisco jumped to assist, saying, "Good day, I hope you find a less expensive seamstress."

Measuring a sleeve length, he said, "No other will charge less than twelve. She'll be back."

Elbows on sewing machine and palms on forehead, she answered, "I hope not." It was a trying day. Imagine harlot Louise living in a mansion and being blessed with a child.

At this point Mrs. Carlton poked in, "I need only a moment. I must have this design from Vienna. Look at the crisscrossed pleats over the bustle but do you advise such a long fishtail train?"

"As is, the train will swish back and forth but a ribbon can be attached to it and your wrist. You can lift it for ease in dancing. A dust ruffle is advisable."

"I'll be back on Friday for choice of fabric. Look at the clock. Almost five."

Mansions and Mills

Elizabeth's weary eyes looked at the clock. She wanted to end this day, but as she was about to lock up, a bag pushed against her. A tittering voice said, "Ten dollars will be fine. I'm told your work is superior and worth it" She didn't admit to quoted prices elsewhere.

Dark clouds feathered the night as Elizabeth finished dishwashing in the galvanized iron sink. The scent of Mr. Hood's tobacco still clung to a thigh-soothing armchair. She told herself, "This situation must end." Francisco deserved the comfort of his own bed. Daily classified notices discouraged. Lodging in her price range no longer existed. She should have "grabbed" Ben. Now the tart had him but if Louise wanted his money, why hadn't she "grabbed" him in the first place? She told herself to forget Louise and get some sleep. Tomorrow she would start on the ten dollar mess.

The following dawn slate clouds shrouded the sun. Before breakfast, rain-pelted pavements darkened. Sounds of rushing water dimmed a tentative knock. Francisco stood in the rain holding her umbrella over his head, saying, "You left this behind a week ago. I forgot till I saw today's weather." Taking note of the classified pages, he asked, "Any luck?"

"No and I can't abuse your kindness any longer. I must go home and learn farm work and milking cows. I hope they don't kick. I have no other choice."

With mouth as dry as desert sand, he said, "You have another choice though you might wonder if it offers the fire or the frying pan. They say two can live as cheaply as one. We are friends. You could marry me."

Her shocked silence held longer than expected. His embarrassment spoke, "Perhaps that proposal wasn't a bright idea but I'm told friendships make comfortable marriages." He backed towards the door as small twitches jumped in his jaw.

She found her voice, "Wait. You can't walk back without an umbrella." Her trembling hands steadied on an armchair. She fell into cushions while she weighed the proposal. She was twenty-six and penniless. He would be a responsible father and women had children into their forties. Babies! At least she could have babies. Compensation. She stammered, "There is one problem. My family wouldn't..."

"Your family wouldn't what?"

"They wouldn't approve of marriage to someone of Catholic faith." She didn't add that they wouldn't approve of an immigrant from the Azores. In fact, she wouldn't want them to know she had married beneath herself. How could her children be accepted in Anglican circles with a name like Castro?

Shifting position, rearranging pillows, she murmured, "Your religion must change and there is the other matter."

He kneaded the rosary beads, asking, "What other matter?"

A whisper somewhat mollified her answer, "Your name." Words rushed, "Your name would reveal your religion. Doesn't it mean Castle in English? You could change it to Castle. We would need to relocate to succeed in the ruse but Boston is a growing city with a growing population."

Blinking, open-mouthed, he protested, "Relocate? That means starting all over."

"There will be no other choice anyway. Declining clientele will continue."

He moved towards her, brushing wet twigs from his coat. "What makes you so certain?" How had it gone from a hesitant proposal to business?

"Francisco, wake up. Discrimination thrives everywhere, especially in Boston. Homer knew you couldn't make it but hesitated in telling you. A change in name and location is mandatory. Together we can build a new business and have a prosperous family."

He scrutinized every feature from auburn hair to green eyes to dimpled nose and shook with craving. A family? She was accepting him? Why hadn't he thought of discrimination when faced with haughtiness and declining business? In faltering voice, he asked, "With met conditions, is this acceptance of my proposal?"

"Yes. With met conditions, I think we may do well."

He planned better. He would earn her love. If it became half of his, it would suffice. He would work as no other man had to fulfill her every wish. With her, this twenty-one-year-old could accomplish anything!

"Elizabeth, you won't be sorry. I promise." He pulled her forward. As he bent his head, she raised a restraining arm.

Dark brows shot up towards his hairline. Quizzical eyes met her lowering ones. "Did Mrs. Blackwood or anyone discuss what marriage entailed?"

Without mentioning the Colpitts girl's hayloft trysts, she answered, "All girls raised near farms know what marriage entails but please remember we are not married yet."

Ben displayed no surprise at the engagement. Elizabeth must have recognized the man's qualities because this marriage was no money match. She had spurned that opportunity. One thing was certain, this couple needed financial help. Both warranted it.

"Listen to me," he said, "I have checked out ready-to-wear clothing and sales of paper patterns which will appeal to the middleclass. For the wealthy, more high fashion houses are opening. Paris is working to remedy setbacks caused by that disastrous war while Vienna will attempt to further fasten its grip. You have made drapes and you need to branch out. Home décor, upholstering. I'll be honest, Francisco. It would be easier if you weren't an immigrant."

Elizabeth spoke up, "On our wedding day, Elizabeth Gilbert will marry Francis Castle and both the couple and the business will relocate."

Ben's mouth formed a happy, curved shape. "Smart. I'll be seeing Bill Klass. You must remember him." At their nods, he continued, "His mills turn out material suitable to all your needs. He can be talked into a deal. Say, when is the wedding date?"

Half intoxicated at the thought, Francis Castle answered, "Monday, December the thirty-first at ten o'clock."

"So soon? Marvelous. You just might beat the birth of my baby. In what church?"

Elizabeth answered, "It will be performed by a judge."

On his way home, Ben muttered to himself, "Don't know much about Catholics, but I recall hearing none of them feel married without a priest mumbling the words. This can't be his idea."

Louise gave birth on the twenty-eight day of December and Ben could not take his hands off the daughter with coal-colored eyes. "Look," he yelped, "she has your black hair too."

"That will fall out. It might come in red."

"Fat chance. Am I holding her right? Might we name her Susan after my mother?"

"Susan Jane after both our mothers. Ben, put her down before you wear her skin off."

He placed her in the cradle before saying, "Why not Susan Jane Morgan Davis?"

"I suggest you leave Morgan out. Do you want your vaulted friends to hear grandpa was an executed horse thief?"

"Who executed him?"

"Irate former horse owners."

"It's going to darn near kill me, but I must leave both of you for meetings in New York. I want to look in on Bill and talk about helping our tailors. He doesn't keep in touch as he once did."

Elizabeth found a house to her liking. It had dark paneling, a large entrance hall and a barn in the side yard. The man now called Francis Castle hated it. Surrendering the bayside house smarted especially since the cost of the new house took every dime.

On the twenty-ninth day of the month, the groom penned a note to Amos reporting wedding plans and name and address changes. Still harboring hope for Amos' relocation, this information was vital, but Francis requested that no other shipmates be informed. He wrote that as silly as it might seem, he didn't want clan-conscious John to know, fearing Scottish contempt. With regret, he would terminate all correspondence with former comrades. Amos was the exception. Every word agonized. He closed asking if any protecting Federal troops remained in his area.

That same day, Elizabeth visited Richard's grave for the first and last time. Chilling winds brushed lengthening shadows. A purple skirt twirled around iced feet. She marveled that a weapon could end a life with speed while unfulfilled dreams never perished. They remained imprisoned in the prism of memory.

For the wedding, she wore a copper and gold skirt in diagonal stripes with a gold overskirt and side-buttoned jacket. A cone-shaped hat trimmed with ribbons tilted over her forehead and she carried a gold parasol. She took her vows composed and expressionless; the groom effervesced.

Elizabeth vetoed a honeymoon, stressing the need to move with utmost speed. She said, "We must get started as soon as possible. Time is money." He insisted on a wedding picture. The photographer attempted the familiar pose of seated groom and standing bride. He gasped as Elizabeth pushed her new husband aside, seated herself and spread the striped train. Her Lilly Lantry bustle collapsed as she sat and sprung back to position when she rose, facilitating adroit gymnastics. She instructed, "Be sure to include the entire train in the picture." The astounded man moved the camera backwards. His skill managed to depict the groom.

Francis celebrated with a sumptuous meal, waving away her question, "Can we afford this?"

Reaching to sandwich her hands, he answered, "No, but we don't get married every day."

He carried her over the threshold into a house decorated with ribbons and banners. "How sweet of you," she said, "everything decorated in pink."

That evening, Mr. Castle sat in the only room he liked, designated as his inviolate library. The walls wore cream-colored, flocked wallpaper. Treasured books assembled in oak cases while blue drapes picked up the color in a multihued rug. He could breathe in this room, although at the moment, breath and serenity eluded.

Shaking fingers pulled out a pocket watch. What is a groom's prescribed waiting time before climbing the stairs? He recalled Elizabeth could be heard in her boardinghouse room for at least thirty minutes before light vanished under the door. What do women do during that time? Do their manes receive one hundred strokes? Do they cream their toes? He decided to wait thirty-eight minutes. Various emotions assailed from panic to eager anticipation that sent blood flowing in pulsing surges. It had been a momentous but exhausting day. Perhaps this matter should be put off till tomorrow night. Bad idea. Tomorrow she would push work preparations which meant lifting and dragging and an aching back. No, it had to be tonight. With postponement, what would be her opinion of him? Imagine a former seaman lacking salt. He checked his watch. Time's up.

As he climbed the stairs, he reminded himself to curtail overenthusiasm. Her trepidation could surpass his. His first glance into the room revealed a form resting on one side and facing the window with a Balsamic moon bathing her white-clad, curvaceous figure. She hadn't brushed her hair. She hadn't unpinned it. It remained knotted. He placed a gentle hand on her shoulder and turned her toward him.

She did not stiffen or cry out. When she closed her eyes, she didn't think of England. She thought of babies, lots of babies and submitted to this unavoidable, foreign invasion.

Chapter Twenty-Four

In mid-January, under a warm overcoat, Ben wore a stylish suit complete with waistcoat and tie around a stiff, standup collar as he ventured through a cold morning. He pulled up the coat collar in a futile attempt to warm ears reddening under his fashionable hat. He left early. Had he postponed, he would have seen the telegram placed in a maid's hand.

After three days of unproductive meetings in New York, he set off for Bill's Fifth Avenue mansion only to be greeted by a black wreath on the door and a red-eyed butler. He said, "Sir, services were held four hours ago." Ben pulled out a calling card, turned up the left, lower corner and positioned it on a tray before retreating. What else could he do except leave that message of condolence? Outside his hotel, a paperboy sold details. She was thirty-three. How old were the Children? Why hadn't Bill informed him?

Back home, his eyes fell on the telegram amid piles of mail. He telegraphed Bill explaining the missed message and stating a letter would follow. He did his banking, dithered between purchasing an emerald or sapphire brooch, bought a gold, baby cup and rushed home for an early dinner. Fatherhood changed a man's habits.

That evening, Louise's tears over Susan's colic sidetracked letter writing, "Honey," he said, placing the baby stomach down on his knees, "be glad that she has such good lungs. Don't cry so."

She countered, "You should have seen me cry when they put red-hot frying pans on cattle's brands."

"Educate me once more. Why did they do that?"

"They did it on stolen cattle, covering the burn with grease. Later they applied their own brand."

"Such preferable associates." He couldn't resist the slight dig. She wiped away tears and smiled.

Ben approved of the tailoring shop's name change to Castle Fashions but frowned at evidence of minuscule activity. Finished and unfinished garments once crowded racks, now wooden poles sat unclad. He consoled, "Starting anew is difficult but things will be buzzing again." Bill had invited him. Was discussing business with the grieving man possible?

If he left for New York on Friday, the first of February he could see Bill on Sunday. As luck would have it, on the last day in January, thirty inches of snow visited Boston. Another delay at assisting the beleaguered tailor. It was mid-February before Ben visited the haggard and dejected widower. Ben began, "I need to talk business but perhaps anoth..."

"No. Now is fine, but what brought you here last month?"

"Meetings on those new ore mines in Michigan and meetings on copper mines. People think this newfangled telephone is just a toy, but Edward Savage, our police chief, had one installed last December. It's just the beginning. There will be need for wiring."

"You're right. Another issue is steel. Railroads will crisscross the West as they steal more land from Indians. We will need discussion on pig iron and this Bessemer smelting method. Means must be found to produce stronger steel."

Ben shifted his weight in an overstuffed chair, saying, "Agreed, but at the moment I'd like to cut a deal on fabric for Elizabeth Gilbert, or rather, Elizabeth Castle."

Astonishment engulfed Bill's face. "She married! Who is this lucky fellow?"

"Francisco, though practicality changed his name to Francis Castle."

Bill understood, "She made a good choice. Couldn't have found better."

"She could have found better. She could have married me but that's a long story. The issue is they have to start over. I may have talked you into cotton mills but you raced ahead and I've heard you are manufacturing various materials."

"That's true and two small mills on the Blackstone River are creating distinctive textiles." He scratched his forehead, features washed with conjecture. "You married Louise and she married Francisco! I have been out of the loop but there was..." A sob seized his throat. Regaining composure, he asked, "Why this interest in her welfare? She must have turned you down."

"She's still a friend." Thinking of Susan, he added, "I'm going to owe her a favor. I suggested a loan but Francis tells me her pride won't allow it. I thought quality fabrics such as you produce, at discount, would give them a start."

"Fabrics? Did you say discounted fabrics?" The older man rested both hands against his cheeks before continuing, "Forgive me, these days my mind tends to wander."

"Of course, we can put this matter off. I'll understand if you aren't the least bit inter..."

Slapping a fist into his palm, Bill answered, "If this is what you want, I'll sell at cost, not discount. Elizabeth deserves some good fortune after that Spencer scoundrel. I understand your marriage proposal. She is a refined and alluring creature."

He circled the room, his expression veering back to gloom, "Janet is of great concern, being inexpressive since the loss of her mother. I was thinking of changing her present tutor. Perhaps a younger one would animate her. Our mutual friend, Hugh, has recommended a young woman. I hope twenty-one is not too young."

He adjusted the black, mourning band on his sleeve before opening a cabinet and pouring imported fluid into glasses, saying, "As I recall you like rum. Let's drink to tailoring."

On a glorious morning, Elizabeth attached herself to a window and contemplated the wonder of snow. Amazing how tiny flakes accumulated into embankments. Somewhat like life's tiny decisions becoming heavy weights. If she had not married, would existence in New Brunswick have been less troublesome? If Mr. Hood and the Blackwoods had stayed would she have continued on that same daily track? If Richard had married her would he be alive? If she had married Ben——.

Her husband had his tortured "ifs". If not for Mr. Hood's fall, his path and Rufus's murderous one would not have crossed. If not for embedded Amos, he'd have carried cargo, accrued a fortune and never known of Susan's birth. If not for an inscrutable, adored woman, he would not be a cash-strapped tailor.

Elizabeth surveyed how sunbeams on snowdrifts caused iridescent sparks and felt sparks of anger towards Ben and his upbeat attitude. How did he think things would be buzzing again?

Snow withdrew under the bombardment of sunlit days and a smiling Ben nudged Francis towards a filing cabinet. "Make a list of all the material you need, even include some upholstering fabric. Plan lavish weekly advertisements. I have found the right man for upholstering. His name is Eric Kirkwood. Hire him and he can teach you."

The tailor fell backwards. "Impossible, I can't supply wages for an employee and I can't afford stock like that."

"Listen, Bill Klass is selling fabric at cost, all kinds."

"Why? How do I pay for even that?"

"I'll pay him. You can repay me when cash rolls in."

Francis' head shook a solid no, "Elizabeth would balk at charity and where do we get the customers?"

"Louise will get the first ones. She knows lots of gir..." He swallowed, "I mean ladies and they know lots of other ones." He hesitated under the younger man's knowing expression before explaining, "You know how it is. Men let them select things and the bills are paid on time. You just send the bills to business addresses. You keep all the accounts, don't you? Tell Elizabeth nothing."

Gripped with doubts, he scanned the broad-shouldered man asking, "What's in it for you?"

Ben crossed his fingers behind his back before answering, "Believe it or not, this is Louise's idea." He uncrossed them and continued, "She has always liked Elizabeth and that is gospel truth."

When Elizabeth inquired about money, Francis replied, "Money is my problem. You are no wizard at handling it."

She wrote home saying that her new husband controlled finances. She could no longer assist. Besides she planned to have a large family.

But where was it? Her mother conceived within a month. Why had she not done the same? It was not from lack of effort. She managed to convey fervency but eschewed tenderness. After achieving the intended purpose, why stroking or unnecessary murmurings into her bored ears? Francis discovered that she was the one who wanted to roll over and go to sleep. Crocuses journeyed skyward as Elizabeth's calendar scored another disappointment. She circled a date twenty-eight days from this one.

At times Elizabeth chastised herself. Her spirits should parallel growing business success. Mr. Carlton lost weight and carted in boxes of clothing in need of major adjustments. Mrs. Carlton whooped, "He no longer wheezes. Leave narrow seams so he won't dare gain weight."

The once paunchy senior edged away from his wife, passing through a throng of stylish, giggling girls surrounding Eric to whisper in the owner's ear, "This place has the tone of a brothel."

"Don't say that to my wife, please."

"And don't tell my wife I said it."

"They are just exuberant, young women looking for a husband and Eric is easy on the eye." Scissors whistled as he went back to work.

Louise delivered customers. It was just a matter of sending Betsy, who had abandoned skin sinning, in pursuit. She said, "There is a new bunch. The moneybags will grant all their demands. When replaced, the girls will send the latest ones and so on. These men shed women like snakes shed skin."

Louise replied, "Just keep them coming. I've always had a special liking for Elizabeth. I'd like to see her rich. Heard you married a bookbinder. Good!"

So the woman that Elizabeth called hussy sent wealth producing hussies. She questioned her husband, "Where are all these customers coming from?" Francis shrugged, innocence spreading over his face like melted butter.

Summer dispersed its last floral perfume and veered towards autumn. Days became insultingly short. Maternity eluded Elizabeth. On Friday, October eleventh, at fifteen minutes past five, she hurled a forlorn look at the sky as the sun set once more on hope. What was wrong?

On the following Monday, Ben swaggered in, whispering, "It may be improper to say, but I can't keep it to myself. Paternity will visit me in April." Ben missed Elizabeth's expression of unadulterated hatred. She missed seeing Francis slip him a folded check.

Before departing, Ben said, "I'm sending Louise to examine that gold fabric. What is it called?"

In a frigid tone, she answered "Shantung."

Once his benefactor was outside, Francis asked, "Do you harbor resentment towards him?"

"Of course not. It's her. I would tell Mrs. Blackwood the truth except for Ben, and except that no matter how she laments having no daughter or granddaughter, she doesn't deserve to know. She said I was like her daughter then went agog over a harlot and deserted me to..." Remembering that man's breath and slobbering mouth, she shivered. With acid smile, she continued, "Frankly, I'd love giving Louise grief."

"She is your friend and Mrs. Blackwood left because of crippling arthritis. In both cases, charity is in order."

"Louise isn't worth a decent woman's friendship and I'll never forgive Mrs. Blackwood. Don't you dare sermonize again, Francis." All said with the dismissive swish of taffeta petticoats.

Wednesday, January first ushered in the year 1879. Within a few days, the year ushered breathless hope. Did her husband's face plunge at the news? Maybe surprise explained facial contortion. Elizabeth counted on fingers standing up like tin soldiers. August or September! She'd be twenty-eight. Still time for several more.

On the sixteenth, ten inches of snow fell on the city. Eric suggested that shoveling should be his responsibility. He said, "You have a home. I don't. You take care of that and I'll take care of shoveling here." On February the twentieth, fresh snowfall measured ten inches. Eric scooped snow as a well-dressed man intent on affairs walked up, panting, "Are you Mr. Castro?"

"No, be careful, don't slip." What possessed this man of at least sixty to be trudging through snow?

"Do you know a tailor named Castro?"

"I know only one and his name isn't Castro."

"Do you know anyone named Blackwood?"

Eric stifled impatience. "Please move to the side. I'd like to clear this out for customers, should they venture out. Blackwood? Unusual name." Moping perspiration from his brow, Eric said, "Don't know any."

When Francis arrived, Eric said, "There was a man here asking about Blackwoods and Castros. Told him I don't know anyone with those names. Do you?"

Stiffening, he answered, "No. Did he say why he was asking?"

"Didn't say," Eric mumbled, housing the shovel behind the door, "but it must be important to send him scampering through snowy streets."

Francis speculated. Could this be a search for information on Richard's murder? Unlikely, but what did he want? Would he return?

The stranger didn't, but he canvassed the old neighborhood tenanted with fresh inhabitants. After verbal boxing with the boardinghouse keeper, he reported to his employer that the search was useless. He moved on to the next case.

In March, Elizabeth awoke to the sound of gossiping birds and abdominal cramps. Doctor Mason's efforts could not prevent fetal loss. Consumed with despair, Francis' obvious relief antagonized her. She interpreted it as joyful deliverance from fatherhood. She didn't hear him say, "Doctor, you did your best and the important thing is saving her. I don't know what I'd do if I lost her." The tortured thought manifested in his voice. But she did hear him say, "Doctor, I'm grateful." Misconstruing those two words, her jaw tightened.

Attempts at lifting her depression misfired. Flowers brought forth the question. "Have you ever wondered why flowers are sent to funerals? Shouldn't they be reserved for happy occasions?" Depression turned to fury at all his rompish efforts. Her moods would have worsened had she heard of Louise's premature delivery of fraternal twins at the exact time of the vernal equinox. He spared her the knowledge. She would learn soon enough.

Francis knew of her eagerness for children. She had not known of his aversion, but he was determined to avoid repetition of her recent ordeal. He had no intention of jeopardizing her life when too many women died of this birthing thing. Old seamen like Harry learned means of prevention in various countries. The entire universe was not inhabited by puritanical Americans. He would visit Harry. On the day he left Boston, young buds were springing to attention and Elizabeth recuperated on an olive-green sofa, the New Orleans pillow cushioning her back. "Dear," she cooed, "do hurry back. The wallpaper in the bedroom is depressing. In your absence, I'll have it changed to a cheerful color."

"Pink would be cheerful."

"I was thinking yellow. Never pink."

"Whatever pleases you." Picking up a jacket, he stooped to kiss her forehead. She clutched his cravat, eyes narrowing in a

Mansions and Mills

mysterious way as he raised his head. He drew in a gulp of surprised air, halted in his farewell by her delayed release.

"As I said, hurry back." The tenor was seductive, the feline smile inscrutable. "I'll be fully recovered soon."

Questions jumbled as he hurried to the station. Has his wife turned coquette? Was his breathlessness a result of her behavior or a steep incline? Guidance from Harry could come none too soon.

Harry waited in a buggy at the foot of Central Street in Fall River. Francis elbowed and shouldered his way through passengers going and coming. Newly arrived immigrants bound for work in the mills and jabbering in foreign languages jostled him. The Fall River Line had brought them from New York.

A smiling Harry drove them up the steep hill. Scrutiny displayed a grimy city, streets garnished with cotton dropped from bales and leavings from overworked horses doomed to early deaths. His host reassured him, "I'll rush through the smelly places. All waste goes into the river, from mills, people and animals. There's even a direct drop for unusable fish parts."

Francis held his nose. Soon the fresh air of Westport mingled with the sounds of clucking chickens and the moos of Harry's cows. The tailor shook a welcoming, slate-colored, feminine hand. "Glad to meet you." she said, returning to plucking feathers from a headless chicken. "This fellow is supper. How come it took you so long to visit?"

"Up to my ears in earning a living."

The following morning the two men went through fields and barns. Pointing, Harry said, "See that bull, best around. By the way, do you know John hasn't heard a word about Rufus? With his disposition, someone might have heaved him over the side."

"I was always scared stiff of him." he replied, vaulting a fence as the bull approached. "Is this brute dangerous?"

"Only if he doesn't like you. Why did you fear Rufus? The captain had his rules about you but every sailor knew that one hand on you and they would be dealing with Rufus. Nobody wanted to ruffle him. The Hausas from Africa were fierce to begin with and he was heated about something. The Bantu tribe, like me and Amos, took to the Baptist faith and prayed for freedom while his breed made uprisings. Guess if it wasn't for Abe, we'd still be praying."

"Guess you are right. Harry, I need to ask you," he shook a fencepost as if to gauge its sturdiness before continuing, "it's about women."

"Women? I'm no expert. You should ask the skipper. Now, there's the expert. Didn't leave bastards behind though, so it's said. Our captain knew means of avoiding all kinds of shipwrecks."

"That's what I..." Bewilderment flowed over his features. "Captain Addison? Our Quaker skipper a seducer?"

Now Harry registered astonishment, "During those chess games, he must have told you about women."

"He said to respect them all like queens."

"That's no surprise. Story was he adored his Hawaiian wife. Her death hardened him the men said, but he softened before he left the sea. Must have been because of you or your chess games." He chuckled, "That game civilized those brine rats a bit."

The sun climbed the sky and Francis removed his jacket. Absorbing the warm rays, he shook his head, "I never knew any of this. How did you find out?"

"I tasted salt for years with men who knew him when. The mongrels love to set you right about captains." Looking across the field, he said, "Look at that frisky calf."

Having wandered away from the subject, Francis squirmed over means to return. Rose-cheeked, he reintroduced the topic, "Harry, I need to know how to avoid shipwrecks, as you put it, with women."

Harry's eyebrows shot up. "Have you got a filly on the string?"

"I don't have a filly. I have a wife."

"Wonderful. Why didn't you bring her?"

"She is recuperating from a mishap. By the time I get back she'll have recovered."

Harry's eyes flashed, "I understand. You want to wait because you are so young. Francisco, you've heard the saying that a prudent cavalryman keeps a sheath on his sword."

"That won't do. She's not stupid. You must know other ways. The passing of the Comstock law made getting information difficult, but it's out there and if anybody knows, you do."

"Well," he said, rubbing a pain in his back, "it's a violation of the law but I will explain the French method, the Indian method and the Chinese method because if you see hungry, ragged, mill children, exhausted and dying mothers you know the laws are foolish."

When Harry drove his friend to the station, the buggy wheels made sucking sounds as they forced their way through mud. As Francis swung one foot on the train, he said, "We went too long between meetings. No more! See you soon, pal."

Rubbing throbbing pain, Harry answered, "I hope so."

Before he left Francis knew the name of every cow and the nasty bull named Rufus. He knew the New Bedford and Fall River milk routes. He hated the city of hills and mills. He decided only a catastrophe would make him live there.

He arrived in Boston with knowledge of Yin-Yang harmony, Indian potions, coitus obstructus, coitus reservatus, and coitus interruptus but with uncertainty of mastering any method or of their effectiveness. The birth rates in India and China promised little.

Daylight had deserted the city when he was greeted by smiling Elizabeth. "Look, dear," she said, while leading him to the yellow-papered room, "I have purchased all these pretty things." Sheer, lacy, ruffled feminine garments adorned every piece of furniture in shades of blue, green, yellow, white and black. She purred, "Choose the color."

He moaned, could he remember Harry's instructions?

Chapter Twenty-Five

A sizzler, the first day of June hit one hundred degrees by one o'clock. By midnight, the thermometer recorded eighty. Saturday, the twenty-eight waited till two to reach the one hundred mark. One person appreciated the heat, a wilting Francis using the excuse of temperature to beg off from a newly predatory wife. What happened? Did miscarriage bring about this change? Within seven years she had traveled from jubilant, heel thumper to cool aloofness, to suitable wife. Now this. At times, she regarded him with inscrutable, dilated pupils. What twirled in her brain?

In July, a yellow fever scare kept many home. Elizabeth believed seclusion would initiate conception. August came and went. Flowers exhaled their last aromas, drooped and dropped. Orange, red, gold then brown leaves polka-dotted what grass remained. Still no pregnancy. Snow sat on rooftops and 1880 inched closer when Ben announced another expected family addition. This one was due in June. Elizabeth whispered to a bored firmament, "I hate that woman." She jabbed scissors into felt intended for a hat, "Four, this will make four, Ben."

"Yes, isn't it wonderful? I've dropped by for Susan's birthday dress, but I'm still going to get her a doll even though

Louise warns me not to spoil them. Tells me we can't raise spoiled brats like the Spencer boy, but one doll won't hurt."

Casting a tense glance at his wife's stiffening spine, Francis said, "Ben, I've been thinking of moving the upholstering to Charlestown. Eric could handle it."

"Need capital?" Ben asked, taking the dress from Elizabeth while turning the doorknob and tinkling the bell.

"No, but thanks anyway." Blasting cold skated through the closing portal.

Elizabeth hissed, "Need capital! We don't need anything from that woman." She chafed over Louise's condition and criticism of Richard's son.

"Dear, it's his money."

"His money is her money." She removed an empty spool of thread from the machine and threw it into a wastebasket with unaccustomed force, emphasizing, "We need nothing from a woman like that."

He flinched, eyes boring the floor. If she knew how helpful Louise was, fury would erupt like a geyser. Did she despise Louise because of an unsavory past and a possibly bigamist marriage or was it pure jealousy? Did she hunger for a gown of Chinese pongee as worn by Louise instead of the serviceable fabric now encasing her figure?

He envisioned the landscape of that figure outlined in moonlight. There was a gibbous moon tonight promising to illuminate contours of her demanding form. Nine months had elapsed since the miscarriage, but in view of her lascivious behavior, could his best efforts bar fertilization forever?

Discouraging news arrived of Harry's health. He wrote of increasing pain which he attributed to tending cattle stricken with hoven, but the doctor speculated on a kidney problem.

The next letter came from Harry's wife. It was kidney failure. Because it would mean more to Francisco than her, the widow included an unopened letter from John. In it, he asked if Harry knew how to reach Francisco. Every step weighed as Francis ambled towards hungry logs eager to devour the Scot's letter.

Elizabeth expressed surprise at his sorrow over the death. "For heaven's sake," she complained, "he was just a shipmate like this Amos you fret about."

"For four years, along with John and the captain, they were my only friends. For that matter, what friends do I have here? Well, it can be said that Ben has become a friend."

"He's a consumer of our labor and talent." Kneeling before a manikin, pins between her teeth, she went on, "Why do you fret about Amos? If he doesn't want to move, so what?"

"This is an election year," he said, rubbing the back of an exasperated head, "Democrats don't want darkies voting. Amos is in particular lynching danger this year." Before noticing his wife's incredulity, he walked to a desk, picked up a pen and said, "I'm writing again, pressing the point."

"Are you saying that Amos is a pickaninny?"

He grimaced, "Please don't use that expression." Forcing modulation in agitated vocal cords, he added, "Harry was too. Didn't I ever say?"

"No, I thought we were of the same color. Do you intend to have Amos reside in our home?"

Before he could respond, the bell on the door tinkled, "Good day," tweeted Mrs. Carlton. "I understand that the bustle is larger this year! I'm dreaming of summer. This lawn material, does it mean it comes in green only?"

Elizabeth laughed. "No, it comes in many colors and it will be cool, but you are rushing the season."

That evening Elizabeth returned to the interrupted subject. In vinegary, soft tones, she said, "Francis, under no circumstances will Amos spend one night in this house."

On Sunday, the twenty-seventh day of June the temperature reached one hundred degrees and after nine hours of labor, Louise gave birth to an eight pound boy. At fifteen minutes before midnight Ben rushed in, whooping with joy as his day's swelter dripped on her sheets. Sweetly, she asked, "Darling, have you had an uncomfortable day?"

On the tenth of July, the sun broiled Boston again with another dose of one hundred degrees. Louise and baby enjoyed Bar Harbor while Ben coped with whining children and Mrs. Murphy who refused to serve anything requiring heating. Charles relished his week of vacation at Hyannis while the Davis offspring filled on cold chicken and ice cream.

Autumn nudged summer aside when Bill Klass accompanied Ben. They viewed the Charleston shop managed by Eric with two added employees. "Bill, they have been turning a considerable profit since summer and you are part of their success. I'm happy seeing Elizabeth having things she deserves like fine china and silverware. She works only three days a week now. Needless to say, paper patterns decreased demand for her services. She's working today. Why not check the Boston place while you are here?"

Elizabeth looked up from color samples as the two men walked towards her. Bill had lost weight. He was narrower than Ben and an inch shorter with hair whitening at the temples. She had never noticed the chiseled profile and the cleft in his chin. In fact, she hadn't noticed his handsomeness at all. The black band on his arm jumped at her, "Mr. Klass, I'm so sorry. One of your parents?"

"No, but thank you for your condolences. My, how you have expanded." He strolled around, inspecting everything from floor to ceiling. She raised questioning eyes at Ben. He lowered his lids and shook his head. Thinking of how many parents lost children, she wondered. Could it be?

With Bill out of hearing, Ben pulled her aside, "It was Mrs. Klass but don't mention it. He is having a rough time."

"Men don't mourn for long." Compressing her lips, she continued, "The Russian Czar has remarried after two months. The first winking petticoat will get him."

Ben tensed, clamping the back of his neck. "He's been wearing that band for close to three years. It will take an exceptional petticoat to get him. At present, he is consumed with his children. You know you have changed from the appealing girl that enthralled so many of us."

Prolonged silence deafened. There was a penetrating, cold stare, which masked torment. At last, she said, "If you are referring to those days of youthful exuberance, that was eight years ago. As they say, much water has gone under the bridge. Some murky."

She took a wide berth around him, "Please excuse me. Mrs. Cole has an appointment."

Remembering their friendship and remembering what he owed her, he regretted his words. He recalled having overheard her telling someone of how she knew of his marriage long before anyone else did. She was protecting his children and Susan in particular from scorn. Boston reeked with scorn.

Bill watched her movements. Putting a hand on Ben's shoulder, he whispered, "Ravishing beauty remains. Let's say goodbye and stop at the coffee shop down the street."

Mrs. Cole's heels cooled as Elizabeth dallied at a window while watching the two men stroll away, both dressed in Prince Edward style coats. She saw a growing breeze lift the corner of Bill's black one as he raised a manicured hand to catch his top hat. Widowed for years! Hungry spinsters must be drooling. A man with handsomeness and wealth is tempting. Yes indeed, she ruminated, very tempting. The two men faded into darkening day. She leaned closer to the glass, catching artful reflections of ignited lanterns when she heard a sharp voice, "Mrs. Castle, I'm waiting."

"Sorry, I was watching lanterns chase away darkness."

"How poetic, however that won't get me home for dinner." She leaned against Elizabeth's ear, "I can understand lingering glances over those men. I have a thirty-year-old daughter. Is the arm band mourning a wife? If so, could you arrange an appointment for her synchronized with his next one?"

"Afraid not. He's from New York. Can't say when he'll be back, if ever."

"In that case," she snapped, "let's get on with this."

Mansions and Mills

Meanwhile, as daylight yielded to darkening skies, Amos ran up the porch stairs in eager anticipation of reading a letter from John. He lit a lamp, settled under it and cut the envelope open with a knife. It said all had lost track of Francisco and this matter could not wait. His eyes widened as he read. Tearing off his brown jacket and throwing it on a chair, he snatched writing material. He would send this news to Francis first. John's answer could be postponed.

He turned at the sound of moving hinges. The noose slipped over his head as struggling hands and scrambling feet splattered ink on John's letter. Angry boots stomped on it as one man growled, "You won't be voting in no election. Before this night is over, there ain't gonna be no darkie voters."

Another shouted, "Let's hang him from his own tree. Let his wench find him."

News from Bella arrived just before Christmas. So many of her people were going to try life in Kansas, and without Amos she would do the same. Things might be better there.

Francis stared back at the face in the mirror staring at him. He didn't think Bella would find life better in Kansas. He felt older than twenty-four. Elizabeth would not understand. Was there anyone to talk to? He knew the answer. Another thing to bottle up. Another world of silence. There is no true friendship between races. Everyone knew that. Everyone except a man named Amos and a man named Harry and a man named Francisco Castro.

He wished he could spill his feelings to Captain Addison or for that matter to anyone. Slipping the rosary beads into a pocket, he donned a heavy coat over his blue vest and jacket and lifted a hat from the hall rack. His wife's head spun around, "Where are you going at this time of night?" The answer was a turning key.

He took no interest in Christmas decorations. She mocked, "See, all you do is drape strings of cranberries, like so. I'd understand if you had a runny nose, but you are having a childish fit, over what?" Ivy tumbled from bowls filled with holly and apples. She stamped a foot, "It's Christmas. We are supposed to be jolly. I'm jolly over the new, crystal chandelier. Why aren't you? Francis, you are trying my patience. What is wrong with you?"

He pushed himself up from the olive sofa, saying, "I'm tired." and climbed upstairs. If he told her about Amos, would he hear, "What, all this over a pickaninny?"

Wearing plaid pajamas, he lit a lamp and walked to a bed ornamented with a lacy, white gown. Holding it up before his eyes, he spoke to it, "No, dear, not tonight."

The year 1881 brought the presidency of James Garfield only to be ended by an assassin's bullet. It also brought expansion of Boston by over one hundred acres of filled land. Hooped skirts, discarded years ago, supplied some filling material. Elizabeth snorted, "Just what this city needs. Room for more illiterate immigrants, as if we aren't jostled enough already. Shopping is an exercise in dodging menacing elbows."

"Elizabeth, more people, more business."

She snapped, "Not for us. They are not college professors!"

When spring peeked around corners, her mood soared. He wondered, could spring be working magic? She blossomed with each iris and every rhododendron bush. Roses faded before she congealed his blood with news, proclaiming that he would be a father by the end of the year. She smiled, "An anniversary gift." Light coming through a window caught triumph in her emerald orbs while revealing despair in his brown ones. Certainty displaced suspicion. He didn't want children. He would have cheated her of them if he could, but there would be more if she had to play coquette for years.

He insisted on her seeing Doctor Mason. A midwife would not do. Her tone dripped syrup as she answered, "If you say so, dear. I'm certain of your concern for our child's welfare."

That night she had a vivid dream where her baby was being held by Richard. He swayed back and forth, crooning. Awakened by overwhelming emotion, she held her head against shaking hands and implored, "Please, Richard, don't let me dream of you again. Please, never again. I can't stand it." Why was it impossible to hate him? Nothing excused that night's derision. For hours, she stroked the life within her.

Francis escorted her to Doctor Mason's office, his pace matching hers. It was a gorgeous day. They had started out early in a brisk, cooling breeze which pressed against her burgundy colored parasol. Stopping under an elm, they watched swans swim towards bread-tossing boys.

Francisco reflected on what had gone wrong with his method of prevention. It had worked for nearly two years under unrelenting enticement. What would he do if she didn't survive childbirth? Louise thrived on repeated deliveries. He sought comfort in the thought, though his hands were quivering by the time they arrived at the old, colonial house.

He sat in a waiting room rotating one crossed leg. He changed seats, slouching in an armchair with both knees cuddling a table in an effort to stop shaking. After an interminable time, a red-faced, flustered wife swept by, snarling, "I can't believe this. You insisted on a doctor didn't you?"

She ran out of the office, onto the pavement, cracking open her parasol. He rushed after her, "What's wrong? Was it that bad?" She stopped, turned to face him, closed the parasol and hit him with it, uncaring of shocked onlookers. This fringed on the girl he had once known, a collar shaker of the first order. Did her condition reverse behavior? In recent years, she had displayed little emotion, unless you considered tartness emotion.

Her rapid stride stopped at a restaurant where she ordered bouillabaisse, steak, potatoes, asparagus, tea and peach pie. With caution, Francis approached the table, "Madam, may I join you?" She calmed enough to point at a chair.

"Do you know what woman I have been exposed to?"

"A woman?" He relaxed and signaled the waiter. "I'll have what she ordered. Elizabeth, did you finish a sentence with a preposition?"

"Do not be facetious. I'm expected to bear an unbearable woman. I won't do it!" She slapped a napkin onto her lap as the first course arrived.

Picking up a spoon, he asked, "What woman?"

"A deranged, gossipy one who has run around the country pushing suffrage and temperance," she took in a deep breath before continuing, "now this unmarried fool has taken up midwifery. Your exalted doctor promotes it."

"He's the best in Boston for this sort of thing. If he trusts her, she must be proficient. How does he use her?"

"He said she attends the birth and sends for him if necessary. If I'm to have a midwife, I prefer another." She stabbed the steak.

"Dear, that beef has already been stabbed to death. Another midwife won't have an excellent doctor at her immediate disposal."

She capitulated. If the baby was endangered, wisdom dictated having a doctor with his credentials available.

Francis relaxed. The doctrine of save the baby not the mother didn't wash with this backsliding Catholic. He asked, "Would you mind if I celebrated with a bit of distilled fluid?"

"Are you celebrating fatherhood?" She appeared dubious.

"Of course, my dear, of course."

But he had nightmares, one instigated by a newspaper article published on November twenty-seventh regarding Jesse Pomeroy. Francis dreamt that he had twin boys, one resembling Jesse and one resembling Rufus. In a cold room, he awoke dripping perspiration. Would a so-called clairvoyant predict that a murderous child was in his future? Stability returned after irrational rumination. He shook his head to further clear his thoughts, dark curls tumbled into his eyes. He brushed them aside telling himself, "You need a haircut but not tomorrow. Mondays are too busy." The clock, at one o'clock told him Monday had arrived.

Elizabeth opened the door to Helen Manchester. She scrutinized her patient with nearsighted eyes, "You look familiar. I've been racking my brain trying to place you."

Mansions and Mills

"We met in a painting class about seven years ago. You left to save suffering women."

"And a few orphans. Would still be doing it if my father hadn't died and left my parsimonious brother in charge of allotments." Moving closer, she said, "I do remember you. You used wishy-washy colors. Are you still painting?"

"Can't find time. May I inquire as to the reason for your visit?"

"Let's see." She opened a notebook, flipping pages. "Castle, no, this is Cavanaugh. Castle, you should be here. There you are, right where you belong, after Carver. This is her ninth. I see this is your first so I must start at the beginning. Like preparations. We tell husbands to boil water. Keeps them out of the way." Narrowing her eyes and drawing pages closer, she said, "Due at the end of the year." She scribbled on the sheet.

Elizabeth squeaked, "How long have you been doing this?"

"Two years and six months." Removing a hat and shawl, she suggested, "Better get down to business. I must check out Mrs. Castro today. She's due in a week." Elizabeth winced at the name.

She informed Francis of the call, warning, "We must never let her know any of our affairs. She gossips so, and I declare that woman's ceaseless chatter could have distracted the crowd at President Garfield's funeral."

Close to her due date, heavy with child, Elizabeth's gait swayed back and forth like a rudderless ship. On the third of January at three o'clock in the morning, she awoke to a warm deluge. Shocked awake, Francis pushed blankets under her before pounding on a neighbor's door. He yelped, "Please hurry. Get Miss Manchester. She lives in the second house around the corner, the one with blue shutters. My wife needs her." The neighbor pushed her husband out while he was still struggling to fasten his trousers. She threw his coat and hat after him.

Within minutes Helen rushed by. Concerned that Mrs. Castle was overdue, the midwife had slept dressed for days. She ran practiced eyes over distraught, disheveled Francis. Convinced that he would be as useful as wings on an ant, she said, "Boil water. Lots of it and don't stop till I tell you."

After a few hours, Helen realized something was wrong. Strong labor after membrane rupture should be more productive. Helen called to Francis, "Get Doctor Mason."

The men could hear Elizabeth's screams from the yard. Francis, white-knuckled, reined in the horse. The doctor kicked off buffalo robes and raced by pots of boiling water. He speculated the humidity would clear sinuses and the extreme heat would warm his fingers before examination. After assessment, he whispered to Helen, "As you have no doubt noticed, she isn't dilating." Labor continued through reducing daylight. The doctor ordered Francis to bring in a kerosene lamp. "Mr. Castle, you will need to hold up the lamp. Keep it away from the ether. We don't want a complicating conflagration."

With his shaking hands, Francis doubted his ability to hold a steady lamp. After removing a marble bust of Queen Victoria, he brought in the elevated stand, positioning it as directed. Helen snorted, "As useful as all the others. Well, at least now, we can see."

Hours passed as he blamed himself for Elizabeth's ordeal. He heard Doctor Mason say, "This one has thrown out a fist." Skillful maneuvers brought forth an infant without an injured shoulder.

Francis heard a slap and an indignant cry. After deep intake of breath, he bolted to Elizabeth's side. Stroking her dripping head he asked, "How is she?"

"With time, she will recover but she needs two weeks of bed rest." Helen scribbled in her notebook as the doctor explained all the problems of the difficult birth. He recommended a woman be brought in to tend to mother and infant. After several minutes, Miss Manchester scrawled "case closed" and popped the notebook against her armpit.

Dr. Mason pealed, "You have a fine son to carry on the family name." Francis stifled laughter. Someone to carry on which family name? The doctor went on, "Don't know if your son wanted to shake my hand or to tell me to hurry up and pull him into the world. Stay put, Mr. Castle. I will drive myself home and have someone return your horse and buggy." A rooster crowed as the door closed behind him.

Within hours, Doctor Mason slipped on ice, striking his head against a picturesque, New England, stone wall. He survived but with limited memory. Cobwebs laced his office before his wife, surrendering to the unavoidable, closed it, entrusting records to Helen—the woman who recorded every detail from mail deliveries to conversations, to observations, and to her personal opinions.

Chapter Twenty-Six

On the day of his son's birth, Francis had no worry about the tailoring shop. Capable hands held the door keys. Weeks before, an Irish seamstress named Rosie rolled in as wide as she was tall. She not only rolled, every uncorseted ounce bounced as did her voice. Her words, "Are ye of a mind for willing hands?" ricocheted off the walls. Folds on her chin sat over each other like round stairs.

Mrs. Carlson blustered at a change in dressmakers, asking, "When is Elizabeth returning from confinement?"

"She will only be making hats at home."

Sullen, she said, "At least I can rely on stylish hats."

Louise's reaction differed. She uttered, "She's a riot. Ben, did you notice how all sides hang off a stool? If she gains anymore, her borders will sit on the floor."

Francis and Elizabeth disagreed over naming the baby. He wanted to name him Antonio, after his maternal grandfather.

She smirked, "Now won't that go well with Castle? He must be named after the Prince of Wales. Edward is a noble name, most fitting for our little prince."

Casting a sidelong glance, he declared, "It is not a name I fancy. Shall we choose another?"

She stepped in front of him, held his chin and simpered, "Are you going to suggest Amos?"

Wincing, his face the color of paste, he answered, "I would like Peter or Caleb. The name Thomas sounds appropriate with the name Castle."

With caressing knuckles, she purred, "Dear, you didn't hear me. He will be named Edward."

Tender touch and tone contradicted the volcanic flash in green eyes. Captivated once more in emerald ovals, he relented. What difference did it make what she named him?

With vigilant eye on Edward, Elizabeth fashioned hats. No other had her creativity. Ben and Louise visited, cooing over the new arrival. Louise said, "Though we miss seeing you, my daughters and I are satisfied with Rosie's workmanship."

Throwing an admiring glance at his wife, Ben declared, "In truth, my wife would look good in potato sacks." Unfazed by Elizabeth's presence, Louise wrapped both arms around him and nuzzled under his chin. Still a shameless hussy, Elizabeth thought. Such a brazen display!

On their way home as Ben slapped a gentle whip on the horse's haunches, Louise expressed her admiration of Elizabeth, "She is so talented. I am happy the wolf is no longer at her door. Think I'll advise some soon to be discarded females to suit up now. Some new household finery might be prudent also."

Elizabeth stormed that entire evening. She despised that immodest, perhaps bigamous garbage. If not for Ben and those children, if not for rewarding disloyal Mrs. Blackwood, she'd expose that mongrel. "How dare she," she vented, "display wantonness in my home?"

Inflamed by her husband's attempts to placate her and assure her of Louise's friendship, she locked him out of the bedroom. He shrugged. She had reverted to shrouding sleepwear and he approved of sustained postpartum abstinence. Time would pass and things were subject to change. And change they did but not by dictates of nature but by dictates of a calendar. Elizabeth wanted children spaced in order to insure adequate parental attention. Fifteen to seventeen month intervals would offer sufficient time for a sizable family. Believing that having given birth once, conception would come on demand, she exhumed the nocturnal finery in June. A newly acquired, painted screen protected Edward from carnal exposure. A perplexed male pondered renewed interest and a perplexed female pondered unpromising result.

Spellbinding information came in September when Elizabeth leaned over the fence, asking her neighbor, "Aren't you Mrs. Fox?"

"Yes." she answered as she hung diapers on a line stretching from poplar tree to barn wall. A toddler played with clothespins, scattering them on the grass and placing one in a baby's mouth. "No, Roseanne, Eliot can't eat that. Give it to me. I hear your baby crying sometimes. What did you name him?"

"Edward." How did she know her baby was a boy?

Roseanne screamed in protest as her mother picked up all the clothespins from the lawn. "No, darling, Mommy needs them." In anger, the girl dumped the basket of clean diapers on the grass. "This one," the frazzled woman said, "is worse than six others." She walked towards Elizabeth, pushing damp hair away from her eyes. Looking around to make sure nobody was within earshot, she whispered, "I'm going to nurse this little fellow till the last drop so there won't be another in a hurry. Hope I can keep it up for two years."

Baffled, Elizabeth asked, "What did you say? Did you say there would not be another child?"

"Indeed, I'm going to keep it up till I dry up like an old cow. Besides, mother's milk is good for him. Have you noticed that babies taken off too soon get sick? Like mill babies."

"I don't know much about mill babies."

"You don't? My sister can tell you awful stories. Those mothers dragging back to work right after birth. They need the paltry wages and the babies lack nourishment."

"Aren't the babies brought to the mothers for feeding?"

Mansions and Mills

"What, stop machines for that? Those money hungry owners don't care if babies are starved or fed bread and water. They have hearts as crisp as dead flies."

Elizabeth reeled. Ben invested in everything. Steel, coal, railroads, oil and cloth producing mills. He wouldn't kill babies. Not in his mills. His had to be different.

She jolted back into the day when Mrs. Fox asked, "You look pale. Have I upset you?"

"No, it's the heat. Hot for September. Inside will be cooler. Would you care to come over for lemonade?"

"Thank you, but Eliot needs feeding and Roseanne needs her nap. Frankly, I need her nap. Good day, Mrs. Castle."

"How do you know my name?"

"I heard it from my sister, Helen Manchester."

Elizabeth dropped on the sofa, fanning herself with one hand while holding a glass of lemonade in the other. Did she understand it right? Did nursing prevent conception? Her only example was her nursing mother. All her siblings were spaced two years apart. It seemed that Mrs. Fox was right, but if so, it shattered her timetable. She could stop nursing, but Edward would be deprived at eight months. She would turn thirty-two in February. With fingers raised like a candelabra, she recalculated. One at thirty-three. Two years between brought her to thirty-five. She could shave off three months, maybe two. No, six weeks. She used all ten fingers for counting and ceased efforts when Edward woke hungry.

Francis slid into bed that night, noting she was back to the buttoned to the collarbone mode. He developed his own headache.

At her insistence, he asked Ben if he invested in mills and gratified her with the answer that he had sold out to Bill. She grunted, "At least, Ben has principles."

One Sunday night, Francis awoke alone. Where was she? Stairs creaked in protest under his weight. A narrow ribbon of light led him to the parlor. The fireplace threw a rosy glow on the back of Edward's head and on her exposed flesh as her rocked son took deep gulps from his fountain of life. She nuzzled his hair, crooning lullabies as candlelight revealed a radiance not seen since the days of Richard Spencer.

He stepped backwards into shadowed solitude observing a vision reminiscent of his mother. He had thought his only fear had been the prospect of losing Elizabeth, now he recognized the fear of exclusion. He felt so alone.

She didn't hear him leave. A breeze ruffled his hair as he unlatched the barn. The horse stomped in impatience while he attached the harness and buggy. He guided the animal towards Beacon Hill, passing the house that had once housed Richard Spencer. He weaved through lanes. He passed two blacksmith shops on Lime Street. Tomorrow morning, bellows would set flames twisting upwards and sparks would fly as a red-hot horseshoe formed under hammer blows. On Union Street, he looked into the windows of the Union Oyster House. He arrived at a shipyard where the *Penobscot* was being built. He went on to Chelsea where the ferry *City of Alden* was under construction. A ferry would go back and forth, traveling the same course, as he did. No riding trade winds or days of battling storms and winning over wild seas. He guided a weary horse home, slipped a feedbag over his head and toweled him. A drained and lonesome man, fingering rosary beads, climbed the stairs, counting each one. In his dawn-filled room, he stared at his bewitching torment, Elizabeth asleep with one arm draped over the cradle.

On Edward's first birthday, he was introduced to a cup and beguiling lace reappeared from perfumed drawers.

In March, Elizabeth, resplendent in burnt sienna, feathered hat and kid gloves brought completed hats to the shop. She flicked through pages in a Montgomery Catalogue, saying, "Francis, how many more catalogue companies do you suppose are in the making?"

"Who knows? At least they can't compete with the manual labor in upholstering." But readymade clothing infringed more and more on tailors. "For now, I'm not too worried. Eric and I are kept busy and Rosie has as much as she can handle."

She gave Elizabeth a cold stare, hearing her say, "Dear, should I order new furniture for the dining room?"

"Whatever you please." Pointing to a bolt of rose print, he asked, "Would you like drapes made of this?"

"A bit too pinky for my taste."

With effort, Rosie stifled a scowl. That woman, she thought, so spoiled. French china, marble tables, silver tea sets. She muttered, "You'd think she entertained royalty, may the saints preserve this man. Next she'll want ermine."

Elizabeth and Francis were leaving Trinity Church, having heard Bishop Phillips Brook speak of days spent in Jerusalem, when they noticed Ben and Bill, elbow to elbow rushing through the crowd. Bill talked at a swift pace, gesticulating in a manner suggesting agitation.

Skirting a dead horse left in the street, Francis said, "I wonder what's wrong."

Sneering, she answered, "Maybe he can't raise mill production or lower wages."

Bill was actually saying, "How can I get rid of her when Janet follows her around like a puppy? She still has nightmares of her mother's final hemorrhage." A chill wind blew up his cravat and he pushed it under his vest before saying, "She's seventeen now. They talk nonstop about fashion and her debut. I don't like this woman's influence on her, not to mention the other problem."

Wrapping left arm over right, hugging himself warm, Ben remarked, "Seems like fall's chill is early. What's the other problem?"

Bill's lips compressed, tense muscles deepened wrinkles on his forehead. "How do I put this? She crowds me. For almost six years, I can't turn around without bumping into her."

"Ho, ho, the lady has designs on you."

Dragging Ben into a tobacco store, Bill went on, "Designs on something. Perhaps not me." He bought his favorite brand of pipe tobacco and steered Ben to their usual coffee house.

"You underestimate your charm." Ben ordered coffee. "You still take it black?" After an answering nod, he asked, "Bill, is marriage still out of the question?"

"I don't know that the children would benefit with a step-mother. Besides, I don't want marriage."

Sipping welcomed warmth, Ben retorted, "That's what Elizabeth said and look what happened."

Bill paused. Over the rim of his cup, he asked, "Does she seem happy?"

Fighting to find punched out breath, Ben answered, "Don't know. Never asked." He looked out the window at shivering citizens. "It's getting too cold for walking. I'll hire a hack. Louise will be thrilled to have you over for dinner."

"I won't impose. I'll have dinner at the hotel. I have a meeting tomorrow then I'm going to Fall River to go over mill books myself. Let's get that hack, first to your house then to my hotel. Give my regards to Louise." He wanted to be alone. He had a feeling of doom. He could not shake off a black cloud hanging over him.

Puffing smoke, the big monster pulled into the Fall River station, its wheels grinding to a deafening halt. The conductor, shifting tobacco around in his mouth, explained the color coding of the horse-drawn trolleys, a service to disembarking passengers. Bill half elbowed and half shouldered his way through clusters of chattering newcomers to the city of hills and mills. On arrival at the Hotel Mellen, the clerk handed him a telegram. "Mr. Klass, this arrived an hour ago." Bill tore it open, his features turning pasty.

"I won't be staying. I must return home."

The trip back seemed interminable. He recognized the doctor's horse fastened to his hitching post. He hurried by a white-faced Miss Benson, pushing faltering words aside as he rushed to Janet's room. The doctor took one look at the exhausted father, before saying, "How could you have permitted this surgery?"

"Surgery? What surgery?"

Janet turned a flushed face towards her father, "I wanted it. Don't be angry with Miss Benson. I'll be fine."

Doctor Hendricks and a confused father locked eyes; the doctor inclined his head towards the hall. Distraught, Bill asked, "What surgery did she have? What is going on?"

"Infection and I fear it is in the bloodstream. It's septicemia."

Bill dropped into a hallway chair, "Doesn't that mean?"

"I'm afraid it does." He placed a comforting hand on Bill's shoulder. "Vanity, female vanity. They destroy their bodies in the name of fashion."

Shaking his head as if to clear his thoughts, Bill inquired, "What did she do?"

"She had four of her lower ribs removed in order to have an eighteen inch waist. The wasp waist is the most irrational dictate of fashion." He lowered his head, "Not all doctors have scruples."

Bill's eyes boiled. Rage, his first manifestation of grief sent him flying downstairs. Miss Benson backed away. "You waited till I was away. You knew I wouldn't allow it. Where did the money come from?"

"She saved from her allowance." With palms covering her face and shivering like an Arctic explorer, she attempted explanation, "She wanted to have a tiny waist for her debut. She wanted to be the belle of the ball."

"She would have been the belle of the ball anyway. You can stop shivering. I won't pound you senseless though I want to." Rage spent, another symptom of grief struck. With an animal like howl of anguish, his knees struck the floor. Then billowing surges of guilt assailed. It was his fault. "God," he sobbed, "why didn't I send you packing on day one when I felt you spelled trouble?"

In racing exit, she knocked over a lamp while cursing her bad luck. Servile flattery of that silly girl accomplished nothing. The way to the father was through the daughter. Had things gone well, the teenager would be eating out of her hand and that might have led to a more welcoming attitude from Daddy.

After scant years, a black wreath hung by the door and the black band hugged his arm. Services were private.

Bill saw no one except Louise and a hat twisting Ben, who said, "I know there are no words of comfort for this, but there must be something we can do."

Silence saturated the room as Louise, pushing away his tray of uneaten food, knelt on the floor, grasping his hands. "There must be something that would help. Anything!"

The eyes staring at them were as lifeless as those in fishnets. At last, he answered, "Ben, there is something you can do. Be my proxy. I trust your honesty and judgment. I don't want to attend meetings or see anyone. Because of Grace and Robert, I can't let everything go to the dogs."

"Bill, what of the mills? By now you must have interests in half the mills in two states."

Gripping his forehead, he answered, "Closer to one third. One problem is I didn't get to check the books in Fall River."

"I understand that city has had more than its share of treasurers with itchy fingers. Grover can help me look into it. He has an excellent reputation."

"He does no free favors. Tell him to bill me."

Ben thought they should leave, but Louise placed a hand on Bill's arm. "What about the children? Is there something we can do for them?"

He slouched forward in the chair, arms going limp. "I hate to admit it, but their presence is a burden for them as much as for me. Could you get them enrolled in good, private schools where they will have the uplifting company of other youngsters?"

She revolved towards her husband, one brow cocked, "We know of schools in Boston. Ben, could they stay with us and attend school there?"

"Good idea, if they can stand our rambunctious brood. Bill, if that suits you, just say when."

"Your brood may be the best thing for them. I'm sure they would like escaping me. Let's make arrangements as soon as possible."

A servant held their coats. They had not climbed into the carriage before Bill fell into a coma like state. Hours later he stood with dark ringed, bloodshot eyes staring at Isabel's portrait. Her hair, accentuated by a pale, yellow gown was as black as coal nuggets. He ran a finger over the painting, feeling its raised brushstrokes and whispered, "Love, I lost our child."

On the return trip to Boston, voice bouncing in harmony with the train, Ben asked, "Do you think anything will rekindle the spark in the man?"

"I'd like to think that someday the right woman might come along."

Unbuttoning a coat straining against a growing middle, he suggested, "A woman like Elizabeth would be right for him."

"No, dear. You know I have always liked her and I believe that everyone is entitled to one fault or weakness. Have you heard her say she danced with the Prince of Wales? She believes she is close to royal blood. Her failing or sin, if you see it as sin, is pride. She can put on airs now. Can you imagine what insufferable airs she would have if married to wealth? I wish I had met Isabel. Even related to nobility, as she was, I'm told she was down to earth. Anyone like Elizabeth would be wrong for Bill."

"How come you don't put on airs?"

"How can I? I never danced with a prince. I'm the daughter of a horse thief who died stretching rope."

Chapter Twenty-Seven

On Edward's second birthday, the short day had a ghost-like pallor. Sunshine hid behind clouds and the sky donned gray, but ground compensated by wearing a fluffy, white rug. Sleighs crunched through snow and skates whistled on frozen ponds.

Bill's children, brought in from a snowball fight, exalted at the number of hats they had knocked off the Irish team. Robert bragged, "Grace kept score and we beat them." They loved the schools and the opportunity to make friends once denied by being tutored in a Fifth Avenue mansion. They urged their father to move to Boston and Ben reminded him of the boon of being closer to mill interests.

The New Yorker trekked memory-filled rooms, the streets which held multiple memories and after much thought, made the fateful choice of relocating to New England.

From 1884 to 1886, building plans, construction and trips to Fall River engrossed Bill along with efforts to placate mill workers resentful of wage cuts. One cut took place in 1884 with an additional cut of ten percent in 1885. Mule spinners organized. In January 1886, the market improved and employees hammered for wage restoration. They reached an agreement by November.

He hoped this spelled the end of labor problems but in view of the Haymarket Square bombing, he feared labor unrest was just beginning.

Construction in Back Bay progressed at a slow rate. Grace looked forward to her debut, however, ribs remained intact. When Robert wasn't engaged in study or instructing a rapt Susan in anthropology, he sat on the docks fascinated by seaman from different cultures. Otherwise, he rode Ben's stallion. Ben told Bill, "I planned to keep him on the gelding but soon realized he could handle Tornado. What a boy!"

In these years, Elizabeth saw drapes close over the next door windows. Mrs. Fox's system appeared to work. Nurse two years and have a family addition in three, give or take a couple of months.

By Christmas 1885, under a toy-strewed tree, Edward faced his fourth birthday, drilled at this tender age to speak to elders only when spoken to and never speak at all with a mouthful of food. He removed his hat when entering establishments or homes and tipped it to ladies. He knew table etiquette and correct place settings for sterling.

Approaching thirty-five, Elizabeth harbored desperation. Marriage provided security, but where was the family? She behaved less inhibited in spite of pulpit-prescribed behavior, confusing her besot husband in the process. In light of obvious tactile aversion, how to explain eager participation? With a wide grin like two arrows targeting his ears, he managed to bear the burden of a seemingly wanton wife.

In January 1886, Elizabeth and Florence Fox, children in tow, ambled to the grocery store. The oversized owner wearing baggy trousers, a handlebar mustache and an apron, eyed Roseanne with suspicion. Last summer, while mothers appraised fly covered chickens hanging from hooks along a wall, she had dug six pickles from a barrel, dumping them into a barrel of flour. She had also removed a loose cover from a container of molasses tempting flies from chickens to an abbreviated swim. A bloodstained butcher engrossed with taking an order over a newfangled phone attached to the wall, didn't notice her toss sawdust, scooped from the floor, into a barrel of loose tea. Mrs. Fox paid for damaged goods.

This glistening, wintry day she struck the butcher with a concealed snowball, knocking off spectacles. On hands and knees, scrambling to locate his second set of eyes, he said, "This is too much. Keep this undisciplined child away."

"I'm sorry, but with so many now..." She pulled blankets around the infant and pointing at Roseanne, said, "This one is always a problem."

"If you cannot discipline your children," he said, wiping snow from his face, "I suggest you tell your husband to make his bed on the roof."

Mouths flew open. The butcher's helper covered a blood-red face with a blood-covered apron. Elizabeth stammered, "That remark is ill-mannered."

"As is this child!"

Swiveling on one foot with aplomb while wrenching the doorknob, she said. "Come, Florence. There are other stores."

The butcher answered. "Let us thank the Lord for large and small blessings."

Later, while sharing a pot of tea, Florence said, "Helen is coming for a visit. Did you know why she didn't come sooner?" She scrutinized Elizabeth's lack of curiosity but still continued, "Being master of the family assets now, she is free to lecture and do exemplary work for women and children. True she is hard on men and blames them for everything but do come over for the fun of listening to her gossip. It is always the drunken and licentious husbands or vagabond sons causing problems. She can be nonstop about the sins of men while sympathetic to women in trouble and their fatherless babies."

"I recall she was engaged." Elizabeth replaced her empty cup in the saucer. "Pity he didn't live up to her standards. Would you care for a refill?"

Mansions and Mills

"Yes, please. Meeting her standards is difficult but he is dull. He shares time with pigeons and chats with a one-legged, colored man, a well-known character. You must have seen him at some time."

Pouring tea, Elizabeth asked, "Seen which one?"

"Every Bostonian has seen the one-legged man."

"It's a large city. Some areas I avoid." Before Mrs. Fox could ask why, Edward rushed in, animation personified.

"Look, Mother. Roseanne found these. She asked me to swallow them. I can." He opened a hand containing several buttons.

Proud of herself, Roseanne gushed, "I climbed up on a table and found them in a cupboard at the tippity top."

Elizabeth ran her index finger around the inside of Edward's mouth. She looked down his throat. "He couldn't have swallowed them."

"He did. I can count to five. He ate five. I can't count to ten so I don't know if he ate ten."

A frenzied mother began slapping his back and a mortified Mrs. Fox suggested it might be the wrong thing to do. "They might come up all at once and choke him."

"Oh, then I'm taking him to a doctor."

As she rushed the boy to the door, Francis walked in. Told of the situation, he said, "Everyone calm down. Mrs. Fox, at this point, perhaps you should take Roseanne home." He held the door, saying, "Cute baby."

A collected father picked up the remaining buttons and faced a distraught mother. "They don't appear valuable, but if they are to you, just search for them in a couple of days. They will show up. Considering the unpleasant search, I suggest you forget the incident."

"Forget it?" She was sputtering. "That monster fed him buttons. She is banned from this house just as she is banned at the butcher's."

"What an accomplishment! Few are banned by butchers."

His laughter incensed her. "This isn't funny." His eyebrows arched in quizzing fashion when she added, "She endangers my son."

Helen visited, carrying her familiar, threadbare bag. While sipping tea she told stories of despoiled and abandoned women and of a tenant of School Street being carried home every morning. "He is drenched. Others empty their bladders on him as he lies in the gutter. Can you imagine the misery of his wife? Florence, has Roseanne's behavior improved? You know, your husband should contain himself. You have enough. Consider this one."

She threw a malignant eye at innocent-looking Roseanne who had crawled under the table and tied the laces of her aunt's left shoe to the laces of her right shoe. She reasoned, how does one learn to tie knots without practicing?

Florence said, "I will take the children the Lord insists on sending even if they crop up like fertilized weeds."

"The Lord's will mystifies me," Elizabeth said, "I keep hoping for a little girl."

Helen had opened her mouth to divulge more gossip but her jaw fell silent. Elizabeth squirmed under a prolonged stare.

Florence broke thundering silence. "I baked cookies. Let's all have some. Here, Helen, you have the first."

Deep in thought, Helen failed to hear her sister or see the cookies. Edward ended strained muteness, asking, "Mother, does Mrs. Fox want me to have a cookie too?"

"Of course, but remember to thank her." She checked the clock. "It is time to leave. We both appreciate your hospitality." Managing a smile while vowing to avoid this weird do-gooder, she lied, "It's been a pleasure seeing you, Helen."

Lifting a heavy, wool skirt with one hand and holding Edward with the other, she stepped out into whirling snowflakes, wondering if Helen had a husband, would she discover a woman's place. Maybe women's rights would fly out the window. Elizabeth pulled her shawl closer as the wind picked up.

Mansions and Mills

Late that night, she watched snow gather on the trellis made by oak branches and gauged white inches climbing up its roots. Francis, book in hand, walked towards her. He asked, "What are you pondering, fair princess?"

She postponed the answer by asking, "What are you reading?"

"A book by Charles Darwin entitled, *Descent of Man*." Feeling a chill at the window, he tightened the belt on his robe. "Now, answer my question. Why so pensive?"

"It's rather foolish, I suppose, but I wonder why this long stare from Helen when I said that I would like to have a little girl."

A floor rocked under his feet. He needed to meditate on words. Simple words flowing over his teeth, words sliding over strangling tonsils. Sucking in air, he began, "Helen was..."

They heard a clinking sound as stroked rosary beads fell from nervous fingers. "What is that?" she asked. "Mrs. Blackwood had one like that made of wood. It's some superstitious artifact!"

"It's a rosary. Haven't you noticed in all these years? I carry it at all times in my pocket."

"Francis," she said, drawing in a sharp breath, "fishing your pockets is not my favorite pastime." Her voice commanded, "You'll get rid of that thing immediately!"

"What?"

"That heathen, medieval object. Neither Edward nor his schoolmates should ever see it. He must have the advantages of being Anglo-Saxon stock. How could he advance if his Azorean blood became public knowledge?" A feline smile preceded her saying, "Rest assured, Ben and Louise will never reveal your lineage. They are clever enough to know what this is about, and clever enough to know I have the Blackwood's address. A natural father might claim Susan or blackmail them."

With each sentence disbelief permeated. Did he know this woman at all? Weak kneed, he stammered. "I hope you are not holding a gun to their heads. You said the name change was about hiding my religion from your family and attracting moneyed clientele but it is more. You are ashamed of this marriage."

"Don't be silly. I am thinking of Edward's future." She stepped from window to window closing drapes, shutting out a violent exterior storm while hoping to avoid a violent interior one. She crooned, "You must be aware of how immigrants from certain countries are distained. That's what it's about. It has nothing to do with this marriage but you must admit the English are dominant here and abroad. They are an accomplished race."

"They were wallowing in ignorance when Spain and Portugal ruled half of the world."

"Francis, you read too much. Some is nonsense. We got off the subject." Her modulated voice toned down to a conspiratorial whisper, "That whatnot in your pocket, I can dispose of it for you." An inviting hand rose from folds in her robe.

"That whatnot is the only thing I have of my mother."

"Does that remark constitute a refusal to discard it?"

"Precisely."

Green eyes flashed like emeralds under candlelight and enraged fists clenched, leaving semicircular fingernail marks on outraged palms. Discussion on Helen or on a strange stare evaporated in a seething atmosphere.

He retrieved his book from a chair and said in a calm voice, "Goodnight, my dear."

"Don't you dare turn your back on me in this fashion. Who do you think you are?"

"The godchild of a Portuguese Dona. You fancy yourself as being royal but your prince danced with fishwives also, Lizzie."

"Don't call me Lizzie."

He returned the book to its rightful place, above historical ones, below navigational ones. He went to the window where white, feathery flakes whirled around tree-lined streets, making elms look like novitiates bowed in prayer. What happened to the bright-eyed girl on a stair, inveigling more food, saving a kitten and rushing, always rushing? He longed for those pounding, hated heels instead of her regal stride, swallowing the thought those heels had pounded for Richard. Tonight her enmity was preferable to cool detachment only dissipating at her flirtatious mood. Perplexing dichotomy.

Someone once said when a woman is adored by a man, she despises him. Who said it? Was it Napoleon? Did Elizabeth surmise how he adored her? She should since he did all to please her. She had a house he hated decorated in green, gold and blue. She purchased place settings for twelve, marble and teak but with the exception of the Fox family refused to entertain. Was it preserved for visits from the well-placed? Impossible.

Strained from tonight's argument, he lingered in the library as windows gathered sleet and snow, blocking views of frozen, praying trees while angry shutters rattled and growled in punishing wind. He fingered the rosary beads. For a few seconds, he saw his mother wearing her potato sack apron. One blink and she was gone. Without doubt, this apparition was caused by fatigue.

He wiggled into a chair by the fire, planning to sleep here tonight, lulled by the sound of cracking logs and howling wind. Elizabeth was, without question, still sizzling and that type of sizzle he could do without.

Two days later, Francis' feet crunched snow as he started down the street, deep in thought. Yesterday, Ben had stopped at the shop with a slew of children jabbering of the forthcoming dedication of the Statue of Liberty. Grace said, "We will see President Cleveland there." When they surrounded Rosie with tales, Francis took Ben aside relating how Elizabeth wanted his heritage submerged from everyone. He asked, "What do you think?"

"I think she is smart. Bigotry surrounds us and Edward will suffer from discrimination."

He mulled it over. That meant lie after lie. At the last census, he had reported his true place of birth. In the next census he would need to lie. That would be in 1890. Should he say he was born in Boston? What if he ever needed to produce a birth certificate? He had to find a city that lost records in a fire. Well, he had four years to find one.

Fate stepped in. He didn't need four years. The Fall River City Hall burned with substantial loss. He had his story for the census or anyone. He was born in Fall River, Massachusetts and his birth record was destroyed.

He had his story but was he comfortable with it? No, he wasn't. He had always had unease about casting aside the name but he had justified it because of a failing business. Talking to himself, he said, "Face the truth, you did it to get Elizabeth as well." But who was he? A Castle on the outside but always a Castro in the inside.

One morning, determined crocus glanced through fresh snowfall as Francis walked by his neighbor's yard and saw Roseanne in tears while engaged in making snowballs. He asked, "Why are you crying?"

"Because I have nobody to play with. Eliot and Edward are building things with blocks and Mrs. Castle won't let me in. She even locks the door. She says I'm a menace. What does menace mean?"

"I think it means you are too smart for playing with blocks. I heard you tied the boys to a tree. Why did you do that?"

"Because we were playing cowboys and Indians and they were the Indians." She wiped overflowing tears on a navy-blue jacket sleeve. "Father says Indians are always killing people with bows and arrows and sometimes hatchets. They are bad and I was a good cowboy. Edward and Eliot were the bad ones."

"I see. Will you stop crying if I make some snowballs with you?"

"If you do, I can give everybody one. They might be so happy that they'll play with me again. Do you think Mrs. Castle wants one?"

"No, she thinks they are too cold, but let's make them for everyone else." He stooped and made several while Elizabeth watched through a window, vexed that he wasted time on this horrible child and vexed that time is money and he would be late for work.

With a stacked pile, Roseanne had an inspiration. When her family fell asleep, she would sneak out and carry them inside. Even though Christmas wouldn't come again for a long, long time, she would play she was Santa Claus and fill their shoes with snowballs. They'd have a happy surprise in the morning when they put on their shoes. Roseanne wanted everyone to be happy. She didn't understand why they were always angry instead.

In early April, Elizabeth, pencil in hand, checked dates on her calendar for the next three months. December would mark their tenth wedding anniversary and they would celebrate with only one child. She wondered if she would care to celebrate it at all if the year ended without a pregnancy. Her panic at times seemed unbearable. Bitterness entwined with panic. She concluded she might as well have spared herself this marriage thing and gone off to feed chickens, but then the vision of healthy, happy Edward calmed her, at least for a while.

In May, Rosie looked up from lining a coat. An impressive man in a three piece suit with valise and a swinging cane asked if she knew a tailor born in the Azores. She answered, "Not a one."

Prepared to ignore all but clientele she pumped the treadle but the man didn't leave. "Have you ever met anyone named Francisco Castro? This is important."

"Is it now? Ye be wasting time here. Eric is too blonde to come from the Azores. He ain't no Castro and Mr. Castle was born in Fall River."

He growled, "Told them this was a waste of time. Riffraff never stays put."

"That's for sure, but ye'll find no riffraff coming through these doors." No reason for this man to know the riffraff that did come through the doors.

The stranger jammed a hat on his head and complained that it was too warm for May.

"Come back in August. Belike, ye'll find an Azorean then."

When Rosie told Francis of the fine gent, he asked, "Did he say what it was about?"

"Didn't ask. It ain't me business." She gave him a scathing look. Did he think she was a busybody?

Francis asked himself, "Who could be looking for Francisco Castro?" Elizabeth's correspondence with the Blackwoods had ceased. It appeared that they had abandoned a search for Louise. Sam would never mention Rufus so that authorities couldn't be attempting to find the murderer through Francisco Castro. Seamen could be impossible to track, more so shipwrecked ones. It couldn't be important.

Chapter Twenty-Eight

*E*lizabeth read *Little Lord Fauntleroy*, and for Edward's fifth birthday party dressed her son in the outfit bearing the same name. All neighborhood children had invitations, excluding Roseanne would be impossible. She tittered at first sight of Edward, swiveling towards her mother, asking, "Must Eliot ever wear a funny suit like that? Edward looks silly."

Elizabeth's face reddened in anger and Mrs. Fox's face reddened in embarrassment. She blubbered, "Edward looks beautiful. Hush, Roseanne."

"No he doesn't. He looks awful." Children giggled, Edward cried and his mother fumed. A slew of presents dried Edward's tears, but he refused to allow Roseanne a piece of cake. She howled in protest before slamming the cake on the floor.

"That's it," Mrs. Fox cried, "tomorrow you will spend the day in your room." Unfazed, Roseanne planned to climb out the window.

Children bundled in hats and mittens left with cookies in compensation for a desecrated cake. On the way home, Roseanne's pigtails suffered repeated twists from a cake-deprived Eliot.

"Great party," said jovial Francis "was it not?" With gallant flourish, he clowned, "Allow me to help clean up the mess."

"How do you manage to find this amusing?" Elizabeth asked in a glacial tone as she reached for a bucket of water.

"The girl is right," he answered, as he removed the lace collar, "he does look silly." Edward's tears flowed again.

"See what you are doing. Edward, you look beautiful and you shall wear it. Francis, this is the fashion these days. I'll bet Louise puts her sons in the same thing."

"I hope not. One atrocious exposure is enough. Please donate it to charity." Through drying tears, Edward tossed questioning looks back and forth between parents. He didn't want to wear the velvet suit again but he did. That day he learned which parent had the final say. Did Father lack interest or fortitude? Neither reason commanded esteem.

Accounts of Queen Victoria's forthcoming Golden Jubilee appeared giving Elizabeth the opportunity of introducing royalty to a son perched on her knee. He heard of her dance with the Prince of Wales. Light laughter wafted from the library. "You tell him all about it, Lizzie, and the vital importance of being a loyal subject."

"Don't call me Lizzie. This is of more consequence than your interest in slave rebellions in Brazil."

He stood in the doorway, appraising her in amber silk with a smaller bustle than in the past. Always fashionable! "Rosie tells me the newer fashions are plainer with straight skirts, flaring below the knee. On your next visit, consider going over fashion with her." He pulled a box from his pocket, "Saw this in a window. It's made from a whale's tooth." It was a scrimshaw bracelet, each square depicting a different nautical design.

"How enchanting." Lifting Edward from her lap, she rose and wrapped her arms around her husband's waist, tucking her head against his cheek. The embrace, so startling by daylight, was like rain on parched earth. If scrimshaw was the magic formula for producing a tactile wife, she would have tons of it.

Mansions and Mills

The small gift awakened her old feeling of comradeship. He was the best friend she had ever had. She pledged to attempt displays of appreciation. The pledge lived a short life. Soon disagreements arose about Edward's schooling and whether she would curl his hair in rags to complete the Lord Fauntleroy look. As usual, Elizabeth won.

The year vaulted from season to season, arriving at the holidays and the faithful gift of Mr. Bruncken's sausages.

At Edward's sixth birthday, Roseanne, constricted by a gritty flicker in her mother's eyes, managed to be an asset, introducing pick-up-sticks, jacks and old maid. Elizabeth's eyebrows rose when noticing Mrs. Fox's expanding waistline. Catching the hostess' eyes, she nodded.

"When?" Elizabeth asked as she retied a girl's hair bow.

"May."

Her method worked. Little Harold, fingers covered with frosting, was born in 1885. No method worked for Elizabeth as she approached thirty-seven.

Though dubious of Roseanne, Elizabeth volunteered, "When the time comes, I'll take the children."

A wail escaped Eliot's throat, "I was not cheating, Roseanne. You were."

Florence said, "When the time comes, I'll send the wild one to my cousin in Medford."

On Friday, March ninth, Eric remarked on escalating business, "This morning we took in furniture needing upholstering from two mansions. Look at the ebony from Ceylon and check the rosewood on this settee. I'll be careful not to mar the wood."

Days before, Francis had strolled through Boston, enjoying unseasonal warmth. But this day, a false prophet, foretold early spring. Inhaling sunlit air, he counted blessings. A thriving business and a bewitching though bedeviling wife. No hint of disaster loomed.

Two unpredictable storms rushed to meet and on the eleventh day of March, it struck a crippling blow to New York. Like a marauding savage it hit western Massachusetts and moved eastward startling Boston with heavy snow and sixty mile an hour wind. Caught unaware, some died on the way home, one man froze to a post. Trains and street cars, mired in snow, left passengers stranded. Rebelling snowplows stalled. Ships wrecked and telegrams had to be rerouted. When the storm abated on the fourteenth day of March, losses of life were in the hundreds. Roscoe Conkling, an acquaintance of Bill Klass and former senator from New York died from exposure.

Francis and Eric trudged between mountains of snow to assess loss. The tailoring shop had scant damage but the other, containing expensive material and valuable furniture, sat in shambles due to the roof caving in.

Bill left to attend the senator's funeral but Ben checked the damage. He asked Francis, "Is there enough insurance to cover all this?"

"No, but I'll use insurance payment to reimburse furniture owners. There won't be enough to cover the building and equipment too."

"I'll give you a loan."

Francis wavered. Then running a tongue over dry lips, said, "Elizabeth wouldn't approve."

"Again, this is something she need not know. You can repay it at your own speed. No interest, of course."

"Let me give all this some thought. Bill hasn't ever requested full payment. He still supplies material at cost. Why?"

"Because I asked him to help you." He gripped the younger man's clenched fist. "As for me, I appreciate loyalty. You, as well as Elizabeth, valued Mrs. Blackwood. Denying her a grandchild burdened you, I'm sure."

Chagrin flashed on the tailor's face. Yes, he would have liked to bring happiness to the woman who saved his life and treated him as a son. One more secret for Elizabeth's sake added to the weight of that first one. He had no love for Richard but no one should die like that while his murderer walked away. If Rufus, so filled with hate, murdered again it would be because his silence enabled it.

He was jarred from painful recollection by Ben's voice, "Did you hear what I said?"

Shaking his head, Francis responded, "Sorry, I got lost in thought."

"I said that Louise would insist. She'd sell her jewels for Elizabeth. Considering gems are gifts from me, it would cause an unsettled household."

"A known loan from you would cause my unsettled household."

"You have kept your wife's nose out of everything before."

Scrubbing a hand before a drained face, Francis said, "That's true but other than an undisclosed secret, why is Louise so fond of Elizabeth?"

"Your wife was the only girl she admired or liked in..." He stopped, having almost said "the days of Richard." After a moment, he continued, "from the days when they first met."

"I'll go through everything tonight from debts to expenses and what will be required to start anew, but Elizabeth must never know. She harbors such majestic pride." Slapping a tan hat on his head, Ben left with a knowing nod.

That night, Elizabeth found Francis, elbows on table and palms against his forehead surrounded by ledgers, receipts and statements. He raised black rimmed, bloodshot eyes. "Elizabeth," he said sucking air still pungent with spices, "our finances are bleak."

Turning white, she asked, "How bleak?"

"Very. We are bankrupt."

Remembering the days of calculating to pay a lecher's rent, she moaned, "I'm poor again."

"No. We are poor again. You will need to remove Edward from private school."

"Never, I will go back to work. Edward must have every advantage."

"Public schools have turned out scholars and other determined minds have self-educated. Without schooling, Lincoln became president."

"That is atypical. Edward must have credentials and benefits from proper social connections. He must become a professor. He will stay in that school if I have to sell every piece of furniture and every stitch of my clothing. If that doesn't suit you or my leaving a six-year-old to work fulltime, come up with a solution. You do it, Francis. You just do it!" With a gigantic swish of taffeta, she marched out. The slammed bedroom door managed to cling to its hinges.

His pencil had dropped to the floor and had rolled across the room. Rubbing a back aching from removing wet debris, he retrieved it and with resignation added tuition fees to the loan.

Ben inhaled a huge portion of air when presented with the total. Regaining composure, he said, "It will take you years to repay this but that's fine. You will make it good."

"I will, if I have to dig ditches."

"Aren't you a bit old to start that?"

"I'm going to be thirty-two in June. Maybe it is a job for an eighteen-year-old fellow. A skipper told me a fortune could be made at sea as long as a man stayed afloat but it's too late for that also."

"If you go by some of the residences in New Bedford it must be true, but you do need to stay afloat. If that ruined building is an indication of your luck, you'd be at the bottom of the ocean."

Francis sold the empty lot to a bank looking for a place to build and handed the income to Ben as first payment on the loan. He moved the tailoring shop to larger space three doors to the east, enabling him to encompass the upholstering business. That involved another deal with a man named Doyle but Edward stayed in private school and discouraged Francis started anew for the second time.

At Edward's seventh birthday party in 1889, Mrs. Fox brought all four children. The only blight on Elizabeth's day was news that Louise expected another family member. "My," she said to Francis, "isn't she close to forty?" She quizzed interstellar space, "Why does that woman get everything?"

Wool prices increased yearly and in 1889, the government prohibited the killing of furbearing animals in Alaska thus raising the price of fur. Francis moaned over carping women while explaining he had no choice but to raise prices.

The previous year after the devastating storm, Eric and Rosie accepted wage cuts for one year but the year was up. Readymade clothing grew in popularity and Elizabeth offered to produce countless hats to compensate. In truth, she enjoyed the task and Mrs. Fox provided more time by having Edward stay at her home after school.

At the time when Francis thought nothing else could go wrong Mrs. Fox terminated daily care of Edward due to a complicated pregnancy. Her birth control method had failed. Hat production slid again.

Louise gave birth to a daughter in July and Mrs. Fox gave birth to a boy in December. Still no child in the horizon for Elizabeth.

By 1890, Elizabeth consoled herself with new fashions. "The bustle is gone," she said, "and sleeves are enlarging over the upper arm. I love this tulip shaped skirt. I'll start with that."

Birds struck a mustering, fall chorus and flexed migrating wings as wind billowed smoke from the train carrying depleted Helen to Boston. Every fragment of her being needed rest after all the heartbreaking work following the Johnston flood, which caused so many deaths and so many orphans. "From now on," she told her sister, "I'll stick to lectures for Suffrage and the abolishing of liquor. No more midwifery either. I've seen too many stillborn babies and too many women die." She rested for days and showed delight at Roseanne's interest in braille. She said. "Aunt Helen, see this dot, it means A, these mean B. When I grow up, I'm going to help the blind."

Florence said, "See Helen, she has your spirit and you thought she was hopeless."

As much as she dreaded it, Elizabeth, in neighborly fashion, paid a call. Reluctant feet dragged down the hill, slipping on wet, fallen leaves. While Helen ranted on injustices, she played peek-a-boo with Martha, uttering, "Little girls are adorable. I do keep wishing."

In a blazing voice, Helen said, "It's inconceivable that you have never been told. It's not my place to tell you but you should know. You were asleep and didn't hear but your husband did. He should have told you. Men! Dastardly creatures!"

Florence's surprised teacup clattered to its saucer. The braille instructions slid off Roseanne's lap as her aunt flashed, "Roseanne, take all the children out to play. Now! Florence, go peel potatoes and close the kitchen door." She refilled Elizabeth's cup and placing a gentle hand on Elizabeth's arm said, "Mrs. Castle, you sustained considerable injury at Edward's birth. Poor Doctor Mason despaired for your life."

Through a constricted throat, Elizabeth asked, "Are you saying?"

"Yes, but there are so many orphans. You could have adopted a baby girl years ago. Would you consider it now?"

At first, Elizabeth's dazed brain didn't function. Numb fingers found the doorknob. Speaking to deaf ears, a subdued voice said, "You are forgetting your shawl."

She passed unseen children. "Mother," Edward began, then stopped. He watched her climb the street lined with elm and oak trees. Darkness closed around her as she walked. Left foot, right foot, left foot.

Florence asked, "What was that about?"

The answer stunned, "Don't you know minding one's own business is a virtue?"

After depositing the shawl and finding a dark kitchen, Edward skipped down the hill for an offered dinner.

The same darkness greeted famished Francis. His wife sat immobile in the parlor with fireplace flames casting leaping patterns over her figure. Moonlight glanced through a window, soon excluded by closed shutters. He struck a match. Now a kerosene lamp scattered its shadows. Finally, her tightened lips moved, "You should have told me."

An index finger ran over his brow. How could she have found out? Ledgers resided in a locked drawer. "I didn't want you to worry. I wanted to spare you."

"Didn't want me to worry? I worried about it every day, every month, every year. And spare me? From what? Behaving like a strumpet?"

What in the world was she talking about? He paced the length of the papered room. Green. Everything green, blue or yellow. Never rose or pink or even ruby. "Elizabeth, I think red-haired women look stunning in pink. Why do you hate that color?"

The vision of the pink, feathered gown shredding and burning harpooned her. She caught the arms of the chair. Could he have found a worse question to ask at this moment? "Are you demented? How could you ask such a foolish question in view of your behavior? No, you are not demented. You are trying to avoid answering. There is no answer. No justification."

Her usual style was cold sarcasm or a cool putdown but now she boiled as she had over the rosary beads. Sniffing in vain for promised stew, he said, "What contemptible sin have I committed to deprive me of dinner?"

"Your contemptible sin is not telling me there could never be more children. That, Francis, is inexcusable."

He wondered if bones could bleed. He felt something drain from his skeleton. Words perched midair for several seconds then rushed forth, sentences tumbled over each other, "At first you were too weak to bear the news. Knowing how you loved babies, I feared you would fall into deep depression. I thought with time gradual awareness of a problem would make discussing it unnecessary and you would accept it. I thought seeing the disorder in the Fox household might even turn you against a large family. You do detest disorder and there were times when I thought you didn't want to know."

"Perhaps I didn't. I needed hope. There is ham and cheese in the icebox. I'd like to stay here for a while." Dawn found her asleep, curled in a fetal position.

In December, undetectable kernels traveled to Boston from New Hampshire. These small seeds of destruction flew over buildings, fluttered like butterflies in the streets, swirled in alleyways, invisible to all but microscopes. They soared across the moon and planted themselves in humans. It was called diphtheria and sometimes called the strangling angel of death. With a high fever, swollen glands, sore throat, difficulty in swallowing and breathing it planted itself in Edward. A quarantine notice hung on the house while sleepless Elizabeth hung over her son, checking for the slate-colored membrane that could grow in his throat, strangling him. Elizabeth believed her diligent care would guaranty survival and it did.

She lost weight, looked haggard and Francis said, "You are going to have a servant. An add goes in the paper this week."

"Remember to say no Irish should apply."

"If you take no Irish, you may go without. One advantage is they speak English. You would need to brush up your French to hire a Canadian. Let's see what we get."

Elizabeth turned down one Irish girl after the other. Francis told her to give in.

To afford the servant, he went to work nights at the docks, loving the sights, sounds and smells. Rosie groused, "Ye'll be too done in for this place. Is an angel going to take the measure of men?"

"Isn't Saint Peter supposed to do that?"

"Funning he is. 'Tain't funny." She entangled thread caught in the foot of a sewing machine. "This devil machine tangles. It wants fixin'. Ye'll be staying late enough tonight to measure Mr. Lewis. The dandy might come with his bandog."

"His what?"

"Ain't ye ever heard of them? 'Tis a dog ye keep tied. Course with his coins..." She shrugged then went on, "For sure, his wench looks like a dog."

Mansions and Mills

"Rosie," he said shaking his head, "don't use that term or any such term in the presence of Mrs. Castle. She has no notion of the habits of many of our clientele."

Rosie sniffed her own thoughts. Beyond his hearing she murmured, as she had many times, "For sure, that hoity-toity only lifts her skirt for her bladder."

In the abbreviated days of February, Francis' unused muscles screamed in rebellion. Once calloused hands blistered. Moored ships bounced as waves dashed against them and he placed a hand on a rusting chain and reminisced. Oh to hear the words "hoist sails" but there was gaunt, hollow-eyed Elizabeth to consider.

One evening the *Roulette* moored. He recalled her construction in 1884. A man with a basket of fish passed by. "Aiming to go to sea?" he asked.

"No, all my coiled rope is on land."

If Elizabeth didn't settle on a girl, he would do it for her. Irish or Canadian didn't matter as long as her cooking surpassed his wife's. For years, he had surreptitiously sprinkled condiments and seasonings in her dishes, making ghastly food palatable. Mr. Bruncken's sausages remained a treat.

On Sunday, the first day of March, 1891, two Irish girls sat on a park bench discussing plans. One would be nineteen in three days. The other, born on the same day as Richard's son was seventeen. Snow blanketed their shawled heads, concealing brown hair on one and light blonde hair on the other.

They engaged in friendly argument. The brunette said, "I'll get meself to Lawrence bloody quick. Come too. In mills, husbands are in the offin' for us."

Cracking newspaper pages open, the other answered, "I'm going into service. Three dollars a week, all clear. Husbands! I'll have me none. Ye thought that sailing man, swelled with his uniform was a prize. Off he is with a rouged limey, didn't I tell you meself?"

Ignoring the question, Annie snatched the paper, jabbing the ad, "Look what it says. No Irish. Ye'll be bowin' to a bloody high and mighty, if she takes ye on. She won't. Let's go for the mills. Me uncle works there. A mule spinner he is with good wages."

"Annie give me his address. I'll send mine."

"Ye have none!"

"Fiddlesticks. 'Twont be long afore I do." She reclaimed the newspaper and turning pages said, "For sure, I'll be having one."

The doorbell summoned as Elizabeth napped. Seeing the girl through the oval window, it was obvious she should have come to the back door. Nevertheless, Francis swung open the massive, front door. He appraised shabby garb on a shivering teenager. Her chin was small and pointed and her hair thick and light. Her eyes impressed, being long-lashed and royal blue. Lengthy fingers denied her stature. She was no taller than Elizabeth. He watched her take in the marble-topped table, the bronze umbrella stand and the oak-framed mirror.

He said, "Child, you look frozen. Come by the fire." She stood by the fireplace, stretching fingers to the flame which pulled the cold from every ice-tortured digit. He reached for a chair, "Do sit and warm your feet." He waited till trembling stopped and a warm glow brushed her cheeks, before saying, "I believe you have seen our advertisement." He continued after her nod, "My wife needs assistance in regaining strength having been through a trying ordeal. Your youth speaks of no experience but is it possible that you are proficient at cooking?" Her blank expression revealed no understanding of the word proficient. He rearticulated, "Is it possible that you are a good cook?"

"Indeed, I cooked for the priest and at times for the bishop."

That was all he needed to hear. An idiot can dust, iron clothing, wash windows and swing a carpet beater. "Now that that is established, tell me about yourself. What part of Ireland are you from?"

Mansions and Mills

"Not born in Ireland. 'Twas in Liverpool. Had little truck with the limeys. Me father wanted it so."

"I see, well let's start with your name."

"Bridget. Bridget Rafferty."

A bell rang in his head. "Many years ago while in Liverpool, I came across a man named Rafferty. I believe he was a dockworker. I recall him well. Short and balding. No relation, I suppose."

"Ay. 'Twas me father, for sure."

"Really? My impression was of a man of firm opinions." He wasn't going to wait for Elizabeth's views, not this time. Nothing was available but Irish girls. They swarmed off boats daily. Besides, this one could cook! "Miss Rafferty, I think you will do. Could you start tomorrow? I'll tell my wife that you will be here at nine-thirty, if that suits you and someday, you can tell us of life in Liverpool."

She nodded for the second time and saw herself out the front door knowing that in the morning, and every day forward, she would enter the back door. That night, in a rented room, she counted every coin in her possession. At eight tomorrow, she would buy the blue dress in the downstairs store window so he would not see her looking so shabby. She washed her long hair. In the morning, she would braid and twist it into a bun. She closed her eyes and saw him. Not freckled, red-haired, pasty skinned and smelly like boys at home. She saw his smooth, olive complexion, his warm brown eyes. She heard his words, his gentle voice. With long eyelashes resting on cheeks, she conjured the smell of the soap he used and the aroma of the good wool he wore. At seventeen, in this strange country, there was no foretelling the future, but she knew one thing with certainty. This day and the flame-lit image of this man would remain forever knitted in memory.

Chapter Twenty-Nine

*E*xcitement and apprehension swirled through Bridget, preventing sleep. Emotions spiked and ebbed like tides flowing beneath marauding seagulls. She would have her own wages and a roof overhead, but what if the mistress of the house displayed contempt? No, she must be as genial as her husband. But, why no Irish need apply in huge lettering?

By nine thirty the following morning, little doubt survived with the words, "My husband engaged you because of his pressing concern for my welfare. Time will tell if this works out. You may begin by washing this morning's dishes." Twenty minutes later, Elizabeth sauntered through the kitchen door, keys jingling from her hand, "Place settings are kept locked in this drawer. Silver tempts thievery. I'm sure you understand." She placed each piece in its slot, counting, implication clear. "You and Mr. Castle forgot to mention wages, I'm told," she said, scrutinizing the inexpensive dress, "but I'm sure you'll be pleased with his offer. I should show you your sleeping quarters. Kindly follow me."

The quarters were six feet by ten, furnished with pegs along one wall, a cot, an armless chair and a two foot high chest with narrow drawers. Index finger aiming at it, Elizabeth said, "Letter writing can be accomplished there, I suppose." Bridget looked through a small window which faced a barn. Below, on a curve, the silhouette of the Fox home masked woodlands. The arched voice continued, "I noticed you carried a small bundle. The pegs should do and the drawers will hold intimate apparel and writing material." Pulling a sheet of paper from inside a sleeve, she extended it, saying, "This is your list of duties."

The girl gasped, "In one day?"

"Of course not. Just do your best."

Elizabeth walked out with a self-satisfied smile. If the list didn't send her out the door, nothing would.

Hours later, the kitchen door opened, admitting nine-year-old Edward. He stared at the household addition. "I never saw anyone with hair that color. Will it be all white soon? Are you going to be all wrinkled like my teachers?"

She laughed, "Not for a bit, laddie."

"My name is Edward. Mother says to call you Bridget. Not Miss or Mrs. I'm hungry."

Pointing at the icebox, she said, "Have some bangers."

Bewilderment covered his face. "Bangers! What's that?"

"These. Bangers."

"Those are Mr. Bruncken's sausages. You call them bangers?"

"To be sure."

Edward roared, holding his sides. He liked this Bridget who called sausages bangers. "Yes, Bridget, let's both have bangers."

Before the first week ended, they played checkers, joined heads over "*Black Beauty*" and he helped with chores to free her for playtime.

Bridget noticed that Mr. Castle left early and returned late. She didn't see him till the following Sunday when he inquired if a salary of three dollars and sixty cents satisfied. She agreed without delay. Since Maggie had plans to marry, she would send most to her mother.

The wage and the pleasure of Edward's company compensated for the anathema of his mother. She told the boy tales of Irish folklore but there would be no chats about Liverpool.

On nights when winds crashed against shutters and raked clapboards, memory marched across her pillow. When sleet skated across her window, it came, dragging voices. Her father's, "Ah, me precious sons." Her mother's, "Pay no mind, the whiskey takes him." Words from cloistered Eileen. Words from Maggie, "Ye did a sacrilege." In vain, she held hands over her ears.

When she didn't hear their voices, she saw them. The nuns, Father O'Toole's lost look and Father Cavendish, the righteous, acclaimed of the bishop. Introspection couldn't take place in close quarters of a ship ringing with Annie's chatter but it could in the confines of a small room in Boston.

She wished she didn't hear the ranting of her father enraged at his parent's starving in the potato famine. "I lived," he roared, "because they gave what little food they had to me. Those damnable Brits stole our good Irish grain. Our grain could have saved us. I followed it. I had a right to it."

Thus, he explained his move in 1849, never mentioning that the Irish Sea was all the sea he could stand. The perils of the Atlantic discouraged him from seeking gold in streets. In Liverpool, the sea supplied livelihood and for several years he dispatched duty with utmost honesty, alert to ships attempting to conceal true tonnage with deeper and wider cargo space than deck width revealed. He exacted every fathom owed England for tonnage and taxes, taking pride in efficiency while retaining hatred of the British.

Bridget never saw him as a happy man, situated among other Irishmen, living a stone's throw from a pint or two of Guinness and marrying the lovely Ellen Malone. By the age of twenty-three he had two sons, Peter and Simon. He brought both to the docks boasting, "Have ye ever seen the likes of these?" The next child was a girl, named Eileen. This one was also taken for viewing. One seaman said, "A bonnie lass, the image of her mother."

Mansions and Mills

But disaster, named cholera, struck Simon. In short order, dehydration took him to a plot. Ellen grieved but staunch faith sustained her, "Paddy, 'tis God's will."

The next infant was a girl named Maggie, willful and demanding from birth. When she was three months old, her brother, Peter, went to the aid of an eight-year-old chimney sweeper caught in a flue. Peter slipped off the roof, both he and the wedged boy perished.

It was then that Paddy took to whiskey, sometimes blending it with his Guinness. "Two girls, 'twas God's will, was it? Me boys, me boys." But hope rekindled when in 1873, Ellen, at the age of forty-one, conceived again, though he stated, "I'll have no part of another girl. I swear by your saints, it best be a boy." He was as good as his word for when a midwife attempted to place his daughter in his hands, he backed away, saying, "Throw that slimy thing off a dock. Me wife is past forty." Rubbing palms over baldness, he rushed for the pub, roaring, "There be not one boy left in her belly."

The midwife watched his rapid departure, remarking, "A disgrace he is. Worth naught but his empty bottles."

Eileen tended the new arrival, crooning, "Pay no mind. Ye be a rosebud." The newborn raised wavering, blue eyes, grasping her sister's finger with a tiny fist. Maggie didn't view this tiny intruder as a rosebud. What was this minuscule thing to her?

Argument came over her name. Ellen wanted to name her Brigid in honor of the Irish saint, Paddy would have none of it. Aromatic breath wafted over family heads as he bellowed, "She'll have no name from the old sod."

"Ye have no use for any saint!" his once revered wife shot back. Paddy would have his way. When baptism took place, he inserted the name Bridget. He could blame error on the priest's state, no more sober than his own.

Bridget, an affectionate toddler, attempted to climb on his lap, only to be pushed aside. On such occasions, her mother or Eileen rocked and cuddled her. By standing on a chair, Bridget watched her father's route to work. One day she followed, attempting to match the speed of his wobbly gait. He ignored her at waterside, allowed wanderings among strangers and disregarded a possible plunge into the brine. Sunlight shifted to horizontal beams before her mother found her, screeching, "Paddy, ye'll burn for this!"

As young as she had been, she remembered. In Boston, she turned off the gaslight, attempting to forget the painful rejections, but she couldn't.

She tossed and turned as faces of nuns invaded her small world. She recalled how they reminded her to make a good confession before receiving first communion. Maggie sang, "You best not forget any sins or you will go to hell."

She rehearsed and rehearsed hoping to get the good priest, the stumbling one. She stared at the two black boxes with a priest seated in the middle and drapes hanging over each side. She knew when someone exited, the next person in line was to step behind the drapes, kneel and wait for a screened door to slide open. It was obvious that both priests were engaged. She hoped the person confessing to Father Cavendish was sinful, requiring considerable time. She preferred confessing to Father O'Toole. It was said that he sometimes fell asleep and gave you light penances, such as two Hail Mary's. Eyes glued to the drapes, she moaned when an elderly gentleman stepped out of confessing to Father Cavendish while Father O'Toole had a serious sinner. She confessed the original sins and of breaking all commandments. He stopped her at coveting a neighbor's wife. "Child, why are you saying all this?"

"Me sister said I had to make a good confession."

"You have. For now, just honor your mother and father."

"Not me father. He takes to the whiskey."

"Ah, yes, the whiskey." He was well acquainted with the problem. Father O'Toole! Father Cavendish had taken to locking the wine after parishioners complained that baptismal water was being poured on their clothing while missing the intended target. A locked cupboard wasn't the solution. He was beginning to suspect a private supplier. His attention came back to the confessing girl when she coughed. "Your sins are forgiven. Say one Our Father."

On first communion day, Maggie hid Bridget's shoes. The frantic search lasted twenty minutes necessitated a mad dash to church. Panting and thirsty, Bridget drank from a faucet, whose covering had been removed three minutes earlier, a covering placed by nuns to remind seven-year-olds not to break fasting. Pursuing Maggie sang, "Ye broke fast. Ye can't make first communion. Ha. Ha. Sister Adrian will swat ye head tomorrow."

Sister Adrian did worse. She instructed Sister Joan to remove Bridget from the children's choir. "She has lost her portamento."

The perplexed nun replied, "I don't believe so."

"I say she has."

Bridget didn't know what portamento was or how she could have lost it. She looked around her feet, turned, looked under desks till Sister Adrian swatted her with a ruler. "Stand still, fool girl." She used the wooden weapon on a windowsill to emphasize her point as Bridget's eyes shifted back and forth, looking for a lost something. Sister Joan acquiesced. Bridget was out of the choir.

Management, wary of pints and quarts, reduced Paddy's position to unloading cargo. He missed more days from work. The girls made lace, but the income never compensated for expenditures at the pub. He staggered home roaring drunk each morning at two, awakening all shouting of glorious Charles Parnell, known as the uncrowned king of Ireland. "Now, that's ye saint, wife."

There were days when streaming tears, Paddy dragged his daughters to stare at gravestones, "Me sons lie there. Don't ye know?" Neither Bridget nor Maggie remembered them but Maggie would hug her father's legs while Bridget stood apart, leaning into Eileen. At times they remained for hours through pelting rain or biting insects. In winter, they stood in freezing cold, wrapping arms around worn coats. Bridget hated his tears and soon hated him.

The Father O'Toole situation worsened when altar boys reported that he raised the chalice in order to stop the pouring after only a few drops of water, then kept the goblet lowered till the wine overflowed. After the superb taste, he yearned for more.

One day, Father Cavendish followed and observed a meeting. A quick exchange of cash placed a supply of golden fluid under a cassock. He followed the enriched supplier to a pub. "What is that man's name and where does he live?" Informed, he came to a door opened by his young confessor.

"Where is your mother?" A graying, worn woman stepped forward.

"Do you know your husband supplies whiskey to a priest? No doubt at an inflated sum then spends the profit at a pub."

"No, Father, but what me husband will do for the whiskey is small surprise." She wiped embarrassed tears from her eyes. "Father, prayers to Saint Monica do nothing but Father O'Toole said 'twould."

He looked at the meager furnishings, at scraps of food resting in dinner plates, "It appears that miracles are needed here."

"Father, I'm forgetting meself. Do sit for a bit of tea." She wiped her hands on a patched apron and reached for a dented teapot.

He ran a tongue over teeth dried from his trek through the city, but taking anything from this impoverished home would be unpardonable in this world and the next. "Thank you, but no. Are there boys old enough to work?"

"The boys rest in the graveyard. There be only these three." She waved a thin arm towards her daughters.

"And their ages are?" he asked, surveying them.

"Eileen is fifteen, Maggie is twelve and Bridget is seven."

"If the oldest can cook, Lord knows we have a need. Father O'Toole confuses spices." He grimaced, knowing this priest had to leave before the faithful did and he would need a cook.

"Father, she can make mush taste like a king's feast and she can make lace for the altar." What an honor if her daughter cooked for priests and the bishop. Almost as good as having a nun

Mansions and Mills

in the family. Maggie would never be a nun. Maybe tender Bridget.

Adjusting a pinching, clerical collar, Father Cavendish said, "Good. You will serve the church." The girl is fifteen he thought and winsome. How to get around possible disapproval from the bishop? He had taken a fancy to the youngest in her hilarious confession. Perhaps if she came along as chaperone, he could point out the charity of feeding two girls on the brink of starvation. It would take all his considerable charm on the prelate, but that old mind was softening, becoming forgetful.

Bridget tailed Eileen to improved conditions, escaping Maggie's taunts, a drunken father and a mother's incessant reminders, "A good man he is. 'Tis only the whiskey."

Bridget regretted Father O'Toole's departure, leaving not for rehabilitation but to a place without access to liquor. Tears glittered in swollen eyes as he was whisked away, muttering, "I know it was sinful to take money from the poor box, but I couldn't help it. I just couldn't."

"Eileen," Bridget asked, "why couldn't he stay? He was so nice and so sad."

"Hush, ask no questions. Remember, 'tis the food. Belike we can send leftovers home. 'Tis the food that matters and fine it is. Best mind ye tongue. Best do what's told."

Bridget began sampling spices, rolling food over her tongue, reveling in flavors. She developed discerning taste buds. On occasion, Father Cavendish received foreign foods and Bridget's palate deciphered every ingredient. But, within three years, she deciphered something else. Father Cavendish believed a man should conquer his vices. He couldn't conquer his own.

What did he do about it? He did what all do from kings to paupers from warriors to fishwives. He rationalized. The questions for all the same. Don't I contribute to the needy, don't I defend my country, don't I heal the sick, don't I change messy diapers? Aren't I entitled to one secret pleasure of my own? Maybe just a short-lived, long remembered moment. Why not, when I don't beat babies or kick dogs?

Bridget saw Father Cavendish remove his clerical collar, lead a hesitant Eileen into a room and close the door. She remembered Eileen's words, "Hush, ask no questions. 'Tis the food."

Several months later, the priest and the bishop discussed the Sisters of Charity and the Sisters of the Good Shepherd. There was a convent in Angers, France. Did those nuns take a vow of silence Father Cavendish wondered. The bishop didn't know. Nuns were of little importance. His mind wandered. He stared at an ant making his way along a wall. "What were you saying? Oh, I remember. Some girl in your parish. Does she know the baby must be given up?" He stood up to watch the ant's progress. "Look, here comes his friend. This one is named Oscar. That was my father's name. Wasn't it? No, I think that was my uncle's name. Let's have lunch or did we already have it? Are you here to discuss some problem?"

Father Cavendish handled it himself. Eileen would surrender the child and enter a convent. Bridget squealed, "Ye'll be gone from me. Can I take the veil and go too? I can't stay here with his like."

"Ye must stay. Remember 'tis the food for ye and for home. Methinks ye are not suited for the veil, and what? Go home and starve? Be wary and never do what I did. Stay and cook. Just cook. If he says he'll throw ye to the street, tell him ye'll tell about me. I expect he'll hold his tongue if ye hold yours. Like as not, he'll keep ye here." She pressed rosary beads in Bridget's hand, "Keep these in remembrance, I know not where I'll be."

Paddy Rafferty railed at the priest, "Ye got her to take the veil, ye say, and not a word to her sainted mother. Not even good-bye. Bridget, is that the way she wanted it?"

"Yes, 'tis what she wanted." However, thoughts raced. Some fathers, who didn't live in pubs, protected daughters by sending them to other cities, passing them as widows. Seaports were full of such widows.

Paddy said, "Bridget, ye best get yeself home, away from bloody priests afore ye have a bloody veil on ye head." He started tugging her from the church steps.

A peg-legged, drinking buddy said, "Ye tell him, Paddy. Real men go to sea. His kind climbs into skirts." He cackled at his pun.

"Bridget, that best not be the case. They push them in nunneries then."

"No." When would this nightmare of lies end?

Father Cavendish spoke up, "Enough from you and your kind. You realize your manner could disqualify you from church rites."

"If ye mean me funeral, 'tis best. Though 'twould show if I be really dead. If I ain't, I'll jump out of the box afore I go in ye bloody church."

Bridget refused to return home. The priest ate well, rejecting leftovers and giving her the opportunity to bring healthful food home. If cooking pots were overfilled, he didn't notice.

Months later the reprobate father, in the darkness of a moonless night, staggered into a sawpit. The more he struggled to right his intoxicated self, the deeper he went into dust.

Workmen carried him home, neighbors washed and dressed him, a crucifix rested on his chest and rosary beads entangled fingers. Mr. Burke said, "He must be dead. He'd be jumpin' like a frog if he ain't."

One woman said, "Where is twine to tie his toes? We'll have none of his ghost roaring in the streets. 'Twas enough hearing him when he had breath in him." A slab balanced on four, old, chairs shuddered as if unwilling to bear him. A cooper asked, "Are candles to be found? Spread salt so his soul won't be taken, for what it's worth." Keening began, prayers rose skyward and Mr. Kernan sat the night.

The following morning, chairs were kicked over and Paddy left home feet first. The parade of mourners and spade carriers marched in proper order to the church, but something was wrong. Father Cavendish did not meet them. He stood before the church's locked doors, saying, "Take him directly to the graveyard. He cannot enter God's house."

Bridget, eyes blazing with pent-up resentment, cried, "Ye must not do this to me mother. 'Tis enough what ye did to..." He cut her off, placing restraining hands on her shoulders.

"Not another word. She chose to live with a blasphemous husband. I protect the house of the Lord."

"Ye should protect it from yeself. Open the doors and have a mass for me mother's sake."

"Never." With three steps, the space between them closed. She raised her right arm and swung it forward, striking a blow which sent him stumbling down the stairs.

Maggie screamed, "Sacrilege. Ye did a sacrilege."

After righting the priest, all trudged to the sod that held Peter and Simon. They nestled him with his sons, but none came back to the house.

Her mother said, "Bridget, ye must leave. Naught is here for ye now. Maggie will care for me but never own up to ye. None will. Belike, ye can do service in Manchester." She held Bridget as she did when a hurt child cried for her father. "Think kindly of him. 'Twas the whiskey, just the whiskey and two headstones."

Deaf to the last sentence, Bridget answered, "Manchester 'tis not far enough. I will take meself where gold lines the streets."

She boarded a ship crowded with the hopeful and befriended a girl named Annie who was soon attracted to an officer. "Pay him no mind," Bridget advised, "he is full of his uniform." On deck, escaping human stench, she continued, "Men are full of themselves, not caring a farthing for any but themselves. Be wary."

In that small, Boston room, memories came in all shades. Kaleidoscopic colors twirled in the margins of her mind. She had warned Annie. All men felt entitled to vices. They were all alike except, maybe, the one who slept with a beautiful, spendthrift, haughty wife a few feet beneath her floor. So near, so far.

Chapter Thirty

In April 1891, Ben burst in the door, the picture of style from cane to the bowler hat which he swept off in a mock curtsy to Rosie. "Good day, fair lady, and where might I find your employer?"

She gave him a head gesture indicating that Francis was in the rear. Delight in the demise of the bustle was replaced by the new demands for puckered sleeves. Soon she'd have deeper complaints when sleeves enlarged into massive, mutton shaped ones.

Ben found Francis unpacking with sporadic pauses to rub his back. "Whoa," Ben roared, "you look like blazes. What goes?"

"Working the docks nights to afford a servant for Elizabeth. Edward is bouncing back from diphtheria but she languishes."

"Francis, think of investments."

"I couldn't afford investment in horse manure."

"Too bad. Good fertilizer, I'm told. Look, you are doing fine on reimbursements. Don't sweat it and quit that other job before you burden Elizabeth with widowhood. I'm serious." It was obvious to Ben business here now flourished. Why a problem?

Guilt drilled Francis. He had written Ben a sizable check but then he opened the mail to a bill for glassware trimmed in gold-leaf and one for a riding habit, boots and a tennis racket. His wife asserted, "Edward must accompany his well-connected classmates." He tore up the first check and rewrote a much smaller one. His family was growing more and more expensive.

Having followed Ben's advice, he was home nights, enjoying Bridget's tasty fare fresh from the stove with his forty-year-old wife, who looked no older than thirty-five, but who remained pale. An impenetrable melancholy encased her, making her more inaccessible than ever. Why was her health not improving?

Summer 1891 passed. The calendar publicized fall and green-clad foliage prepared for a color change. In a blue haze of twilight, Francis, surrounded by books, magazines and newspapers, indulged in his favorite pastime. Elizabeth joined him in the library, asking, "Do you think Edward spends too much time with Bridget? Besides hopscotch, there are marbles, checkers and jump rope."

"I doubt such activities will corrupt him." He folded the newspaper and reached for a book on Field Marshal von Moltke.

"Yesterday, they made molasses candy and he tells me she had deciphered the recipe for Mr. Bruncken's sausages."

"Time well spent. Ask her for the recipe."

"She wouldn't write it down least an evil elf sees it. This talk of elves is superstition."

"If you want me to say he won't outgrow this like all fairy-tales, I can't oblige. At his age, I thought God had nothing to do than watch me and record wrongdoings. Forget it, sit down and read this book."

"Read this? It's about a general!" She pushed it away as if burned.

"Elizabeth, this is history and unknown history is a menace." He picked up a newspaper and remarked, "Now this is a tragedy. This Russian persecution of Jews is causing refugee problems."

"You read too much. I don't care about refugees. Jews are not my problem and never will be."

Mansions and Mills

He read every detail from the House of Rothschild withdrawing from participation in the Russian Conversion Loan to Baron Maurice de Hirsch donating funds to establish Jewish colonies abroad. Saying that his horses ran for charity, he donated all of their winnings. Francis concluded that his wife was right. Migrating, homeless Jews would never impact them.

On that same day, a man named Solomon Goldstein and his young, pregnant wife traveled towards Woodbine, New York where a five thousand acre farm set up by the baron anticipated Jewish settlers. In October, under a balsamic moon, the Goldstein's son was born, blinking unfocused eyes at his parents. The father said, "Is good he wait to be born in America!" The exultant immigrant continued, "His name will be Jacob and he will be rich man in America!"

In Boston, with Edward's coercion, Eliot collaborated in annihilating Bridget's list of duties, freeing her not only for playtime but giving her the opportunity for an early bedtime. Elizabeth marveled at the girl's efficiency. How could she complete the ironing while doing the grocery shopping? The boys took the shopping list to the store while Bridget did other chores hidden behind a closed, bedroom door. The boy's trips to the well for buckets of water shortened window washing. Deception was fun and rummaging in stores delightful. Monday's washing was done on Sundays while Elizabeth took her walk and attended Sunday affairs. The boys enjoyed turning the paddles on the washing machine. Edward said, "This is not work. It's fun. I can crank faster than you, Eliot. We'll hide the wet clothes in the cellar. When Mother sees them on the line, she'll think Bridget got up really, really early. Let's play marbles." Francis noticed all three scrambling on the ground. Bridget didn't look like bad influence.

Francis' soothing reassurances lasted two more weeks till Edward reported the enthralling visit to the nuns. Mother lectured at length then catching Bridget's arm, she hissed, "No one in this house is Catholic. If you expose Edward to anyone or anything of your faith, you shall be dismissed."

Taken by surprise, Bridget gasped. Unbalanced, her skirt brushed her employer's. Elizabeth snapped hers back, "Keep your distance and remember your place."

On the day in 1892 when Edward turned ten, Francis noticed that Elizabeth, in beige wool, had gained little weight. In spite of having all chores lifted from her, the lassitude persisted. He was chaffing inside a stiff, high, choking collar when Bridget walked in, carrying the cake. He saw her every evening at suppertime, yet for some reason had not noticed that she was no longer the thin girl fresh off a depleted ship. His raised eyebrows registered surprise and concern. Concern that the policeman walking the beat or the postman might notice the curvaceous girl. The thought of losing a good cook to another man unsettled.

January snow visited several days later, layering the ground with white frosting, and to the tailor's surprise, Ben dragged unenthused Bill in, saying, "This man once said I needed sprucing up, now I say he resembles a vagrant."

Neither Rosie, nor three absorbed men heard the tinkling bell. Ben checked material, Francis oiled a machine, Rosie inspected colors in a spool delivery but Bill battled distracting concerns over Fall River Mills. The mule spinners had obtained wage increases causing the weavers to organize a union. The Spindle City triggered headaches. He wondered why he should concern himself with his wardrobe.

Bridget, unnoticed and unheard, opened and closed the door again. The second bell tinkling caught Rosie's ear. Raising her massive weight, she took a bag from the girl's hand. Completed hats peeked through.

"Ah, she be up to this labor to her liking? Belike she ain't so frail. And ye be the colleen born to serve her likes. Could not this errand wait a fairer day?" She looked out at a darkening sky, promising more snow and inspected a shivering girl in a threadbare coat. Rosie vowed to find enough leftover material to make this ragamuffin the warmest coat in Boston. "Come, warm yeself by the fire. Ye look frozen to death."

Mansions and Mills

The men noticed her when, gloves clenched in shuddering teeth, she warmed her hands, rubbing them with vigor. Francis withdrew the hats, attempting to explain, "She wants them sold fast so she can design more. Elizabeth takes such pleas...." He stammered into humiliated silence as the staring men noted how the weather warred with the servant's worn clothing.

Ben stepped forward, "Allow me to offer the warmth of my carriage for your return trip."

"Sir, it might be amiss. 'Tisn't me station to ride in fancy carriages, but 'tis much obliged I am."

Rosie pushed her toward the two men, "Nonsense, mind ye go. If I don't mistake, a storm is blowing up."

Bridget requested to be dropped off a block before the house. Bill hopped out to help her alight. Embarrassed eyelids lowered, she said, "I'm beholding to both of ye gentlemen."

"My pleasure." Ben said, tipping his hat.

Bill watched her trudge up the hill, exclaiming, "I forgot about my wardrobe in those fantastic eyes!"

"So did I."

On Tuesday, the twenty-second day of March, Elizabeth read a newspaper account of the mortality rate in Chicago the previous summer from typhoid. Clutched by familiar fear for Edward, she proposed having him out of Boston as early as May to avoid a typhoid, cholera or diphtheria epidemic. She said, "Francis, I would like to take Edward to New Brunswick through the summer and until mid-September. Ann has a new husband. I will have the opportunity to meet him and Edward will become acquainted with his Canadian relatives."

"A wonderful idea. It will get you away from summer heat." Then he thought of his fabulous meals. "However, what about Bridget?"

"She can do chores in early morning, leave your prepared meals in the icebox and spend nights in the convent. I'm told nuns accommodate Catholic women in every way. Bridget visits often enough."

Mother Superior agreed. Such an arrangement would offer opportunities to persuade Bridget to take the veil. "Yes, child," she said stroking her crucifix, "come when Mrs. Castle leaves. I expect you will arrive in time for evening prayers."

Elizabeth and Edward left in dawn's awakening sunshine, but fickle weather delivered a downpour by late afternoon. After checking a clock and realizing she was late, Bridget packed all her clothing, except all her socks, in a satchel. Clutching it to her chest she ran under an oversized umbrella. A cold, drenching splash from a rushing carriage hit her. The shock caused her to drop both the umbrella and the satchel which popped open, spilling all the contents into a puddle. "A pox on ye." she shouted at an unconcerned driver.

She heard a voice, "Bridget, what on earth happened?"

"Oh, Mr. Castle, everything I own is wet." Streaming strands of hair clung to her face.

He held his umbrella over her sopping head, "You are wet to the skin and cannot proceed. The convent is blocks away. Come, you must turn back."

While her skirts wept rainwater in the rear hall, he went to the front hall, retrieving an overcoat from the stand. "Here, go upstairs and put this on. I'll light a fire and dry your clothing."

She stood uncertain, shivering, and apprehensive of dripping over Mrs. Castle's polished parquet floor. "Glory be, I'll drip water on the floors and the stairway."

"The wood will survive but you might not survive pneumonia. Get upstairs, child, and get into the coat. Do you have another pair of shoes?"

"No, Sir, but there be dry socks."

"Hope you have two pairs up there." he said, fine lines puckered from smiling eyes. "Move, you look like a drowned cat. I expect you had supper."

She nodded, "The nuns said to fill meself to the brim here. 'Tis a convent on short rations."

Once more, a smile lifted his features, "Small surprise. I'll enjoy my solitary meal. Did you hear me say move?"

After the sound of his rattling dishes, came the sound of footsteps towards the library. Ears strained to follow his trail, but the dwelling's creaks and mutterings along with swelling rain smothered acoustics. She didn't hear footfalls on the stairs nor the closing of his chamber door.

Once inside, he looked at walls mourning an accustomed shadow. He wanted the Elizabeth he had not had for over a year as she traveled through exhaustion, frailness and depression. Relieved of household duties, she appeared to have bloomed anew enjoying designing and producing hats, but she still claimed ill health. What kind of ill health? Was she so affected by that terrible time of fighting for Edward's survival? Was she concealing deep fear? What had happened to that lustful wife? Where had she gone? In such a large world, how could a man be so alone?

From deep sleep, he was awakened by a load crash. Did the storm cause damage? Hurrying, he checked the rooms on the second floor. All looked normal. Buffeted by wind and rain, the honeysuckle bush bent and swayed, but no broken oak or elm branches rested on the lawn. He was certain the sound had not come from downstairs. Attic stairs flew beneath his feet.

The door to Bridget's small room stood open and he was only a few feet from her kneeling figure. He asked, "Did you hear a crash?"

"Me apologies. 'Twas me knocking over the chair getting me beads in the dark." The light from the half-filled lamp he held fell on the rosary beads.

"Those look like mine, or rather like my mother's."

"Did ye steal her beads?"

"No, she is no longer with us. Do yours come from your mother?"

"No, from me sister but she has aplenty in the convent." There was no concealing bitterness.

"You sound angry. If it was the life she wanted, why?"

"Cuz 'twasn't the life she wanted. Me father could have saved her if not for his whiskey." Gentle tears turned into violent sobs.

Placing the lamp on the floor, he dropped to his knees, brushing the tears away with his fingers. In a shocked moment he realized she still wore the unbuttoned overcoat. There was nothing between them but one layer of his pajamas. He rose to leave but long fingers restrained.

He wanted Elizabeth. He had hungered for over a year. No, he hungered for her since he was sixteen and the doubt was always there. Once more, he tried to extricate himself and once more Bridget held fast. Groaning, he kicked off his slippers.

Captain Addison had said, "If you have one woman, you have them all." Tonight, for a short time he had Elizabeth, but in coiling suppleness, Bridget was not Elizabeth. She was someone, something he had never imagined and he could not tear away. What made it so different?

She did not look at him as he reached for his discarded slippers, but murmured, "Ye be Catholic. Please, never confess me."

She awoke before dawn filtered in the window. The storm had traveled westward plaguing others, but left clouds behind veiling the moon's condemnation.

Though midday delivered soft breezes and cheerful sun, Francis wallowed in misery. How could he have done such a thing? The girl was eighteen and despoiled at his doing. Guilt. Didn't he carry enough? Guilt that he had assisted in depriving a woman who had saved his life of her grandchild. What choice did he have in that matter? But still it hounded him. Each day he prayed that Rufus would not kill again. He carried guilt over deceiving Elizabeth by locking up ledgers. Now he had added this. He clawed his hair. Apologizing to the girl was the least he could do. Heavy steps carried him home at two thirty.

He found her sitting on a ledge, enjoying sunlight and combing her hair. Strands captured golden sunbeams as the breeze lifted filaments. She brushed them off her face while humming an

Irish ditty. After many starts and stops, apologetic words dashed from his mouth, but she held up a warning hand. "Now don't be saying what grinds ye mind. 'Tis always the woman's fault. Don't ye know that?"

"No, I don't know that and don't believe that. You are a child. This is my fault. I can only beg forgiveness though I don't deserve it."

She flounced from her perch. "I'll be taking meself to the convent now." She gathered her belongings without a backward glance and strode down the hill. He didn't see her again. He saw her handiwork. Washing was done, shirts were ironed and meals required heating only, including morning muffins.

In New Brunswick, Elizabeth heard Ann's views, "Did you notice that farm people don't get all the sickness that afflicts city dwellers? I think it is fresh food and well water." She churned butter with zeal and continued, "I think it's what goes in people's stomachs."

In July, Francis saw a hearse in front of his neighbor's house. Though the infant survived, Mrs. Fox did not. Due to travel restrictions, Elizabeth could not attend services and Helen was not at her residence. She was somewhere across the country on a lecture tour.

Elizabeth returned on Wednesday, the seventh day of September determined to follow Ann's advice. When Bridget renewed residence, the mistress of the house handed food instructions. Everything had to be carried or delivered from local farms. No more choosing from fly-covered chickens hanging from hooks but a delivered chicken's price was seventeen cents a pound instead of fifteen cents. Milk, if fetched and carried by Bridget, still cost six cents a quart. She grumbled, "Next, her ladyship will put me to milking the cows."

Increased food prices seemed natural to bill-paying Francis. After all, Bengaline silk rose to one dollar and fifty cents per twenty-one inch width. All the bargaining still left the price of a new sewing machine at thirteen dollars and fifty cents. Bridget watched him, palms pressed to forehead as he juggled accounts. She could spare him the price of lard by saving more bacon grease. Mrs. Castle wouldn't know the difference. She ate everything, perhaps she'd eat sawdust marinated in butter. As long as she didn't eat the stove. Bridget loved the semicircular, side attachment which held water warmed by the stove's potbelly.

On the twenty-first day of the month, Bridget's eyes rested on a stethoscope encircling a doctor's neck, while saying, "Methought 'twas consumption. Never thought this for just one time. It took me sister how many years, I don't know, but 'tis for sure 'twasnt done just once."

"Perhaps her health was not as good. Strikes me you had good nourishment, forming what I call good, maternal soil."

"That me had for ten years. Took meals with the priest."

Having made calls to ailing men of the cloth, he smirked, "If you shared the same fare, you were well-nourished indeed." He had treated many cases of indigestion in rectories and seen many priestly hearts damaged from obesity. "Will the rake marry you?"

Her gaze shifted from the stethoscope to crowds outside the window herding like sheep through narrow streets. Where would this lamb go? Not to adoption. She'd not surrender her infant to strangers. She'd write Annie. Maybe she knew someone who would take her in. Eliot's aunt helped women in trouble. Could she be found now?

The doctor questioned again, "Will he marry you?"

"No, Sir." She picked up a jacket fashioned by Rosie and handed the doctor several coins. Noticing how few were left, he returned them.

Annie had nothing to offer. She hated mill work and was going to try New York's offerings. The grieving, next door widower had no idea where Helen was, "You can write her at a Baltimore address but heaven knows when she will get it. She is always away. Are you planning to join the movement? You know, that lifestyle requires adequate funds." Under his questioning gaze, Bridget beat a hasty retreat.

Mansions and Mills

The only resort was nuns and adoption. That wouldn't do. She wanted the baby. She would have to turn to Francis. When she told him, he paled and stumbled backwards. If that possibility hadn't crossed his mind, it might be because twelve years had passed since he had caused a pregnancy. Didn't potency wan somewhat at thirty-five?

"Have you considered the Home of the Good Shepard?"

"No, because they will want the child for adoption. A way needs finding afore Mrs. Castle notices. 'Twont take long." A tight corset and loose skirts would not hide it much longer.

His mind raced. If he managed to keep Bridget segregated in the country, added expense and all, Elizabeth would expect another servant. With upholstering booming and with the fancy ladies' demands on Ben's aging friends, he was doing well. Elizabeth's hats sold well but Rosie and Eric deserved raises. He needed to upgrade equipment. Could he manage to support a household for Bridget? He had to find a way.

On Columbus Day, Edward wanted to attend the four hundred year, Italian celebration. He bounced to music at the band concerts and applauded the unveiling of a statue at the corner of Washington and Malden Streets. He dragged parents to a parade. He anticipated the evening's fireworks. Amid banners and flags, a gray-faced Francis answered his wife's question, "Have you noticed Bridget's weight gain?" He stammered the facts. A candied apple fell from Elizabeth's hand.

Edward picked it up, brushed dirt from its sticky sides, and said, "Don't be upset, you can still eat this part." She didn't hear him. Using the gloveless hand, she dug fingernails into her husband's wrist. He stood motionless as blood garnished the walk. She twirled on one foot and elbowing, pushing and stepping on toes made her way through the throng.

Watching her disappear into hordes of revelers, he said, "Sorry, Edward, but we won't be going to the fireworks."

The boy's yelp could be heard above the cheering crowd as the Italian flag snapped in the wind, "I want to go! You promised! Where is Mother going?"

As they headed in Elizabeth's direction, they met Eliot who shouted, "Edward, come to the fireworks with us. Our cousin is taking us. Mr. Castle, let's go together."

"I can't but Edward can go, if it's all right with your cousin."

"Sure thing," said the twenty-two year old, "I'll see that he gets home in one piece."

Francis crawled home. Might as well go home for his fireworks. But there wasn't one. No one was there. Bridget must have gone to the celebration with Rosie. They had formed a close friendship. A warning bell sounded. Would she tell Rosie? Would Bridget name the father? Panic creased his forehead. The scandal would ruin his business. In a cool house, perspiration ran from head to toe.

The outside door closed and Elizabeth walked in holding Bridget's arm. "I found her just as she met Rosie. We all had chocolate and cookies together. In fact, we enjoyed each other for almost an hour. Didn't we, Bridget? Now go to your room and stay there." She pushed the girl towards the staircase and waited till she heard the attic door close.

Elizabeth asked, "Where is Edward?" Once informed, she said, "How convenient." Then, in pianissimo, continued, "Now, Francis, you started this little play and I will tell you just how it will end. Bridget will not leave this house. She will not tell her sad story to anyone. Can you imagine if she told Rosie or sought help from Helen, the friend of the wanton? She would have figured who the father is and enjoyed crucifying you."

He slumped in a chair, looking through the window and fixing on a rose-colored puddle, a remnant of a brief shower. Thirsty sunrays sipped it skyward. He wished a beam could sip him from this room. She had not finished, "We will close the drapes and you can say I'm the victim of a difficult confinement. Only Helen would know it is impossible, but with her sister gone

Mansions and Mills

and with her dedication to saving womankind, she has no reason to return. Neither Bridget nor I shall be seen by anyone."

"I expect I'll have to fetch groceries. Won't that cause conjecture when we have a servant?"

Suffused in golden light of late afternoon, she said, "It's 1892. You must have heard of the telephone." She went on as if speaking to a child, "You know, they fasten a box to a wall with a speaker and a receiver attached to the side. You tell the operator what number you are calling and she connects you. The big bells ring when someone wants to talk to you. Simple. We get a phone. Do you understand how it works?"

"Elizabeth," he said, sinking lower in the chair, "I know all about phones."

"Even Bridget should be able to phone in orders."

He wondered why is she so calm? Why isn't it possible for this woman to wail like a banshee or smash things? But then, British ladies like refinement.

Nevertheless, she was seething. "How dare you jeopardize Edward's future? How dare you chance disgracing this family? How dare you insult my sense of propriety and in my home? Did you consider what a scandalous affair would do to the business?"

"It was not an affair. It happened only once and will not happen again. I never meant to hurt you."

"Hurt me? Don't flatter yourself. You can't hurt me." Words sprayed like puncturing shrapnel, "One time or a thousand times, one harlot or a thousand harlots. Do you think your body is that valuable to me?" It had been when she thought it would produce a child. What galled her was that body produced a child for another woman. Adultery she could ignore but she could not ignore another woman having her husband's child.

He comforted himself with the thought that she spoke from rage. He believed it possible to avoid disgrace and still protect Bridget. That old story of widowhood in another city could succeed again. In time Elizabeth would get over this and things would return to normal.

327

She sliced his thoughts, remarking, "I hope it's a girl. She will be named Victoria after the queen."

He unbuttoned a strangling collar, "What if the mother prefers to select the name?"

Green eyes roamed the room in silence, taking in the costly furnishings before her lips settled in a determined line, "As I said before, you may have started this drama but I'll write scene three. Bridget will not name it. Francis, understand something. This child is mine."

Chapter Thirty-One

That evening, Elizabeth stood inside the doorframe, erect, stately, a dome of rage surrounding her. The servant, expecting a pitch to the street, sat on her cot, belongings bundled at her feet, planning to seek Rosie. She would not finger anyone. She would only state her condition. If pressed, she would claim an indiscretion with an irresistible, naval officer. She rose to leave.

"Where do you think you are going?"

"I thought Rosie might..."

The arched voice interrupted, "She can't help you. She can't afford to feed your condition nor can she cover your disgrace. Only we can do that. You will stay here, seeing no one until the infant arrives."

"Then what?"

"That solution must wait. One problem at a time. You will retire at nine and arise at five-thirty. At the end, a nap will be permitted, but no game playing and no association with Edward. You are not to be seen even by delivery men. If you speak to anyone about this, you will rue the day. Have I made myself clear?"

Bridget nodded. What better solution was there for now? She had to have a strategy for when the baby was born. Going home was impossible. Maggie hated her. She had asked Eileen why and been told, "Methinks because ye be prettier." That couldn't explain it. Eileen was the prettiest. She'd have to think of something. She had about four months left to plan. Could she count on Mr. Castle? Would he care or would he act like her father, minus whiskey?

In truth, unhappiness and dread haunted Francis. Although his intention had been to offer protection for mother and child, he never intended an enlarged household. Elizabeth's planned domesticity seemed unimaginable, even perverse. She would become knitted to the child, one that Bridget could cart back to England, carrying that widowhood chestnut with her. She could say, "Me husband is gone to Davy Jones' Locker." Elizabeth may not have considered that, but his wife must be spared emotional devastation.

Weeks later, leaves, having deserted trees, crunched beneath feet hurrying to a jeweler's store. This Christmas, Elizabeth would be gifted emeralds. A guilty conscience present? No. The plan framed last year, had finances this year. Excluding Bridget, the family celebrated the holiday with strings of cranberries on the tree, exchanged gifts, caroling and game playing. Francis convinced himself that Elizabeth, like many wives, would forgive and forget.

The following evening, a crimson-robed Francis stepped aside as Elizabeth entered his treasured library. Fingering and twisting a red tassel, he said, "Elizabeth, be realistic, does this living condition make sense?" The long silence provoked another question, "Have you considered how you will feel after you become attached to the infant and Bridget finds better accommodations and departs?"

She watched the quickened rise and fall of his chest with a catlike grin, "She will not be able to take it anywhere, not when the birth certificate lists you as the father."

"Have you lost your wits? My name, listed with hers!"

She kicked a footstool aside. "For all your self-education," she waved an arm at stacked volumes, "you haven't an ounce of shrewdness."

"You can't link our names on an official document. Haven't you been adamant in concealing the linkage?"

"Yes," she answered with a musical chime, "I told you this child is mine and so it shall be. Five minutes after delivery, you will register the infant as being biologically ours. It can be done since she's too stupid to give certification any thought."

He rose from his chair, poked embers and added logs to the holly-decked fireplace. "That's fraud."

"Which will never be discovered. Will she rush to City Hall to acknowledge illegitimacy and adultery? Adultery is a crime. She's at our mercy."

He faced the fireplace, preferring it so. She couldn't see his anguish. How much injustice was to be heaped on this girl? And he an accessory again, a perpetrator of lies, an instrument smothering so much, even murder. This time, however, it was all his doing.

She walked up to her husband, wrapped her arms around his waist, pressed her head against his and whispered, "Worry about nothing but the business." Her longing for children had been the main motivation for marriage to this tolerated man and she would have his children regardless of the incubator.

As his nostrils drank the essence of her cologne, his mind traveled to the first sight of her so many years ago. Nothing had changed. He laid a head against the mantle in agonized submission.

Beginning on Columbus Day, Edward sensed swirling, negative emotions in the household culminating on that snowy night when he heard Bridget's tortured cries. He had been outraged when his father locked him in his room. Confined there, he concluded that Bridget was injured and the scissors were used to cut bandages. Pressing an ear to the keyhole, he managed to hear muffled voices.

"You must do it now. We don't know how soon Helen will arrive."

His father's raised voice said, "No, that's too cruel."

"There's no choice any more. Just do it! Do it now!"

Edward tried the knob. He tried seeing through the keyhole. Trembling with cold, he wrapped himself in a quilt. There was the sound of heavy footfalls followed by a moan. Within minutes he heard the horse's hoofs and the swish of runners through the snow.

The following morning, Edward listened to his mother saying, "Your father is taking you to a different school in New Hampshire. You will stay there and not come home every day. They are expecting you." She put a warm coat over a heavy sweater, tugging sleeves which wouldn't budge over thick cables. "Now, you mustn't write to Eliot. Soon his aunt will be here and she will destroy letters before he sees them."

"Why would she do that?"

"Because she doesn't like any of us." she lied as she won the sleeve battle. "I'm sorry, but you can never see Eliot again."

Tears began flowing, flying off his cheeks as he shook his head in denial, "He's always going to be my friend." Through the kitchen window, he saw bloodstained snow, "Where's Bridget?"

"She has been injured in a fall and has gone for care at the convent. She might stay there because we are moving and she doesn't want to move with us. You will find new friends."

His grim-faced father sat in a chair, head in hands. Pouncing from a footstool, his feet began a pacing march while ten fingers paraded through his hair.

"Elizabeth, why that hellhole? Can't we get lost in Everett?"

"It's too close. We can get lost in that hellhole. Who would dream we'd go there?"

Edward wondered why they wanted to be lost. That was scary! He heard a kitten-like sound from upstairs. Wrapping a scarf around him and pushing him, Mother said, "Go now. Let me see how fast you can run."

Father shook his head when Edward asked, "May I say goodbye to Eliot and Bridget?" and sunk in thought, was silent during the trip to New Hampshire. How could he make another new start? And in such a place. Without Ben, Bill, Louise and the "ladies" they sent the last one would have been impossible. The horse plodded along but his mind raced. Payments would go to Ben even under austere living conditions and living conditions would be austere until he became established in a strange, friendless city. He could not sell the house with speed and still get the asking price. Storage bills and Edward's tuition would dent the budget. Remorse and guilt burned like jungle fever. Neither woman deserved the fate inflicted on them. His fault. All his fault.

They packed, sold the house, put much in storage and found a place on South Main in Fall River with the swiftness of greyhounds. The new house had tailoring space downstairs and living space upstairs.

Brought home, Edward choked at reduced circumstances, including public education, but Mother seemed delighted as she said, "Look at what the stork left here. A baby sister." She recorded the birth in Fall River, Massachusetts, listing the parents as Francis and Elizabeth Castle.

Edward walked the streets of hills and mills where the wealthy lived on the Hill and the poor lived below the Hill. It was a city so full of mills that tiny City Hall appeared to occupy too much space. There was a triangular area where mills embraced one another, bordered by Hartwell Street, Pleasant Street and Plymouth Avenue. Standing on the corner of Rodman Street, Edward could see mills before him and to his left and right.

In mills, carders sent lint into the air, causing cotton fever, twisting machines caught hair, causing scalping and the sound of slamming, metal parts deafened workers. Spinners lost fingers, burns resulted from contact with burning steam vents. The mill owners profited on cheap, child labor.

Edward watched boys skimming rocks on Crab Pond. They jeered, "Well, look at fancy pants." Then they threw rocks at him. It was late, with the moon sitting on treetops when he first saw her striding on North Main Street. Her pointed chin reminded him of Bridget but her eyes were brown and her hair the color of sable. Maybe the girls were friendlier than the boys here. As he followed, she frowned. They had reached Brightman Street when she stomped her foot, "Why are you following me?"

"I'm curious. You work in that mill back there. Why don't you go to school?"

"My father said it was more important for boys to go but my brother got kicked out for sticking gum on the nun's habit. When he gets work as a doffer, maybe I can go instead." She waved him away.

"Where are you going?"

"Are you a dummy? Can't you see everyone going to church? It's Friday." He took his eyes off her and noticed people climbing church stairs. "Why are they going today?"

"For the stations of the cross. You don't know? Don't tell me you go to church on Rock Street."

"Yes, I do."

"Then you are a dirty Protestant. Go away. My father will whip me if I talk to you." He forgot about friendship with the sable-haired girl.

He didn't like this unfriendly place where they spoke in strange languages. Had they moved here because this is the place where storks drop babies? Victoria was all right, he supposed, but now that they had her, why couldn't they move back? That stork might never leave another anyway. Besides, she was strange. Mother fussed over her but her blue eyes followed Father. Most times only he could stop her perpetual crying. Edward wanted out of the Spindle City with its stench, with a river polluted with manufacturing waste, garbage and slop pots and where even girls weren't friendly. Most of all he wanted Eliot and Bridget.

On a cold, overcast day, wind puckered Mount Hope Bay and tussled with Edward's hair. He saw his father in a shoeshine parlor. Spending money on this he fumed while we live with dingy walls, dark wainscot and uneven floors. Francis hoped that a professional shine would make his last pair look presentable. A man stopped and asked, "Aren't you Mr. Castle's son?" After an affirmative nod, the stranger continued, "A fine man and bright. I suggested politics for him."

Mansions and Mills

Crimson suffused the portly, Celtic face as Edward spat, "Mother says only the Irish go into politics."

Continuing his trudge home, he sickened at swarms of chimneys like ugly, red phalanges seeming to pierce the sky. Thick, cloud cover refused to allow today's soot to dissipate, so grimy air winged in and out of lungs and fell on houses painted either brown or gray. No white houses could be found.

That evening he complained, "I hate it here. I want to go back to Boston and see sun again. I'm sick of loud, morning bells shaking the city awake every morning at five-thirty. I want to see Eliot and find Bridget."

"Edward, don't mention this again." His mother stood firmly before him, hands on hips. "You cannot see Eliot and Bridget. Chances are she is wearing a habit. Finding her is impossible." He noticed Father sinking his face into his hands.

In Boston, Rosie had washed the inside windows, balancing her huge frame on a stepladder. Mr. Castle had paid her to make things look presentable. While sweeping the floor, fighting to catch every scrap of material and thread, she was distracted by a jingling doorbell. Stunned faces looked around the vacant shop. Ben asked, "What happened? This place was buzzing three weeks ago. Where is everybody?"

"They left, not saying where and not one word from Bridget. She is me friend, or so it seemed. What got into her?"

"When did they leave?"

"They left days ago. Bridget, there ain't no saying. Saw her last on Columbus Day. Not one word since." A tearful polka-dot design formed on a wooden floor.

"Did you get to ask Mr. Castle anything?"

"Indeed, not an answer in the man."

Ben reeled. This didn't seem like the man he knew. Something must have happened. But what? It didn't seem plausible that the man would run out on a loan.

At first, astonishment rendered Louise speechless. For suspended minutes she leaned against a wall, wishing for a chair. Finally, she asked, "Rosie, are you going to need employment?"

"That I am." She caught a fresh batch of tears with her sleeve.

Louise wasn't concerned about Eric. He was young and a man. If worse came to worse, he could go West and shoot Indians. "Ben," she said, "I've never had a lady's maid. Doing my own coiffure is trying. Perhaps Rosie would care to help me."

Rosie bit her lower lip, "Mrs. Davis, 'tisnt in me nature."

Undeterred, Louise answered, "If Mr. Davis agrees it soon will be."

He put a finger on Rosie's arm, "You have our address, try it."

Darkness fell soon after they left. She could learn to be a lady's maid. Pleasing one woman as opposed to several tempted. She muttered, "A rich lady's maid! I'd be bettering meself."

Reaching for keys in a jacket pocket, she looked around before locking up for the last time. A cutting voice sliced her nostalgia, "Is there a Mr. Castle around here?"

"He moved away."

"Moved away? Not far I hope. Where to?"

"Ye be asking the wrong person. Did ye not come before asking for some other man?" She reached for her shawl. Now all the pegs stood naked. "If me don't mistake the name was Castro."

"One and the same. It took this long to find out. Can you direct me to anyone who knows where he is?"

"No, he up and left."

"Good Lord. I told them to close this case. Thought it impossible, now I know it is. This bloke might have taken off for the Azores where he came from." Oozing impatience, he shoved a briefcase under his arm.

She watched his stiff-backed retreat before putting the key in the lock. It made a loud, final click.

Chapter Thirty-Two

On the day of the move to Fall River, cold infiltrated every organ in Bridget as her eyes opened in a room illuminated by a small, corner light embracing a diminutive figure, shrouded in white. Through shivering teeth, Bridget said, "I'm cold. I'm so cold."

"That's because of so much blood loss. Make no sound and I will find you more blankets." As she opened the door, light flowed in from a corridor. The tiny figure looked to the right and to the left before hustling away. Returning with arms full, she said, "Mother Superior wants to speak to you but that can wait. What she doesn't know won't hurt her so let's whisper. She'll think you are still sleeping."

Bridget, squinting in the dark, realized this white-clad figure was a novice. She murmured, "How did I get here?"

"Just before dawn last Thursday the bell rang and a man deposited you on the floor inside the door. He rushed off in a sleigh and Mother Madeline wants to know where the baby is. Did it survive?"

"It must have. I heard her say, 'I have a lusty daughter' but 'tis mine. She took it."

"A note was attached to your waist. I was instructed to give it to you." She reached for a shelf and produced a sealed envelope with the name Bridget standing stark against the white background. Recognized handwriting said of how sorry he was and how he hoped her depth of forgiveness equaled his depth of remorse. He promised that the child would have the best care a father could provide. Giving it thought, she concluded this outcome preferable to other options. As parents both Francis and Elizabeth excelled.

The following morning Sister Madeline stood at the foot of her cot. A huge crucifix dangled from a belt encircling a huge frame. Hazel eyes blazed as she asked, "Where is the baby?" Head bent, the novice tidied the room, placing fresh towels on a rack and opening shutters. She pretended oblivion when the question was repeated, "Are you deaf? Where is it?"

"The baby is safe. 'Twill be raised by the father."

"A likely story! Too many babies are found in ashcans, rivers and alleys to believe that and how many fathers assume responsibility? I'll submit a report." She whirled out, skirts flapping behind her.

The novice said, "It is not my place to question, but didn't you say that a woman took it? Now you say the father has it. Which is correct?"

"The father has it. The note says he will raise her. 'Twill be best. I can give her nothing." She could see wheels turning in the white-clad head.

"But is the woman claiming the baby your mother or sister? Sit up, your hair needs brushing. You know, Sister Madeline will not believe the note. She will say someone else wrote it." Turmoil swam through Bridget during the long process of hair braiding. Before continuing, the novice searched Bridget's countenance, "If you stick to that story, Mother Superior will insist on the father's name."

"Name him? Never! 'Tis best not to shame me child's father."

"Then Sister Madeline will believe you disposed of it." She warned, "There is this matter of authorities."

Bridget, wild-eyed, contemplated escape. Rosie's house was close to the tailoring shop, but how far was it from here? A long, paned window faced a brick wall. "Where am I?"

"You are in a home for unwed mothers." Patting Bridget's hand, she said, "I must excuse myself for prayer. There is much to pray for."

Clarion thoughts raced through Bridget. Escape seemed impossible because she was familiar with nothing in Boston but the route from home to shop to Rosie's. Which direction to pursue even if she could flee this imprisonment? Holding and circling the cot, she wobbled to the solitary window. She saw nothing but a forbidding wall and heard nothing but the cry of a street peddler. Her head plunged into anguished hands as the sun plunged into the horizon.

Her white-garbed guardian returned, and after placing Bridget's washed clothes on a bureau, said, "Took two days of cold-water washing to make them presentable. The brown plaid conceals any remaining color. Let me help you back to bed. Not thinking of jumping, are you?"

"I would if I thought 'twould offer safe landing. 'Tis a thing I never thought he'd do. Give me baby to her, leave me on a floor." She vacillated between grief at loss and gratitude that her child was in safe hands.

"An uncaring man would have left you in a snow bank instead of bringing you here for medical care. Even one responsible parent is better than a foundling home. However, had you died of exposure you wouldn't have to face authority. No one is a fool. Your hems were free of oil, unlike mill workers, and you were well-fed. You no doubt worked in a home containing an unscrupulous male. Having seen so much, Sister Madeline has figured that. At present, she believes the baby has been deserted. As it stands, if you don't escape or name the father, you fry alone."

"Then I fry by meself for 'twont be no mention of a name. They'd take the little one if he swore off being father. That sweetie would make him say 'twas not his." Her shoulders drooped. "There's no escape. I've got not a farthing."

Sister Bernadette smiled, "Oh, but you do." Reaching into the bowels of a drawer filled with histories of saints, she retrieved one of Edward's marble bags filled with cash. Lowering her voice, she said, "I found it inside the door that night. It must have dropped from your wrappings. As for escape, with money, all you need is help. Mother Superior works till nine. Fifteen minutes later, you can set a clock by her snoring. She had a phone installed two months ago and the telephone operator can ring up a hackney for us. Do you feel strong enough? If you don't she'll be back with a posse. Do you have someplace to go?"

Bridget hesitated till a stunned mouth resumed control, "I have me friend Rosie's address. A driver could find it." Looking into animated, dark eyes, she asked, "Why are ye doing this?"

"Because I believe you and I know how hammered you will be. They want the babies to save souls. No doubt from sinful mothers, but sinful ones leave them in gutters. Most mothers in here don't have a chance at seeing their babies again, but you do. I didn't have a bag of money, but you do. At least you might see her in a playground. I suspect her father is married. My son's father is and didn't care a fig about the infant."

Bridget wrapped her arms around the white habit, asking, "If they find out ye helped me, what of the novitiate?"

"I have no intention of taking final vows. I will be leaving. Without a suckling in my lap, my father has decided to forgive my wrongdoing." She walked to the window and stared at blank cement. "You know, Bridget, the things we do by two and two, we pay for one by one."

Uninvited questions trespassed through Bridget's mind. She and Sister Bernadette had chosen their actions, but had Eileen chosen either her sins or her cloistered life?

Sister Bernadette's skill created a flawless flight. The punctual hack driver stopped before Rosie's house as dawn painted horizontal, gray streaks across the winter sky. The door opened to a slack-jawed, robe-clad former seamstress. Framed in a halo of light from flickering candles, she secured the purple belt around her abundant form, before sputtering, "Just where was ye, dearie?"

"Taking care of Mrs. Castle."

"Tush! 'Twas said she was having a sick confinement but not so mighty as to stop a move. No word of a birth so 'tis for sure they quit before. They had skullduggery in them. Why change a name if 'twasn't so?"

Bridget fell into a buff-colored settee. "They moved? When did they change their name? What did they change it to?" She swallowed air in an effort to ward off drowning sensations.

Rosie scoffed, "Like as not, they'd not take the name Castro again. Suspect 'twas the name that got them into deviltry. Might behoove them to take an uppity one like Vanderbilt. 'Twould suit the likes of her. How can ye know nothing of this?" Noting the girl's pallor, she said, "I'll get ye nourishment."

"I was in hospital. Pneumonia. Is their name Castro or Castle?"

"Both, but methinks the true one is Castro. He was born in the Azores. I expect that he'll skulk back home." She positioned a cup of tea next to a plate holding toast and scrambled eggs. "Do ye think the Castle or Castro blarney came from the missus?"

"For sure, 'tis likely. A cold one she is like New Brunswick where she was born." Eyes locked with the same thought. Refuge there?

Rosie discussed her plans to work for Louise. Bridget said, "I might as well move to New York and live with Annie. She writes that she earns five times as much in one day then she earned in a week in the mills."

The older and wiser woman's brows shot up. "Best be wary of that. Methinks hers is a nasty profession. Ye went in service once. Go in service again. All can't be bounders, changing names and running from gents with bags of papers."

Bridget twisted her skirt. Being under the thumb of another self-styled, royal woman rankled. What did being in service get her? The delight of playing with children and one magical night, but at what price? Had Sister Bernadette not intervened, the price would be higher. She decided to leave Boston, go to Lawrence and work in the mills.

Rosary beads from Eileen stuffed in her pocket, she set out for her destination chilled to the bones. She fought to keep coat and scarf close to her body, but the wind tossed them in every direction while piercing her body with bullet-like precision. Rivers feeding mills boiled past, transporting debris. Each step carried her closer to the looming brick building waiting to hold her captive for endless hours each week but she would taste independence. Annie had said the air in mills was kept hot and wet for the sake of the product. Summer with its prickly heat had driven her out. She had stated that the lot of the cotton worker was worse than the lot of the cotton picker, but Bridget gambled on it being durable.

She was fortunate in finding immediate work for by midyear the panic and recession of 1893 struck and continued employment resulted from nothing more solid than an overseer's heated, though unrequited, romantic interest.

On a blistering day in August, Bill Klass, consumed by managerial problems, strolled through brick and granite buildings gleaning working conditions. He saw shoeless doffers, feet wrapped in rags in useless attempts to prevent puncturing splinters. He felt vibrating floors as crashing sounds reverberated in eardrums. He asked how a girl had acquired semicircular scarring on her forehead and was told, "She was a lucky one. A nearby loom fixer cut her hair free." No wonder the Jews won't work the mills, he thought. Too smart. Two years ago, the Fall River mills had planned to hire immigrant Jews, but when funds provided for them by Baron de Hirsch went afoul, they chose charity to mill employment. The years 1886 through 1892 had brought profit but this year's financial crisis could be devastating. He halted his ruminations at the sight of an eight-year-old doffer. This child labor had to stop! Somehow the clink of his pocket change sounded less musical.

In his fact-finding tour, Bill didn't notice Bridget. On that sweltering day, unmindful of modesty, she shed petticoats, stuffing them under bins reserved for flawed material which was free for laborers. She considered it poor compensation for heat rashes in armpits and groins. Tending eight looms, she scurried back and forth, unable to wipe dripping perspiration from her chin or free a sodden skirt clinging to her legs.

As the sun rode westward, the day's closing bell sounded. She retrieved petticoats and chose a length of defected cloth. Walking over a gravel path that still radiated heat, Bridget looked backwards at a slender, male figure entering a buggy. He seemed recognizable. Had she seen him before? He oozed management as the ornate buggy swung out of the mill yard. Impossible to have met him, but something seemed familiar. She couldn't remember. Well, if she didn't, he was not memorable.

Summer relinquished golden days and flora settled in for winter napping when Rosie noticed the envelope resting on top of Ben's mail. She identified the handwriting. She withdrew a reaching hand when she heard footsteps. Ben greeted her, "Good morning, Rosie." Scanning the mail, he said, "As expected." before slipping the stack in a valise. Hat in place and coat buttoned, he said. "Please tell Mrs. Davis I won't be here for lunch."

Rosie rubbed the bottom of three chins. As expected? Did that mean he heard from Mr. Castle often? In the future, she'd make a point of meeting mail delivery. One month later, she saw the distinctive scrawl. Squinting, she made out the postmark. It didn't make sense. If avoiding a sheriff, he'd be on foreign soil. She muttered, "Fall River, 'twont do for much."

The following spring when robins returned searching for worms, nesting material and mates, Bridget and Rosie met in an Irish Club with a conventional lady's entrance. The mill worker exclaimed, "It be a long time since our last meeting but Rosie, 'tis worth your trip for the best corn beef and cabbage in Lawrence. How do ye like being a lady's maid?"

"Better than me thought, but Mr. Davis must have a deal."

Digging into her meal, Bridget questioned, "What deal?"

Rosie took time to savor cabbage before answering, "With Mr. Castle. He must know why the two-faced one took himself off to a Godforsaken place." With crestfallen face she chattered on, "Me thought Mr. Castle an upright man. Goes to show." She paused at Bridget's florid countenance, "What ails?"

"What Godforsaken place?" Dropping her fork, she pulled her chair forward. A hand gripped Rosie's, "If ye know where, tell me!"

"What's taken ye? 'Taint New Brunswick or the Azores." She winced as Bridget's grasp tightened.

"Where is he?"

"The letter marks say Fall River. Why would a man the likes of Mr. Davis have truck with him?"

Bridget's mind galloped. There were mills aplenty in Fall River and she could pack in ten minutes. Other than a few years as a seaman, he had done nothing but tailoring. A snippet would find him.

A puffing train deposited her at the North Main Station. Babbling, foreign languages intensified frayed nerves. None understood her question. Pushing her way through masses and reaching for a harassed porter's arm, she shouted, "How do I get to Hotel Mellen?" In the melee, she didn't hear instructions. She dragged a flabbergasted, red-haired, freckled man away for accurate information.

Enclosed by hotel walls and freed of a corset, Bridget counted funds. Mill girls in Lawrence spoke of high quality goods produced in the King Philip Mills. Did high quality produce higher wages? However, on April ninth weavers and carders went on strike. She found work elsewhere, settling in unsanitary, factory owned housing.

Labor problems escalated. By the end of August, management locked mill doors to all operatives. Laborers' hardships mounted and Bridget's money stash diminished. By September merchants donated food to the needy and a coal company donated fuel as the weather chilled. Bridget obtained a ticket for bread bestowed by the McWhirr Department Store and searched bulletins for free distributions of pea soup or clam chowder.

Trudging towards the location of several mill-owned tenements on Flint Street, she heard hoofs slamming pavement. Buggy wheels screeched as the horse reared. That same man, she thought. In Lawrence, in Fall River. Is he treasurer of all the mills or does he own them all?

He asked. "What are you doing here?"

"Minding me own business. Are ye off to the Stafford Mills checking on locked doors?"

"I'm minding my business, trying to end this misery. But I asked what are you doing here? Why aren't you in Boston, working for Francis Castle?"

Through a famished haze, she evaluated him. Yes, she had met this minted one but she didn't care. The donated loaf under her jacket beckoned and a shrunken stomach wanted to eat it all, gambling on finding food tomorrow. One hand clutched a fence as she listed to one side. A swift movement brought him beside her. He steadied her saying, "Good Lord, you are a laborer. Why? Why did you leave the Castles?"

Shaking and clearing her woozy head, she answered, "They left me. Didn't ye know that?" Pushing him away, she added, "Now, go mind ye mills."

"I'll mind my mills after I see to your nourishment. Come along. You could use a steak."

She wanted no part of him but she wanted steak. Empty innards craved it more than Paris had craved Helen of Troy.

Captivated by her unmatchable eyes, he said, "Tell me what brought you to Fall River."

"Did I not say 'twas me business?" She attempted to smooth a tan bodice in need of pressing, but without coal to heat the stove, how could she heat an iron? "If ye fixed the strike, ye'd be tending to ye own affairs, not mine."

"I'm trying to do that, but I am only one and all have different views. Let's get you a meal." He admired her impertinence while she gobbled his steak. He also admired her exquisite table manners and asked how she had acquired them.

"Listening to Mrs. Castle teaching her son proper deportment. That's what she called it. Deportment. Showed him how to bow and curtsy to royalty. Ye should hear her blabber 'bout dancing with the Prince of Wales. Uppity airs, for sure."

He flinched. The image of Richard returned. Once Elizabeth percolated charm, innocence and friendliness. He visualized the obvious adoration when gazing at the man who had callously used her. The flexible stride, the mirthful wit and the exuberance lost forever, replaced by stiffened haughtiness. "I have a great regard for that woman. Seems you don't."

"I have me reasons and that too is none of ye affairs."

"Perhaps with maturity, you will see her qualities. Would you care for dessert?"

"I'll see none of her. I'll be thanking ye for cream and strawberries. Might as well fill up now on ye bankroll." She laughed, "There be no eggs and rashers to be had by morning."

He admired her honesty, her spunk. Imagine laughing over no forthcoming food. In spite of bitterness, he sensed warmth and deep empathy. First she required elocution lessons. Examining her attire, he changed his mind. First she required suitable clothing. Playing Pygmalion would entertain. She was the first fetching woman since Isabel, but she was almost a child. He reached for the hand vacant of the serviette, asking, "Would you consider marrying a man more than thirty years older?"

"If he took me fancy, I'd make him think himself twenty again."

"Then you'd consider marrying me, if I took your fancy?"

"Ain't no way your kind marries my kind. 'Tisn't marriage ye have in mind. Ye men are all alike. Look to ye overseers!"

"Can't change them but marriage is on my mind."

Doubt covered her features, "Is it joking ye are? Ye ain't funny." She rose to leave snatching the bread hidden under her outsized skirt. Then rotating on one foot, sat again, looking concerned. "Could ye be an omadhaun in need of the infirmary?"

"What's that?"

"Ah, 'tis the only Irish word of me knowing. Me father called me it. It means fool." He noted painful quiver in her voice.

"I tried entering a mental institution but they wouldn't have me. Said I was only half an omadhaun. Would you consider marriage to one?"

"Bejesus, if ye ain't joking, no way will I marry a cold-blooded cod who don't give a fig for starving people. Fix the strike? Not by anyone's bloody arse, ye won't!"

"I swear. I'm trying." Bill Klass smiled as he escorted her to the buggy.

Chapter Thirty-Three

On Monday, October 29, 1894 seven months of strike ended and bells rang again calling operatives to their daily grind. It offered Bill time to court a dubious Bridget. Why should she trust any man in light of past experience with a rejecting father, a lecherous priest and Francis Castle? In half-light allowed by an overhanging elm, he suggested a refurbished wardrobe, piano and elocution lessons before the marriage.

"There is to be no marriage but I'll be thanking ye for lessons if ye be willing to wait a bit for payment. No need for other lessons. Her royal majesty wanted table settings like the ones in palaces." Her lips puckered as she said, "Her ladyship wanted fingerbowls and tatting on napkins and tablecloths."

"If you know anything of Charles Stewart Parnell, we can pass you off as a relative."

"Everyone of Irish blood knows everything about him."

She listened with one ear as he advanced plans for life out of sight in a Swansea cottage. "What makes ye think I'd be sharing an indecent roof with the likes of yeself? In Swansea, ye say? Pish."

"Are you insane, girl? Have my reputation ruined by an unholy alliance? Unmarried cohabitation? Never, besides

Mansions and Mills

business calls me elsewhere. You won't see me till your teachers report you are presentable as a relative to an uncrowned king. But, please, apply yourself to study. I'm not getting younger. After the wedding, we can live in Boston."

"I'll do no living in Boston."

"So, where do you want to live?"

"Fall River. Naught else will do."

"You are insane. Why this cursed city?"

"How many times must ye be told to mind ye own affairs?" She boosted up from a log, saying, "No right thinking lass marries a man not minding his own business. I'll not be marrying the likes of ye!"

His laughter radiated to every vital organ. Good God, the girl had gumption and somehow he would have it in his remaining years. This girl might be a headache but she'd never be a bore. Besides, he wanted to make a rich widow of someone worthy.

Mount Hope Bay smothered the sun as he held both her ears in his palms. "Bridget, you'll have me."

She worked hours each day on perfecting English and succumbed to affection unknown from any but Eileen and her mother. After the wedding, he said, "At my age, you won't find marital expectations trying."

Placing her hands on his cheeks, she replied, "No, I won't, but I expect you will."

Ben rejoiced at the wedding. Bill's grown children felt their father had spent too many years alone and welcomed it. The only objection came from Grace's son. Five-year-old Bradford believed his grandfather was his and his alone. He refused to be the ring bearer and refused food at the affair till offered three scoops of ice cream.

At each visit, Bradford insisted on filling the well-worn pipe and sitting on the aging lap till the last puff while sparing Bridget none of his resentment. She told the cook, "If looks could kill, I'd be in the same state as that fish you are scaling."

Bridget was still a bride when Bill came in the door roaring mad. Holding her away with a firm grasp on her arms, he hissed in her ear, "Please join me in the sitting room." Sun filtered through lace curtains as he whirled around to face her, face florid. "What were you doing in the mills?"

She checked the door, making sure it clicked shut before answering, "The servants mustn't hear. Isn't that considered gauche?"

"I'll whisper. Why did you go there? It is not fitting."

"I wanted to bring sandwiches to the neediest children. Bill, some are as young as eight."

"I know and I want to change that but I am only one voice. Do you understand that overseers lie about their ages? Children are paid less which pleases many. The French Canadians seem to want them working in diapers. Some save every penny for repatriation to Canada which is but a hop and a skip for them, unlike the Irish, Portuguese or Italians. Unless they build a ship, they had better be good swimmers. At least, money hungry as they are, Canadians aren't willing strikers. Enough of that, you are to stay out of the mills. It's dangerous. You could slip on oily floors or bits of wet cotton. Mills are no place for my wife."

"Are you forgetting that I worked in them? In rain or snow, anyone could slip on the street from cotton which falls off drays. Bill, I want to see those children in school."

"You can't drag the French to English speaking schools and parents of all lineage need child income. I can't make you forget the children but I can have you evicted from the mills. I'm sure you will not subject either of us to such humiliation."

Her dark green skirt hid his legs as she settled on her favorite spot. "Bridget, one of these days, you'll break these old bones, although I can't think of a better way of becoming a cripple."

"I fear bouncing Bradford will do it first."

"I checked out jewelry today. Would you prefer sapphires to match your eyes or diamonds to match everything?"

"I have no need for jewelry. Just having you is enough, but thank you anyway. Any chance you can sleep later in the morning?"

"No. Cummings wants an early morning session about water rights. Can't imagine why. As far as I know, Fall River owns water rights all over the place, even in Rhode Island. But may I make an appointment with you for tomorrow evening about nine?" The setting sun's pink rays, streaming through the window, lit her light hair. He picked up a strand with an index finger, sighing, "I wish today had sapped less, by the way, you will have jewelry if only to please me."

While Bridget resisted trimmings of royalty, singing mill bells woke Francis from troubled slumber. Scant morning filtered through curtains as he held a pencil between grinding teeth, reflecting on how he could find another source of revenue. One attempt at hanging a door revealed little carpentry skills. He felt he could construct simple things such as a table, stools and benches. The financial crash of 1893, arriving only a few months after their departure from Boston, devastated and the Fall River strikes of 1894 worsened affairs. Books and magazines rested near worn soles as he sorted through columns. By the end of 1895, sustaining income came from Elizabeth's exhausting endeavors at hat making. Servant women had seen them and spent meager incomes on the luxury. She had paraded through the highlands of the wealthy in cumbersome, though attractive, mutton sleeves hoping some lady would inquire about a dressmaker.

At thirteen, Edward could work delivering telegrams. Elizabeth would object, believing Edward should study. She still dreamed of a profession for the boy. He knew as she did not that Edward joined the colored help from the Fall River Line in playing craps. Weather permitting, they played under the wharf. He was beginning to show interest in Faro also. Time would be better served in employment.

Reduced payments to Ben compelled again. It was a wonder the man didn't hunt him for immediate repayment. Could some other bill be deferred till next month so a larger check could go to Boston? With all his calculations, nothing changed except the hands on his watch. Frustrated teeth cut furrows into the pencil.

Elizabeth didn't complain. No recriminations about the life once enjoyed before his transgression. She strove to attract more business with her modish, Sunday promenades complete with parasols in summer and fur accentuations in winter. After attendance at the Church of the Ascension, she strolled through sections of the privileged.

One Sunday, while turning southward onto Belmont Street from French Street, a matron approached, "Pardon me, but that hat! Did you acquire it from that milliner on South Main Street?"

"I am that milliner."

"Then I want one just like that in royal blue. My maid tells me you make adjustments also. I've lost some weight. This frock no longer hugs the body." She opened her coat and pulled at the bodice of an orchid-colored dress.

"If you come to the shop, I can accommodate all your needs."

"No, my dear, we do not venture into certain areas. I will give you my address. Please bring samples to me." Thus, Elizabeth acquired a consumer with five fashioned addicted daughters-in-law and four daughters.

"Francis," Elizabeth asked, "how come they all came to us in Boston and these ladies of the "Hill" won't go beyond The Brown Building for library books or trot further than Gifford's for jewelry?"

"Mr. Hood told me it was all Mrs. Spencer's doing. It was like a party to her dragging her associates along and escaping some dull afternoon. Somehow, it became established habit for all. It did make it simpler for us. It could be Fall River aristocracy prefers to avoid proximity with the mills and those impoverished ones who furnish their luxuries."

Mansions and Mills

Two weeks later, Francis gazed at sallow light coming through unwashed windows while serving supper as an apt househusband should. How much time did elite women need? Were they fussing over tassels, fringes or lace? Did entitlement include working Elizabeth on an empty stomach?

Victoria pulled at his leg, "Papa, ice cream for me?" Then she remembered. "Please."

He reached into the ice box where the ice cream melted along with the cake of ice. "Edward," he asked, "will you be delivering telegrams on Saturday?"

Through his son's grumbling affirmation, he wondered why am I here instead of on a deck? Elizabeth, of course, but she was worth it. Closing on forty-four, with a few added pounds, she still held magic. As a bonus, he had found unexpected joy in a child who worshiped him, in contrast to his son's contempt.

That contempt had begun to manifest in Boston. He felt it had accelerated as a result of his now unrewarding career, but how could he expect respect from a son when he had none for himself?

Supper cooled. He filled time in the cellar, working on benches. Victoria played with wood shavings. As he planed wood, she retrieved the curled droppings and placed them in her hair, "Papa, see yellow hair."

Later, Elizabeth ate supper unheated. When Francis stroked her long hair streaming across the pillow, she whimpered "I'm so tired." As his hand withdrew, she thought, this is not what I planned when youthful and hopeful. I have neither time nor energy for the children I wanted. I'm eating cold meals instead of presiding over lavish foods. From the start I knew I'd never inhabit paradise, but did it have to become so bad?

Francis arose, treading to the kitchen. Under feeble light, he read catalogues and leafed through ads of readymade clothing guaranteed to fit. Standard sizes, of course, but if it's too long, hem it. If it's too tight, let out the seams and if it's loose, take them in. He supposed that if you had five daughters of varying sizes, one party gown would do for all, as long as they weren't expected to attend simultaneously. Just keep taking in and letting out seams till the material expired. He approached dying embers, dropping all catalogues in the stove. One flashed rose-colored life and then perished. "Damn them," he said to a cold room, "they don't even burn."

Diaphanous, icy crystals covered dreary ground and pebbles crunched beneath his feet when Francis saw her in January 1896. Burst of wind threatened to blow them across South Park and into the Taunton River, but undaunted, Bridget approached, "Good day, Mr. Castle, or is it Mr. Castro? What name are you using these days?"

A gloved hand almost lost the grip on Victoria's collar. Tiny fingers freed themselves from a velvet muff and reached out to shake the lady's hand. She said, "Hello, my name is Victoria and I must wait two, long weeks for my birthday. That's a long, long time."

"I know. It is a long, long time."

Seconds passed before words tumbled from him, "Castle. Where did you hear Castro?"

"From Rosie."

"How is she?"

"She is fine. She has lost poundage. Mrs. Davis insisted on a diet."

He fell backwards. Did she say Mrs. Davis? The same Mrs. Davis? Did she use the word poundage? Did she speak with but a hint of a brogue? Edgy, he wanted to end the meeting. He didn't ask what she was doing in Fall River. Her chiseled gaze at Victoria told him. "It is getting colder. Nice seeing you." He swiveled, rushing diminutive feet through frigid air, hoping the little blabbermouth would forget to tell Mother about the nice lady.

Hope was pointless. Two hours earlier, Elizabeth had stopped at McWhirr's. Approaching the glove counter, she halted, ice invading every capillary. It couldn't be, but it was Bridget, elbow on glass countertop. A saleslady fitted and massaged a leather glove onto her upraised, right hand while saying, "These fit but would you prefer the pigskin ones? The shade is darker."

Mansions and Mills

"Let's try them. I suppose I could use both pairs."

Elizabeth couldn't leave without her change. She averted her face while waiting for it to come down in a cage sent winging down on a cable. She looked up at the cashier seated in a raised balcony at the rear of the store. What was taking so long? Bridget, selection made, left before the cash glided down. Sighing relief at not being seen, she approached the saleslady, "That lady looks familiar. Could you tell me her name?"

"She's a faithful customer, saying how marvelous it was when the store helped in feeding hungry strikers. I don't imagine you know her. She is Mrs. William Klass."

"Isn't she from Boston or New York?"

Bending to rearrange cased gloves, she answered, "Don't believe so. All charges go to a Fall River address."

Staggering up the stairs to their second floor tenement, she encountered Francis on his way down. She sputtered. "You won't believe this. Bill Klass married Bridget and they have a Fall River address. How do we prevent her from knowing we live here?"

"We can't. She knows, but did you say Bill Klass?" He gaped, "How could that have come about? What will happen if Edward discovers she's here? He has always bemoaned her loss and I suspect he put the blame on me."

With catlike grin, she asked, "Is it not?"

"Admit it. Had you found a British girl, you would have discharged her in spite of Edward's supplications. You insist green is their proper color and how many times have you said that their blarney is your version of perpetual, barefaced lying?" While waiting for a nonexistent reply, arrows of guilt shot through his viscera. How could he have robbed a poverty-stricken immigrant such as himself of her baby? How could he have left her bleeding on a floor? He knew why. For the same reason he sheltered Richard's murderer.

He knew with certainty that this night of all nights he would hear I'm tired or encounter the immobility of a dutiful wife.

He settled in for soothing reading where in a halo of light, he read of the annexation of the Hawaiian Islands and establishment of a naval station at Pearl Harbor. He reflected on how Captain Addison would no longer recognize the beaches where he had frolicked with a flower-clad native. His saturated brain closed his eyes over the poems of Walter Whitman and Oliver Wendell Holmes to dream of Hawaiian maidens as they once were.

Bees flitted around cornflowers and sporadic clouds obscured a smiling sun when Elizabeth and Francis took Victoria to New Bedford to view whaling ships. Sniffing the air, she grimaced, "Papa, you said it would stink fishy." She slid on oil-covered, ballast stones, delighting in the novelty as her father stared into lapping water.

Elizabeth said, "Come, Victoria. Let's take a walk. We can return and buy fresh fish for supper. Francis, why are you dawdling here?" The toddler skipped along sometimes between them, sometimes ahead till stopped by a muscled voice at the corner of Union and Purchase Streets, "Ay, mon, is that you, Francisco?"

Excited, Victoria asked, "Do you catch whales?"

"That I do. Ken every whale that ever was." He was so galvanized at the meeting that he didn't notice the peg-legged sailor and stepped on his only foot. The man waved off apologies and ambled to the nearest saloon.

"Elizabeth, this is the John you have heard off. John, this is two-thirds of my family. My son is working and this little madcap is Victoria. What news do you have? Let's move under the awning of this store." It sold hats and caps. Elizabeth pretended interest while hoping for brief news from this distasteful foreigner.

"I need to wipe my broo." He scrubbed his forehead with a cloth drawn from a back pocket before remembering to whip off his cap. "Apologies Ma'am. Been too long at sea. A verra bonnie lass you have here, Francisco."

Elizabeth squirmed at the name while Victoria asked, "Papa, why does he call you that?"

Mansions and Mills

John looked confused, but began, "Ay, news. Hall got sparky for money. Drove ships. Clutched wealth but the sea clutched the mon first. I went handfasting. Didn't want to slip a bairn but no strangers to brew, I'd have a pint to my lady having a mutchkin. Did not hold it well so the bairn came along. Went to the kirk, hard benches and all and got my own lady. Been nigh on eight and ten years." He shot a pleased smile, thinking his lady was soft and warm while his former shipmate had married a fine specimen but one as stiff as a spar.

Elated that his wife would not understand the jargon, he asked, "What do you know of Rufus?" His voice sounded muffled.

"Thot one hit a jackpot, I ken. In tobacco, after hooshing a mon who beat a lass named Jessie. The mon didn't like her blood. Rufus did. Took the filly to Cuba and tobacco farming."

For Francis, a rising, warm mist turned cold, "When you say hushed a man, do you mean..." He glanced at Elizabeth.

"Met Davy Jones. That makes two." No, Francis thought. That makes three. The first two, I could do nothing, but this one I could have prevented. "God, please," he prayed, "if there are others don't let me know."

Victoria's voice cut through, "Papa, let's go for lemonade."

Round, wet rings formed on the table as each hand elevated a glass. Bored, Elizabeth folded and unfolded a napkin around her glass as if diapering a baby. She hadn't understood much from this man.

Still, he continued, "When did they cotch you?"

"Catch me for what?"

"The money, mon, the money. They had the wurst time fetching you. That was no mean sum, you lucky bloke."

Elizabeth understood the word money. Boredom winged like a scavenging eagle. "Money. Did you say money? What money?"

"Left to Francisco from the skipper."

"We never got it. How do we get it?"

"Dinna get it? Fetching Francisco wasna easy, they said, but it was done, finished in 1893. I was of a mind that you had it."

Francis said, "John, explain this, if you can."

The seaman told of regular visits to the captain and when his wife predeceased him, he rewrote his will. "The auld mon left it to you. If you dinna get it, maybe his niece did. Her barrister said it was done with. Forget it, he tauld me. You shud have got it and you shud have wrote to the auld mon. He loved you well."

"I didn't want him or you to know I changed my name to Francis Castle. That's why they didn't find me. They searched for Francisco Castro."

"You denied kinfolk! Why deny clan? Jaysus, you bollixed it."

"I knew you would find it contemptible. That's why I never let you know."

"Aye." John fell silent, sipping lemonade when he wanted brew.

Victoria chattered but they rode home in silence. Without the change of name, Elizabeth would never have married him. Now Mrs. Blackwood's warnings about pride vibrated through her ears.

In despair, she walked the streets of the majestic Hill. It wasn't Beacon Street or Back Bay in Boston but it was Rock Street or Highland Avenue in Fall River. All inaccessible.

She suggested they sell all stored valuables, "We will never use them. I had hoped but we will never prosper again."

Francis said, "I want you to keep the things you love, but if you decide to sell other things, remember to bring the wedding picture home. It should be on a wall and not in a box."

She stared for several minutes before saying, "The wedding picture. Of course, Francis, the wedding picture."

Chapter Thirty-Four

Gloom penetrated Elizabeth when she learned of the massive treasure lost to the skipper's niece. The girl's barrister insisted for years that Francisco Castro had probably drowned at sea. Dividends alone would have kept Elizabeth in a Newport mansion. Why didn't Francis share her misery?

The children must never know. Edward would be furious. How could she make them understand that the name Gilbert couldn't dovetail with that of a man whose father sheared sheep on some nondescript island?

At home, Edward's communication shrank daily. He chafed at the meager allowance granted him from his wages. Other youngster's stipend of a penny sent that gleeful penny to a candy store where it took five minutes selecting. Should it be a peppermint stick or a gumball? Sympathetic store owners waited behind counters aware of the major importance of this weekly ritual. Edward, however, required all his earnings. As a child, he threw dice with coins offered by tolerant black men, but now with employment, they asked, "What's your wager on this toss, boy?" Having been called "boy" so often they enjoyed flinging the term back.

While Edward fretted over his allowance, Bridget implored a meager one, "Bill, I love the jewelry that you insist I must have but I have only one neck, two ears, two arms and ten fingers." She pulled out a drawer displaying a glittering array of every jewel ever mined. "It's easy for me to say 'send the bill' but without some change, I can't invite an acquaintance I meet on the street to join me for coffee and muffins. I promise I won't donate to the suffragettes or temperance movement."

He puffed his pipe and studied its glow. "You are right. You should have a muffin allowance. You must believe women should vote but please don't donate to abolish my good, Irish whiskey."

Minding his own affairs as agreed, he knew nothing of her aversion to Irish whiskey and nothing of Annie. The magnanimous and unquestioned muffin allowance permitted hiring a detective to search for the attractive woman lost to her for months.

Annie had lived outside the law, inveigling victims into alleys where a blow on the head and a missing wallet resulted. She worked in unison with a silk-shirted thug named Willy who also served as her pimp, but after her arrest in 1895 by Police Commissioner Theodore Roosevelt she adopted a safer and more lucrative "parlor house" and walked New York streets by daylight finely gowned, avoiding oil and ash stains from overhead streetcars. Willy, abandoned and forgotten in an airshaft tenement, found a new accomplice but not for long. Bridget's detective learned of his fatal fall off a roof in the summer of 1896 where he and others attempted to sleep, escaping from the stench and stifling heat of overcrowded tenements.

Undaunted, the investigator found Nell who warily scanned the well-dressed man, asking, "This ain't no setup, is it?" Reassured, she agreed to deliver a note when she met Annie on New Year's Eve. "For sure, 'twill be a special night this year. 'Tis said even the fuzz will pay for merrymaking. 'Twould be a change." A ruby-faced detective caught the first train. Obviously, Mr. Roosevelt hadn't dented police corruption or prostitution. It was said that he roamed darkened streets attempting to ferret out malfeasance. By gosh, the detective thought, a man like that should be president.

Mansions and Mills

On the last day of the year, Nell met Annie by a corner firebox, saying, "Annie, why so late? Been freezing me arse leaning on this thing. Let's go to that hoochie coochie saloon for a bit of warming. The bluecoats will pass us brew through the backdoor. Now, why so late?"

"Saw a doctor. He was the late one." She swallowed a small cry of pain.

They halted for a horse and carriage struggling through gathering crowds before passing under a cable car loaded with revelers. "Ye look pale. What did the doctor say?"

"That I'd be fine."

"Have a letter for ye. A man brought it from Fall River. Maybe from the lady who killed her ma and pa." She giggled.

Annie attempted to place it in a small pocket, managing to squeeze it in by folding it in four. Nell asked, "What have ye got in there? In this bunch, hope 'tisn't last night's earnings. Look, 'tis Officer Lowney. He'll get us hooch. Owes me. By the way, where's Willy?"

"Fell off a roof last August same time a bunch of horses died from heat. You remember that? I've forgotten Willy."

"Forgotten? 'Tis best. Open ye heart, they'll push in hurting. There was a politician. Treated me like something afore winning a place in congress. Got hitched to a senator's widow. Now, he's hoity-toity. Anyone ever treat you like somebody?"

"Nell, you must be daft. We are nobodies." Patrolman Lowney handed them two bottles of red wine. "Best I could do. They are celebrating two-fisted, like they needed another excuse. Don't be telling where it came from." He winked at Nell.

Crowds thickened, stretched necks viewed the parade and sang along with bands, impervious as rainfall turned to torrents. Umbrellas fought gusting winds which turned icy before jelling to snow. A man wearing a rain-streaked, silk hat and a frock coat bumped into Annie. She moaned before making an instinctive grab at her pocket, dropping a wine bottle. Spilling on snow, its redness looked like blood. Annie recoiled, while Nell, appalled at the loss, asked, "What do ye have in that pocket? Gold? Now we have half a bottle to celebrate with New York all aglow at getting the Bronx, Brooklyn and what else for themselves. Ye must have whiskey money in that pocket. Cough it up."

Her eyes glued on reddening snow, Annie confessed, "I have only five cents for the cable car."

"Methought ye made more in a house."

"When working. Ain't been up to it of late." A vicious explosion of wind blew her shawl from her head, revealing hair shorn close to her scalp.

"What did ye do? Ye look like a nun!"

"I want to be a nun or a maid or a ring spinner, but..."

"Jesus, Mary and Joseph! There be no fun in the likes of ye. It's Lowney for me tonight. Go home, read ye bloody letter."

Smoke rampaging from chimneys became heavier as revelers deserted deepening snow for extra fire logs. They could celebrate New York's growth to three hundred and twenty square miles in fairer weather. The weaving and jostling mass dwindled to a lone figure. Reaching into her bulging pocket, she swallowed the potassium cyanide. None were left to see the snowcapped mass on the corner of Twenty-Sixth Street.

They found her in a red pool, a Sacred Heart Medal pinned to her camisole. The autopsy baffled. There was suicide, but pelvic examination showed a botched abortion. They concluded she regretted her choice and taken poison not realizing she was already doomed.

An incensed coroner bellowed, "These butchers! Why not learn to do it right? Another exploited immigrant. Her coloring says Irish." He ran a tender hand over the lovely, cold face. "Let's hope the note identifies her and let's hope she will be spared a pauper's grave. There are days when I wish I dug ditches." He threw the scalpel into a tray. The sound resounded through the morgue.

Mrs. Lapointe handed her employer the telegram, face wrinkling into a gigantic question as Bridget rocked with each word.

"Say nothing of this to anyone. Please bring tea to my room." Thoughts raced. How much would it cost? Could muffin money cover it? What excuse could she give Bill to justify a trip to New York without him? If she told him the truth, how would he react?

Bill returned from the bank walking into a room vibrating with emotions. He said, "By your leave, my dear, I think I'll have a spot of tea, though absent a cup I'll help myself to yours." She summoned for another. It arrived, yellow roses hand painted on china. "So, what is the terrible problem?"

There was no way of concealing inner turmoil from this intuitive man, there had never been. She spilled everything except Annie's occupation. "I don't want her in a pauper's grave with a number. Without her, I would have been so alone on that ship. She made me laugh even while seasick. Her letters were funny. She can't make me laugh anymore." At last, tears overflowed, dampening his soothing shoulder.

"Bridget, identifying her will be an unpleasant task. I wish I could go with you. Being the third day of January, a wage reduction of over eleven percent begins. That could spell huge problems. I need to be here for negotiations. I'm sorry I can't go but whatever you want for her, have them send the bills and please call me daily. Take Maria with you, but leave all jewelry in the vault. You'll be safer appearing less affluent."

Bridget and Maria traveled on the Fall River Line in spite of Maria's trepidation of water. After identification, Bridget asked, "What was the cause?"

Unwilling to state either suicide or abortion, the coroner temporized, "She was found unresponsive in snow. One might suspect exposure." Arrangements followed, including a monument engraved with roses.

Once home, tearful and nestled in Bill's lap, she asked, "Why did you do this for someone you never knew?"

"Dear one, I did it for you." He burrowed her head under his chin. "Anyone who comforts and brings laughter is, as you discovered, priceless."

Within a month, Louise and Ben attended a birthday party for Bradford and Ben took the opportunity to call on old friends. Looking over a sewing machine, Francis said, "I've wondered when you would show up demanding full payment."

"Payments are fine. Since I'm in Fall River, stopping by for a glimpse of you and Elizabeth seemed fitting." He noted the smallness of the shop. "Is business poor here? Aren't you making drapes and upholstering?"

"Eric had the talent and the young back. Takes two to lift a couch. As for drapes, have you looked around this fair city? Drapes? Most residents are dirt poor. They use the same newspapers to stuff under their coats for warmth that they used the night before to stuff in broken windows. Keeps some cold out. The city's grand ladies don't project far from the highland area unless it's to project to Europe."

Ben began, "Then why in hell did you..." Then he saw the reason looking up at him. He studied her from booted feet to saucy hat as she walked in, holding Elizabeth's hand. Those unmistakable eyes, the pointed chin, even the slim, elongated fingers spoke of Bridget. The difference was the dark hair, the olive complexion. She extended her hand in customary precociousness.

"Good day, I'm Victoria. I just had a birthday. Now I'm five." She held up five fingers. "And I can count to twenty. Papa thinks I'm smart."

"And I think so too. Meeting you is my pleasure." The radiant, dimpled smile tossed in his direction was Bridget's smile, but the coloring? Was this the reason they left Boston in haste? Elizabeth's icy stare punctured. Ben said, "Nice seeing you. We are all visiting Bill, except Susan. I'm sure you remember Susan."

Elizabeth relaxed, understanding the message. He would keep this secret as she had kept his. "Ben, would you care for tea? Would you like to try it seaman style with molasses?"

Mansions and Mills

Saying he was expected for dinner, he declined. He chose walking blocks in order to ponder. Why did Bridget walk away from her daughter? Or did she? Was this her reason for insisting on life in Fall River? Was it possible that Bill knew? Was it possible that he didn't? If he didn't and found out, what then?

When apprised of a five-year-old daughter, Louise sent a gift of an embroidered, pink dress and a matching coat secured with pearl buttons. Victoria, joyful, tore the box open. "Papa, please help me with the buttons." She waltzed before a mirror, admiring herself.

They jumped at a slamming door. "What is this? I return from working with impossible women to a daughter in a pink monstrosity. How did she acquire this, Francis?"

He stuttered, "It's a gift from Ben."

"You mean from Louise. We need nothing from her." Victoria cried as Elizabeth removed the outfit.

"We have had much from her!" He bit his tongue. Elizabeth must never know of Ben's loans and assets once produced by kept women. It would shred her dignity. Why was his life secret after secret?

Elizabeth scoffed, "What did she give us except the dubious honor of producing family attire and they got their money's worth. Stop crying, Victoria, I'll get you another dress and coat. Blue would be nice."

Victoria wailed, "I like this one."

"You cannot keep it. You will have another."

"Elizabeth, let the child have it. She likes it and another won't be the same quality."

"Are you reminding me of my part in a lost fortune?"

"Never, I could have refused to go along with—changes."

Twirling petticoats climbing the stairs settled the matter once more.

Francis sighed. She was more remote since the meeting with John, knowing the life she had wanted slipped through her fingers. Once she had tantalized but that was before the Bridget matter. As he deliberated on the timing of the chilly bed, he remembered that it began with her extended exhaustion following Edward's illness. Understandable. But fervor hadn't returned in those months before her New Brunswick trip. Why not? Was it an age thing?

That night his dream was of sailing with Harry, following the whaling route. In spring, to the Carolinas and West Indies then to the Azores, Cape Verde, Africa, Brazil and the Falklands. Even after summer whaling in the Grand Banks they had not a single catch. Discouraged, he sat on shore. A dolphin, covered with gold coins and jewels, swam close telling him to give the bounty to Elizabeth, but when he reached out the dolphin turned into a shark. He awoke in panic.

While he returned to reality upstairs, Elizabeth loitered downstairs. Standing over the stove, she incinerated Victoria's pink outfit as she had incinerated the pink gown, piece by torn piece.

The following evening, walking home in the glaze of winter, Bill looked up to see Bridget silhouetted in the lit rectangle of the kitchen window. Bounding the stairs, his nostrils followed the aroma of spices. "So, you are making your sausages. It has been all of three months since my palate has tasted your work of art."

"Out, out. Not even you can view the recipe. The cook is dispatched shopping. Do you know that eggs are up to thirteen cents a dozen and one chicken will cost eighteen cents? Maria is off buying bengaline. That sells at a dollar fifty per yard but it is only twenty-one-inches wide. The price of things! I got rid of everybody and you scoot too."

"Why must your recipe be kept secret?"

"I don't know yet, but someday I will."

"You never cease to delight me. I'll celebrate everything with a topnotch pipe." By everything he meant a tranquil labor force and boosted business because of the Spanish-American War. Though dubious of war, it produced profit as it did for all rich men.

Mansions and Mills

They welcomed 1899 with a party of seventy guests. Ben and Louise arrived early as did Grace, husband and Bradford who guarded his right to fill grandpa's pipe.

On the second day of that year, Francis overcome with melancholy, leafed through Harper's before dropping it to the floor. Tailoring work had dwindled to almost nothing. He stared at laundry flapping on clotheslines and watched bloomers fly free like balloons. Small children hustled to saloons to pick up pails of beer for fathers. Victoria would soon be six and a new library was scheduled to open on North Main Street. In March, he could occupy himself by taking her there. They could walk hand in hand and return with as many books as allowed. Elizabeth might ask, "Are you going to make a bookworm of her also?" while suggesting it hadn't got him very far.

Thoughts of his wife brought him to thoughts of supper. Pots and pans rattled as he began his nightly ritual. She would be exhausted after maneuvering ladies into corsets, producing the now dictated S shape. They both sewed ruffles upon ruffles on camisoles supplying the required full bust, charging extra for flat-chested ones. He pondered, were mutton sleeves of the past or present fashion more idiotic? At that point, Elizabeth complete with hanging fatigue arrived. The evening promised little mirth.

That evening produced mirth in a house on Rock Street. Bill played the piano, urging Bridget to sing. "I can't. I lost my portamento."

"What's that?"

"I don't know exactly but it's gone."

Heaving her over one shoulder, he carried her upstairs, saying, "I suggest we search for it."

At the end of the year, Pope Leo X111 spoke of the century dying and of how many monuments of disgrace he perceived in looking back. Francis, reading the entire ode, asked, "And how many monuments of disgrace do I perceive looking forward?"

Western civilization anticipated marvels as the twentieth century arrived. Cures for many diseases sat on the horizon.

Francis explained Greg Mendel's studies in crossbreeding. Elizabeth took heart in believing Victoria would skip all parental traits, and after training in the niceties be a fit wife for a lawyer or even a professor introduced by Edward.

Conjecture turned to her son. Where did he spend his time? He was an eighteen-year-old content with delivering telegrams. Didn't he understand she wanted the best for him? She would stop that nonsense by demanding immediate college enrollment.

She fumed at Victoria's nightly habit of sitting on her father's lap reading her book while he read his. "Papa," she asked, "what is this word?"

Elizabeth interjected, "He is Father, not Papa. The French say Papa. You are British." Victoria persisted. He was Papa to her.

In May, when tulips and daffodils bloomed, Victoria dragged Papa to the opening of a synagogue on Pearl Street highlighted by the mayor turning the key.

Bridget attended with friends. Bill, pleading fatigue, begged off. Encountering her, Francis tipped his hat but shied away, though not before many heard Victoria ask, "Papa, why don't they take their hats off when they go to church?"

Old men, white beards cascading over their chests frowned but one little boy, yarmulke in place, smiled at the pretty, blue-eyed girl. A hand jerked his to attention, "Jacob, no. Goyem, shiksa." The boy, born in a settlement in New York, pretended deafness. His father had whispered, hadn't he?

By August, streams of sun skittering through lace curtains formed a pattern on Bridget's widow weeds as Louise tried reasoning with the bereaved. She said, "No one will understand why you are having his remains sent to New York. When the time comes, you will want to be with him. Plots are available at Oak Grove."

The neighbor said, "No doubt Mrs. Klass is planning to remarry." A warning shot through tear-streaked eyes failed to caution her. "Everyone remarked about the age difference."

Mansions and Mills

"Are you suggesting that my husband was fool enough to marry someone interested in his money?"

"My dear, it happens all the time."

"I hoped for many more happy years with him."

"Yes, of course." Her expression belied her words. Too surprised to resist, she found herself grasped by the elbow, whisked through the servant's quarters and on the outside of a slammed door.

Louise cried, "Bridget, you don't throw a Borden out that way."

"I just did."

"After this is over, you'll see no calling cards."

"Good. It's a silly custom." Outside the window, a horse flicked his ears at flies while the pavement shimmered in heat. "Three months, Louise. He complained of fatigue just three months ago. Now this!"

"You wouldn't have wanted him to suffer. You made him so happy." She patted Bridget's shoulder. "I suppose you were the love of his life."

"Isabel was. That's why he will rest with her. When I hung her portrait, did you hear him protest? I was not his great love but we had a happy marriage. It was full of fun. Above all, we had a deep friendship. How many marriages have that?"

"I don't know. Perhaps not many but you are so young. You might find more than friendship."

Bridget looked through the front door as union leaders came to pay respects. Mill workers seeking shade stood outside with caps in hand. Invited in, one praised, "Mighty good man." Another said, "Real fair chap." Through the throng, she saw Francis climbing the stairs. He had shaved off his beard. The skin no longer clutched the bone structure, but he was more appealing than ever. Did Louise say she might find more than friendship? She had found it years ago.

Realizing Francis' discomfort, Ben approached, shook his hand and led him to the widow. "Bridget, I don't believe you know that years ago your husband and Mr. Castle formed a bond. They held each other in great esteem."

"That is true, Mrs. Klass. I wanted to come here and show my deep respect for him."

Francis didn't know how he would have handled the awkward situation. Once more, Ben had furnished much needed aid but how did he know it was needed?

Bridget said, "Mr. Castle, this explains your flowers. I am pleased at being able to thank you personally." All three were aware she couldn't send a note to his house.

After retiring, her ears picked up stealthy sounds. Upon investigation, she found Bradford in Bill's chair, tobacco-filled pipe resting on the adjacent table.

"Bradford, what are you doing?"

"Waiting for grandpa to smoke his pipe. If he knows it's ready, he might wake up. I want him to wake up."

She carried the tearful boy to bed, resting beside him as he cried himself to sleep. In the morning he told her, "I don't hate you anymore."

Alone, she accompanied Bill's casket in the train to New York, coveting those final hours, dwelling on all he had done for her, even to what he had done for Annie. He must have concluded her occupation but it hadn't mattered. She was a human in need.

Condolence telegrams arrived from far-flung places. Servants, distracted from chores, received each one, but one day the doorbell rang as Bridget stood in the foyer. Two footsteps put another missive in her hand. Her tearing eyes didn't recognize the youth but he recognized her and his eyes saw Victoria. He backed down the stairs, thunderstruck.

Elizabeth found her son with head sunk in hands. He boomed, "Now I know why we left Boston. To escape his vileness. Now it can be seen in this city. It was big of you, Mother, to salvage both Bridget and Victoria. I hate him. I hate him for leaving Boston. I hate him for what he did to Bridget. Get a phone. I will call you but I'm not staying here with him. I'm leaving and I'll never be back."

She followed as he rushed out. "You must be going to Providence. Edward, you are enrolled in college there!"

"Forget Providence and college too. I'm going back to the city I love. Boston."

Chapter Thirty-Five

Panic engulfed Bridget at the scope of her inheritance. Bill had set up a trust fund for Robert who, in the outback of Australia, didn't hear of his father's death till months later. Bradford had one also, but Grace, married to wealth, had made but one request—her mother's portrait. The young widow believed that her husband's business interests began and ended with mills and was floored by stocks, bonds and overall possessions. Broad-shouldered Ben attempted to calm her.

Her modish, bell-shaped skirt pivoted toward a bay window. She watched as fall showered flying leaves on glass panes. "What will I do with all that money? I can't manage to spend all the muffin money."

Forehead lines indenting in confusion, he asked, "What is muffin money?"

"It's a long story, but with Annie gone, I can't spend it on her."

More bewilderment flooded his features as he asked, "Who is Annie?"

"The best friend a destitute, seasick colleen could have." Fresh tears spilled on the bengaline skirt.

Mansions and Mills

Whoever Annie was, he accepted explanation and whipped an immaculate handkerchief from his pocket. Handing it to her, he continued, "There are valuable paintings stored in Boston also."

She wailed, "This is too much. Grace has houses galore. She should have them. Ben, I've never managed money. I don't know how. I want to give it away."

A carried tray revealed that tea and cookies were joining them. Ben salivated, "Good, my stomach is speaking." He waited till the servant closed the door. "Bridget, don't worry. It can be managed for you." He smiled encouragement, "And you can indulge favorite charities."

Her eyes widened. "Charities? Yes, that's it. I'll know how much I can spend on charity. Right?"

"Right, and what might that be?" Picking crumbs from his lap and placing them on an empty plate, his head jerked up at her answer.

"Mill children. Yesterday's paper told of a twelve year old boy whose arm was broken when a belt broke and knocked him over. Ben, those children belong in school, especially the bright ones. Bill didn't want me in the mills. Said it was unseemly. Do you know anyone I could hire to go in the mills and select smart children desirous of education?"

"I know a local man in need of employment. He could do that and be trusted to balance your check book." He looked up as she circled the room, her blue eyes envisioning an oasis of opportunity for children. "However," he continued with trepidation, "you may be reluctant to employ your former employer. Perhaps your association produced some resentment." He knew he had ventured into deep water.

"Francis Castle?" She readjusted a dropped jaw. "He doesn't need a job. Not with his tailoring talent."

He unbuttoned his jacket, buttoned it and unbuttoned it once more. "He is not doing well in this fair city. People are pouring over catalogues, ordering by mail. A regular salary would benefit his family. Have you seen his daughter? A prize." For sure, she would care for the child's welfare. "Tailoring has gone the way of the dinosaurs, Bridget."

"What of drapes and upholstering?"

"For starters, the place is too small even if demand existed in this hick town. As intelligent as he is, he has nowhere to go but down. A shame. I fear that entire family will continue on a downward spiral." Ben wondered if the relationship had been so poisonous that she couldn't rise above it, not even for the girl. He asked himself, "What in blazes happened in that house and how?"

Mind twirling, she massaged her wedding ring. If there was no place for him to go but down, the girl would be in want. She didn't care if Elizabeth starved but Victoria was a different story. "Is the boy employed?"

"Don't know where he is."

She arranged flowers in a crystal vase. The day was graying. "Mr. Castle would refuse my offer."

"A drowning man will grasp seaweed."

"Fine, but you talk to him. If he agrees, we'll work it out."

That night, long after Ben had dined with Louise and three of his five children, Bridget sat at a window, gazing at the firmament and its display of stars shimmering against moonless black. Could Bill see her from there? What would he advise? Would he say help the girl directly? She would answer, "Elizabeth won't allow it." Would she allow her husband to accept the position?

Bridget contemplated on how embarrassing it would be if he refused. But then, how embarrassing would it be for him to accept. She wished she hated him but had it not been for the thoughtful currency he had left behind, she would have faced authorities' questions without acceptable answers. She was certain Elizabeth had no suspicion of that scrap of kindness. She wouldn't have permitted it. Not even that. Ben believed a working relationship with Francis Castle would succeed. So much that virtuous Ben did not know. Still, he could be right. After all, two adults should be able to work together but was the possibility gossamer thin?

The clopping horse and rattling bottles of milk deliveries alerted her to the hour. Fall's gray dawn stroked the horizon before she arose to another day of mourning. She thought herself prepared for eventual widowhood. It had just come too soon.

When informed of the job offer, Francis' eyes expanded. He asked, "Why, and at such a generous salary?"

"Perhaps to benefit your family." Ben curled wood shavings around his fingers and cemented his gaze on the floor as he asked, "Another occupation, Francis?"

"One for which I have little talent." He noted the avoidance of eye contact. "Ben, she spent less than two years in our employment. Why would she be interested in our benefit?"

The tailor's fudging lacked aptitude and Ben was too busy for games. In a sharp voice, he said, "You tell me!"

Francis crumbled. "What did she say?"

"Nothing, but it's obvious why you left Boston in a rush. Seeing both of them together would have shouted truth to the world. If she had wanted to protect her reputation, why would Bridget not have traveled in the opposite direction? Forget it. I don't need details, but rest assured that girl's welfare concerns her. If you won't take employment, accept donations."

Francis looked out the window at November's shortening day and lengthening shadows. Heavyhearted, he answered, "Elizabeth would not accept such employment and I cannot accept donations. Victoria is my responsibility."

Ben waited while this crushed man regained composure before continuing, "Louise states that Elizabeth's weakness is her pride. Stand on yours and your wife slaves and your children strive in poverty. How can you refuse her generous offer of a worthwhile position? Anyway, think about it. I must sail to New York tonight on the *Priscilla* so I must bid you farewell." He paused, giving Francis a reassuring pat on the shoulder although he would never understand how this came about. Francis did not seem to be the type of man to commit adultery and with a mere girl.

Francis spent Thursday assisting Elizabeth by sewing seams on gowns and Friday carrying boxes of completed finery to the "Hill" ladies. Damn them, he thought. Mrs. Carlton could buy all they owned without a blink yet she sent her maids for pickup, if she didn't come herself dragging a retinue of friends. They made a day of it like children at a circus.

On Saturday, he offered an excuse to be gone for the day. "Going to check on a job." he said. In a sense it was true. He wanted thinking time and the beloved sea always cleared his head. A young sun peeking through skeleton trees cast shadows across his path and a brisk wind tossed sylphlike branches back and forth as he journeyed to Newport.

Cold, greenish-gray waves capped with white foam washed the beach then rippled back in merriment. Seagulls squealed. Two pulled at the same prey. His lungs relished inhaling the salty spray as it tantalized his nostrils. Moving on, he came to a spot where the ocean crashed against jagged rocks, flinging sunlit drops of water like diamonds into turbulent air. The sun glared warm but his ocean-seasoning warned him against tarrying.

Nevertheless, hunger demanded a sandwich. As he sipped wine, he deliberated. Staring at the tin, embossed ceiling as if an answer hovered there, he asked himself, "How can I face Bridget day after day but how can I allow Elizabeth's drudgery to continue? Do I need to decide on this darkening day?" Sunlight had made its brief, curtain call and disappeared. Small, hexagon flakes began tumbling. He checked his watch and decided. He could never discomfort Elizabeth, not at any salary. He would find something else. Perhaps a bank position or bookkeeping. Why had he clung to tailoring, a dying field?

Two inches of snow brushed the walks before he arrived at wood-crackling warmth. He struck a match. Sudden flame sucked oil from the wick, burning with gusto and casting a dark image of him upon a wall. He carried the lamp upstairs before hearing frenzied rustling as his wife attempted to conceal a small bundle behind her. A red ribbon rested on a table. He reached around her, taking the parcel from a hand whose veins pulsed from one emotion or another. Elizabeth sputtered, "I didn't expect you so soon."

"Obviously. Does he still affect you so? I wondered if you kept his letters." He pulled out his mother's rosary beads hidden in the space under a drawer. "You wanted me to dispose of this. I didn't because I couldn't. I disposed of my name though, but you kept those precious letters." Shifting them from hand to hand, he weighed them. "I won't ask how many there are or how often you read them. I suspect many times." He handed her the ribbon. "Secure them well, seems the snow has subsided. I'm going out."

"Such a fuss over letters. All women keep letters. Where are you going?"

He roared, "To Rock Street!"

"Don't shout. What's on Rock Street?"

"Have you forgotten? Bridget Klass and she offers a good job."

"You can't mortify me by associating with that shoddy woman."

"I'm not planning to associate. I'm planning to have worthwhile employment."

After pinning the rosary beads inside a pocket and rubbing them for courage, he set out for Bridget's home, his thoughts fixed on Richard's letters. After eighteen years she still treasured them, reread them. That knowledge added one more twist in his contour of pain. He wondered if he would ever stop hurting over Elizabeth.

Bridget wore a black, wool dress which clung to the landscape of her form. Francis looked away, took the offered chair, and glued embarrassed eyes on the rose-colored rug.

"Mr. Castle, it was good of you to come. I imagine if you take this position, you will come to enjoy it."

She explained its simplicity. He was to ask mill personnel which children were bright and anxious for education. When parents declared they needed the child's income, she would offer them whatever the child earned. She didn't want partiality, but advised screening the French children. Were the parents planning to hop over the border? She said, "If the parents are happy in this country, they'll stay, but there is no sense in teaching them English if they plan a return to Canada. I believe girls should have the same opportunity as boys. One day, women will get to vote and they cannot be low information voters. I have considered opening a school for five-year-old youngsters to give them an early start. Half of the carriage house could be converted into a classroom. I would like to find a solution to mothers returning to work too soon after delivery but that might require forming another union!"

When he left, snowflakes whipped by wind flew like confetti around him. He tasted them on his tongue. Yes, he decided, this job would taste good also.

Foraging through the mills for candidates, his eardrums protested the clanking of machinery, and in the hot, humid, working conditions of summer, his skin objected to the constant dripping of salty fluid. Otherwise, he loved interacting with immigrant families. One asset was his fluent Portuguese, the other was that he learned French.

He understood her desire to elevate Victoria's situation but what explained her apparent benevolent attitude toward him? He questioned himself, "Will I ever dare to inquire?" He maintained a professional distance.

Though gratified by the income, Elizabeth's words rang often, "Do nothing to bring a whisper of scandal to this family." Clamping the back of his neck in agitation and tossing a magazine into a corner, he said, "I have no such intention and you know it." Changing the subject seemed like a good idea, "Have you heard from Edward?"

"Yes, he has acquired a position as an assistant manager. I urge better but how often can I say it?"

"Elizabeth, how many children fulfill parental aspirations?" He stooped to retrieve the magazine. "He might change his mind and enter college. Many work their way through. His salary is sufficient, I'm sure."

The following week, Edward's news devastated. A beaker fell from shocked fingers. It had all been needless. The move, the loss of an expanding business, the sale of possessions. Helen could have been no threat! All revealed in Edward's letter.

After an unproductive search for Eliot, Edward savored Boston beginning with a meal at the Union Oyster House, followed by standing outside Fire Engine Company number ten at Mount Vernon and River Streets admiring the dappled gray, fire horses. He held his nose at the stench of horse manure being tossed into carts for fertilizer, but this smell was perfume compared to the odor of Fall River.

He hopped over brick sidewalks on Beacon Street and reminisced jumping from ice cake to ice cake on Frog Pond. He chatted with the wooden-legged man famous for frequenting the Public Gardens. On the west side of Charles Street, he inspected hardware in one store and fruit in another. On the east side, he had the choice of purchasing fish or going to a bakery which served soup at five cents and a chicken sandwich for ten. He spent one penny for a pickle speared from a barrel at Mount Vernon Street. Back on Charles Street, spending a nickel on a shoeshine, he saw a familiar face. "Eliot," he called, "I've been searching for you. What happened to your house?"

Old friends entwined arms, jumping with joy. Eliot's derby bounced into the street landing under crushing cart wheels. Neither noticed. Eliot responded, "Just two months after you disappeared, during wedding festivities, Martha went upstairs for a nap. A candle must have caught a curtain on fire. With the door closed, and the merrymaking, we didn't notice the smoke soon enough. Everyone else got out, but Aunt Helen noticed Martha was missing and ran back. They were found together on the stairs. Dad married a shrew with a house and we all left home as soon as possible. We would have been so happy with Aunt Helen. She was remarkable, you know, and Martha was a good kid."

Feet on brass railing, they sipped till the moon rode high, Edward disparaging Fall River and Eliot praising Roseanne who taught the blind and deaf. "She wants to help people just like Aunt Helen."

Edward wrote the entire tale. Elizabeth ranted, "We didn't need to move. We didn't need to leave a growing business for this! If I had spent two months with Victoria in New Brunswick, the fire would have covered our secret."

Francis consoled, "There was no way to foresee such a calamity. Besides, the nuns might have uncovered it."

"Nuns? How did they get involved?"

"Didn't it occur to you that I would take Bridget for good care? Did you think I'd deposit her in an alley?"

"Why would I give it thought? Why would you have any more integrity in disposal than you had nine months earlier?"

One summer day as sunrise chased night's dampness away, Francis set out for the carriage house in a happy mood. If he could teach Amos and Harry, he could teach five-year-old pre-schoolers. Hammer in one hand and a box of nails in the other, he intended installation of amateurish but serviceable bookshelves, in spite of dawning, abdominal discomfort.

Curiosity drew Bridget to hammering sounds just as he collapsed in pain. Bridget sent Maria for a doctor. Skirts held to her knock knees and legs pumping, she found one at home three blocks away. The doctor's buggy raced to Rock Street.

He said, "I fear this is appendicitis, a fatal problem as a rule. However, Doctor Fitz has advocated removal of the organ."

Bridget, frantic, said, "Who is he? Where is he?"

"In Boston, but following his suggestion many surgeons have effectively performed the operation. I know of one. Where is your phone?" He adjusted his glasses and found the number in a frayed notepad. Linked by the telephone operator, he held the receiver to his good ear. He prepared to shout into the mouthpiece but luck prevailed for the connecting lines had minimal clicking.

Urgency demanded surgery on a kitchen table before transportation to a guest room. The surgeon cautioned, "He is not to be moved any further. I recommend twenty-four-hour nursing care." Bridget sent word to Elizabeth informing her of the situation and inviting her to visit her husband. Elizabeth declined, but requested regular reports.

Mansions and Mills

In truth, Elizabeth seethed at her drudgery while Francis luxuriated in prepared meals and skilled care. The night nurse begged off as her improving patient slept the night. The doctor called daily leaving orders in arpeggio along with bills. Mrs. Klass could afford it.

Light from the hall outlined Bridget's form and her scent knitted the air as she stoked the fire. Inundated with hours of sleep, soft sounds awakened Francis. "Why are you so kind to me when my treatment of you was so cruel?"

"Perchance I learned kindness from a master." She twirled the ring around her finger.

"No. That's not it. You were rainwater soft on the day you were born, but I don't deserve a drop of it."

"You do. I know my treatment was not your wish. I may have been lightheaded that night but aware of her instructions. You could have left an Irish immigrant in the street to be picked up the next morning by trash men. With no identification, what can the authorities do but number them and dispose of what remains of another scorned immigrant?" She smothered tears. Satin slippers peered from under long skirts as she settled into a horse-hair chair. "I know it is done that way."

His eyes puckered, "I never could have done that. Bad enough I ravished someone so young. Good Lord, I was nearly thirty-six. There is no excuse."

"You ravished no one. Did I slam the door in your face? Please don't carry unnecessary guilt. As for Victoria, had she stayed with me, she would have waited in breadlines. It was gratifying that you wanted her."

He punched the pillow. "I should have wanted her. I want her now but I didn't then. Elizabeth wanted her."

Confusion inundated her face, "Why would she want another woman's child?"

"Because she couldn't have her own and she wanted children. Had you had triplets, she would have taken all three, but she is a good mother. Because of you and this employment, soon she will end working endless hours. We owe you much and you owe us contempt."

"You did the best you could for me. The generous funds you left gave me a fresh start and protection from authorities."

Readjusting a coverlet, he said, "I didn't think of authorities that night. I thought of pleasing Elizabeth and maintaining our business and our status. I so regret it."

"Please don't regret. As I have said, this was my doing." The message still eluded him.

She patted his hand. A prickling sensation starting on his skin pierced veins and traveled onwards. His eyes flew open as realization struck that he was recovering with rapidity. Undisciplined fingers grasped hers for a moment then guilt-ridden, let go.

He mumbled, "With assistance, perhaps tomorrow I can manage a return to my home. It will ameliorate Elizabeth's distress."

Separating her torso from the chair, she said, "Yes, we must ameliorate distress." Quick steps brought her to the open door where her light hair caught the dim, hallway light. She paused. "Tell me one thing. Mr. Castle, did you ever confess me?"

"No, you asked me not to."

"Thank you, being of the faith that must have been difficult."

"On the contrary, I never saw a reason to."

The door closed with a soft click, but to him it was like the clank heard in jailhouses. He was alone again. He wanted her back. Radiating warmth, her presence filled vast years of emptiness. What explained her huge appeal? Was it unquenchable spirit or bottomless kindness? Was it lack of pretense or was it human accessibility? Emotions twisting into pretzels, he reached for the magical rosary beads.

On his return home, Elizabeth scrutinized every feature, every gesture indicating change and was emboldened at seeing none. "Francis, I have been so concerned because of all the mortalities from appendicitis. I would have been at such a loss in the event of..." She adjusted a hairpin. "Well, I mean had you not survived. I would feel more secure if we had a plot at Oak Grove Cemetery."

"I'll attend to that matter, don't concern yourself. Having just gone over accounts, I am happy to say that we can afford better living conditions. Select a house you like and plan to enjoy well-deserved retirement. Bear in mind nothing as lavish as in Boston."

Elizabeth found a two-story house with stained-glass windows. It was in a respectable if not opulent neighborhood, one not bordered by mills or mill tenements. Her disposition improved.

Elizabeth envisioned an unburdened future. Someday, the girl would marry and supply a host of grandchildren, compensating for the children she didn't have. Passing the park on their way to further inspect the new home, neither Elizabeth nor Victoria noticed a boy flying a kite. In the shadows cast by the newly erected Saint Anne's Church, he alternated between pulling the attached string and casting sidelong glances at Victoria. Forbidden fruit. A shiksa.

Chapter Thirty-Six

On Rock Street, the air electrified. Once the windows of communication opened, both Bridget and Francis craved opened doors. In the weeks of Elizabeth's house search, they fought to keep distance between them. They ignored clawing eyes. But for years, he had hungered for speech beyond the weather and today's menu. He wanted to communicate tales of the fickle sea, of Mrs. Blackwood, Amos, Harry, John and the captain to a human who would grasp the significance. He wanted to talk to someone who would never dismiss his mother as someone clinging to a superstitious religion. He longed to unfasten the door of guilt. But he knew he couldn't. He would maintain distance, somehow.

Bridget had never spoken of her father, the priest, or of her cloistered sister. Before now, she had never wanted to. But that was impossible. She changed her daily routine, avoiding Francis.

Meanwhile, two young hands assisted Elizabeth in cleaning and unpacking. Francis planned to spend the following weekend discarding unwanted items from the old building. An ancient sewing machine which had taxed pumping legs faced banishment.

Mansions and Mills

He told Elizabeth, "By Sunday evening, the dismal place will wear a for sale sign."

Late on Saturday, as he was about to leave, a broken windowsill caught his attention. He muttered, "Better fix it before the sign goes up. This place is shabby enough." The temperature plunged. Because of the move, he hadn't ordered coal for the coming season. Was there a shovelful or two remaining? A quick peek around the cellar stairs revealed the bin held enough to warm him for a couple of hours. As the shovel touched bottom, it made a strange, crunching sound. Investigation exposed a sodden, cardboard box containing a water-stained wedding picture.

Drumming pain pitched him against the wall, the timpani grew with each breath.

Long strides took him to the new residence, photograph in hand. Elizabeth shrank, saying, "Victoria is on her way home. Shall we speak of this later?"

"No, now! This you intended to abandon. How long has it been in the bin?"

"Since we moved here." She brushed a strand of hair from her dampening forehead. "You weren't thinking of a wedding picture when you merged with the maid."

He blocked her attempt to climb oak stairs littered with unpacked boxes. "Other than injured pride, I fancied you unmoved by my so-called merger."

She tried bypassing him, but his grasp of her gray sleeve restrained. "I am unmoved. Francis, at this late date, this conversation is idiotic." Freeing her arm, she picked up a box of toys.

"It isn't. Explain it all, Elizabeth."

"Very well, since you must awake sleeping dogs. I thought I made it clear once. Let me try again. I didn't covet your person, only the fruit you gave to another woman. All my husband's children belonged to me, not to anyone else. Had there been five maids in the same circumstances, I still would not have cared, but there would be five more children in this house. Now, do you understand?"

"What I do understand is how little you value me." Pushing the damaged picture against her cheek, he continued, "In fact, this shows me the depth of your contempt."

Conjecture whirled in his brain. In spite of her denial, why did he persist in believing that Elizabeth turned icy because of Bridget? Allowing for a full year of illness, why the Arctic environment from January to May of 1892? Fool, he told himself, she just made it clear! Colorful lace and perfume took flight with hope for another child. Why hadn't he considered it before? Years of her contrived behavior humiliated him.

Soundless door hinges made his departure imperceptible. He passed an immigrant's shanty and sleeping mills waiting for awakening by clamoring bells. He trudged to the juncture of North and South Watuppa Ponds and back along Bedford Street. The moon sat above blackened, brick, mill chimneys when he found himself climbing Rock Street. At the corner of Walnut Street, he turned back but at the corner of Pine Street, he turned around again. The clock in the tower of the new Durfee High School told him the day would end soon. Breath quickened with each quickened step. Would Bridget still be awake?

A well-lit parlor revealed her dressed in Gibson girl fashion, reading a history book. A light tap on the window brought her to the back door. He asked, "Maria?"

"She is discreet. She will say nothing of this late visit." In a voice vanishing to a whisper, she asked, "Elizabeth?"

Face crimping in pain, he said, "There is no Elizabeth. There never was. She's unreachable. I tried. Oh, how I tried."

"I know." Long fingers unbuttoned the top buttons of his stiff collar.

"I shouldn't be here but the emptiness and the..."

"I know." Nimble fingers released another button.

"I must tell you. On that night, I wanted Elizabeth."

"I know." She freed the last button.

She was as she had been years before. Inviting, yielding, encircling. He had forced himself to forget while becoming accustomed to stiff, dutiful response.

Mansions and Mills

Propped on an elbow, he brushed drenched, tangled hair from Bridget's sleeping forehead before slipping out into a nascent day dying gold color across the eastern sky.

They were discreet. None suspected, not even Elizabeth. Bridget purchased a cottage surrounded by Swansea's foliage as a secluded retreat and a horseless carriage produced by a man named Ford. Francis became a driver, christening the new-fangled device, with its mule-headed crank, Magnolia. He explained, "Reminds me of a jackass of my acquaintance. This thing has cussy moments too."

Before long, in hushed conversation, he unveiled his guilt at ending correspondence with a captain who prized him enough to bestow prosperity. He spoke of deceiving Elizabeth about the source of past wealth. Without mentioning names, he told of the unavoidable pain of deceiving Mrs. Blackwood and of the avoidable anguish of another man perishing because of his silence. Rufus survived, three met untimely deaths. He could have saved one.

"All this for Elizabeth even destruction of your identity. Don't you resent the loss of inheritance?"

"No, I didn't deserve it. Did I offer comfort to the skipper in his old age? With him, I was always on the taking end." Discourse yielded to fusing stillness as night slithered across the room.

Years passed as howling, winter winds raced down chimneys, summer flowers smiled, foliage withered and spring buds emerged under balmy breezes. The miserable S shaped figure saw a sensible demise along with ruffled, bust improvers. The fashionable replacement of a hobble skirt had women shuffling like geishas. More cars startled horses and Victoria approached eighteen before the motoring couple mentioned marriage.

"Impossible," said Bridget, holding a feathered, flapping hat in a bouncing car, "Catholics can't divorce."

"I can. A priest did not preside." He laughed, "The Church considers me a bachelor."

"One problem, I will never remove my wedding ring. I promised Bill, even though he thought me foolish. You might not understand the commitment to one who supplies every human need."

Eyes liquefying, he answered, "Perhaps I do, but it's no problem. Your long finger can accommodate two. The burning problem is Victoria. You are mirror images. Are you prepared to explain?"

On that day, ripening Victoria noticed a Jewish boy engaged in teaching youngsters the art of kite flying. At sight of her, enthralled fingers released the string and the freed missile soared over the Taunton River accompanied by dismayed groans from juveniles.

Wind velocity perfect for kites raised mischievous havoc on large-brimmed hats and Victoria's burgundy one skittered downhill with a male in hot pursuit. Recapture offered his first opportunity to speak to the dark-haired, blue-eyed teenager.

She looked up at his head as he handed her a now featherless, felt lump. "Your hair looks like a porcupine."

"Enchanting thing to say to someone who rescued your finery," he said as he resorted to spit on his cowlicks, "some appreciation would be nice."

"I do appreciate it but look. What a mess. Don't do that." She jerked his sleeve. "That's germy." She pinned on a shapeless hat. "Spit is always germy. Mother says so."

"You should take the hat off. It looks silly." She stomped off. Fine beginning he thought.

Two weeks later, he appeared at South Park again as she watched children glide down Sliding Rock. He asked, "Want to try it?"

"Gave that antic up years ago. You try it and where have you been for two weeks?"

"Been doing inventory, checking assets and liabilities. I can't account for two shovels and a pitchfork so my father says I'm a putz." His eyes twinkled in amusement. "Missing items are no doubt borrowed by Uncle Izzie on a permanent basis. Have you missed me?"

She stirred pebbles with one foot, making circles before answering. "Miss you. No way."

"No, when I'm so bewitching! Let's walk to the bandstand and watch the sunset." They watched its glow that evening and many others before he caught her by the shoulders, pulling her forward. His lips bruised.

She placed a hand over her mouth, "Look," she said, holding out a pink-tinged finger, "tomorrow I'll be swollen. How do I explain it to Mother?"

"I'll be in hotter water if you explain it to our poppas. I might even get dead. Real dead."

"Don't be funny!" The Irish blood in her rose as she kicked him in the shin.

He rubbed the injury, "That hurt!"

"You hurt me!" Her effort at extricating one clear drop of blood proved useless.

"I will make you two promises. One is that I will never hurt you again and the second is that I will never touch you again unless you ask."

She turned on a scuffed heel, "That will never happen." But, it did.

He soon confessed that he had been blind to any girl since he had seen her at the opening of the synagogue. "I knew then that it had to be you. My father will become deranged if he discovers us."

Father didn't discover but Uncle Izzie did. To hear him tell the story, "Sol went meshugah. Three times, with mine own eyes, I saw him bounce off the ceiling. I said, enough already. He plays with shiksa. It's bubkes, but Sol is kohen."

Sol blew skyward when Jacob informed him that Victoria would be his wife. He shrieked, "You don't marry a shiksa. You screw a shiksa."

"Not this one. This one I marry."

"Feh, I should live so long. Yenta find you baleboosta. I vant you should think of the mishpocha. I vant you should listen."

"I'm not listening. You can have a shiva. Shammatha won't stop me." The mezuzah shuddered as Jacob slammed the door.

Elizabeth heard of the matter when Uncle Izzie visited with cash believing the goyim could be bought off with Uncle Samuel's New York cash. She poured ice water on Izzie's lap.

Victoria arrived home to a colder dash of maternal fury. "Our kind doesn't mingle with Jews. How dare you carry on with one? Besides, he only wants to make a fool of you."

"Mother, no man makes a fool of a woman. She makes a fool of herself."

"This from a girl your age. You must have heard it from your father." After discovery of Richard's letters, did her husband think her a fool? Impossible. Unlike Victoria, her association had been with the most worthwhile man in Boston, not a substandard one.

Both families triumphed. Uncle Samuel traveled from New York assuring Jacob that his father should have remained in farming. "A businessman he is not. He needs your brains. You vant him to starve already?"

Elizabeth's relentless pressure on Victoria forced her into marriage with a British blooded, scrawny Congregationalist. She told the defeated girl, "He is of good family and your children will inherit. You must always consider the children."

Her consideration hadn't shaped her son. Convinced that Prohibition would become law, he stored liquor. "Someday," he told his mother, "I'll make a fortune."

"But that will make you a lawbreaker." At the sound of his laughter, she slammed the telephone receiver. He was supposed to have a profession. Well, Victoria would produce grandchildren.

As she poured consoling tea, she gave no thought to the powder keg in Europe, the arms race or the possibility of a Great War to end all wars.

Mansions and Mills

Because of the outbreak of war in 1914, the demand for material increased. As he drove the crank-free car, thanks to an invention of a self-starting crankshaft, Francis said, "Bridget, this boom will only last the war. Southern states are building mills, sensibly so, since cotton grows in their back yard. Fall River's heyday will end. Investment changes are in order. For myself, I'm free of debt and will invest in property." They hit a rut and clung to the car doors. "Wish the roads improved along with methods of transportation."

Righting herself as flowing, egret feathers flapped on her hat, she said, "People will never give up horses. This is a toy for the rich."

"Don't bet on that." Falling silent, he mulled worrisome war thoughts. "I hope we can avoid the fray, but I doubt it."

The sinking of the Lusitania and Germany's submarine attacks changed American, isolationist minds and a declaration of war came in April. The draft bill passed in May and an Army uniform incased Victoria's husband.

He didn't die smothering in bombed, muddy trenches, or amid the squealing cries and tortured eyes of men or bullet-ridden horses. He never inhaled poison gas but expired from a clumsy fall in August, 1917 while a doughboy.

Victoria and Jacob met by chance in early November inside a kaleidoscopic world of red and gold leaves. Jacob shuffled through fallen ones. Faltering feet led Victoria towards him. A hesitant hand rested on his shoulder. He wrapped both arms around her before saying, "This won't die. How do we kill it?" She made no answer. They walked hand in hand toward a coursing river, melting into acceptance of the inevitable.

Ice stitched trees and masked ponds before she suspected it. March winds rattled shutters before she admitted it. Jacob turned his back to roaring winds, hugged scarf and coat before backing Victoria into scant protection of shrubbery. "We closed it from our minds but it was bound to happen. There is only one course of action now. We will work it out." But he knew the obstacles. Accord among Catholics, Protestants and Jews never happened. Not in Fall River!

Made aware of the situation, pronouncements from Elizabeth stung. "Francis, I want her out of here. You have experience at this sort of thing. Don't you, dear?"

Her husband sat, inspecting his fingernails, trimming off a hangnail and opening a newspaper. "Have you noticed that they still don't get off the subject of Jesse Pomeroy after all these years? How come this old copy is still here?" Reaching for yesterday's issue, he said, "Now this is better." He perused each page ignoring her tapping foot.

"Francis, didn't you hear me?"

"Yes, but don't do what you might regret, Elizabeth. If tossed out, has it occurred to you that she may never return? Why not a vacation in New Brunswick instead?"

"Go to my family with this disgrace? Make proper arrangements and after, she'll have no choice but to return."

He chuckled, "You may discover otherwise." He instructed Victoria to box her belongings. With two passengers, the snow covered buggy traveled to Swansea.

"Papa," Victoria said, "I couldn't help it. It was like trying to hold the tide with a broom. You probably can't imagine what it feels like to sacrifice everything for one person."

Pausing at a rail crossing, he brushed one hand over his forehead. What makes each generation think the preceding one had blocked blood flow? He recalled heat rising in his veins like mercury in a heated thermometer, but he answered, "No, I could probably never imagine it."

Hammering wind from Mount Hope Bay pushed the buggy forward as it sliced through muddied slush towards the cottage. He would remain there tonight and leave at dawn for Rock Street.

The following morning Bridget distrusted her ears. She rolled up a window shade. Morning beams entered. "Where did Elizabeth think Victoria could go?"

Mansions and Mills

"No question, she expected me to deposit her as I had deposited you, but at her age, Elizabeth couldn't expect to palm this one off as her own. She expects a forced adoption followed by submission to another arranged marriage, this time to a thirty-year-old widower named Elton. Jacob wants marriage, but they will be cut off to starve by both groups. Any ideas?"

Bridget sat with feet curled under her while emotions played on her face. After several seconds, clouds lifted from her brows, "Time for a new venture." The stylish, shortened skirt streaked up the stairs. Bridget returned with a paper fluttering in one hand. "Bill always laughed but I told him there was a reason for guarding this recipe. Do you think it will taste the same with kosher beef? If not, he can change his name and make it with regular beef. Since if they marry, he'll be dead to the Jewish communities anyway, he may have to change it. You did. Louise tells me people in Boston are clamoring for those sausages since that German retired to his homeland. Francis, talk to Jacob."

Jacob had one remark, "Tell me where that business was located. We can live in that neighborhood."

That evening, Bridget and Francis relaxed by the cottage fireplace watching fading logs sink into darkness. He reached for her hand and said, "I don't think it's because I'll be sixty-two in June that I find such comfort in your presence. I found that at the start. Leaving you each evening becomes more and more oppressive."

"You can move into the Rock Street house."

"No, and foul your reputation and Bill's for that matter. I owe that man too much."

"Then let's leave this city. Do you think Ben and Louise would be shocked if we eschewed marriage and cohabitated in Boston?"

He stifled laughter. They could be bigamist! "I doubt their censure. There we could spoil our grandchild if you are prepared to tell Victoria the truth. If you want marriage, that too can be arranged. Whatever suits you, suits me."

393

Several weeks later, Francis stood at a window watching dawn ease in another day. He had spent the entire night gathering his personal belongings and packing them.

While waiting for Elizabeth to awake, he read the newspaper. German defeats made it obvious the war was winding to its close, but another monster, first noted in German troops on the twenty-sixth day of June devoured warriors and civilians. The monster had a name. It was called the Spanish Flu, and playing no favorites, felled people of every race around the globe.

Sleepy fog still prowled Elizabeth's eyes as she reached for a coffee cup. At the news he was leaving, her upraised arm, cup in hand, froze in position. Within seconds, chilled cells flamed and the cup crashed against the side of his head.

"My dear, such a unique, emotional display." He shrugged, "Would have been more effective with scalding coffee."

"How dare you consider this abomination? I'd be the laughingstock of the city. You will not do this!" She swirled cream in a new cup, ignoring smashed stoneware on the floor.

"You have options. A move back to Canada would camouflage the entire thing. Habitation with sons is common practice. He may hate me but he is devoted to you."

"My relatives are scattered now and I will not impose on Edward." She didn't mention his bootlegging plans. "You might rethink this when Victoria returns from confinement."

With brisk movements, Francis prepared his breakfast. "Having married Jacob, she is not returning. They have started a business. Care for any pancakes?"

She barged past him into the sitting room, nestling against the cushion from New Orleans. Strange, he thought, how she valued it. When troubled, she always nuzzled it. It seemed that she had prized nothing but the pillow and the fruit of his loins while he had surrendered his soul. Once he had deluded himself that her love would grow, and in time he might reap one grain of Richard's harvest.

Mansions and Mills

A cold voice reached him, "Am I to return to my former occupation or seek alms?"

He stiffened, "Ah, your poor opinion of me surfaces. Neither will be necessary. Monthly funds will arrive from my attorney. You are the sole beneficiary in my will which he will have along with the cemetery lot."

He was jamming a hat on his gray head when her voice detained him. "Does any of this," she asked, rocking a chair in fury, "come from the generosity of your cherished Mrs. Klass?"

Taking deep breaths and counting to ten, he countered, "No, I've invested in rental property and followed Ben's advice regarding investments. I consider you my responsibility."

Jumping from the rocker, she blocked his escape. "Then it is your responsibility to protect me from mortification. If you don't abandon this foolishness, I'll call Edward."

A gentle hand removed her restraining arm, "Edward and I have faint influence on each other. Movers refuse to remove my belongings till this flu ends. Understandable since it is annihilating so many. Elizabeth, please remain safely at home."

Sunset stained the western sky when the phone's shrill ring beckoned Francis. A gruff-voiced Edward said, "I knew where to find you though calling the magnificent, Klass mansion is impertinent, but I wish to speak to you. Where might we meet that is contamination free?"

Lips taunt, he answered, "No amount of conversation will change my decision. I'm sure that is your purpose."

Edward persisted, "It seems that speaking to your son, under these circumstances, is warranted. It does involve my mother and between us we might find more pleasant arrangements for her."

There was the Swansea hideaway up for sale and vacant for weeks. The citizenry, concerned with an epidemic, had no present interest. He furnished the address. After a prolonged, charged silence, Edward said, "I can meet you there at two on Wednesday if that is convenient."

The older man answered, "That's fine with me." He wanted Elizabeth as content as possible. He twisted in despair and guilt. More guilt! When he provided trifling income, Elizabeth had provided. What she wanted, she never received—a large brood of distinguished children. Neither Edward nor Victoria brought a sense of accomplishment. He wanted her happy. He had always wanted that.

Francis settled into a horsehair chair while removing uncomfortable shoes. Bridget watched his torment from the doorway. She said, "Francis, you are always free to change your mind. Be certain."

Geese migrated in unmistakable formation and an impatient October wind rushed ballooning clouds across a sun struggling to warm a day of chilly discomfort. Discomfort was the functional word for the Castle family as well as humans and livestock buffeted by biting air.

Edward, in diabolical mood, sat at Elizabeth's kitchen table, alternating between pounding on its oak surface and sipping coffee. "Are you certain he will not change course? You must be certain, do you understand?"

"I am certain." she answered, wiping a ring deposited by a creamer. "Look at his belongings, packed and sealed, waiting for this flu to burn itself out. I hope you have not risked exposure."

He waved flu concerns aside. "He cannot humble you so. He has brought us disgrace by violating a mere girl and poverty by forcing the move from Boston. How long was I deprived from association with Eliot? I can't forgive any of it. I have brought the means to prevent this move." He withdrew bottles of whiskey from his coat pockets, one full and one with two draughts removed. "As long as I don't confuse the bottles, I won't kill myself."

Elizabeth cringed, "What are you planning?"

"Frankly, Mother, to make you a respectable widow."

"You can't mean..." Elbows on the table, she raked her hair. "You'll be executed."

Mansions and Mills

"I won't be caught." He replaced the bottles, one in the left coat pocket and one on the right. "One has ricin, brewed by my dainty hands. Enough that he won't suffer too long."

Blasting air flow aided his downhill rush. He didn't hear Elizabeth's parting words, "Don't, please. You could confuse the bottles."

Edward's first words to his father were, "You are as well dressed as a politician."

Francis said, "The discussion is your mother's happiness not my apparel."

"You could make her happy by staying put." He drew a bottle from his right pocket. "Without heat in here, let's have a warm up." Finding glasses on a counter, he poured two drinks from the bottle.

"Edward, I can't stay put. My decisions are now in concrete. Living in constant scorn without Victoria as a buffer is unbearable. Your mother has destroyed their relationship."

Taking sips of whiskey, the younger man snapped, "Victoria should have used sounder judgment. Your glass is empty. It's getting colder. Have a refill. I'll catch up." Francis didn't notice that the bottle, missing the equivalent of two drinks, was taken from a left pocket.

Knotted fingers clutched the rosary beads when he fell.

While Edward tended to murder, Elizabeth, curious as to what her husband valued, unsealed a box. There she found diaries dating back to seafaring. Flipping through those boring pages, her eyes fell on the word Richard. She read of brutality, an avaricious marriage and Rufus' revenge motive. She learned of Sam's disfigurement and its perpetrator and how her husband had shielded her pride against knowledge of generosity from Ben, Bill and Louise while his pride rode in dust. Page after page showed guilt over its concealment from her. He covered Richard's murder to spare her mockery from those who knew of their association and he wanted her shielded from investigation. She squinted at a marginal scrawl that he had no headcount on heyday attendees. He wrote of agonizing pain over loss of contact with Mrs. Blackwood and Captain Addison—the wished for father. She read of his enduring shame over Bridget and how years ago she had been a substitute but now, through her he learned that love in pastel shades supplied more comfort than one in fiery tints.

The room's empty space smothered. While longing for an undeserving man she had lacerated a commendable one. Mrs. Blackwood had warned her about pride. Without it, she would have valued the name Castro, inherited, and avoided crushing work. She would admit all of her folly to Francis. Francis! They were meeting today. Where? She didn't know. She couldn't stop it!

Hours later, the phone summoned. Before collapsing, Elizabeth heard the words, "Mother, you are a widow."

The Federal Bureau of Public Health stated that in the two weeks prior to October twenty-sixth, forty thousand flu deaths occurred. Overwhelmed doctors, morticians and city clerks listed Francis Castle as one more flu victim.

It took eight months of recovery before Elizabeth inquired at Oak Grove Cemetery, finding no record of internment. The attorney assured her of compliance with Mr. Castle's will. "You are the sole inheritor of his estate." A nervous cough preceded further explanation, "You see, Mrs. Castle, your husband purchased two lots. You own the one at Oak Grove, but he designated burial in a Catholic cemetery."

"In a city where Catholics and Protestants don't mingle that cannot be. Catholic cemeteries don't admit Protestants."

"He didn't abandon his faith. A funeral mass took place. A pity your illness prevented attendance."

Elizabeth, carrying flowers, approached her husband's grave and stopped short. An engraved monument said it all. Sandwiched between the dates 1856-1918 was the name Francisco Castro and carved beneath and to the left, the date 1874 preceded the centered name Bridget. No last name. To the right, a date waited.

In granite, he disowned her, for all time. She wanted to cry but she could not. Tear ducts had cemented on that night years ago. How could he have done this to her? Didn't he recall that she was a Gilbert, born on a land grant bestowed by a British king? Nobody heard her as she howled, "Lord, nothing was supposed to be like this. Did you not notice? I danced with the Prince of Wales!"

Made in the USA
Middletown, DE
25 August 2023

36932602R00241